DEUSETTA

by

Hal Enzinga

Disciples of Eden Book One

To all: I owe you the moon, stars, and Mars.

Chapter One

It officially began.

Eleven aching heads lay groaning on the oak table, some in a more dismal state than others. Parisa sat at the far end, already awake, saying nothing. She fiddled with her veil, eyes wide, mouth tight, trying not to stare at the head of the table, where a man lay slumped with his face cradled by a gold plate. He was different. The unconscious others were undoubtedly alive. Breathing, grunting, eyes fluttering. Not him. Probably dead. He hadn't blinked once in the few minutes she had been awake.

One minute after she awoke, she bolted to each of the four steel doors. All locked. In two minutes, she scoured the room for something to arm herself against her fellow captives. Fruitless. Five minutes later, panic-stricken and slightly sheepish, she returned to her seat and spent her anxiety by pulling out the loose golden threads in her veil. Drugged, kidnapped, locked in a room with a probably-dead body, surrounded by strangers, but at least her unknown captors didn't snatch her veil and jewelry from her. She darted her eyes around her periphery.

It was a dining room, or at least pretended to be, full of unlucid bodies and dusty books shoved into a wide, blackwood shelf. Dark red walls housed the steel doors, one on each wall. Heavy curtains hung over lightless, copper-framed windows. An ugly, yellow wash flickered from crusty bulbs dangling from the brutally low ceiling. The thick carpet suffocated all the gurgling sounds leaking out from the strangers.

Being kidnapped was a terror, but so was the painting leering down from the far end. A massive scene of a stag hunt, beautifully composed and colored, if a bit viscerally grim. The poor creature was being eaten alive by the hunting hounds, ripping limbs from the joint, shredding the skin from the muscle. Grotesque, but a decent enough distraction.

She found a precious three seconds of tense calmness until the man sitting to her right grunted into consciousness.

Wassermann shook the last bits of grogginess from his eyes, gave a loose once-over of his surroundings, then proceeded to panic.

He cried in something foreign, frantic, and apparently requiring much spit. Parisa only shook her head. Falling mute, he gave her appearance a frank scrutiny, and she stared at her lap as though to expedite his judgment. Small, barely an adult, with a complexion suggesting an Arabic heritage, the bracelets and silken finery suggesting wealth, and her composure suggesting innocence.

A moment later, Parisa reciprocated the stranger's scrutiny. Tall, gangly, clean-shaven, painfully plain, an unassuming, middle-aged European. A caricature of the everyman. His cheap and ill-fitting suit implied a career in the lower levels of government or a mediocre academic. A person one would immediately forget after glancing away.

Without overt threat, he sniveled at her, and she sniveled back. The dreadful terror melted into dreadful awkwardness. Entirely his fault. He was the awkward sort, not knowing where to look, so he opted to look everywhere at once. He stood there with a dim, tight-mouthed expression, fidgeting with his hands, about to say something again, but a gurgle interrupted him.

Another sobered up. Morrelli lifted her head off the upper side of the table with a yawn. A thirty-something: sturdy, sun-burnt, and wind-whipped. A thick braid tamed a shock of black hair that ran down her back, dusting the top of her seat. A heavy, rubbery smock covered her muddy dress. When she smacked her gums to conclude her yawn, the realization settled in. Immediately, she became loud. Frightfully loud. Hysterical, even, but the situation deemed hysteria to be appropriate. Shouting and jamming her finger towards Wassermann's dour face, her lung capacity knew no limit.

He grew pleasantly surprised, hazarding to brighten into a smile. He switched into another tongue, and Morrelli responded, but didn't dim her histrionics. Instead, her shouting grew louder, angrier, and she bolted up and began to slap him across the temple, without shame for assaulting a stranger. He responded in the only way one could by cowering back down in his seat and putting up his frail, office-worker's hands to defend against her pounding fists, gurgling out more and more foreign gibberish.

Something he said must have been effective, and Morrelli sat down with a huff, yet the shouting endured. Parisa only watched, which was likely the best course of action.

Finally, as Wassermann pathetically moaned a question from under his hunch, Morrelli screeched her name, then said, "*E tu?*"

"Wassermann," he responded.

There was a brief pause as the two looked each other up and down. Only one thing was understood: they found each other faultless and unattractive. The man then turned his attention back towards Parisa, "Speak English then?"

"A little."

"Who are you?"

"I'm Parisa Shahidi."

"Well, then, Miss Parisa, I'm Wassermann. Wouldn't happen to know where we are, would you?"

She shook her head, a tremble twitching her eyelids, "No. I think I am kidnapped, but my memory fails. My head hurts."

The eye-twitch blossomed to a full-body shake as Morrelli leaned over the table to give Parisa a scorching look. Yet, Morrelli reclined into her seat after a snort, maybe finding Parisa as faultless as Wassermann, but not as unattractive.

Wassermann continued, "Kidnapped, certainly. Do any of the other fellows here look familiar to you? They are all strangers to me, and to her, the banshee."

Parisa shook her head.

He asked, "You think that fellow is dead?"

She responded, "His eyes open. He does not blink."

"Well, that certainly doesn't bode well, does it?"

Parisa said, "I say no."

"Ah," Wassermann mumbled, then let out an inappropriate chuckle. "Ever seen a dead body before?"

Parisa responded with a grimace and a violent head shake.

Another awkward minute passed. The groaning from the other heads grew louder, threatening to awaken. Morrelli sat in a nonplussed frown, and Wassermann sat in a pitiful bashfulness, rubbing the red marks on his temple. Talking appeared to be another fruitless endeavor, even a painful one, so no one could blame Parisa for maintaining silence.

Morrelli, shedding her sudden bout of violent temper, picked up the gold plate before her, gave it a quick inspection, whistled at its finery, and stuffed it down into her smock. It rested for a minute before she pulled it out again, admired it some more, then re-stuffed it. Her hands wouldn't sit still. She began to un-braid and re-braid her hair. At once, Morrelli's anxiety was all but lost. She almost approached friendliness, sitting all self-satisfied and cheery. She turned her head towards Parisa and said something that was maybe amiable, but there was no reason to give her the benefit of the doubt.

Wassermann said, "It's Italian, she's asking you if she can have your plate as well. She likes the design."

Parisa slid it across the table. "All people here Italian?"

"Don't know, but I'm from Zürich," Wassermann said, and nervously chuckled again. "Nice place, ever been?" It should have been a welcome reprieve, but his screwy face and warbly voice betrayed the friendly intention, and it just made the whole exchange heinously uncomfortable.

The discomfort was expounded by another man rubbing grogginess out of his eyes. Dr. Oberst was of a sickly pallor, decorated with neatly trimmed dark hair and an accompanying mustache. He sported a well-worn but otherwise fashionable suit, instantly putting Wassermann to shame. A conservative guess placed him in his early thirties, marked by the youthful charm in his otherwise anxiety-racked face. Had it not been for his thickly German voice and egregiously German obedience to good posture, he could have passed for Parisian.

As expected, he immediately began to sputter in that coarse inflexion native to German speakers, and Wassermann eagerly responded. Three or four sentences in, and Dr. Oberst switched into English.

"I have no time to be kidnapped," Dr. Oberst said. "I'm expected to be at an onboarding reception in two days! This will reflect horribly on my bulletin. I'm already treading shallow waters with the board. What could they think of me now? Unless this is a part of the onboarding? Is that it? Is this some rite of passage? Are you all medical practitioners as well?"

Wassermann said, "I am no such thing. Morrelli is a cow

maid. You, Parisa? Actually, you don't look old enough."

"I am not," she responded, "No employment."

Dr. Oberst slumped forward and began to moan. Wassermann leaned across the table with a flurry of consolations, but Dr. Oberst only moaned with more anguish.

"What was your name again, sir?" Wassermann asked.

Dr. Oberst gave his name, then began to frantically pat his chest, "I should have my card somewhere on me."

No time to exchange business cards. A new voice, a crisp and elderly male growl, emerged from the top of the table, "You look like no doctor to me."

His accent was undeniably English, as was his appearance. Pudgy, pale, papery—from his hair to his face to his scowl. His sun-spotted hands vibrated as they grasped around an old mahogany cane. His small, watery eyes glared behind his crooked reading glasses, shooting tepid rage down the length of the table. His name was Gage, and the name suited him.

He continued, jerking his head to the young doctor, "What is this then? I knew I had enemies. How cowardly. It was you, wasn't it, cretin."

Dr. Oberst flapped his jaw, "Me? No! I have just awoken, and I have nothing to do with any of this! Please, I'm a doctor, you must believe me, not a criminal. Where's my damned card?"

"No. I am a doctor, and I know a fellow doctor when I see one. You are no fellow doctor," said the senior. He butted the end of his cane down the table, pointing straight at Wassermann, "Are you also of the Kaiser?"

"Me? No, I am Swiss."

"That's almost worse. Work for the bank, do you? Worse."

Wassermann fidgeted with his hands, and after ensuring the subsequent silence was overbearingly awkward, said,

"How about we wait for all to get up, and then we can continue this. Please, I want no trouble, I'm as lost as the rest of you."

"I'm not lost. I know what this is," Dr. Gage said, swiveling his cane to point it at Dr. Oberst, "Spies, the lot of them, all spies, and I am sure the rest are as well. That's their game, drugging, kidnapping, and then yanking targets into dungeons."

Suddenly, two seats down from Morrelli, a lithe, scruffy, auburn-haired young man jolted to his feet, his eyes darting and fiery, his fists clenched in anger. None knew it yet, but unfortunately, that was Kovacevic. Kovacevic was dressed shoddily like a newsboy, despite being a bit too old and much too enraged to be one. Dried blood splattered down the side of his temple. He whipped around, set his sights on the door underneath the stag hunt painting, dashed over, and before Parisa could warn him differently, he slammed his body against it. All he won was a pink bruise on the cheek. With a snarl, he kicked it, then trudged back over to his chair but did not sit.

He stammered in a heavy Slavic accent, "I was not drugged, I was taken. Dragged. Against my will. Shoved into a car. Not drugged."

Wassermann squinted, likely trying to sound out the choppy sentence, which apparently upset Kovacevic so much he huffed back down with a leer.

Dr. Gage said, "Well, I certainly did not come here of my own volition, I'll tell you that. What do you want from me? If it's money... well, no. No, you may not bully your way into my savings."

Dr. Oberst began to wring his hands. "Ransom? I have no money. I was told that Paris was safe! There's never been any kidnapping in Paris!"

Wassermann lost all of his color, not that he had much to

begin with, "Paris? Is that where you were? But I was in Zürich! Have been for most of my life! The farthest I have ever gone is Lugano."

He switched to German and attempted to confer privately with Dr. Oberst but was halted by the violently irate English doctor.

"Stop that right there, don't you dare conspire in front of me! I'll have you know I picked up quite a few German words in my time. Don't you dare try anything; I'll know it."

Wassermann stuttered, "Apologies, it's easier for me, and I just wanted to know if there's some thread between us that —"

"I don't care what's easier for you, don't you dare keep me in the dark!"

Wassermann committed to his stutter, "But Ms. Morrelli here doesn't speak English very well! We can't be expected to only talk in—"

"That's just too bad!"

Kovacevic proclaimed, "I was in Paris too. Where I was beaten."

Dr. Oberst asked, "Do you know who beat you?"

"No."

Dr. Gage grumbled, "If you have nothing helpful to say, then remain quiet, and let me collect my thoughts in peace. Oh, this man here…is he dead?"

He gave the dead man an indelicate poke on the temple, "Yes, surely dead. Well, that's grim."

Parisa murmured, "He does not blink…"

Kovacevic was about to restart, but he was once again cut off by a loud shriek.

A malnourished man, or maybe a boy, he was somewhere between fifteen and forty, began pounding on the table with his fists. He sounded Slavic too, and Kovacevic squinted at him. The screamer's hair was shaved close to his scalp, or maybe he was bald. The dim lights only muddled his appearance to abject vagueness. But he did have a long, sloped nose decorating a rather angular head on top of a rather tall body. A street-brawler build but missing the vital component of muscle mass.

Kovacevic tried speaking to him privately, but only confused and flustered the screaming Slav more, so he gave up and slumped down in his chair.

Dr. Gage said, "Now that's the last thing I need. A gaggle of Ivans. You, beaten man, tell him to shut up."

"I do not speak Russian."

Wassermann asked, with an attempt at friendliness, "Well, what are you then?"

"Serbian," Kovacevic replied, ignoring the friendliness, and he crossed his arms and began to simmer in a half-deserved petulance. Another side-glance to the screaming Slav, and he spat out, "It's a Soviet."

Without an explicit reason why, everyone save for the Serbian leaned forward to stare at the Soviet as though he were some fairytale creature.

The stare brought clarity to the vagueness. The Soviet was a boy. A weary, fatigued boy, who recoiled under the scrutiny and made another incomprehensible plea to the Serbian. Kovacevic relit his fire and began to shout down the table, which elevated the Soviet's shrieking, which made Wassermann try to calm him, which only made it worse, which only further irritated Dr. Gage. Morrelli plucked up Dr. Oberst's plate from across the table and, without explicit permission, stowed it away for herself.

Parisa, long forgotten in the onslaught of noise, turned to stare straight at the young woman before her, slowly breaking into consciousness. The young woman became fully lucid in a minute, and in two, fell into mute despondency, immediately understanding the futility in speaking. Haggard, mousy, waifish, clad in a tattered red pattern dress. She had a face that would suit any name. Perhaps she could be pretty anywhere else, but then and there, she was extremely unpleasant to look at. But at least she didn't compound the cacophony, so Parisa offered her a weary smile with an obvious hope that it would be returned.

A small blessing—the young woman returned it. But her mouth began to tremble as her eyes hung glistening, "Me? Stolen? None would believe it…"

The next ten minutes were a very painful affair as the remainders awakened with increasingly ear-shattering shouts. For whatever reason, the dead man slumped over the head of the table commanded no particular attention.

Instead, a petulant Asian man sitting next to the mousy woman slammed his hands on the table and shot up. Everything about him was small, sharp, and shiny. Wax greased his hair back, his eyes had a mean slickness, and his dinner suit was suffocatingly stiff and immaculate. Despite his short stature, he held an air of gargantuan self-importance, squaring his shoulders and tilting his nose upward.

He spoke, surprisingly in perfect English with even a faint hint of a Londoner's accent, "Shouting about will get us nowhere. I must require you all to conduct yourselves professionally and civilly in my presence."

A curvy, graying woman in a heavy French accent with even heavier makeup said, "The hell are you? Did you snatch me?"

The man bristled but continued with a thin shield of politeness, "Heavens no. I am Junichi Kitagawa. If any of you are educated, you must have read one of my articles through Cambridge University Press. If this is an attempt to solicit a ransom from my father, please know that nothing but the harshest punishment is expected for kidnappings." He paused, allowing space for some sort of impressed gasp. He was only met with more confusion.

Another Asian boy seated before him muttered across the table. This was a boy, certainly. Not yet fifteen and dredged up from abject poverty. Grime collected in the corners of his nose, ears, and neck, and his dark hair was thin and long, pulled back into a low tie.

This young boy, named Gao but it was likely that the others wouldn't care what he was called, gazed up at Kitagawa and continued to mutter. Kitagawa waved the words away with the flick of a hand and scrunched his nose like something stank.

"I have never heard of you before," the French woman huffed, crossing her arms over her chest, ruffling the chiffon collar of her evening dress, the sort of garb only suitable for an opera outing. "Now, surely whoever these kidnappers are knows me. Lucie Renard."

Dr. Oberst exclaimed, "Oh. I knew I recognized you! The stage actress. My family used to be patrons." A boyish flush crawled up his collar.

Renard allowed a look of satisfaction to banish her worry. Kitagawa scowled and tried to speak again, but Renard decided to exercise her profession.

She groaned, "Yes, it is true. A treasure of Parisian culture, jewel of the theater. Quite the travesty, such a black mark on the policemen of France, to allow one such as myself to be stolen away. But the world has fallen, so I must descend with it."

Morrelli lit up, reaching over to grasp around the actress' arm with both of her hands like wringing out a towel, "*Celebre!*"

Renard bestowed her with a smug smile, but then sharply

returned to dejection, "Some scandal then, some conspiracy! To steal wealthy persons in Paris."

"But I was in Zürich," Wassermann muttered.

"And I was in London. And as I have said, I am not made of money," Dr. Gage spat, then turned a sharp eye to Dr. Oberst. "My poor wife. I will wring their necks if the ransomers give her so much as a nudge. Here me, you cretin, I, a real doctor, will wring your neck! Then I will reset it and wring it again."

Dr. Oberst cried, "I told you; I have nothing to do—"

"Maybe there is some connection between us," Wassermann said, waving his hands, attempting a sense of decorum, and not succeeding. "Let us all be silent for a moment. Certainly, one of us knows what is going on. Looks like we are locked in, so here, perhaps a more formal introduction?" He then made a vague gesture to Gao to start the required but excruciatingly painful procedure necessary to turn a gaggle of strangers into a gaggle of collaborators.

Kitagawa huffed, "He doesn't speak English."

Wassermann decided to continue his vague gestures regardless, and something must have worked. Gao leaned over the table and muttered to Kitagawa, who didn't seem too thrilled with the prospect of playing translator.

However, after a deeply contemptuous sigh, Kitagawa did render the service. "YiMing Gao. Born, raised, and never left Kunming. South China, for those unaware of the globe. He understands nothing, can't hardly speak his own tongue."

Parisa cleared her throat, initiating a polite introduction, but Kovacevic jolted up, still full of fire, "Petar Kovacevic. I do not know what I am doing here, and I do not know what all of you want from me. I do not like any of you."

He quickly sat back down and seemed very satisfied with his little burst. The ten others then craned their heads to look at the Soviet. Kovacevic's satisfaction quickly turned to preemptive protest.

Wassermann asked, somehow even more gracelessly than humanly possible, "Kovacevic, you may know best what the Soviet would say. Would you help?"

Kovacevic spat, "I do not understand him."

Renard smiled to herself, suddenly proud for whatever reason, "You speak Yugo, no? Surely it is the same. Like Spanish and Portuguese, no? Or Japanese and Chinese?"

Kitagawa snorted, "Japanese and Chinese are not mutually intelligible. I'll have you know I've studied the classics for—"

Kovacevic interrupted with a sneer, "Serbs and Russians, not the same."

Renard only wrinkled her brow and subsequently didn't care enough to provide a verbal retort to either.

"Well, can't you at least try?" Wassermann asked.

Kovacevic rolled his eyes but then asked a rapid spray of questions to the Soviet.

The Soviet only blinked slowly, heavily breathing, scanning the gaggle of strangers. He pointed towards himself. "Pyotr Semyonov Volga."

"Name is Pyotr," Kovacevic said.

Renard said, without an attempt to stifle a smirk, "Obviously. Another Peter? That is what Pyotr is, correct? Like how you are Petar? Such strange odds. Very similar names, in essence, the same."

Kovacevic resumed his grousing and sank into folded arms while narrowing his eyes. It would have suited him if a forked tongue poked out of his mouth, but instead, he just sat there scowling. Semyonov attempted to scoot closer. Kovacevic scooted away.

It was finally Parisa's turn. She cleared her throat, took in a small gasp of air, but a sudden shyness stifled her English capability. With a swell of desperation, she gestured to Renard, and the actress took up the task with glee, craning forward to hear Parisa's fluid French whisper.

"Quite understandable! Saving breath for a more poetic language. Parisa Shahidi is a Persian girl. She is a daughter to, uhh, how you say…" Renard conferred back to Parisa, asking her the same question thrice, then abruptly grew serious, "She is the daughter of an officer of Shah Reza Pahlavi."

Those with university diplomas gasped.

Dr. Gage nodded, "Heavens, connected to the Shah of Persia. My, I dare say we will be quick to escape our confinement then. He will sort the money, yes, he will sort the money."

Kitagawa announced, "So, I seem to be among peers. Some of you, at least. My father is also in such a position of importance. Admiral of the Imperial Navy. We must have been targeted for the wealth and influence of our families. That's it then. Our captors did an excellent job marking at least a couple worthy targets."

None gasped, not even those with university diplomas.

Parisa eagerly gestured to the mousy woman sitting across from her and even leaned over the table to illustrate a semblance of amity.

The woman's face was ghastly, mere seconds from fainting again. Without breath, she said, "Harriet Foster. I'm a seamstress. New Hampshire. Nothing else. Was on my way to Stockholm to visit my brother, he's a student there. I'm nobody of importance, no money. Don't know how I got mixed up in this. Don't even remember being drugged."

Another multilingual murmur shuddered throughout the room.

It must have felt quite rude to a socialite to ignore the horrific boon at the table, so Parisa meekly pointed, "The man that does not blink…"

Dr. Oberst examined the corpse, gingerly tilting his head back up. He poked about the dead man's neck, pronouncing, "Angioedema. The man surely died from anaphylactic shock. See here, Dr. Gage, his throat is very swollen. Asphyxiated through allergy."

Dr. Gage leaned forward again and pried open the man's mouth. Light blue rings circled his orifice. He inspected the man's hands and grunted to himself, "Not a bad assumption, but too hasty. Given our situation, poisoning or murder cannot be ruled out. We may be among some malicious characters."

Dr. Oberst sighed into a smile and must have thought he had won approval, placing an expeditionary hand on Dr. Gage's shoulder. It was sneered at, then slapped away.

Morbidly curious, Renard craned her head over Dr. Gage to gawk at the corpse, "Surely, it must be an accident. Why kidnap for ransom, then kill them immediately? No matter, once my husband receives the ransom letter, he will make quick haste with payment." She sat back whilst nodding to herself, fumbling with the heavy ring around her finger.

"But who is the dead man?" Wassermann asked, "Is he familiar to any of you? Or maybe, he is of some important family, like Mrs. Renard or Miss Shahidi."

Kitagawa said, his scowl borderline comical, "Are you by chance forgetting me?"

The questions went unanswered. Harriet interrupted, "I have no money for ransom. My father is a working man, nothing to our name." An odd, frantic giggle escaped her mouth, and she clamped her teeth on her tongue.

Renard shrugged and began to coil her graying locs around her finger, "You must have been in the way. No worry, I am sure that some request will be made to the embassy.

These criminal types, they do not discriminate on such things."

"And you think Yugoslavia will answer my note?" Kovacevic scoffed, "This does not look like ransom kidnapping to me. You all are spies, I know this, yes, spies caught. This is a prison in France. Yes, you are the bad actors."

Dr. Gage sharply turned his attention to Kovacevic, dropping the dead man's jaw, "Have you outed yourself then? You are a spy? Reveal yourself all you want. I am nothing of the sort. Spy? Me? Never."

Dr. Oberst said, trying to shimmy into Dr. Gage's orbit, and failing spectacularly, "Nor I, besides, this is certainly not a French prison. And do they not separate spies once caught for interrogation? I can't imagine any of us being political adversaries."

As it turned out, many could imagine such a thing, and angry looks darted up and down the table. Parisa, certainly unsure who in the room would be her political adversary, opted to resume a soft, non-contemptuous stare at Harriet. Once again, Harriet returned the gesture.

There was no softness anywhere else in the dining room. Kitagawa said something to Gao in terse, clipped Chinese, but it didn't appear to be an explanation, more so an accusation. A vulgar accusation. Known only because Gao's eyes began to water instantaneously.

Only the Soviet was left entirely unaware. He sat there, frantically surveying the room, hunched in a familiar dejected posture. Kovacevic markedly avoided eye contact.

Wassermann slapped the table, "Well, no use sitting around staring at each other. We are not bolted to this table, are we? There must be something of use around this room."

Dr. Oberst asked, "Wait, the doors! Why not just leave?"

Wasserman responded, "Locked, as I said."

Dr. Gage spat out, "How are you so certain? Did you do

due diligence?"

Wassermann said, "No, but she did. Him as well."

Parisa's face reddened; a humiliating thought—he was awake for her earlier bout of frenzy. Kovacevic didn't seem similarly humiliated, but did rub his flushing bruise.

Wassermann paced over and began examining the bookshelves. None followed—too ludicrous and too inane an activity.

Gao started to nervously swing his feet. On the second swoop, a loud clunk rattled the dining room. He kicked something ten times before hazarding to check underneath the table, and only because Kitagawa snapped at him.

A small mahogany chest, fastened together with intricate golden leaflet locks. Gao studied it with gentle curiosity, resting it upon the center of the table for all to see.

Kitagawa whispered something to Gao, his eyes glinting, the wick of his mouth pulled downward.

Gao shrugged and shook the box. Protests erupted around the room: maybe it was a bomb, or maybe a decapitation, or maybe a pile of excrement. But nothing violent happened. Just the clacking of small objects jumbling around.

"Perhaps it's more books, the room is filled with them. In multiple languages too," Wassermann said without turning from the shelves. He plucked a random novel out, and a plume of dust followed. "This book here may be of some interest."

Before another word could be uttered, Morrelli grabbed the box from the table and ripped the lid off its hinges, the feeble lock being no match for the brute strength of a cow maid. Eagerly, everyone scrambled to see what lay inside, even Wassermann, who dropped the novel as quickly as he had picked it up.

An assortment of cards and passports. Their own.

"I say, give me mine back," Dr. Gage cried out, reaching his thick hand over the young Gao.

Renard asked, similarly clamoring for her identification, "How odd, why take them from us, but only hide them under our feet?"

Wassermann yanked the box away from Morrelli, "Now, now. Some decency. I think it's only fair that I look over all these to ensure you all have been truthful."

Renard scoffed, bouncing her stiff curls with each bob of the head, "And why should you do it? Because you are Swiss? How customary, so arrogant."

Wassermann continued, trying to keep the other prying hands at bay, "Precisely, I don't mean to be rude, but given our circumstances, you know, contemporarily speaking, and now knowing one is a spy, it's only right that it should be me. I shall ensure you all were truthful."

Promptly, he delved into the box and cried out a discovery, "Ah hah. Here. On this passport, it says Agnes Durer. One of you is a liar."

Renard rolled her eyes and snatched the little book from his hand, "That is me, idiot. Lucie Renard is simply my stage name. But please, not one of you is permitted to call me Agnes. Only Mrs. Renard, thank you."

Wassermann pulled out several more passports and identification cards. So far, Dr. Gage, Dr. Oberst, and Kitagawa had all been truthful about their nationality and their name.

Wassermann did comment, "Mr. Kitagawa, here it says your birthday is January 1902, you really are thirty-four? You don't look it. I assumed no older than twenty-five."

The eternally youthful Kitagawa raised his brow in slight appreciation and plucked his book back, "I suppose being indoors most days lends itself to aging with grace."

Dr. Gage grumbled, "As does being a permanent student, never knowing a full day of work."

Kitagawa scrunched his top lip but didn't respond. Not verbally at least. He just whipped out a comb and aggressively raked his hair back.

Then followed the verification of Morrelli, Harriet, Parisa, and the two Slavic Peters, but not for YiMing Gao. No such identification for him, but one passport remained. Polish.

Wassermann read aloud, "Stanislaw Nowak, born in October of 1906. Tell me, doctors, does that man look around thirty?"

"Yes, yes, I'd say so," Dr. Oberst said before Dr. Gage could.

But Dr. Gage claimed the final, albeit redundant, word, "So, dead man is a Pole named Nowak. The unlucky sack."

Wassermann asked, "Mr. Kitagawa, ask YiMing Gao if he has any sort of documents, anything that was taken from him?"

Kitagawa rolled his eyes. "I doubt it. They are disorderly in the south. He's probably forgotten already by his clan."

The snideness transcended language, and Gao ducked his head.

Harriet, glumly aimless, looked straight ahead to Parisa. "Ever been kidnapped before?"

"First time."

Harriet responded, "Hopefully our wardens come quick. I don't like that painting. Makes my gut churn."

"Wardens…I remember no wardens," Parisa said, then nibbled on her lip. "Do we have wardens?"

Harriet began to blink erratically. "I would assume so."

Parisa muttered, "Assume…we assume…"

While the others snatched at the passports, demanding to

conduct their own verification, Parisa tilted her head towards the painting. The stag hunt. The mere image of it was suddenly arresting. She sniffed as though a strange odor filled her nose. A strange but familiar odor. She drifted her gaze over to Wassermann as though he were that strange but familiar odor.

She repeated, "Assume…" Her gaze drifted back to the painting. The stag was in so much pain. But so were the hounds. Their eyes were bulging and frantic. Her mouth slackened. There was another in the scene. A serene man, watching with his hands folded across his gut. So happy, so content, so blissfully aware yet apathetic of the stag's mutilation.

A loud, metallic screech followed by the sound of a hammer striking an anvil cut her trance, and made all the others snap their jaws shut. Not overtly obvious but silently understood—the doors had unbolted.

All were stunned, except Parisa. Like the unreal scent still lingered in her nose, she lifted herself out of her chair, tapping Harriet on the shoulder—a beckon to follow. Harriet obliged, still consumed in her trance.

Parisa came upon the door behind the dead man's chair. With a light hand, she tugged on the steel handle. It opened.

Morrelli suddenly shrieked something and slapped Renard on the shoulder.

Renard grimaced, rubbing and tugging on her earlobe, adorned with the heavy, golden earring, "Oh, Ms. Morrelli is correct, if a bit too loud, this could be a trap. Our captors may be crafty and wait for us to leave, then punish us."

Parisa and Harriet peeked their heads out of the door anyway.

A dark, iron-wrought hallway that disappeared into a dark void.

Dr. Oberst hobbled up behind them and took in the sight. He blanched, then ran to the curtain at the side of the room. He ripped it away and yanked up the windowpane. All may have believed, simply and subconsciously, it was nighttime. However, no night lay beyond the windowpane. No sunlight. No horizon. More iron wall.

Dr. Oberst shrieked, "I know this. We are underground. A bunker!"

Dr. Gage began angrily coughing and hacking, "I knew it. I knew you Krauts were up to something. I had my suspicions. This place reeked of a German bunker."

He tried to clamber his way over to Dr. Oberst, no doubt with some violent intent, but doubled over coughing and flushing red.

Those who understood English were soon beside themselves in a renewed panic. Those who didn't understand English figured it out for themselves.

Harriet was about to succumb to the hysteria, but Parisa placed her hand on her shoulder. Parisa sucked in a breath whilst turning her face up to match Harriet's eyes. Harriet exhaled, grabbed Parisa's hand, and let out a nervous snort. Together, the two drifted out into the cold and dark iron hallway, leaving the dining hall and its inhabitants to their fear.

Chapter Two

A cramped, metallic intestine. It stank of mildew. Grated vents punctured the underground ceiling. No light, not even a dim old bulb. Yet it was so silent, Harriet's deep breathing created thunder. Parisa gave her another analysis through the corner of her eye. A safe sort of woman. Very common, like any one seen dawdling out on the surface. Parisa wrapped her arm around the crook of Harriet's elbow.

Twenty strides from the dining hall door, Parisa halted, then yanked on Harriet's forearm with a surprising amount of grip strength. She drew in a heavy breath, bracing herself to do something even scarier than venturing into darkness—speaking English to a native.

Parisa whispered, "I think I know something. The man, his name I cannot pronounce. Switzerland, Zürich man. I think he is familiar, yes, I saw him before here, I was in Switzerland. Family holiday, do you understand?"

"Wassermann? Bleak fellow? Looks like a...well, I don't want to say frump."

Parisa fervently nodded, increasing the tension in her grip like she was strangling a chicken.

Harriet allowed her arm to go numb without protest.

"Familiar? In a bad way? He did something wrong?"

Parisa shrugged, "No, he was nice. I think. Barely met. Nice, but I did meet. And I'm not certain he saw me try doors. He woke up after I sat down again, I think. But I don't know."

"Maybe this is not random, then. But if by design, why me? I'm nobody. Things like this don't happen to nobodies," Harriet whispered and continued treading down, the vice grip still clenched around her arm. "Should we say something about that? Think it would help?"

"No. They will just yell at me, and I am shy of yelling."

"Well, drat, I don't like to be yelled at either."

The corridor's hollowness was suffocating. The passage narrowed with each step, yet the ceiling never grazed the tops of their heads. But it was the noise. The eternal amplification. The draft, the steps, a low scrape and groan as the metal seized under the cold.

Another fifty-odd paces later, they came across the next obstacle: another wrought-iron door with a strange engraving. A hound. Saliva dripping from its fangs, tears dripping from its eyes, a globe being crushed under its feet.

The two deliberated through a volley of grunting and gesturing who would give it a go. The winner of the silent deliberation was Harriet. Parisa crept her hand out, hazarding to grasp it. Locked, but gave the slightest hint of a budge.

A whimper escaped Parisa's lips and grew into a deafening cry as the iron bounced the noise.

Harriet muttered, "No worries. No worries. We can try the others. Let us do it together. Better than hanging around all those…people."

As if by some misplaced ill spirit, the bunker decided to bounce around only the latter words.

Harriet said louder, "Those people, I mean, are too

dignified for the likes of me."

The bunker decided not to bounce the correction.

Parisa drew her fingers along the engraving, then pressed her nose against the door hinges. "A scent."

Harriet gave it a quick sniff. "Smells like air."

Parisa whispered so lightly the words evaporated, "Like the painting. The stag hunt?"

"I reckon you're right," Harriet said, then licked her thumb and pressed it against the door. "Metal's clean. Wouldn't a bunker be dirty?"

"I don't know…I don't know such things."

"Well, double drat. Say, think it's worth getting another look at that painting, then? A motif like that in a place like this is odd."

Parisa nodded, then patted her chest as if to cease a flutter.

Uneasily, they started their return, each step bringing them closer to the dim yellow light on the opposite end of the corridor. Rancorous sound escaped from the dining hall, the bunker metals did their duty and announced that a new argument emerged. The two slowed their pace.

❋ ❋ ❋

Harriet and Parisa entered into a strange sight. A fight erupted between Dr. Gage and Kovacevic. It must have been pre-ordained to have such a fight, as both spoke like they had rehearsed in private.

"I have admitted to nothing, I have heard stories. This is how the West rounds up spies." Kovacevic said, backing into the corner at the opposite end, shoulders hunched up to his ears. "I am captured by mistake. This is the West, they see me and think I am villain."

Dr. Gage shouted, his face bulging red, jutting a sausage-like finger out with each sentence, "You made the first mention of treachery, don't lie to me. You must be some agent, tell me now, the King of Yugoslavia's agent. That's why your English is so proficient. King Alexander has eyes and ears everywhere."

"The King Alexander is dead for years. Not hard to believe that I may be talented in language. The West is like that, turn virtue to sin. Yes, I saw spies in Paris, but they were not Serbs, they were German," Kovacevic shouted back, jabbing a finger at Dr. Oberst. "Why is a German doctor in Paris?"

"For the *Société Psychanalytique de Paris*," Dr. Oberst said without true alarm. He had a rather flat look about him, resigned defensiveness at the feet of an accusation.

Dr. Gage grumbled, "Both of you are dastardly liars as far as I am concerned."

Dr. Oberst was about to make a concession, or maybe even agree in a vain attempt to restore peace, but was cut off by Kitagawa, who had been not-so-patiently waiting for some opportunity to orate.

"Oh yes, I hear many stories from colleagues, even in the Muslim world. Germans have infiltrated everywhere," he said in a feigned boredom befitting an aristocrat. "But I will not blame you, doctor, for this situation. I have also received much suspicion being from the Far East. Oh well. Once our captors present themselves to us, you all can go on and ask them. I say it hardly matters whether or not Kovacevic or Oberst are spies, I highly doubt this is a prison, all that matters is that my ransom is paid."

Dr. Oberst's face drooped, his mustache twitched, but he said nothing.

Morrelli, Gao, and Semyonov remained unaware of the argument's contents, but it was apparent enough that no progress was occurring; thus, they must not have cared. Gao instead joined Wassermann in examining the books on the shelves, copying every maneuver. Wassermann couldn't look any happier and was apparently ready to instruct Gao on the science of librarians. But as soon as Wassermann gained a companion, he lost him. Not five seconds later, Gao yelped, clapped, then dashed over to Kitagawa with a book gripped between his fingers.

A book in Chinese. He tried to present it to Kitagawa, who only pretended the vaguest interest. The man gingerly plucked the book up, mindful not to touch the boy's hands, shuffled through a couple pages, handed it back, and then flippantly responded to Gao's questions.

Dr. Gage asked, "What's this? What's he got going on there?"

Another feigned yawn, and Kitagawa rubbed his temples, "The Chinese boy cannot even read Chinese. He wanted to know what it said. It's simply some old picture book. Nothing worthwhile. My studies of the Mandarin language are more elevated, the ancient Eastern tomes of philosophy, epic poetry, and historical insights. Never spent time on products made for the illiterate. Would be a waste to my benefactors."

Wassermann said, thumbing through yet another crusty novel, "But that is a precise purpose, correct? Why have books in all our languages if not for a precise purpose? Certainly, there is a plot here. Come look at the shelves, all of you. See if there is anything you can read. Maybe there may be something of note among the pages."

Renard moaned, stretching her arms and legs out, slumping in her chair, "Oh, we are held captive for ransom, why bother? My husband will pay, and I will be free shortly."

Wassermann continued perusing the bookshelves as though he was spending the weekend leisurely at a library.

Kovacevic decided his time was best spent hunching up like a gargoyle and snarling at Dr. Gage, who reacted like a mother to an infant's tantrum. The rest sat around the table, crossing their arms and sucking their teeth. The dead man still lay at the head of the table. No point in giving him further attention. None save for Renard noticed Parisa and Harriet's return.

"I assume that our salvation is not down the hallway?" Renard asked, her disappointment thinly veiled, but fleeting.

Harriet said, "No, no, just a locked door with a dog on it. But these three other doors, we may as well try them. At least nobody was waiting for us, nobody to punish us for leaving this room."

Parisa tugged on Harriet's sleeve, and she pointed to the canvas painting hanging on the wall. The longer she noticed it, the more obscene it became. It was regal, but in decay. The right-hand corner wilted down. The frame was too large for the canvas, and there was no glass covering, allowing the paint to peel. The painting begged Parisa to rip it down.

Parisa walked beneath it, the urge to tear it down strengthening with each step. But her short stature curtailed her. Three mighty hops, but her fingernails barely brushed the base. Parisa attempted to frown the painting into submission. A strategy abandoned after a full minute. Harriet gave it a go. A similar failure, more ego-bruising, as Harriet had a head of height over Parisa.

The only other captive intrigued by the attempt to defile the painting was, quite strangely, the Soviet Semyonov. He walked up, reached, easily ripped the painting from the frame, and presented the tatters to Parisa with a shaky twitch of the mouth. Maybe it was an attempt at a smile, or maybe it was the beginning of a seizure. He didn't even look to see what he unveiled, only waited for Parisa and Harriet's response, perhaps a precious mutter of gratitude. But the two women became slack jawed.

A mirror. There it was, etched in the mirror glass, smeared over with red ink.

Dic veritatem ut ex inferno egrediaris

The air thickened. Several stiff seconds passed. Semyonov never got his gratitude. Finally, the squabblers took notice.

Dr. Oberst said, "It's Latin. I had to study it in medical school."

"As did I," Dr. Gage interjected.

"Me as well," Kitagawa said. "Not medical school, through love of learning."

"Well, then, you geniuses, what does it say?" Renard said. As quickly as her attention had been commanded by the mirror, it faded. She resettled in her seat and fiddled with her jewelry, which was now understood to be her most loyal companion.

Dr. Gage started, "Well, it has been a while for me, you see, but *veritas* is truth, and *veritatem* must be some sort of conjugation."

Oberst quickly interjected, "Say truth in fire leave."

Kitagawa jolted up, "No, no, not quite, it must be *speak from truth and out of fire leave*. It does not appear to be grammatically correct."

He nodded to himself, overtly overjoyed with his translation. Dr. Gage and Dr. Oberst pondered it, probably agreed, but refused to confess it.

Morrelli spoke to Renard, who promptly relayed the thought, "Ms. Morrelli is certain of its meaning: *Speak the truth to exit Hell.*"

Dr. Gage nodded, "Oh yes, yes Inferno, that is what we were missing. The cliché, Dante's Divine Comedy. I was just about to say that."

Kitagawa struck up a finger, "As was I."

"Oh yes, how plain it actually is," Dr. Oberst added.

Harriet hurriedly interrupted, "Sure, that's what it may say, but what does it mean?" She inspected the etching, pushing up on Semyonov's shoulder to draw her face closer, "The ink isn't very dry. How long would you say we have all been conscious? Fifteen minutes? Twenty? It must not have been very long. It must have been expected to be uncovered. But why?"

Dr. Oberst's face sank deeper into fear. "As I suspected, this is no ransom kidnapping. I never assumed so, for only a few of us bring any promise of money. Furthermore, for any kidnappers, such a group of strangers would be too cumbersome to ensnare."

"I was not ensnared. I was beaten then forced," Kovacevic blurted out, energetically bobbing his head with each word. "I knew it. We must be political prisoners, or you all are enemy agents."

Kitagawa drummed his fingernails on the table, pouting, "But what of the Chinese boy and the Soviet, or even Foster and Morrelli? They are worthless, politically speaking, of course. Or the Polish man? Stanislav something… If he were a political prisoner, wouldn't they know of a severe allergy? Wouldn't they avoid an accidental murder?"

He snapped his head to the side and sharply spoke to Gao, who shook his head eagerly.

Kitagawa lilted a distraught sigh. "No, as I thought, Gao is a peasant, son to another peasant. Why steal a Chinese boy from Kunming? Why bring him here, to some German bunker, among Persian and European celebrities?"

Renard said, "It matters not. My husband will notice my absence and find me. If not him, then the police, surely. I suspect this is purely entertainment for us, something to keep the mind busy while we wait for the money to be delivered. Or it means absolutely nothing. Vandalism maybe. That is why it was covered with that ugly Renaissance pretender."

"You twits," Dr. Gage grumbled. He pointed his cane back to the mirror etching, "You are asking the wrong *why*. This is not a matter of why we are here, no, right now the question is *why* we are left to deduce this, *why* we must speak truth."

Before any could answer, a clang violently echoed down the iron hallway. A slow hiss punctured the air. Vents leaked a cloudy gas, filling the room before a single blink. Nobody had sufficient time to react; they only choked and coughed. Soon, all were out as cold as they arrived.

Chapter Three

Parisa awoke first, the others several minutes apart from each other, all seated in their original arrangement. No dead Polish man. The etching remained in the mirror; the ink fully dried. Panic faded to snarky apathy. The painting lay crumpled on the floor.

Dr. Gage grumbled to himself between hacking coughs, cursing his poor fitness between breaths, "Thank goodness the body has been taken. It would start to smell soon."

Dr. Oberst similarly wheezed, but quietly. His eyes frantically bulged, and he pounded his fist on his chest. Harriet ran over and helped swat him on the back. In any other life, she would have made a wondrous cow maid, as just about every single bodily fluid expelled from Dr. Oberst at once with a single harsh slap.

"Are you alright?" she cried.

He faintly nodded, clutching his throat with his sinewy hands.

"Yes, yes, I believe the gas is laced with traces of morphine. I am also allergic." His weak voice strengthened with each cough, "But a good constitution allows me to survive such small doses. Hopefully, this isn't frequent."

Semyonov hysterically chattered to Kovacevic, who shook his head with unnecessarily pointed irritation.

"*Ne govorim Ruski*," Kovacevic responded.

Semyonov repeated "*Ne govoryu po Russk?*" with a foolhardy glimmer of hope. The unveiling of cognates only served to further irritate the non-consensual companion, and Kovacevic scooted his chair further away from the Soviet.

As though his feelings were an impenetrable fortress, or just didn't exist, Semyonov spoke again to Kovacevic, who listened with great displeasure. However, the displeasure did give way to some understanding, albeit begrudgingly, and Kovacevic pouted but started to engage Semyonov in something resembling a proper discussion.

It was anybody's guess what the two were trying to communicate. Kovacevic made ample use of every facial muscle possible, contorting into a smile, then a sneer, then a grimace, then a look of abject confusion. Semyonov attempted the same. All that could be said about it—an attempt. But the clumsy attempt bore fruit.

"I think Semyonov says he wants to look around too. If the two women venture out again, he wants to join. Don't know why. He must be stupid," Kovacevic spat then returned to his brooding.

"Well, look at that, the boy is asking for permission from his fellow prisoners," Dr. Gage chuckled, "Yes, though, I agree. You two. Girls, be sure to take him with you if you do try to be adventurers again. Much safer in the company of a man, I do say, even one like him."

"Another door then, shall we?" Harriet looked behind her at the right corner door. "What do you think, Parisa? That one next? Perhaps going in the opposite direction will give something new."

Once again, Parisa readied an answer but was cut off by

Kovacevic.

He muttered, "Why not try all at once? What's the worst that can happen?"

Dr. Oberst said, "Why bother? It will only be more locked doors. There's no use in getting up. If anything, it may bring punishment upon us, like when you all ripped the painting. We must be more cautious, especially those of us with medical conditions worth considering."

Dr. Gage and Kitagawa wordlessly agreed to the sentiment, which must have stung. Fellow kidnappees, yes. Intellectual peers, never. But unfortunately, good reason made good reason. Yet, the others did not listen as nothing explicitly compelled them to.

Soon, the group split up, and all four doors leading out of the dining hall cautiously opened. Some ill-founded sense of discovery lingered tantalizingly in the metal tubes, and Parisa held her breath.

Those who rejected that sense only sat staring at each other. Dr. Gage bounced his eyes between Kitagawa and Dr. Oberst, measuring which one would be a more engaging companion for argument. Dr. Oberst chose to stare specifically at Kitagawa. Kitagawa decided to stare at his fingernails, then decided to elevate the effort by migrating to the mirror, in which he commenced to continuously re-flatten his glossy dome.

Nobody accompanied Gao as he opened the wide iron door on the right wall behind Kitagawa. He did quietly request Kitagawa to join him, but the request was expectedly refused. Luckily, it was not a far journey. The iron corridor was only roughly fifteen steps long, came to a massive opening, and that was it. One peek inside and Gao returned a mere minute after he left.

He gave a small report to Kitagawa, who moodily translated, "There's a standard industrial kitchen behind me.

Barren inside."

Gao then darted over to the discarded stag hunt painting and frantically sputtered words as he tried to present it to Kitagawa. Kitagawa listened intently for all of twelve seconds before dismissing the boy with a wrinkled nose and an eyeroll.

Morrelli and Renard ventured out of the door on the left wall. After an uneasy thirty or so paces, the hallway sharply cornered left before presenting them with two more doors. A narrower steel door on the left wall, crested by a steel grate akin to jail cell bars. Morrelli gave it a firm grasp. Locked. It actually brought a small relief—an abdication of further responsibility.

Morrelli turned her attention hesitantly a couple more paces downward to the center door that marked the end of the hall. Again, she gave the knob a shake. Open. No relief. Now she had the responsibility of doing a proper survey. Quietly, she peeked inside with Renard clinging to her back.

Small, stony, circular, and soulless. There was a small step stool under an opening in the ceiling, only wide enough for the crown of the head to fit. Curved mirrors lined the dark room's walls, reflecting an ugly gray light back onto each other. Everything looked wet, and it smelled like filthy rainwater.

Very quickly, Renard grew frightful and begged to hurry back to the yellow glow of the dining hall. She waited for no response before she started tugging Morrelli's braid back down the hallway.

Renard reported back what they had seen, with an impressive amount of theatrical flair.

Dr. Gage nodded to their brief yet artistic description, "Sounds like the observation room. Grab a sheet of paper, I have a pen here. Make a note of that. And don't forget to put the kitchen on there as well."

The passage that Parisa and Harriet optioned was much

shorter but much more bothersome than the previous. It presented a choice via a forked path: left, right, and straight. They opted to go straight. Kovacevic and Semyonov veered right.

They regrouped maybe three minutes back in the dining hall, relaying the expedition. Parisa and Harriet found some sort of armory, all articles inside gated and locked.

Dr. Gage leaned forward. "What sort of armory?"

Harriet shrugged, "The type with weapons."

"What sort of weapons?"

"I think guns."

"Well, what sort of guns?"

"I think the type that shoots."

Dr. Gage stopped with his questions.

To the right was a boiler room. Kovacevic, in a fit of caustic cooperation, stated that the boilers appeared to be in use—steam and fire poured from active machinery. The two did not describe the room any further; Kovacevic out of spite, and Semyonov out of inability.

"The left?" Wassermann asked. A mild question, but all at the table jumped regardless, because they had certainly forgotten he was even there. So pale and gray, he almost vanished into thin air.

Harriet responded after an uncomfortably long pause, "We haven't checked yet. The hallways absolutely wreck the nerves, to be out there even a minute is too long."

Wassermann attempted some level of bravado, which came out as a pitiful chuckle, "Well now, let us go check. I feel like we have nothing to worry about, if someone wished harm upon us, then there would be harm upon us."

Renard said, "One could say there already is harm upon us."

It was a joke, a poorly executed one. Wassermann gave it

a sympathetic laugh, an effort no others attempted. His laugh died in its infancy, and a sudden shame seized up his throat. He chose the remedy of turning on his heels and walking out into the hallway.

Parisa tugged on Harriet's sleeve again. "We must see. We do nothing, then we will be forgotten. Forgotten, then die."

Harriet shrugged her concurrence. They followed, came to the same impasse, and veered left. After twenty steps, the hallway cornered right. Peculiarly, in this corner rested a mounted radio set: old, dirty, and lifeless. Wassermann, at the helm, scrutinized it, rolling it in his palms with a curious eye before setting it back in place.

"Broken," he groaned.

The three continued right and walked for another twenty steps before coming to yet another godforsaken door. At least this door was different. Not iron. Either brass or copper. The handle was no utilitarian knob. Decorative and expensive. Worst of all, the door was ajar. Harriet and Parisa hesitated, waiting for the other to take first action, but Wassermann continued on, slowly peeking his head in.

"Looks to be the navigation room of sorts," he said, diving into the room and beckoning them to follow. Neither woman moved. Another quiet deliberation.

Parisa whispered, "Think he's safe?"

Harriet responded, "Yes, a bit of a drip, but safe."

"A drip?"

"Reminds me of my brother. A charisma vampire."

Parisa nodded, and elbow to elbow they followed after Wassermann. From the odd twitch in his face, he heard his moniker yet provided no protest.

The pressure felt unusually high and was much warmer than the bunker's cold confines. No room for a bunker but fit for the quarters of a ship captain. A ship's wheel stood central in the small, square, brass-emboldened room, with a golden box lodged underneath. Various old graying maps lined the walls. Towards the back cowered a desk encompassed in razor wires like a spider's thread around a wasp. Deep inside the tangles waited another mirror. Another etching smeared over with dry ink.

Parisa and Harriet hesitated to venture any further, as though an unsaid embargo was placed on disturbing the settled dust. Wassermann felt no such embargo, walking straight towards the desk.

"Look here, more Latin. We must go fetch someone who may understand. I think the Italian woman may know it best."

Harriet nodded in agreement, obviously eager to leave. Wassermann unnecessarily relayed the same information to Parisa in shaky French, accidentally peppering in some Italian and German. Parisa nodded, nevertheless, and rewarded him with a delicate upward tug of the mouth. It would have been condescending to commit to a full smile to one like him.

Before departing, she studied him, overtly picking apart his utterly mundane face for the faintest hint of any malice. None. The average bureaucrat: disheveled, dopey, and dull. Yet, there must have been something there; her study drew on longer and longer. Something nameless, but certainly not fangless. A charisma vampire indeed.

She accidentally frowned at him.

Wassermann said after a flaccid chuckle, "You alright, Miss Shahidi?" His face retained its gray flatness, but his neck veins shivered.

"Why do I know you?"

"Haven't the fuzziest idea. I certainly don't know you."

Harriet wiggled Parisa's arm, "Well then, let's go give our report to the flock."

Parisa vacantly mumbled her concurrence and followed

Harriet out of the door.

✶ ✶ ✶

Dr. Oberst took it upon himself to draw a crude map of the bunker's layout under the watchful eye of Dr. Gage and Kitagawa. He even bothered to use a book to straighten the lines and used ornate calligraphy to name and number each room. With great glee, he presented his handiwork to his self-selected supervisors.

A beautiful map. Central dining room. Upper wall passage leading towards a locked door and an observatory. Left wall passage leading to yet another locked door with the dog engraving. Lower wall passage leading to a kitchen. Right wall passage splitting to a three-way aisle: navigation, armory, and boiler room.

Dr. Gage griped, "Drawn a bit small, wouldn't you say? Not all of us have young eyes." Dr. Oberst's mustache bristled as he scratched out his penmanship and hastily scrawled large letters overtop.

Harriet asked, "The door that we first went to, the dog one, do you think that was the exit?"

Dr. Oberst shook his head, "No, no, I don't think so. In my experience, an exit would be this one near the observation room. It makes the most tactical sense for the access points to be condensed. But I'm no architect."

Dr. Gage added, "You're also no doctor."

Renard said, "It's stranger still that we have access to an armory, even if they are locked. So odd, whether we are here for some political or financial purpose, why not bar all doors and remove weapons?"

Dr. Gage groaned, "No. No. No. You twits. We have been given an order, don't you all understand? Speak truth and exit? Now then, who here has the truth? One of you must be a suspect in some crime, or rather, we all are. Come on then, fess up."

"I have committed no crime, sir," Renard replied, "Unless you have something to confess yourself. No, rather, I think maybe the Yugo was right; maybe more of you are spies. Once you reveal yourselves, then we may leave. Yes, I think that is right. Who else besides the Yugo is a villain of the state?"

Kovacevic was about to protest the accusation, but stopped with a sudden twist in his face, then said, "Then why Latin? Why not ask in our mother tongue separately? It must be a great cost, stealing away people from all corners of the Earth to be brought to some German dungeon."

"How could all of us be suspects?" Kitagawa continued the thought. He furrowed his brow in a deeper contemplation, scratched his small head, and muttered something to himself in some other unknown tongue.

Gao tried to copy the posture, but a venomous sneer from Kitagawa curtailed the exercise.

Dr. Gage grumbled and rocked himself in his chair. A slumbering agitation bubbled to the surface. In a jolt, he sharply asked Dr. Oberst, "Let me see your passport. How old are you?"

Dr. Oberst stiffened and handed nothing over. "I am thirty-six. Why?"

"You were fighting age…" Dr. Gage said. His grip tightened around his cane, his gaze unrelenting, something turbulent overcoming him. The deep breaths produced from his gut became huskier, sturdier.

His deteriorating temper stifled the air. Nobody spoke. Nobody breathed.

Sweat dotted Dr. Oberst's forehead, "As were you assuredly."

"Yes, I was a surgeon then, blast it all, stop evading the

point. What role did you play?" Dr. Gage demanded again.

Held fast in place, Dr. Oberst stammered, then looked around the table for allies. There were none. If anything, he only found more detractors.

"I was seventeen in 1916," Dr. Oberst stuttered. He turned to the Yugo, "Where were you during the war, Kovacevic?"

"I was nine at war's end. Sat at home with my family," Kovacevic said, slightly bemused, and leaned back with an acerbic satisfaction.

Dr. Oberst frantically looked around the room and settled on the Soviet—undoubtedly too young to have taken part.

Alone, he refaced Dr. Gage's interrogation, "I was conscripted. And I accepted our loss graciously. Afterwards, I left for medical school in France. That's all, I'm no criminal. I have nothing to be ashamed of."

"Disgraceful...I should have known. You recognized this as a bunker first." Dr. Gage glowered, "No, I think maybe some truth lies there. So, we have a spy and murderer of peace. Who else here has some crime they need to confess?"

Kovacevic exclaimed, "I am no spy."

Dr. Oberst lobbied a similar protest, attempting to join efforts, but Kovacevic's superfluous mean giggle disallowed a bandwagon.

Kitagawa said, his nose high in the air, "No, that cannot be it. Most of us live too far off or are too young. I'd rather not play whatever game our captors have for us. I think we should find a way out. Let us make our own exit."

Harriet nervously asked, "But what if there's more gas? I have no allergies, but I could feel the drugs weaken my chest."

She looked to Parisa, who was still staring at the etched mirror. With more of Parisa's vague yet articulate hand gestures, an unconscious understanding passed through both of them.

Harriet continued, "I think we are meant to look through the unlocked rooms. Just as one of us was meant to rip apart the old painting. We aren't meant to try to escape."

Renard scoffed, heaving a breath over her crossed arms, "Well, of course kidnappers don't want us to escape." She turned with a squint to Dr. Oberst, "You batter France, then settle in France. Hmm, to me, yes, that is a crime."

"I was mainly in Flanders," Dr. Oberst said meekly, "Conflicts happen all the time. It's no crime."

Kitagawa sighed. "I have no use for such spats. All those with rationality must concur that we should not sit around idly. One of you must produce a means of escape. I have no brawn, but maybe the Italian woman can rip a door off its hinges. If it wasn't from the hands of a woman, it would have been quite the impressive display. Perhaps wars would be over in an instant if the front lines were nothing but farm maidens."

Wassermann eagerly tried to engage in parliamentary discussion, "Yes—"

Another jolt in the room. They didn't even realize he had returned from the navigation room.

He continued nonetheless, "The observation room or the navigation room may be good places to start. They, at the very least, may provide some bearing on our location, if not provide a passage out."

He looked around for volunteers. None jumped to their feet. Gao and Semyonov, the two who flatly didn't understand any of the quarrel before them, sat sullenly in shared confusion. Neither Kitagawa nor Kovacevic bothered trying to explain. Wassermann wilted, yet again.

Kovacevic spewed, "Why should I do anything for any of you? All of you, even you all from the East. Done nothing but accuse me and give me insults." He pounded his fist on the table and raised his voice to a shout, "I will do nothing until you all say I am blameless."

Renard said, slightly scandalized, or at least pretending to be, "Peter? Peter, was it? Well, Peter, you did accuse us first of being spies. It cannot be helped." A saccharine, placating grin crumbled the rest of her cracked makeup.

"It is Petar. I was beaten across the head in Paris and then placed here among all you, then tried to place me a criminal. No, I have done no wrong, and I have no blame. I am blamed always."

Renard interrupted, "Regardless, we have been here a mere hour. Surely our captors will make themselves known and give us some manner of explanation. Hopefully soon. I fatigue easily."

Wassermann cast a sorrowful look, "I would not place money on that. No, I think it's best we find our own way, while we are still left alone. There is no room for accusations now; we must collaborate sensibly. You agree?"

No response from Renard. Five seconds of awkwardness. Morrelli shouldered Renard.

"Oh, was he talking to me?"

Wassermann wilted even further.

Harriet and Parisa hesitated to join the congregation's decades-old dramatics. A deliberation passed between them through grunts, nods, and whispering in each other's ear. At last, they shrugged, and both optioned to remain self-contained. The sensible thing to do.

All were silent. For once. For a fleeting, precious once. Silent and unmoving.

Yet, Morrelli, spurned on by something unholy, turned to Renard, "Waiting is boring."

"Oh? Ms. Morrelli, I would —"

"Eh? Ms. Morrelli? No. Alessandra," Morrelli said, "I am no Ms. Morrelli."

Kitagawa snorted, "I'll say. Too much physical fortitude."

Thus, Renard gave the name change her stamp of approval, which, for some reason, was left to her authority. "Well, then, Alessandra, what do you propose?"

Alessandra declared, "Victory!"

Alessandra spoke to Wassermann in Italian, with too many hand gestures. But it at least bridged the gap. A promise to accompany him if he were to venture out again to find some hidden exit. Wassermann graciously, yet embarrassingly desperately, accepted and turned the invite back onto Renard. Surprisingly, she also accepted, but not before delicately licking her thumb and wiping a smear of dirt off Alessandra's face.

Renard said, "Ah, I have no use for fear. I am too valuable a target for harm to befall me. No, this is a chance. I shall be a literary heroine! An adventurer!"

The three talked amongst themselves, free of the burden of conversing in English, reveling in their little code. Quietly and quickly, they left out the back iron door, down the hallway, and veered left. Abruptly, Wassermann started to tremble. Yet, Renard and Alessandra didn't notice. Not four steps into the hallway, they apparently forgot he was among them.

Chapter Four

It was not that Renard, Wassermann, and Alessandra's departure went unprotested, merely uncared for. Personal interests retained supremacy over whatever it was those three decided to waste time doing.

Kitagawa gawked wide-eyed over the Latin phrase, his mouth pressed to the back of his hand in a supercilious academic posture, completely ignoring the pointed, anti-Bismarck derisions uttered by Dr. Gage and the general hateful stare from Kovacevic.

It surely tickled his brain in a diabolically comedic way. Some poor cow maid from the low country of Italy produced a better translation than the literal and clinical minds of the educated, hailing from either end of the globe. Kitagawa held himself above it all, regardless, lording over the table with the social conceit due to being an expert on all things cultural.

He pondered aloud, "A furnace of fire does not carry such evil connotations in Japan. Ignis and inferno, fire and hell, such Western machinations, as denoted by the very cruel and very selfish predilections of the afterlife. Undoubtedly, our captors bely on the occidental. If we are to make sense of it all, then we must know our captors' perspectives. Dare I suggest Kovacevic may actually have a correct assumption? This is a form of punishment."

Kovacevic perked up, maybe thinking about submitting a verbal acknowledgment, but then repledged himself to his beloved companions: apathy and annoyance.

Yet, the pause gave room for Dr. Oberst to warily engage, "Selfish? How can a fiery hell be selfish?"

"Yes, Inferno implies that the world is only for the living, no consideration for spirits. That death is final, a very limiting notion, and the demonization of heat and flame. They are both very natural wonders, yet carry such hateful implications. But I suppose it is not just the West that corrupts the essence of fire, and makes it a punishment?" Kitagawa addressed Parisa, "Sephardic traditions rhyme. I am not so Anglo-minded to forget where some interpretations originate."

Parisa twisted her face up, shrugged, and then ducked her head, which was apparently not a suitable response for Kitagawa as illustrated by the crinkle above his lip.

Dr. Gage coughed to bring attention back towards himself, "Do you not believe that those who do wrong are to be punished? What is not more punishing than intense heat? Spend one day alone in the desert sands, and you will see why it is natural to prescribe suffering to the flame. Fanciful over-philosophizing. Find some real employment, and you may need to alter your manner of speaking."

Kitagawa responded with a lilting sigh. "I suppose I am discontent that the foundation of law of powerful lands is founded upon such a strange preconception. But I guess that is why it is the way that it is. Latin gave birth to modern law and modern religion. The words carry such weight on the framing. I wonder if hell was cold, if the message sent to us would be any different? Any more decipherable? Even further, does wrongdoing need punishment or correction? The lingering of a spirit can be corrected, but not damnation."

Dr. Oberst said, "What do you mean by that? You must have word-smithed many beautiful essays in anthropological journals, but could it not be stated more succinctly?"

Little did Dr. Oberst know that Kitagawa was fundamentally incapable of being succinct.

Dr. Gage croaked from his chair, "It doesn't mean anything. All you young thinkers all sound the same. And it was not Latins that founded law, it was the Greeks. Perhaps I should call up your benefactor and tell him that despite all your time and money spent in Cambridge, you cannot remember such a simple fact."

Kitagawa's eyes sparkled, and his shoulders slackened, "Young thinkers learn from the older masters. Any faults that lie with me were molded by my predecessors, by your contemporaries."

Dr. Gage responded, "Nonsense. My contemporaries didn't need to recite an encyclopedia to express a single thought."

Little did Dr. Gage know that his contemporaries were also fundamentally incapable of being succinct.

Kovacevic broke into the orbit of self-importance, "You all are insane, arguing about stupid school things. Nobody cares about that. Leave your classroom once."

Recoiling back into a stiff spine, Kitagawa's mouth hung in a haughty scoff, "Maybe to the pawns it has no meaning, but to the kings, those that win the game, thought and philosophy dictate wars, dictate the society that pawns must live in. As a spy, you should understand as much."

"I am not a spy."

Dr. Gage laughed, "You have already betrayed yourself. You said you were beaten across the head. Therein lies your confession."

Kovacevic narrowed his eyes, jumped to his feet, and

began to formulate a defense, but stuttered. Pupils rapidly dilating, he inwardly convulsed for a second, gnawing on his bottom lip, and sat back down with a huff.

A smug glee lit up Dr. Gage's face. He answered the question all were too proud to ask, "Immunity to poisons. A learned trait among those who operate clandestinely."

Kovacevic sucked his teeth, "I was born with a good stomach, is that wrong? No use in arguing, you decide my blame already."

None responded. It was just tiring rather than incendiary. More amusement found in plainly staring at the ground.

Dr. Oberst yanked on his collar, crumpling between the angry glares of Dr. Gage and Kovacevic.

Seeking solace in the competition of verbal prose, he scratched his mustache and turned to Kitagawa, "Seems to me you are arguing our captors are Western thinkers. This is good news! Then they must be humane."

Dr. Gage huffed, "We have moved past that topic already, moron."

Dr. Oberst furrowed inward and picked at his thumbs in his lap.

As though by expressed request, Kitagawa began to warble on about his life at Cambridge, living among the kings of the future, talking to nobody in particular. Dr. Gage interrupted often to provide a much-needed but much-ignored humbling. Nobody else was invited into their joint soliloquy. Nobody wanted to be.

Harriet and Parisa sat next to each other, watching the barbs volley back and forth over the table.

Harriet whispered, "Doesn't this feel a bit, I don't know, silly? Given the circumstances?"

Parisa shrugged, "I think geniuses all do this, like bored aunties around a stove."

"Oh, well, I guess so, but I must admit, I do think Mr. Kitagawa has a point, and I have always felt like a pawn, or some small little cog my whole life. Must be nice to be a king. What's it like, Parisa? Being so close to a king?"

Parisa thought it over for a moment, but then shrugged, "Normal."

"Don't give me that. Tell me, when we get to the surface, by any means, do I have an invite to your palace? If you want, you can see the dump I call home."

"I live in no palace," Parisa lied, then turned her attention to Semyonov. "Harriet, do you think he is our age?"

"The Soviet? Can't say, but not far off. Why?"

Parisa leaned in even closer, cupping her words so none strayed into the wrong ear, "I do not trust the others, and I think we need one like him. Maybe protection, yes? As Dr. Gage said."

Harriet bit down on her fingernails, "Sure, I'll take any friendship offered."

Their conversation was interrupted by another embarrassing display around the table. By some stretch of thematic drift, Kovacevic began demanding some sort of apology. Not for any pointed attacks, but for the mere generality of history and reality.

He said, "You. Shahidi. The Ottomans. They brutalized my people. Agree. More so than German to British. Yes, agree, tell them, tell the Westerners."

Stupefied, she blinked and stammered. Her recently acquired reflex demanded she grip onto Harriet's arm.

Harriet obliged, "Leave us out of this. How can we hope to keep up in such a conversation? Shouldn't we focus on figuring out what the Latin means?"

Kovacevic responded, "Answer! Then yes, we figure."

Parisa squeaked, "I am not Ottoman... I don't know."

Kovacevic rendered himself back to muttering, "France and Britain have some violence and must have war over it. We have too much for century and must sleep through it."

Kitagawa conducted another well-practiced yawn, "Yes, futile in arguing with the incapable. My apologies, I thought maybe some light brain exercise might be entertaining, I didn't mean to cause a stir. We shall wait in silence for our rescue, then. May we, upon our return to the surface, resume being strangers again."

Dr. Gage, still full of argumentative fire, coughed himself into the back of his chair. "Oh, confound it all," he said, rubbing his wheezing chest, "Let us resume being strangers now."

❋❋❋

Those three that ventured were safe from the exasperating discourse but were presented with a new puzzle. Upon closer inspection of the ship wheel, it was wrapped thoroughly in razor wire like the desk, giving it a rather fuzzy appearance, and the center housed a thick blade. A funnel leading to a tube connected to an ornate box beneath the wheel, its joints shrouded with a confusing array of machinery. A faint humming noise whirred amid the jumble.

Upon remembering his existence, Alessandra spoke in Italian to Wassermann, "How odd, what could be the purpose of this? The box is not unlike the one under the table. See here, it looks clamped shut by some machinery. Looks too strong for even me to rip open."

Wassermann joined her inspection while Renard turned her attention to the desk, specifically to the etching in the mirror.

Per effusionem sanguinis venustas venit
quae spes dominum habet

Renard beckoned Alessandra towards her, instructing her not to prick herself on the razor wire. Alessandra cocked her head to the side, chin resting on her knuckles, stirring her thoughts, then leaned against Renard with mimed mental fatigue.

Much to Wassermann's dismay, Alessandra spoke in French, "This one is more difficult. Some of the nouns I can translate, but I'm not sure if it would be an excellent translation. I can try, maybe to sound it out word for word, but I cannot promise any sense. By pouring blood, something —don't know the word, comes what—something, something has…. I think. I hate to suggest this, but maybe one of those who studied Latin in university may fill in the gaps."

At first, Renard grimaced, but it melted into a smile as she patted Alessandra on the shoulder, "Maybe we should, once their tempers cool a little. It is such a burden to listen to them, fawning and stroking themselves. I'd hate to think what will become of their dispositions once we ask for their assistance."

Wassermann joined, with his embarrassingly elementary French, "A second Latin sentence, also a command?"

"No, I think it's a question. I cannot say until the entire sentence is deciphered," Alessandra said, glancing around the walls of the room at the old and crusty maps. "These maps here, they aren't like the ones I have seen in school. To be honest, I haven't spent much time in a proper schoolhouse, so I may be mistaken. Do these maps also strike you odd, Lucie?"

Renard squinted at them, drawing her finger down the edges. "Mrs. Renard, you mean. Yes, very strange, there's a lot of little lines and circles, good eye Alessandra. What do all the colors mean? Wassermann, have you a clue?"

"A what?"

"A clue. Do you have a guess?"

"Oh, pardon, no, I do not."

Renard huffed at his intellectual shortcomings. "God must

be challenging my humility. This is something else we may have to ask the others. But I'd rather die here than return empty-handed, without something to boast. How about the wires, do you think there is something worth protecting in the desk, or in the box fastened under the wheel? These are very expensive furnishings for an otherwise drab and utilitarian office. And why is it so stuffy here? My God, it smells."

Wassermann grunted, "Why ask the others? They prefer among themselves argue, erh, themselves argue among…argue among themselves. Was that right?"

"The Persian girl? She seems to have some sense, the first to leave the room, no?" Alessandra asked mildly. "She doesn't look very strong, though. That will likely be a challenge. Oh, but her chosen companion… I get a bad sense from the American one. Just farm sense. Like a wild horse. No, not a horse, a hound. She's going to bite. I can feel it."

Renard chuckled and playfully patted Alessandra on the back, "I got a strange sense from her too, but I thought it was just because she was somewhat ugly."

"Ugly might be too mean a word."

"Fine. Possesses coarser beauty."

"Appearances don't matter here. It is just the general air I refer to."

"Appearances matter more than you'd think," Renard responded, approaching sternness.

Alessandra surrendered to Renard's logic and waited for Wassermann to provide some sort of diversion. He did eagerly, long awaiting re-entrance into their conversation.

"I'd rather we go back with some sort of answer, or, how do you say… clue. Alessandra, you ripped the box open before. Do it again?"

"I don't know, some wires are poking in and around it, connected to something whirring in the wheel. A machine it sounds like, I have heard similar noises on my farm. I would not touch it," she said, even gently lowering Renard's hand from touching the map. "Something bad is here. I sense it."

"That sense is the musk. It reeks and it's hot. Something's burning," Renard replied, wrinkling her nose. "Ghastly. If we are to rely on your farmer's sense, Alessandra, then I suppose all I can offer are statements of the obvious."

Wassermann did not heed Alessandra's warning; in fact, he stooped down to take a closer look at the golden box beneath the wheel. He ignored the dull whirring and the razor wires, and hovered his face before it, as if mesmerized by its humble gleam. He took in a hard swallow. His tremble grew violent.

Alessandra said, "Mr. Wassermann, let us look in every corner. Maybe that big display in the center is some sort of distraction from another window of entry. Let us look for any vents or perhaps trap doors or something." She tugged on Renard for concurrence, but the actress just shrugged.

"Let the man do as he pleases. No use in arguing, we should leave that to the others. Come now, Alessandra, we said we would find answers, so let us look for them, perhaps in a less dangerous place. All these blades and wires are making me nervous. Please, be careful not to nick yourself."

The two women were just about to turn their attention away when Wassermann firmly grasped hold of the golden box, intending to rip it away from its wiring.

First touch of palm to gold, each fiber seized. His eyes widened to a vessel-bursting bulge. His teeth clenched and ground so hard one must have broken. The veins in his neck and hands strained against his skin, threatening to rip through. A stench of sulfuric smoke clogged the air.

"Oh God, electricity," Alessandra cried, and then shoved Renard away to keep her from yanking at Wassermann. "I've seen this before, do not touch him without some barrier."

Alessandra ripped off the old, stained, milking apron that was wrapped around her waist. Barely a hair of rubber's protective sheen on the surface, but it was all the insulation available. She wrapped it around his hands and pried them off the electrified box, almost snapping several of his fingers in the process. Resting him on his back, she pressed her ear to his mouth. No breathing. His face was terribly white. More so than standard. His mouth and eyes outstretched in a supernatural grimace. Both arms stiff. Both hands reeked of fried skin.

Renard cried, "What should we do? He isn't moving."

Alessandra groped around his neck for a pulse. Futile. Her hands shook too much.

Renard yelled, grabbing up the shaken Alessandra and running out the door, "The doctor. The English one. He must have experience with this. We should go fetch him."

Alessandra offered no protest but only looked back briefly at the rigid body of Wassermann. The navigation room seemed to darken. A small shuffle and a cackle.

As soon as her heel crossed the threshold, the door swung shut.

❊ ❊ ❊

Renard broke the uncomfortable silence of the dining hall with her hysterical cry, "Dr. Gage, come to the navigation office! An accident. Wassermann's electrocuted!"

Alessandra, in tow, nodded feverishly yet vacantly. Dr. Gage tried to leap to his feet, but the best he could do was groan and hobble onto the support of his cane.

Dr. Oberst was quicker in action and strangely quite giddy.

"How long ago was this?" Dr. Oberst asked while making his way over to the door.

Renard shrieked, "Just a few moments ago. Please, Dr. Gage must have more experience with such injuries; he should come help. We need an actual doctor, not a psychology student."

Dr. Oberst grimaced but didn't reject her reasoning. He turned his efforts into expediting the elderly Dr. Gage out the door, providing an arm on the back to push him forward faster.

The remainder of the room fell into apathy. Gao and Semyonov, confident that they were perpetually to be left in the dark, didn't bother stirring. Kitagawa, without academic interest in a medical matters, didn't allow the hysteria to bother him. Kovacevic, who had tucked away into a remote corner, allowed shock to prick him but ultimately fell back into his ever-beloved apathy. However, Parisa pushed past her timidness and followed behind the ambling doctor. With just a look, Harriet leapt to join her. Semyonov picked his head up, eyeing their trail. He looked at Kovacevic, who shook his head. The Soviet resigned back into himself.

✳ ✳ ✳

As Dr. Gage hobbled down the corridor to the navigation room, he jut a fat finger to the radio in the corner, "What is that there? Has there been a radio this whole time? Blasted, why did no one think of the easier solution first?"

Harriet called from the rear, "Wassermann tried it, broken." Dr. Gage only grunted as his response.

As the group turned right to round the corner, Renard ran up to yank the door open.

A sick surprise seized her. "It has been locked."

Alessandra tried putting the whole of her strength into yanking it open. No use. Fastened tight. They stood there dumbly gasping like suffocating fish, taking turns hastily trying to rip the door open. After futility set in, they all circled in a pod, blinking at each other, waiting for someone to produce a genius solution.

Dr. Oberst asked through a thin, tight mouth, still pressing his hand into the fleshy mound of Dr. Gage's back, "What was even in the room that gave him an electric shock?"

"A desk and some wheels, all covered in razors and wires. There was this golden box. He grabbed it, and it paralyzed him. The desk had a mirror with Latin on it. Oh, I forget the phrase," Renard quickly asked something to Alessandra before returning her uneasy attention back to Dr. Oberst. "There was something about blood being poured. Ah, we don't know."

"Another Latin phrase? Why didn't you mention this to us before?" Dr. Gage cried, fluttering his hands about in a tantrum.

"Because Wassermann was electrocuted," Renard responded in a similar outrage. "We had to choose a priority."

Before there was a chance to retort, a heavy click reverberated in the halls. All attention was ripped back to the locked door. Slowly, Renard stuck her hand back out and rotated the knob. It opened with a croak.

Alessandra stuck her head inside hesitantly, inciting Renard to protest about safety.

She shrieked, "Body gone," and then flung the door wide open.

The room waited undisturbed, only a faint hum drumming in the air.

Renard muttered as she gripped onto Alessandra's forearm and wormed into her side, "How? How so quickly could his body be snatched?"

Dr. Gage sputtered out, "Snatched? What happened? Did he die?"

Renard responded, "How could we know? That's why we came for you."

Dr. Oberst said, "Body snatched? Hmmm, this means that this room does indeed have some sort of exit point."

Hal Enzinga

Grim optimism allowed itself inside the chorus, but only for a second.

Parisa murmured, "We are watched. The vents…"

Alessandra and Renard began to crane their heads upwards, swiveling around, holding their breath, waiting to catch a blush of sound. The vents: all bolted, all leaking out smelly, moldy air, all too small for anyone of decent size.

Dr. Gage grumbled and shook his head, "A very bold assumption based on so little evidence. Is that what you two had been muttering between yourselves then, fanning your speculations? Nonetheless, one thing is clear: I agree we are being monitored and our nasty captors are clearing away bodies soon after death. This is some horrible game, yes."

Urgency lost, Dr. Gage swatted Dr. Oberst's hand away from his back. He hobbled about as though he were impervious to the material world. "Now, show me this new Latin phrase."

Alessandra uneasily ushered him over to the desk, carefully monitoring his hands to ensure he touched nothing. Renard stood in the doorway, wringing her hands, eyeing up the nearby Parisa. She wandered her fingers out to cling onto her as she did Alessandra, but Parisa slunk to Harriet's side.

Dr. Gage grumbled in an entranced murmur, "*Per effusionem sanguinis venustas venit, quae spes dominum habet.* A strange phrase indeed. By pouring blood comes in beautiful. That's the first part at least. Quite a stupid phrase."

Dr. Oberst peeked over his shoulder, which bothered the older doctor, but he didn't push his face away, despite his expression betraying how much he wanted to.

Dr. Oberst muttered, "No, not pouring blood. I have seen this term used before in Roman poetry. Together, it means bloodshed. With *Per*, it translates *through bloodshed*. This is not a literal phrase, but a poetic one. Unfortunately, Kitagawa might actually have a better insight if he really has studied the classics. Please, Harriet, run and fetch him. If he does not come at once, please speak to his ego. I think that may convince him."

Both Harriet and Parisa ran out the door hand in hand. Strangely, Renard, standing in an awkward posture, patted Parisa's head as they fled, then looked around for something else to do with her hands.

Moments later, they returned, producing Kitagawa's ego. Indeed, it did not take much convincing when Harriet pleaded that his intellect was required.

At first entering with dignified certainty, Kitagawa became very uneasy with the daunting apparatuses fixed in the room and gingerly walked around the razor wires. His wariness only grew once Dr. Oberst recounted to him the disappearance of Wassermann's corpse. But soon he focused on the etching and produced the sheet of paper already scrawled with notes. With foreign murmurs, he jotted thoughts down before finally producing an expert opinion.

"Through bloodshed comes beauty. What hope does the master have? That is the phrase, you all were right to come alert me," he said. "I don't think this is something taught in Catholic Mass to farmhands."

Renard mumbled, "Bloodshed? Master? I don't think I like the sound of either of those things. You don't think this has to do with the 'truth', now do you?"

"A riddle," Parisa said quietly. "Not like the other. The other, a question. This, a riddle."

Dr. Oberst followed up, "So this is just some puzzle for us, then? But why? Why torment us like this if just for a simple ransom, or being prisoners of the state?"

None had a chance to respond. Gas started to leak back into the room. They ran back out into the hallway to escape the fumes, but the vapors permeated all corners of the bunker, ripping away any chance of escaping its effects. Wheezing and coughing, all of their faces went gray and blank.

The last thing audible, but only barely, only to Parisa, maybe a trick of the mind—a slap. A firm hand against a soft face. Somewhere between the metal. A slap between unseen ghosts—the wardens, the kidnappers, the invisible observers.

"I know you see," she muttered, and let ether take her.

Chapter Five

When they re-awoken, all living members of the dismal party had been reset in their assigned seats.

It was a true trial for Dr. Gage to recover. His age and feeble body did not absorb well whatever drug lingered in the air. Dr. Oberst was even more tortured. It took several minutes for his chest and throat to expand normally again. Even those of a more moderate age were similarly accosted. Renard and Kitagawa hacked up phlegm and bile, and did not even pretend to do it in some dignified way. Just right onto the table. Shamelessly. But not remorselessly. Renard did try to set a book over her sickness. Kitagawa stared at his, sniffed, and announced that it wasn't his fault.

Dr. Oberst wheezed, "I am not too sure how many more doses I can take." Within the trite comforts of total despair, he burrowed his face in his hands, "Why is this happening to me? Is this only torture? To play mind games and then rip away our lives little by little?"

Harriet exclaimed through a feeble voice, "Look here. In the center. Bars of some sort."

On a plate in the middle was indeed a mass of brown chunks of something austere next to dusty jugs of water.

"Hardtack," grumbled Dr. Gage. "It appears our captors do care for our well-being after all."

Feebly, some nibbled on the crusts of the tack. The taste itself was a crime. Renard must have decided she'd rather starve and allocated her portion to Gao.

Instead of accepting it, Gao asked something of Kitagawa, who obliged for once, "The boy wants to know how long we have been in here."

"Too long," Kovacevic muttered, "But how can we know? No clocks. No sun. I guess, I say at least a full day." Kovacevic paused and thought for a moment. "What did you all do in the other room? Why did gas come back?"

The information was readily shared, along with the additional Latin passage.

Kovacevic finally shifted his disposition to something approaching genial, "We are watched? Good, someone is nearby. There must be some places where they can watch, without notice. And gas, how it spreads from room to room. That is a matter of, what is word, *termo dynamika*? I am much surprised none of you had thought of that."

Semyonov perked up, "*Termo-dinamika? Kotel'naya?*"

The others leaned in towards Semyonov, who spoke so rarely that he became just another furnishing in the dining room.

Kovacevic twitched his nose, "*Kotlarnica.*"

A bumbling energy bounced between the two, and most understood the dilemma that unfolded: Kovacevic found some sort of mission, Semyonov wanted to join, and Kovacevic very much wanted to be alone. All this passed through furrowed brows and pleading glances. The silent negotiation carried on, and all others watched as if it were a stage production.

Finally, a murky concession was forged.

The two rose up and headed for the door on the backside. No verbal explanations, no final words, not even a glance back. Somehow, it was an insult. Almost as insulting as being gassed half to death.

Dr. Gage protested, "Hey now. Where might you be going? Do not do anything rash. My chest feels like it may cave in; the last thing I need is more of that infernal drug."

Kovacevic shirked off the chiding, "Don't you think that boiler room must be where gas is expelled? It heats all of bunker, yes? A matter of *termo dynamika*. We may be able to stop it. I have found a solution. Me. The Yugo."

Kovacevic gave some sort of instruction to Semyonov. Before the two finally disappeared back into the hallway, Kovacevic turned around to shoot the dining hall and all its inhabitants a glare. "You all call me a spy and put blame on me. But no, I will find answer. I will free us from gas. Then, you all must know true character of a Yugo. You will never apologize, but you will know you are wrong."

The two left. Nobody followed suit.

"No retort to that?" Kitagawa said to Dr. Gage through a flat mouth. Dr. Gage waved it off and shoved hardtack into his maw.

✳ ✳ ✳

Semyonov kept an eager yet healthy physical distance between himself and Kovacevic. It was a delicate balance, not intruding on the halo of scornful solitude Kovacevic seemed fond of but still trying to demonstrate a sort of fledgling allyship. But Semyonov followed behind diligently, like a duckling to their much, much, smaller mother. If Kovacevic was intimidated by Semyonov's lumbering presence he did not show it and instead displayed an extension of his previous apathy. It surely stung Semyonov, but without ill-will. Ill-will was expensive, only affordable to those who didn't need companions.

In only a few long strides, they were there. The boiler room. Skin-searing intense heat. Extremely gray and orange. Rows and rows of metallic cauldrons, each groaning and gurgling with pulsing belly flames. The ceiling was too high to understandably be confined beneath terrain. Long rafters crossed above, with thick chains swinging down, dancing with the heat waves. Yet, it was a familiar place with a nostalgic pang and even prompted some relief. No different than a large factory found in the wintery plains.

Kovacevic scoured the room, hands on his narrow hips, not saying precisely what he was looking for. The scowl, the pose, the orange hue—Kovacevic looked almost matronly. More so than Renard.

Semyonov took the opportunity to ask a question. A basic one. One promising, at least a couple of cognates.

Kovacevic returned with a sour, "*Ne govorim.*"

Semyonov resigned himself to quiet assistance. Daring to sneak glances of Kovacevic, Semyonov studied and attempted to replicate his every move. The Yugo man delicately and deftly bobbed and weaved around each machine, leaning in close to narrow his eyes and craning his head back out. Harrowingly, he was fast. More cat than man, slinking from corner to corner. The reddish bob of hair was a mere peripheral streak. Next to him, Semyonov was an oaf, tall and dumb, and didn't dare disturb him. The best companion was a silent non-nuisance.

It was perhaps a good hour of spryly looking around when Kovacevic cried out with a triumphant glee and pointed to a large vent in the upper left corner of the room. A loosened grate, big enough for a feline, agile man to squeeze through.

Kovacevic exclaimed something in earnest excitement, beckoning Semyonov over, who eagerly complied. At his side, Kovacevic forced Semyonov to his hands and knees, firmly

Hal Enzinga

placed a foot square on his back, and hoisted himself up on his human stepstool. An easy climb, only encumbered by the biting heat of the steaming machine that pierced through clothing.

Semyonov muttered meager protests, despite arching his back for a higher boost. Something in the air was uneasy. Too simple, too obvious. Kovacevic did not feel the same, or if he did, it didn't matter. Escape was inbound. Sole escape. The best escape. He ripped the grate from the vent with a flourish and without further investigation.

Without thinking, he jabbed his right arm in deep to begin pulling himself into the vent. But the excitement was murdered in its tracks. A click and metallic shriek, followed by an echoing snap. A choke clutched his throat as he tried to yank his arm back out. He couldn't. Another ferocious tug, and his shoulder sprained with a pop. Bright red blood began to trickle down the vent onto the walls and sputtered onto the steaming machine. Kovacevic tried to tug his arm out against pained sobs, but only more blood came gushing, accompanied by a fleshy rip. He frantically cried out in more unintelligible Serbian.

Semyonov gripped onto the hot boiler, ripped himself up against the scorching heat, and subsequently seared his knees as the machine's fire began to roar harder. He tried to tug Kovacevic's arm, but it only produced an even louder fleshy rip and was met by Kovacevic biting him on the shoulder in carnal protest.

The second, and certainly stupider thing to do came to mind. He reached his hand into the vent and tried to yank apart the razor wires that claimed the arm. The wires were tight. The serrated edges shredded his palms.

Kovacevic shouted something, desperately craning his head towards the door. With a panicked boot to the chest, Kovacevic kicked Semyonov back down onto the floor. The thud flattened Semyonov's lungs and definitely bruised his skull, but Kovacevic kept on shouting. Semyonov jolted up and tried to obey.

He returned only a few seconds later with Dr. Oberst, Harriet, and Parisa.

Dr. Oberst cried out, "What has happened?"

"Razor wires. In the vent. Stuck," Kovacevic grunted. "Cut them. Cut them now."

Harriet shouted, "With what?"

"Doesn't matter," Kovacevic spat down. He tilted deeper into the vent, trying not to rest his weight onto the machines below him. Cosmically vitriolic, they churned out more and more steam. But the vent brought no relief. The razors had burrowed deep into his flesh, and the squelches dripped down and sizzled to oblivion onto the machines below.

"The only thing we can do is pull you down," Dr. Oberst said through a thin mouth.

"That will rip my arm off," Kovacevic moaned, but as he was forced to rest his weight back onto the boiler, he shouted, "Fine, quickly, quick, now."

Dr. Oberst walked forward, and without a thought, Semyonov returned to his role as step stool. Parisa threw her veil onto the top of the machine, a thin but still welcome barrier, and Dr. Oberst climbed up, followed by Semyonov. Dismissing the scorches on their hands and knees, they tried to pry Kovacevic's arm out of the vent. More blood poured down the wall. Kovacevic's cries grew more exasperated and pained with each tug, and he found relief in biting back into Semyonov's shoulder. Harriet climbed up and lent the necessary third set of hands to rip joint from socket. Like three piranhas to a carcass, they tugged and tugged. Kovacevic stopped shrieking, stopped biting, stopped blinking. Parisa averted her eyes, and her attention was caught by something in the other corners of the room. She drifted away without a sound.

With a final skin-shredding tear, the vent finally released Kovacevic's arm. None needed surgical experience to know that the state of it was dismal. Not much arm left. Ivory bone intermingled with crimson and beige flaps of skin. The fingers were fat and purple.

Kovacevic's lips quivered at the sight of his own arm, "I cannot move it. I cannot move it."

Semyonov and Dr. Oberst carried Kovacevic back to the dining room, the mutilated arm dragging long red streaks along the floor. Parisa pulled Harriet into the backside of the boiler room. At first, she pointed to the chains, then the inflamed machines, then onto the lower belly of one boiler. Yet another Latin phrase.

Harriet muttered, "Jesus… this really is a puzzle."

"Puzzle, maybe. Or test. We have observers. This I know." Parisa knocked thrice with her knuckles on the boiler. No response, but that didn't kill her certainty. As she took Harriet by the arm to return to the dining room, she asked nobody in particular, "Why are we tested?"

In the dining room, Kovacevic lay in the corner, pale, shaking, and mute, clutching at the remains of his shoulder. Renard used her silk shawl to wrap his arm, and sat beside him, patting his head and murmuring comforts. The rest looked among themselves awkwardly. Inhuman to say and do nothing, but foolish to even pretend like they had any agency in the matter, and none would be made a fool. Without discussion, it was decided: no more snooping, no more exploration, no more deciphering. It only promised punishment. They were to wait for their captors to finally release them, despite the fact that likely not a single one thought such a thing would happen.

Chapter Six

They waited. Hours to hours to hours. Even among the most pretentious and unamiable of the group, no one dared say anything sneering. Not in English, or within earshot at least. They all had that much civility.

Dr. Gage made the grim statement: two primary arteries in the arm had been severed. With shoelaces, donated generously from Semyonov, Kovacevic's arm was bound in a tourniquet at the shoulder.

"It will need to be amputated when we return to the surface," Dr. Gage noted with a precious hint of sympathy.

This revelation had no effect on Kovacevic if he even heard it at all. His eyes glazed over, and his breathing remained shallow and shaky. Renard forced him to lean against her, coddling him like a mother, shushing and rocking.

Dr. Oberst concluded they must have been in the bunker for well over a day, and their captors had no intent of starving or dehydrating them to death. Very little comfort, but it was comfort, nonetheless—to Dr. Oberst and absolutely nobody else.

Grimly, the wait stretched on. Time stopped ticking, losing count of itself. The only indicator was the state of Kovacevic's arm. Every so often, Dr. Gage would peek under the shawl to look at the tattered flesh.

Dr. Gage didn't need to announce it, the stench did, but he did so anyway—the limb had begun to blacken with tissue death. Necrosis was inbound, at which amputation would be necessary for survival. When Dr. Gage would carry out these sporadic inspections, Renard would shield Kovacevic's eyes, which was likely unnecessary. He had become numb and unmoving, save for the slight rise and fall of his chest and the occasional blink.

"No one deserves such a fate," Renard crooned. She continued brushing his hair with her fingers, "No matter the purpose for our imprisonment, this is punishment too severe. Even for a spy. No, they must answer to God for this."

Kovacevic just continued to blink, maybe a bit ironically.

Kitagawa had to indulge in his nature, groping philosophy for a slight reprieve, "Why not answer to their fellow man? If one man were not so concerned with answering to some vertical power, but rather to their immediacy, maybe Kovacevic would have been evacuated by now. This is cruel, yes, and as sovereign bodies, we should be answered to and forge our own justice."

Nobody took Kitagawa up on the bid for intellectual discussion. His musing hung awkwardly in the room. So awkward it made everyone shuffle. Even the fading Kovacevic.

"Not spy," Kovacevic sputtered, weakly and disjointed, "Acrobat. Street performer. Scammer. My partner, together, trick cards with people, I distract. Small scam. Nothing much. Never much."

Renard shook her head, "But none of that matters now. And it will not matter much even after, it is a common, petty crime. Forgivable even when one is poor enough and the audience is simple enough. It's true, the gullible keep the desperate fed."

She turned her head to Alessandra and made a request. Alessandra ousted herself up from her slouch and began to peruse the overstuffed bookshelves, reading French and Italian titles aloud. It didn't take one proficient in either language to know the titles were so dull; Kovacevic likely wished he were already dead.

Renard gently shook her head. "English, dear, only English." The first time such a phrase was ever uttered by a Frenchwoman.

Alessandra randomly plucked one from the shelf and tossed it over. Renard nodded for Alessandra to take a seat beside her. Alessandra obliged and also took up petting Kovacevic like he was a soon-to-be-euthanized hound.

Renard said, "Hmmm, *The Sociology of the Rural American Plains,* what an unpredictable topic that may stimulate our senses. Would you like me to read to you, Petar?"

He groaned. She took that as apathetic permission to read the most heinously dull book of the lot. Renard also glanced at the peevish faces of the youngest prisoners, Gao and Semyonov, and pouted in a genuine pity.

Semyonov sat with his head down on the table, raking his hands through his scalp. His palms were shredded and scabbed over, his ribcage creaked and groaned with every twitch, his shoulder bite mark was still pulpy, but he gave no indication any of that bothered him.

Gao's perpetual fright endured. However, he was not as withdrawn as Semyonov; he couldn't afford to be and sat with his feet swinging. He had been trying at least once every hour to whisper something to Kitagawa, but each attempt only bestowed upon him frosty indifference. Thus, Renard beckoned Gao over, who hesitantly obeyed, purposefully diverting his eyes away from the blood-soaked shawl.

She said to Gao. "It is never too late to learn a new skill. Yes, I will speak aloud in English. Perhaps the alphabet is easily understood?"

The boy swiveled a confused frown at Kitagawa, who listlessly gave a truncated translation while directing his eyes straight onto his own fingernails.

Kitagawa couldn't help reflecting his own opinion back to Renard, "It will be a fruitless effort."

She dismissed his opinion with a scoff. He responded with one of his own. Her scoff was better—more operatic.

In any other circumstance, it would have been an amusing sight: Renard slowly sounded out sentences from the book, trying her best to explain to Gao, with some input from Alessandra, which only succeeded in further confusing Gao. Kovacevic was a participant by proximity and certainly not by choice, but his senses were obviously too muffled to care. Every so often, he would raise his eyebrows when Renard would say a surprising fact from the book. This was not often, as there weren't many surprising facts on the sociology of the rural American plains. After one or two hours, eventually Semyonov joined them and kept all of his attention on Kovacevic. Close attention. Nose to cheek attention.

Dr. Gage mused aloud, straddling the line between cynical and sincere, "A true mother goose type, don't you say. The way she preens the cow maid and the boy."

Harriet perched next to him and nodded slowly. "I wonder if she has children of her own. Do you, Dr. Gage?"

He heaved out a breath, which smelled like fading tobacco, "I have two, both sons. Only one remains on Earth. I was not the only one in my family to take up arms."

"How old?"

"Alfred was eighteen at death. In Somme. But my Thomas will be thirty-three this year." Dr. Gage felt about the breast pocket of his vest and produced a large pocket watch. A delicate click, and it opened. The inner lid bore several engravings: *WG, BG, AG, TG.*

"All of my family, myself included, engraved their initials onto this watch I was gifted upon completion of my medical training," he chuckled, "See, Thomas was only six when he wrote his initials. His G is rather sloppy. Bernadette, my wife, tried her best to guide his hand. But he is hasty. Never been one for patience. But see here, Alfred's is perfect. So meticulous. Even tying his shoes, always had to make sure the loops were even. Wanted to be a surgeon, too."

He clicked the pocket watch shut, returning it to its home. He reclined fully into his chair, letting his hand linger on the pocket. Strain finally left his wrinkled face, and he relaxed into memory.

Harriet sat quietly next to him, lacking the experience and the vocabulary to provide any response. Luckily, Dr. Gage didn't seem to expect one, as most elderly sorts don't. The best mannequin for reflection is a silent one. So, mutely, with her left hand, Harriet rubbed circles on Parisa's back, who uneasily rested her head on the table and picked at the table's edge.

Parisa spoke in a murmur, "My father talked about it. He watched from afar, but he still remembers it."

"Tumultuous times we have lived through, dear," Dr. Gage said, punctuating with a croaking moan from his chest and a sputter of coughs. Harriet patted him on the back in a manner known to those familiar with the afflictions that plague avid smokers.

Dr. Oberst tilted towards their conversation and seized up with a choice: whether or not it would be appropriate for him to share as well. Overtly, there was much lingering on the front of his throat, begging to be spoken into existence, but the first syllable of a beautiful soliloquy started and stopped in a blink.

The audience would be unsympathetic at best, and unnecessarily rude at standard, and thus he said nothing.

Every so often, he would look subtly to Kitagawa, hoping for another instigation, but for once Kitagawa seemed content in silence, keeping his unimpressed gaze on his nails, only squinting every so often to Gao and Renard flipping through the sociology book.

❋ ❋ ❋

Countless hours passed. Kovacevic was slipping in and out of consciousness. His skin had turned a blueish yellow, the corners of his mouth had darkened to a violently purple shade, and the whites of his eyes feverishly pinkened. The room began to smell like sewer sludge. Dourly comical, Renard continued reading to him as though he were just an uninterested schoolboy. Although her arms had fatigued and her voice was fading, she still carried on.

Gao still listened obediently to the English quasi-lessons, probably absorbing nothing, as did Semyonov, who maintained his intensely close attention on Kovacevic. Interrupting Renard, he would sometimes ask something in Russian, prompting Kovacevic to provide a response in Serbian, regardless of whether the response was gibberish, as long as just one cognate was uttered. Just one.

Kovacevic would very rarely respond in a raspy breath. More frequently, he was unresponsive. But with some fleeting moments of grace, Kovacevic allowed a spirit of friendliness to pass between him and Semyonov. Not quite a smile, but something just as warm. This spirit alone kept Semyonov fastened by his side.

As Kovacevic's expiration grew imminent, Semyonov took great care in studying every detail of his face; some features so reminiscent of those from the frozen plains, more Slav than Balkan. With some adjustment, Kovacevic could pass for Semyonov's blood relative. Semyonov, perhaps pretending they were kin, started whispering things, perhaps things he wished to say to a favored cousin, perhaps the last rites, perhaps something else entirely. With each unintelligible whisper, he grew more frantic, more desperate, gripping to his bloodstained shirt, trying to get Kovacevic to drink water and eat crumbles of hardtack.

His efforts did not go unrewarded, at least momentarily. Kovacevic, with the last push of a fading conscience, pulled Semyonov in close, pressing his mouth to his ear. Through rasps of shallow breath, he muttered in his last words. As though Semyonov understood it all, he nodded. Clasping the grip of a weak hand tugging on his collar, Semyonov felt every ligament, every callous, and every strand of knuckle hair.

Shortly, Renard could no longer feel the weak rise and collapse of Kovacevic's chest. She faintly called to Dr. Gage, who hobbled over. A peek under the shawl, a poke on the neck, and a pried open eye. A quick yet thorough inspection. Tersely, Dr. Gage declared Kovacevic dead. A statement of the obvious. It was a surprise to no one when gas slowly started leaking back into the dining room.

Before Parisa succumbed to the gas, she pressed her ear against the wall, and unfortunately, she heard a faint argument, then the shuffling of money passing hands. Fortunately, she fell unconscious too soon to pick apart the muddled talking between the ghosts in the walls. Beyond her knowledge, a meaningless side bet has been settled: whether or not Kovacevic would die a liar. He did.

Chapter Seven

Again, awoken at their seats. More water and hardtack crowned the table. Kovacevic's corpse banished. Only nine inhabitants. Nine ghastly inhabitants. Equal in their ghastliness.

This round of gas did a painful number on most, even among the younger ones. Dr. Oberst was blue in the face, trying his best to get his throat and chest to suck in air. Harriet had to drive her elbow into his back seven times, likely cracking a rib or two in the process.

Renard let out a howl and collapsed into Alessandra's arms like a sinner before the Pope, "So, we are going to have to wait until all of us are dead. Is that it?"

Smears of Kovacevic's dried blood crusted the front of Renard's dress, and Alessandra tried to rub it out with her knuckles. It only made the smear worse. Renard bellowed even louder. Limply, Alessandra hushed her. The hush had the opposite intended effect. Alessandra wriggled her nose at Gao.

The boy trotted over, patted Renard on the back, and said, "*Mei shrrr.*"

Harriet, in a strange attempt to make herself amenable to the actress, said, "Don't worry. We still have actions available to us. I will do what I can."

Renard sniveled, "Oh...what do you know?"

Alessandra clucked her teeth in a gentle chide but shot a wary glance at Harriet. The *shut up* universality. Another *mei shrrrr* from Gao did a better job.

Parisa awoke in a strange way. Still gagging, but something about suffocation brought a newfound sense of urgency. She started for the back door again, turning around to beckon Harriet.

Dr. Gage sputtered, "Halt! Where are you two headed off to?"

Harriet offered the explanation, she had to, Parisa was already charging ahead, "When we went to collect Kovacevic, she saw something in the boiler room. Something worth looking into. It wasn't the time to explore it further, given his condition. But now it is, I guess, if that's alright with you."

As she turned to leave, Semyonov jumped up. He tried to pause her with a gentle hand to the shoulder, but all that won him was a reflexive slap against his shoulder right above the bite mark. A grimace served as her apology, and a grunt served as his. They both shrugged at each other, then scratched their noses. Harriet patted Semyonov on the shoulder, away from the bite, and he returned the same. He made a vague wafting gesture with his hand, and she made a vague hammering gesture with hers. Nobody interrupted the forging of the strange new language. Not until the two turned to follow Parisa.

"Wait now. What if you get injured, like Kovacevic?" Dr. Oberst yelped, and then immediately erupted into a body-seizing coughing fit.

Harriet said as she disappeared beyond the door, Semyonov at her heels, "I think this will be like labor pains if that makes sense. There are some puzzles here, we have to work with them, not against them. Go through it, not around it."

Parisa politely waited for Harriet by the boiler room door.

She darted a quick eye to Semyonov, "He still wants to go?"

Harriet responded, "Yes, he wants to be useful."

"He tells you this?"

"No, not really, but I get it. We all want to be useful."

Parisa attempted to shake Semyonov's hand as a welcome into the small assembly. Just the polite thing to do, but it made Semyonov confused and made Parisa somewhat embarrassed. But it was quickly swept aside as Harriet grunted and shrugged at him, which he eagerly returned.

The foul metallic stench of festering blood commanded attention, just as the raw heat punished them for walking deeper into the boiler room. Nevertheless, Parisa all but sprinted to that one machine. There it lay. Almost mocking.

Funes qui ligant sunt confracti

Harriet asked, "Understand it?"

Parisa shook her head but pointed upward towards the chains hanging in the rafters, connecting to the machines. At first glance, the chains seemed lazily strung about, but a second glance assured coordination. There was a certain tension, an energy, captured in the anchoring points. Parisa had swiped the communal notebook and began to sketch the pattern the chains made swinging in the rafters. She scratched and re-sketched over and over, furrowing in frustration at her own artistic ineptitude, using way more pages than prudence would allow.

Semyonov wandered around the room, already acquainted with the vast labyrinth of boilers, and overtly overly wary of them. Steam poured from the boilers in great columns at suffocating volumes and with thunderous laughter. Even the sweat upon the brow began to sting. The stifling heat singed the very hairs nestled in the nostrils. Just existing was a burden, more so than before, as though the boiler room was plopped in the last couple of hours on top of an active volcano.

The fires were barely concealed in the metal furnaces. Harriet and Parisa took great caution in not letting their fabric hems get near the flames, but Parisa's skirt caught fire anyway.

As Harriet stamped it out, she held up a scorched tatter, "Don't suppose you'd want me to re-attach it?"

"It's not necessary, I have plenty at home," Parisa responded, but took back the tatter regardless. Just another polite thing to do.

"It looks expensive. Those threads—gold?"

Parisa nodded, "My veil had beads of sapphire. My favorite has emeralds. I am happy that one I left in Tehran."

Harriet let out a weak giggle and was prepared to say something else, probably a request to keep the tatter for herself to triple her net worth, but Semyonov emerged beyond a pillar of steam and tugged on her sleeve.

Amid the discussion of textiles, Semyonov noticed the myriad of switches and knobs on the machines and embedded in the walls. One demanded particular attention: large and golden with a red knob, placed squarely on the far end of the wall. Chains from the rafters wrapped around the shaft of the switch lever. It required a closer examination, but it was impermissible. It was shouldered by two machines, both of which sputtered out wisps of smoke and steam.

Harriet tried to lodge herself in the foot of space where the vapors completely dissipated.

Tried. Failed. Even the steady air stung satanically. Yet, as she could see in a quick lean, the chain was padlocked around the shaft, announcing to any onlookers that it was not to be removed.

Harriet turned, blotting steam out of her face, and tried to start a sleuthing discourse with Parisa, but Parisa had since been engulfed in something else entirely.

She migrated to the far back end of the room, gazing up at the naked, gray wall. Yet not so naked with a longer look. A small twinkling. Barely a glimmer. Some sheen of a prior ink lettering, since rubbed off. Yet again, something demanding attention.

But of course, there was always something else. Amidst all the iron and brass industrial machinations of the boiler room, planted near the edge of the back left corner was another small, wooden door: humble and easy to overlook.

Parisa quickly buzzed over to give it a closer inspection. The small, rusted iron handle was tetanus incarnate, but Parisa gave it a firm tug anyway. Bolted shut. However, on a metal plate near the crest of the door was another strange, foreign word. Faded and scratchy *die Kaserne*. Parisa whistled above the shrill screeches of the steam, and Harriet and Semyonov paced over like dutiful hunting hounds.

Harriet gave the tetanus door her own tug, Semyonov's grip on her forearm followed with a stern grunt.

Harriet retracted her hand, inspecting it for tetanus, despite Semyonov's continued grip, and asked, "What's it mean?"

"Not French, not Persian, not English, not Turkmen, do not know," Parisa said. "Recognize the tongue?"

"I failed my world languages class. My father wasn't exactly a great tutor," Harriet responded. "There's also this lever, oh, it has a malicious feel to it. But so does everything else. Why must everything here threaten harm? My God, even this grip on me. I understand it probably makes him feel better, but I think it's starting to cut off circulation."

She looked down at his hand and softly tapped it. Finally, he let her loose, leaving deep digs of fingernail bites. Another shrug served as his apology, and she shrugged back her acceptance.

"We go back?" Parisa asked.

"Wait, before we go, do I still have eyebrows?" Harriet asked, patting her face.

"Somewhat," Parisa said slowly to dampen any alarm.

Harriet was alarmed anyway. No eyebrows, hardly any eyelashes, but better faring than being armless like Kovacevic.

Before they headed back out the door, Semyonov turned and muttered a final count of all the boilers, steamers, and machines in the room.

"*Sorok*," he said, and made a gesture of four and zero.

Harriet said, "Forty boilers? Seems quite a lot for a small bunker. But I wouldn't know what's proper."

Parisa nodded. Semyonov blinked. Absentmindedly, Harriet rubbed her arm's deep red indents.

Parisa gave Semyonov a polite once-over. "Do you think he knows something?"

"Like what?"

"He knows there's forty. He knows forty must be important. Think we all know something?"

Harriet responded, "I know nothing. Unless you do want me to hem your skirt."

"Forty...forty is an important number. Religious number in Christianity, no?" Parisa said.

"Failed Bible lessons too," Harriet said, rubbing her eyebrow-less forehead.

"Forty days in heat," Parisa continued. "Is that familiar? We are tested on things religious?"

Harriet shrugged. Parisa sighed and nodded. Semyonov blinked. The best discussion the bunker could offer.

Chapter Eight

They returned to the dining hall, in which Kitagawa was bemused. "Welcome to see no new injury, it's bad for my nerves. Dying men tend to be too dramatic for my tastes."

It was a small blessing that Semyonov didn't comprehend any English. It was unknown to them if he was the brawling type, but such words would inspire a reaction in even the most dovish of people. Harriet conducted the shrugging ritual regardless, which was a stroke of blind luck. Semyonov was the brawling type. Several of the unseen ghosts would testify to that fact.

Alessandra lifted her head from resting on her palm. "Found something?"

Parisa started a lengthy explanation, but it was short-lived. One mention of another Latin phrase, and it was back to the self-assigned intellectual heavyweights.

Dr. Gage impatiently motioned for Parisa to hand over her notebook, "Well, let us see it then. Let us see the Latin."

Kitagawa intercepted the paper. "Remember the navigation room? I may be of most use here. Let us see now." He glanced at the page against the cold anger of Dr. Gage and the slight dejection of Dr. Oberst, "Oh. It is quite easy, actually. The chains that bind are shattered. Or broken, either word works here." Then, he flipped it over to Dr. Gage. "Look and tell me that you agree."

"I concur. I'd go with the word broken, though. The chains that bind are broken. It must have something to do with the chains that loop around in the ceiling, that is what is drawn here, correct?" Dr. Gage said, "And...oh my.. Is that German I see?"

Dr. Oberst sprang up, eagerly trying to glance down at the page. For once, Dr. Gage permitted Dr. Oberst to take the notes from him, but not without a wobbly frown creasing his jowls.

"The barracks? It appears that the barracks are connected to the boiler room. How peculiar. That is not the design that I am familiar with."

"Nor me." Dr. Gage bobbed his head. "Could it be some trick? We are being purposefully led to believe that this bunker is of German design? Meanwhile, we could be in, oh let's say Romania."

He suddenly collapsed into a coughing fit, then said, "Apologies, I am afraid I will be largely relegated to my chair from now on. Any medical emergencies will simply have to be brought before me. If that does not suit you, well then, just don't go sticking your hands into any more wires."

Dr. Oberst grimaced, "You may regret to hear that we have some solidarity. I feel my chest grow tighter by the hour. This prolonged exposure will be the death of me." He rubbed his chest, emphasizing the point. He needn't say anything or do anything; his face had grown veinier and paler with each dosage.

Renard moaned, "I have no allergies and yet I feel it too, Alessandra has said the same as well. Don't know what Gao says, but I know the look of a young boy in pain, and I am sure he is also feeling faint." She pressed the back of her hand to Gao's forehead. "So cold! My God, how much more are we expected to stomach? Here, tell him, tell Gao to seek warmth in me."

She didn't wait for any permission before she wrapped her arms around Gao and stifled his face into her neck. He sighed and patted her on the arm.

Kitagawa sucked his teeth. "Don't worry so much, those people are less household pets, more beasts of burden."

The two exchanged scoffs yet again. Kitagawa had been practicing—for once, his was better.

Dr. Oberst returned his attention to Parisa's notes. "When my strength fully returns to me, I will take a look around the room myself."

Harriet muttered, "I would not be so eager, doctor. It's God awful in there, and I'd feel more comfortable knowing that both medical practitioners are not in harm's way. Both a psychiatrist and a surgeon offer more purpose and expertise than me. If needed, I will offer myself to find new means of escape. It would be morally abhorrent to take medical help away from the rest."

Kitagawa flicked up the corner of his mouth, "How very noble of you, but first, I think that we must pay attention to *the chains that bind are shattered*. And in the navigation room, *through bloodshed comes beauty, what hope does the master have?* Along with that phrase there, on truth. What could it all possibly mean? Are we meant to cobble the sentences together to make some sort of passage? There are similar themes here, masters and the chains that bind. I wonder if it is from some literature that I am unacquainted with. Perhaps literature that is in this very room. Of course. Why else should there be books here? Certainly not just to teach the English alphabet." Kitagawa shot up and began to rifle through the shelves.

Renard said, a defensive arm still wrapped around Gao's indifferent shoulder. "But one is a directive, one is a question, and the last is a statement. Why not collect all Latin from all the open rooms before trying to find an appropriate passage. It would be easier, no?"

Alessandra, through her blossoming English comprehension, did not concur. And she made it known. Not so much through words, but through ample use of her limbs, flailing in every sort of direction. A whole-body activity. With much more physical contact than necessary.

From her nonverbal speech: each room had two parts, an obvious and a hidden. Wassermann had been electrocuted trying to force something hidden into the obvious. To illustrate that point, she just grabbed Kitagawa and rattled him, and surprisingly, he acquiesced to the pantomime.

They had to work with the obvious to unlock the hidden. Like treating a lame cow, using symptoms to find the true injury. That portion she asked Kitagawa to moo, which he unsurprisingly did not acquiesce to. Yet, as her use of limb was successful, had she been a contemporary of Renard, she may have been a laudable stage actress herself.

"Alessandra, you are a genius," Renard exclaimed and clasped Alessandra's face and shook her with effusive glee, before wrestling her into an embrace.

"Ah, Lucie, that hurt," Alessandra cried without resistance.

"Not bad reasoning," Kitagawa said with surprise but forbidding any indication he was impressed. "But how does she propose we go about uncovering this *hidden*?"

Renard beamed, as if all fatigue and pessimism had been wiped from her. "We did not get to that part yet. But still my proposal stands. Let us collect all of the obvious, all of the Latin, and let us take notes of all information presented to us." She was then consumed in a coughing fit, but this did not dampen her spirit. She kept a hand on Gao, now relegated as her sentient walking cane, and tried to force his face into a smile to match her own.

Harriet said, "The kitchen and the armory, the places we have yet to look through thoroughly." She flapped her hands as she leaned over the table. "Parisa. Kitchen. We go?"

Parisa ripped some blank pages from the notebook. "Yes, while I stay in this mind. Things fit. I see some patterns, I think."

As they began to make their way through the short distance to the kitchen, Semyonov joined their party silently after Harriet blinked, shrugged, and vaguely gestured at him.

Alessandra snatched up some blank pages and pointed to her destination. "*L'armeria.*"

It was a given that Renard would join her. Surprisingly, Kitagawa also stood up. He did not offer an explanation. Yet, his presence was welcomed, mainly by Alessandra, illustrated by a laugh and hearty jostle of the shoulder, to which he gave a slight bow of the head.

Dr. Gage and Dr. Oberst remained seated, not for lack of enthusiasm, but bodily incapability. Gao also remained fastened to his seat but began pouring over English books with a great fervor, much to the glee of his self-appointed tutor, Renard. Slowly and clumsily, he began to sound out the basics of the language. Proclaiming a desire to hear his mother tongue spoken appropriately, Dr. Gage corrected him.

Chapter Nine

Despite feeling they set off on some grand expedition, Harriet, Parisa, and Semyonov only had to walk roughly thirty seconds to find their way into the vast, barren, industrial kitchen. Nothing out of the ordinary. Steel and tin clad, complete with rows of cabinets and drawers. Immediately yet cautiously, they each began to rifle through each compartment. Everything was empty, housing only dust. Semyonov found the kitchen sink which stunk like mildew. Rust consumed every spare inch; the spigot so crusted with black grime that it would be impossible for any water to groan through.

It did not take long for the group to turn their attention to the floor. In the center rested a big, mobile table. The structure obscured something painted on the floor in bright red. Parisa and Harriet addressed each other, preparing to engage in a discussion on whether they should move the thing, but Semyonov went ahead and did so. No congressional deliberation needed, not even a shrug and grunt.

No painted Latin on the floor, but a symbol. A big, red circle with a line through it.

Harriet asked in peevish ignorance, "Is that a street sign? No entry?"

Parisa shook her head gently. "No, it is a Greek sign used frequently in mathematics. It is called Theta, a letter in the Greek alphabet. I remember from my instructor. When I see her again, I should apologize. I was such a lazy student. But how could I have known the use would be so practical?"

Harriet chuckled, "Seems like you were good enough to me." But then she started to nibble on her fingernail and her face scrunched towards the center, "Why Greek? Why not Latin? Why is this different?"

Her question went unanswered as Semyonov pointed to the areas surrounding the Theta. Raised edges ringed around the periphery, creating a large square, housing the symbol, too thin to almost discern while standing. He knelt down and ran his finger alongside the divots, motioning for Harriet to do the same.

Harriet muttered, "My word, I believe this is a trap door of sorts."

Parisa responded, "Maybe not a trap door, but perhaps some sort of storage? Common in a kitchen, I think, I am told at least. Never been inside a kitchen, to be honest."

Silently, Semyonov ran his hand along the edge, feeling for the pull. Once found, it took a great show of force to lift the heavy steel door, complete with the metal's creaking and groaning. Semyonov strained to pry the door fully open but managed to do so and rested the lid down with only a dull clang. They poked their heads down into the black hole. All immediately gagged. Fungal rot. The sort of stench that lies thick over the throat.

The cellar was deep, too deep to even consider entering, but not very wide. No way of emerging out from the depths. It was a scarily sharp drop onto a dark dirt and rock floor. The wooden moldy shelves and crates that littered the cellar didn't seem tall enough to climb and escape. Certainly not strong enough to hold any weight. On the ground lay the wooden ladder, likely once used to exit the cellar, but it was snapped in thirds and similarly overrun with fungi. Curiously, thick, open-ended hoses snaked and coiled around the cellar. But other than that, it was barren. Nothing else of note, not even a dead rat.

Parisa jumbled a sentence together, "The, uhh how to say, snakes must be important, no? The only thing uncommon for underground storage for wine."

"You mean the watering hoses? Yeah, I thought so myself. But what exactly? What would hoses and mathematics have to do with each other?" Harriet leaned her head further into the cellar opening, wantonly craning past the point of comfort.

Semyonov grabbed the nape of her dress and yanked her back to safety. She grunted out her apology, he shrugged his acceptance.

Parisa began to scribble down everything in the notebook.

Semyonov turned his attention back to the rest of the kitchen. He poked about each cabinet and drawer again, trying to emulate the mannerisms of Kovacevic. He scoured every surface, albeit much less nimbly. Nothing found. Just dust. Not even a roach.

Finally, he gave more attention to the sink. Despite the obvious age of the fixture, the pipe works underneath the sink were less decrepit, definitely under a year old. Slicks of oil traced around the screws, each pipe was still wrenched tight, not a single leak. Absentmindedly, Semyonov flipped the dial on the faucet.

A deep trembling reverberated through the kitchen. The two women frantically swiveled around and knelt down to feel the floor. Semyonov kept his eye on the faucet. No water trickled from the crusted spigot. But the thunder of gushing water jolted the kitchen.

Harriet shouted, "The cellar. The hoses are flooding the

cellar!"

Semyonov rushed over. Gurgles of putrid, blackened water poured out of the coils, turning the cellar to a cauldron. Semyonov rushed back over to the faucet and flicked off the dial. The waters persisted, continuing to raise the waterline down below. Somehow, the waters began to pour even more rapidly. Semyonov hurriedly tried to raise the heavy steel door to slam over the cellar. He grunted and strained, and Harriet readily joined his effort, throwing her whole back into lifting up the door. Parisa leant her strength, which did absolutely nothing.

With a final push, the two slammed the trap door back down on the cellar. Water still roared in. As the three turned tail to run out of the kitchen, the gushing whimpered to a silent death. However, they didn't care to check.

Frantically, they returned to the dining hall to recount it all, Parisa and Harriet tripping over each other's words in a frenzy, interrupting and finishing each other's sentences.

Dr. Gage helpfully offered, "Well, be more careful next time."

❋ ❋ ❋

Straight out the right door, Renard, Alessandra, and Kitagawa headed for the armory. The cramped iron hallways no longer caused any fright, claustrophobic leering lost its potency, more irritating than anything else. Still, Renard held onto Alessandra out of habit, loudly assuring the younger woman she would protect her. Alessandra patted Renard's hand, being earnest even in the face of the irony. Kitagawa was silent behind them, demonstratively pleased with his masculine self-sufficiency.

It was only a minute or two before they entered the cramped armory chamber and immediately assumed a posture of an awkward gawk. Even to a layman, the room still felt irregular. Perhaps it was the smell. The odor was unusual, but not inherently good or bad. Only different.

Perhaps it was the faint hiss dwelling in the background, so subtle any noise would overwhelm it.

The weaponry was arranged in a bizarre manner—rows of locked gates with imprisoned fuselages. Yet, towards the front of the room were six chained rifles lined up in a row, opposite to a wooden chair backed against the wall, as if it was an area designated for a firing squad.

Good judgment prompted the three not to get in front of the displayed rifles. They skirted it around, paying more attention to the gated weapons. The old padlocks that safeguarded the kept rifles were ancient. Historical relics, more like. With a proper display of force and a crowbar, they would easily shatter. Kitagawa paid closer attention to the hissing noise, tracking the genesis of the sound. It proved difficult but still discovered the four origins, which he made sure to announce as soon as he did.

Each corner of the room had a top and bottom vent. He felt around each vent with his delicate fingers. Thus, he began an unrequested lesson in aerodynamics. Vapor expelled from the bottom, suction produced from the top, the hissing noise the child of the two forces.

"The air is being manually circulated," he continued. "I don't know what is in the air, however, but I don't think it is more of the drugged gas. Mrs. Renard, can you place a guess on the odor?"

"Perhaps I can, my nose is finely attuned to expensive and complex fragrance." She deeply inhaled. "Yes, I can identify that it is not bergamot, lavender, or rose. Further, it is not myrrh or cardamom."

Kitagawa responded, "There's a million things I can say it isn't, but can you identify what it is?"

"Can you?"

Kitagawa did not respond.

"Rose? You look like a Rose, not a Renard," Alessandra said, laughing and poking Renard on the stomach. "You ask to use fake name. That's funny, I want to call you Agnes. No— Lucie! Lucie is better. Yes, I still use fake name. No Renard. You don't look like a fox."

"Too informal, dear. But good work on the English, I see the novels have served you well, as I suspected," Renard replied, patting her on the head yet removing the offending poking finger, "This room has no Latin in it, none that I can see. And, my God, it's so small."

With a grunt of frustration, she put her hands on her hips. "I was so certain we would collect more answers ourselves. Hmm, they cannot trick me. It's so rude."

"Who are *they*?" Kitagawa asked, continuing to investigate the circulation of the vents. He tried to keep his voice steady and slight, as if he didn't truly care to know and only asked the question out of placation. But his perched mouth betrayed his intrigue regardless.

"Why, did you not hear that ugly girl? We are watched, surely. They must know I am resolved to find a solution, so now they remove the answers. They must hate the French."

"All hate the French," Alessandra giggled to herself. It was a strange noise to be heard from her. She did not look like the giggling type, too solid and sturdy.

"Chances are they hate all of us, hence the precarious parameters of our predicament," Kitagawa said plainly, then muttered beneath his breath, "Which one is the ugly one? Not that such insipid characterizations are a benchmark of my practicum, just for my own edification of properly classifying all inhabitants into appropriate strata."

"Mr. Kitagawa, please, we are not doctors nor scholars, you may use simple English to us. We, I can assure you, are impressed all the same. I do not meet many people from the Far East with such a command of a European tongue,"

Renard said, "And it's the Harriet girl. A scarecrow, no?" She pursed her lips and squinted her eyes, probably thinking of something to say to keep her voice busy.

Kitagawa stopped his slight investigation and remarked rather woodenly, "Very well. Forgive me, it is out of habit. I live in a taut environment, you see. One blunder of language and I am rendered incoherent by my peers in university."

"Oh yes, I understand all too well. In theater, forget your line once, and you are so easily replaced. That is, of course, before you make yourself well known and well-loved to the public. As I have. Ask Alessandra here, even a foreign cow maid knew me before we found ourselves in this miserable dungeon," Renard said, then playfully shoved Alessandra.

Alessandra shoved her back, with a bit more force than intended, sending the actress careening against a grate.

Under the strain of recovery, Renard asked, "Please tell me, Mr. Kitagawa, what was your first name again?"

"For me, it is not customary to use first names with strangers, or anyone unfamiliar."

"I do not consider us unfamiliar. Do you not think so, Alessandra?" Renard asked. Alessandra did not seem to fully understand, so Renard repeated slower.

Alessandra shrugged but shook her head, her thick braid flopping around to emphasize the point, "I think we in ground for a long time now. No friends, no, but no strangers."

Kitagawa grimaced but acquiesced. "Junichi, if you insist. But remember, in any other place I'd never respond to that. Not even to my mother."

Renard curled her fraying hair around her finger listlessly while watching Alessandra do the brunt of the searching. "I am sure we won't ever meet on the surface, so you have no need to fret over it. Still, I wonder, why are you in Europe,

Junichi? If you are son to such an important man, why stay here? Why be a poor student? I have seen those impoverished souls in the art institutes. They would paint a family portrait for three scraps of bread, with or without a benefactor. He must be a very generous man."

"Truthfully, I am sponsored with a generous stipend by the empire itself, not by any one person in particular. Upon completion of my studies, I intend to return without a second thought. As to why Europe, well, Europe imposed its presence upon Japan, so I impose my presence upon Europe."

"Sponsored by the empire? Now things make sense." Renard dropped her finger and turned an easy gaze back to Kitagawa. "Is it true you people think the emperor to be God? My husband tells me that is the Oriental way, no? He's an expert on your kind."

Kitagawa heaved in a breath and pinched the bridge of his nose. "Our cultural relics are important to us. As yours are to you."

He mimicked Renard's posture, leaning against a grate, watching Alessandra do the thorough inspection they all committed to. "It is tiresome work. I must answer for every preconception and ill-founded notion from my colleagues, self-proclaimed experts or otherwise. I try in vain to shade their thoughts with nuance, but for them, concession is confirmation. So yes, but also no, the emperor is God. Yet I know, as soon as I say yes, my answer will only be a yes for those who want it so. If I were to outright deny it all, my opinion and my entire depository of information will be disregarded."

Renard half-heartedly smiled. "There it is again, the talk of a scholar."

He snipped, "Why did the French sever the heads of their aristocrats? Their founders and keepers of culture?"

Renard shrugged, "It was the times. You must understand that you bring intrigue to those unfamiliar. Our questions are harmless."

"Not always so harmless," Kitagawa said and looked to Alessandra. "And do you not grieve that what it is to be Italian will only be shaped by how others view a proper Italian to be?"

She halted her rifling through a crate, blinked back at him, shrugged, then started to laugh as though it was the funniest thing ever uttered on the face of the planet.

"Junichi, do not bother. Even if she spoke perfect English, the question would be lost upon her. Farmers are simple people. They do not think on such things. Intuitive people, they rely not on thoughts but senses," Renard said, giving Alessandra another playful nudge.

That sentence Alessandra surely understood and returned with another not-so-playful nudge.

He responded, giving only a passing glance at Alessandra, "Only I will know when I should not bother. Intellectual curiosity and indulgences garner discovery, something you ought to know. But I suppose differing linguistic capabilities is a consideration. But regardless, I will heed your advice, I'd hate to disturb her intuitive peace."

Alessandra finally spoke, "Why care?"

"Ah, Alessandra, he will not understand you, you did not use enough words," Renard said, increasingly smug.

"Do not mock, it is how he has fun. As to how you want to act out each feeling, you express too much. Too dramatic," Alessandra retorted, a bit firmer than usual, but still keeping a semblance of friendliness. "Simple is not stupid, you know. Without us, students have nothing to study."

Kitagawa allowed himself to tightly smile. "I daresay you may be correct. Some would even suggest true culture is held within the soil, tilled by such people. I do find your types beautiful, and exposed, not cluttered by the presumptions of society."

Renard let out a trill laugh. "You only say that because it is Alessandra. If it was, oh let's say Harriet, or some other ugly little thing, you would not sing the same song."

Kitagawa was ready to continue his diatribe when the wooden chair caught his eye again—a red slap of paint against the seat. He quickly paced over, almost giddily.

Renard called out, "Junichi. Careful of the weapons. They may be loaded. It may be a trap."

He waved his hand, dismissing her concerns. He crouched over the seat of the chair. No trap. No weapons set off.

"A Theta, the Greek symbol, here painted on the chair," he said, looking at the back of the wooden chair. Indeed, something was etched into the back, in print so fine he had to squint. "*Quid peccata mundat?* Hmmm. What something cleans?"

Alessandra gasped, "*Peccata?* Oh, ehh, sins. Yes, *peccata* is sins."

The three stood around the chair for a while, silently, like three old crows over a carcass.

Kitagawa repeated the new discovery in its entirety, "*Quid peccata mundat*…. What cleanses sins…"

Renard hummed in an over-effusive attitude, strutting about the room, feigning deep thought.

Alessandra muttered aloud, "Holy water, no? Like priests use? But no, I think too plain and simple, as I say, always the second or third answer, never first."

A twinge flicked Kitagawa's eye. "Yes, I suppose you do have some sort of reasoning."

He flinched as the small, so small none should have heard it, shuffling and clacking echoed out from the ceiling—a new side bet emerging. A side bet that lasted one minute as a gambling ban was emplaced on the observing ghosts.

Chapter Ten

All members convened back in the dining hall and started sharing notes, if it could even be considered sharing. Gao remained resigned near the bookshelves, diligently pouring over picture books written in English. Renard, ecstatic to see him doing so, hurriedly took a seat on the floor next to him, stopping herself just short of cradling the boy in her arms.

The table full of those too enveloped in more pressing adult matters mused.

Dr. Oberst asked, "The Theta... what could it mean? Was it in the observation room or navigation office?"

Renard said half-mindedly whilst peeking over Gao's shoulder to follow his progress, "Not that we saw. Even more odd is that one of the rooms had no Latin phrase in them. Only in this dining room, the navigation office, the armory, and the boiler room. Why is the kitchen any different? Did the observatory? A double check is in order."

"Yes, yes, definitely, but this Theta is strange." Kitagawa pursed his lips. "I am not so familiar with arithmetic or geometry, but Theta usually denotes an angle, correct?"

Dr. Gage grumbled from his seat, his heavy jowls shaking with every word, his hands clasped firmly over his chest.

"Hmm, yes. But don't forget the literal interpretation. It is *th* in Greek alphabet."

Renard cried out in exaggerated exasperation, "God, this is too confusing. All these mathematics. And the new Latin too, very theological. *What cleanses sins*, so vague. Impossible to decipher. Do you not agree, Gao? Too difficult, hmm?"

Finally, she pulled Gao backwards into a superfluously emotional embrace, much to his surprise. He didn't struggle or yelp but just allowed it to happen yet again.

His limp hand patted her on the arm, and he sighed out, "*Hao.*"

"Difficult, but not impossible. No, the first room actually may be the easiest," Dr. Oberst muttered to himself, his eyes wide and fastened upward as his fingers drummed with frenzy. "The blade and the funnel… *bloodshed*… I think that may be the answer. The *hidden* must be in the box. Some answer must be in there. We must open it with bloodshed. Yes, that must be some sort of answer. An intended response. We should go back to the navigation to make sure we have seen all that the room offers."

Alessandra said and steadied Dr. Oberst as he tried to scramble back out the door, "But it killed Wassermann. Shocked to death. Locked us out."

Parisa interjected, "But we are not Wassermann." Her voice was the firmest it had ever been, certainly over-confident that they escaped death easily, through prudence alone, forgetting the haste in which they originally fled. "Go on, Dr. Oberst. I go too. All three of us will."

As Dr. Oberst left eagerly, Parisa and Harriet waited for Semyonov, outstretching a hand. As it dawned that he was finally a part of a cohort, the tension in his jaw relaxed, and he attempted to bestow an approximation of a smile. No longer just a sentient centerpiece, but perhaps a step above.

"Goodbye then, brave explorers." Renard waved them off before turning her attention back onto Gao. "Let us see, my dear, what have you learned in my absence? Incredible how fast young brains grow."

Soon she became enraptured in this activity, as though it were a divinely appointed duty. Gao accepted her fawning— his duty to allow her to satiate her motherly instincts.

Renard chirped, "Yes, yes, perhaps when I am to retire for good, I shall be a great instructor of language. See how you speak now, Alessandra? Almost native. You are welcome."

Alessandra said, "I studied English for few years."

Her words went unperceived.

None had noticed Kitagawa quietly taking his absence.

❋ ❋ ❋

Slipping through the front left door, Kitagawa set off for the observation room alone. A proper inspection he could do without an entourage, without having to answer any nagging questions. The trek through this hallway was more ominous, perhaps due to the sharp left turn of the hallway, implying villains could hide around the corner. He held his breath as he pivoted, exhaling with an uneasy chuckle at the continued emptiness. Soon, he passed the door on the left wall. He gave it a curt shake. Still bolted. A few steps further down the hall, he came across the end of the hallway, and the observation room's door presented itself. A tentative jiggle of the knob and the door opened. Kitagawa cautiously entered.

True to the description previously offered, he was met with a small, round room covered in mirrors with an uncomfortably low ceiling that domed upwards in the center. Therein waited a hole in the center of a ceiling encircled with a metallic shaft, a small, wooden step stool placed underneath. To his delight, the step stool also had a painted Greek symbol on it. But frustratingly, not a Theta. A more statistical symbol

—the population mean, painted in red. A Mu.

"God, I hate mathematics," he murmured to himself, looking up through the metal shaft. "Mu...mu...mu." A small glint, a hint of reflection twinkling a couple feet up the tube. "The looking glass. A periscope."

He was about to stand on the step stool to poke his head through the tube when another faint glimmer caught his eye. Thin wires laced around the periphery of the tube. A morbid curiosity begged him to poke at the wires, but he steadied himself. He undid his belt and used the leather tip to poke at the wire slowly and gently. Thick blades poked out just as slowly from the shaft's walls.

"A devious trap," he said with glee to himself, tickled by a sick pride. "No, foul observers, you will not cut my neck open today. Nope. Nor will you force me to do mathematics."

He stopped himself from giggling in delight at his cleverness. Carefully, he swiveled his neck around the remainder of the room. His pleasure continued. Etchings in the mirror. Different, barely scratching the surface, not emboldened with ink.

Quid dominus videt quod funes non possunt?

Only then he became positively beside himself in joy, so much that he indulged in the childish activity of clapping his hands with a little hop. A simple phrase, needing no assistance with the translation. Kitagawa relished in it all: a Greek symbol, a Latin phrase, and some malicious device. All found on his own. No need for tag-alongs, no need for any of them. Him alone, the best companion, the self.

Once satisfied with the extent of his findings, he jaunted back out the door. Holding on to his optimism and self-satisfaction, he gave the exit door another tug, going back down the hallway. Locked eternally. But that couldn't deflate him. Nothing could.

As much as his absence went unnoticed, his presence went immediately celebrated, if pointed questions on his whereabouts could be considered celebration.

"What does the masters see that the chains cannot. I sense a clear motif here," Kitagawa announced. "The answer may be found looking through the periscope. Similar to the box in the navigation office."

Dr. Gage, eyes closed and hands still clasped over his stomach, grumbled, "We may have to wait for the others. Through everything, it will fall into place. But I may have a theory, a theory of punishment...." Before he could finish his thought, the aged man dozed off.

Alessandra pranced up to take a seat beside Kitagawa, knocking his elbow, and sighed into an overly lax position, "Something slavery, maybe? Follows Bible themes."

Kitagawa replied, "As you said before, it is too simple and plain. Something lurks behind the meaning, surely."

"Fine, I do not know it now, but if I think I know, I will ask you," she replied with a tired smile, pulling out a clump of strangling hairs in her braid and tossing it behind her. She began to comb out her long mane, flipping it around her shoulders energetically, whipping Kitagawa on the side of the face.

Usually a disgusting behavior, but somehow also mesmerizing, and Kitagawa must have decided it warranted an academic inspection.

From his over-pronounced thinking posture, it was so easy to understand how he analyzed such a behavior: it was so vulgar, too crude for polite company, yet it was just so correct. Perfectly befitting the lower class. Succinctly articulating the trifling habits of those who didn't know what to do with their eternally laboring hands. Upon return to the surface, it would be a peasant habit he must share among all his colleagues. Assuredly, they'd find it as odd yet charming as he.

If side bets were not forbidden, some of the ghostly wardens would have won.

Chapter Eleven

The dark hallway had a heartbeat. A slow, fading blink from the corner. Dr. Oberst gave the pulse a name. A radio hail.

He sharply turned to Harriet. "I thought you said the radio was broken?"

"Wassermann tried it. He told us it was," Harriet anxiously replied. "What should we do? Should we answer it? Could that be our wardens?"

Dr. Oberst gingerly picked up the receiver with a twitching nose. Clouds of dirt and dust plumed off the earpiece, making the twitch turn into a hearty sneeze. Turning a few dials, he managed to push a wary *Hello* into the receiver.

At first silence, save for another sneeze, but then a gurgle, then a scratch, then an ear-splitting wail. The dispatch end shrieked alive, and out came a barely audible mumble.

Dr. Oberst spoke again, but in his mother tongue. A lower timbre, a rapid pace, fluid ease, the closest he had come to earnest excitement in the bunker.

A slurry of frantic whispers, questions, and accusations came out with ample spittle. He pressed the receiver right to his mouth, giving it a grotesquely intimate kiss.

A pause for a response. Unintelligible gibberish followed, disturbed by heavy breakages. Dr. Oberst nodded fervently regardless. A tense smile crept up his face, and he sighed deeply with premature relief.

Another lengthy pause, he gave more frantic spews to the caller.

Only providing a spare few seconds for a response, a sharp tone pierced through the receiver, sending all into a recoil. End of transmission. Sharply cut off. Dr. Oberst ground the earpiece into his forehead.

He said, "The signal was very weak, but I could hear him. It was a man, a German named Cohen, he said. He dialed this frequency by mistake, trying to call some sort of emergency services. He doesn't know me or anything about this situation, I fear. It was so strange. He was just as confused as I, and very worried…something about current affairs."

"An accidental dispatch? Impossible, isn't it?" Harriet said. "No, some form of joke."

"Perhaps, but it indicated our location. Close to Germany. But please don't tell Gage. I'll never hear the end of it," Dr. Oberst sullenly nodded. He began to fiddle with the radio. "I know this type, in a trench. Not broken, but heavily damaged. Strange, I cannot see what our frequency is. Strange. Not the manufacturer's standard. Strange."

The three watched Dr. Oberst fidget with the contraption for a bit longer, until he cried out, "Damn thing! Apologies, it has been almost twenty years since I last had to use one."

Harriet limply patted him on the back and offered an apologetic half-smile. Semyonov did the same, without a smile. Harriet patted Semyonov on the back, without apparent reason. Then the two started patting all in arm's reach. Dr. Oberst was neither comforted nor appreciative.

Parisa jostled Harriet's shoulder. "The navigation office, let us go. We may be close to finding something. No distractions."

"Alright, if you say so" Harriet whispered.

All four in the hallway jolted. There it was again. Another firm slap among the ghosts behind the walls.

"The wardens are angry with one another," Parisa murmured, then continued.

Back in the navigation office. Graver than ever. The hum and heat still unyielding. The funnel, blade, barbed wire, and the ship wheel glinted in the dimness. The box underneath the wheel similarly shimmered. The faint humming seemed to chuckle at them. The four inspected the wheel and the entirety of the messy entanglement of wires.

They stared at the box and wheel for no less than five minutes, silently. An inane attempt to intimidate an inanimate object into submission. It just kept humming along.

Parisa bounced between the desk and the wheel. "The wires, they are purposeful. It must be a, uh, the word... circuit. See how they disappear into and out of the wooden wheel? How it connects to the box? That must be electricity."

Harriet said, furrowing into her crossed arms, "So to open the box, we must cut the wires? Easy enough. That's why there is a blade."

Parisa shook her head, "No, it is connected. The desk and the ship. They are not separate. How to say the phrase again... in English?"

Dr. Oberst obliged, "Through bloodshed comes beauty, what hope does the master have?"

Parisa continued, "I think I know something. It is not one sentence. It is two. The first is a command, something of the kind. The second is the question."

Dr. Oberst snapped his fingers. "It is a current redirected. I think I know. The first part, bloodshed, the funnel, and the blade. To redirect the current, we need to pour blood into the funnel. That may be what they want. But I don't know, maybe we can cheat it? Pour water instead?"

Harriet said, "But blood is not such a good conductor of electric current, even I know that."

"Inhibitor, perhaps, prevent the current from connecting," Dr. Oberst said. "Yes, look at how the wheel and the wires are anchored into the floor. It is being controlled underneath."

As if the room were sentient, the humming drummed louder. The blade above the funnel began to oscillate. The four blearily sighed. Harriet and Semyonov did a back-patting ritual.

"Is that it then? A blood sacrifice?" Harriet murmured and darted her eyes around. Something silent and strange gripped her throat—a sentient neurosis strangled her while whispering secrets. Her eyelids began to twitch, and her pupils dilated.

Harriet continued even quieter, mechanically, "Always watching…I think if we try to cheat, we may end up like Kovacevic." In the next instant, her face reset as though temporarily possessed, but that odd giggle of hers jumped out before she could clench her jaw together.

Dr. Oberst grunted, "Alright then. We may as well try." He shot a nervous glance around the room, then reached out his finger to meet the blade. He winced as the blade sawed across the surface of his finger. A trickle of blood leaked down the tunnel. Nothing happened.

He sighed. "The size of the funnel indicates they may expect even more."

"We should take turns then," Harriet said, rolling up her sleeve. She grit her teeth as she prepared to meet her skin to the knife-edge, but Semyonov stopped her. No back patting, no forearm squeezing, just a frown, a frantic shake of the head, and even a harsh tug backwards.

Dr. Oberst limply chuckled, "What sort of man would I

be to permit that? Maybe now Dr. Gage will be quieter."

He stuck his palm onto the blade. The intensity of the vibrations increased and cut deeper than any could suspect. Almost straight into the center of the palm. His hand became a coin purse. Instinct salvaged his hand with a yank back and a shriek. However, very briefly, the electrical humming dampened. Encouraging to all but Dr. Oberst. The gash on his hand dripped profusely, but the wheel was unsatisfied.

He groaned, rolled up his sleeve, and allowed the blade to cut into his forearm. Slower this time. Each layer of skin curling and splitting off before spurting out a hot red wetness. The humming dimmed a bit more, but the fuzzy electrical aura around the box persisted. Dr. Oberst withdrew his limb in a hurry. With a fleeting moan, he paced around the room, sucking in deep breaths. After a thorough self-soothing convulsion and a flurry of unintelligible curses and slurs, he rolled up his left sleeve to try again, but Harriet stopped him.

"Please let me. I have no knowledge of Greek and Latin, and I am not clever, so I am almost useless. It would be dumb to risk injuring you, or Parisa. Then we would be totally blind."

She drew in a sharp breath and met flesh to steel. She didn't even last as long as the doctor. The wound barely released a slight trickle. Yet, she bounced in place, readying to try again, but Semyonov ripped her away from the blade.

He slammed his own forearm down onto the oscillating blade. Cutting and ripping punctured the room. The metallic odor of blood grew heavy, and suffocating. He did not cry, or yelp, but kept his arm fastened, although his mouth began to froth and his eyes instantly became bloodshot. Parisa knelt down to the box, hovering her hand over the infernal thing. Electricity's hot fuzziness snapped at her palm, and she cursed it in turn.

Semyonov's resolve was stronger than Dr. Oberst, but a

body's still a body. His knees clacked and buckled. Harriet had to hold him up by his backside. At first only a hand, then putting her shoulder to his spine, then pressing her back against his.

It stretched on forever. A very thirsty wheel.

"We may be wrong, should we end this?" Harriet called to Parisa, straining under her support.

Parisa shook her head, eyes affixed to the hateful, ghoulish box. A deep gurgling rattled within the hollow ship wheel, and after blood's splatter soaked all in the periphery, finally the humming stopped.

At once, Parisa poked the box. Hot to the touch. No shock. Ripping away the barbed wires and cords from the box, the hot metal seared her hands, but she provided no cry. It wouldn't have been very self-aware to cry at a light sizzle.

Harriet clamped her hands around Semyonov's forearm to hold it together. Muscle and vein laid bare, skin all but minced to nothing. A mute screech left his face wide and vacant. Dr. Oberst unbuttoned his vest, wrapping a tight bandage around the massive wound.

"Lie him on his back. Prop his feet up. He may be going into shock. I have seen the expression before."

Harriet did as she was told, resting Semyonov's feet on the desk despite the razor wires still wrapped around the wood plunging into his skin. A small trouble, in the grander scheme of things. She started a new head-patting ritual, but he, not so unsurprisingly, gave no response.

Amidst the frenzy, Parisa focused solely on her prize. The box opened softly and was rather light. Suspiciously light. Only books, European books. Boring, European books. *The Wealth of Nations, Two Treaties of Government, Discourse on Inequality, Principia, Common Sense.* A painting cowered inside the inner lid of the box—a letter resembling the English under case 'u.' Parisa eagerly wrote everything down in her notes but scrunched her nose at the books. Those stupid, boring, European books, which demanded the draining of a body. It would have been more understandable if they were at least great comedies. But no. Stupid and boring. Yet as she lifted one up, there was the motif again. A crying hound.

Dr. Oberst split his attention away from the gravely injured Semyonov, leaving Harriet to figure out what to do with a mangled arm.

Dr. Oberst said, "These texts are famous, the Age of Reason? And that letter, the Mu, I have seen many times throughout medical school. What does any of this have to do with beauty or bloodshed?"

"Knowledge is beauty maybe?" Parisa said, but then shuddered, "No, no, I think that this has to do with the masters. What hope do the masters have?"

Another swiveling glance around the room. No masters seen. Certainly nothing beautiful seen.

"We have books in the dining hall. What was the point of cutting an arm open for more books?" Harriet said, straining, maintaining pressure on Semyonov's arm. He still mutely screamed.

Parisa said, addressing nobody in particular, and rubbing her forehead raw, "Maybe it must be like the maps. These books. All Western. Many of the maps here. Focus on West. Must be related. What hope do masters have? Through bloodshed? Maps. Books on reason?"

Dr. Oberst interrupted her private conference, "We maybe should head back to the others. Semyonov is certainly going into shock. We need water, and maybe Dr. Gage could help him."

Parisa nodded and snatched up the box. Harriet and Dr. Oberst carried Semyonov down the hallway ahead of Parisa.

Before she left, she took another look around the navigation office. Without a second thought, she ripped the maps down from the walls, stuffing them under her arms. Another swivel around, pinching her nose to stifle the stench of burning blood.

"I can understand it," she said to nobody, "Laugh if you want, but I can understand it."

She turned and left. Not a run, not a saunter, a walk. A simple, knowing walk. The room did indeed chuckle at her exit.

Chapter Twelve

Dr. Gage attended to the wounded boy without unnecessary barbs, an unexpected but welcomed self-censoring. He clicked his tongue as he felt Semyonov's pulse, "Weak but rapid. Not a good sign."

He thumped Semyonov on the eye. No response.

"Automatic sensory responses decreasing. Hmmm. Keep him warm and try to get fluids in him. Without proper medical intervention, we can only hope he stays in the first stage and progresses no further."

Harriet did as told without assistance, slumping into the corner and draping Semyonov on her side. Clumsily she tried to funnel water into his mouth, succeeding in funneling most of it onto the floor.

Dr. Oberst found himself back at the shoulder of Kitagawa, who wasn't even pretending to care for the mutilated Soviet. At least Renard could pretend, good to her prior profession. Not so much to comfort Semyonov, but more so as an excuse to burrow into Alessandra and wrap an arm around Gao. This time, it was Gao's turn to pat her on the back, and even scruffed her hair.

Parisa tactfully waited until the immediacy of Semyonov's condition waned before presenting her findings to the group.

None responded with any amount of tact. Fiery and immediate.

"This must have some militaristic form to it, certainly," Renard called out, "But of course. We are in a bunker, after all."

"Terrain navigation maps, it's likely," Dr. Oberst replied, wiping sweat from his brow, "I know them well. But the books? The Mu? Those are nothing similar."

Kitagawa sat straight up with a sadistic little glee, "I have given that much thought. The mathematical approach is likely faulty; there has been nothing of mathematics presented to us thus far, and so we should not make that our primary assumption. No, instead, we have been accosted with very elementary philosophy. These books here, from the box, are books of philosophy and reason. So, I submit the Greek symbols are used in a similar sense." The group stared at him, and certainly not in the manner he desired.

Renard clicked her tongue. "So?"

"So, there must be some importance on a more linguistic, less scientific level."

"That's not helpful," Dr. Gage jeered from his seat, rubbing his chest. "What hope does the masters have, that is the question presented to us. The answer must be literal, can't you all see. Take this all literally, through bloodshed comes beauty. Beauty here meaning literature, or rather, intellectual advancements. Advancements, see, can have several meanings. The maps, used to charter out land gains by officials of the military. The answer is there. The masters are the officers, hence why it's in the navigation room. They hope for advancements, through bloodshed. Territorial gains. That's it. Territory. Therein lies the tie to the military and answers the riddle."

Renard prepared another scoff, but thought about it, and drew nothing, which must have annoyed her severely by the way her face sunk into a purple. She remedied her mood by furling on top of Gao, and prying open another book for another bout of unrequested alphabet lessons.

Parisa whispered into Harriet's ear, and Harriet parroted, "If indeed territory or advancement is the answer to such a riddle, perhaps it provides the answer to the whole? The 'truth' so to speak."

The contribution went ignored. Alessandra had been thumbing through each of the new books. She found nothing and set them down. "I do not understand how territory is in these books."

Dr. Oberst grunted and pounded his still bloody fist on his forehead, "It's so hard to think, my brain is so groggy. But I will try to recall what I remember when I read these books so long ago in school."

"Why not re-read them, you have the time," Renard said, continuing to encourage Gao to sound out words found in the English picture book. "Nothing to do but enjoy dreary literature about dreary national debt."

Dr. Oberst muttered, "I fear I may not have much time left. I feel my chest and throat tighten as time wears on down here. The gas is persistent; it lingers in this room still."

Dr. Gage nodded, "Yes, I daresay you'll be the next to go if the Soviet pulls through." He said it as though it was not a poke, but an earnest, helpful insight. Dr. Oberst found it neither helpful, nor insightful.

Finally taking her full concentration off of Gao, Renard heaved as well. "I feel it too. Maybe not as severe as you, for I have no allergies. Perfectly made."

Nothing but silence. Somebody was probably supposed to agree.

For an unnaturally long stretch of time, the only noise was Gao clumsily sounding aloud words, "Cat. Dog. Rat. Mouse."

Renard commented, breaking the silence at last with inappropriate giddiness, "The little boy is so clever. Do you hear him?"

"I'd hardly call him a little boy, and don't praise such small feats. It's poor for the ego," Kitagawa scowled. "You don't submit your praise appropriately. One receives accolades for being able to pronounce basic words, another receives scorn for referencing classical literature."

Alessandra laughed, slapped the table, pointed a finger at him, wagged it, then laughed again. Renard told her it wasn't a joke, but that only made Alessandra laugh harder. Kitagawa flushed, reshuffled in his seat, then offered an actually helpful thought, "There must be a Greek symbol in the boiler room. Those three must have overlooked it. It would make no sense. It would break the pattern if there wasn't one. We should go corroborate."

Alessandra lightly chided him, "Not too quick, risk of injury," followed by an ungraceful, unsubtle tilt of the head to the very blue Semyonov.

Dr. Gage groused, scratching the white hairs poking from his ears. "But just what is the fault with my answer? Why waste time? It is more prudent to act than to sit around waiting until he bleeds out and the Kraut suffocates. The chains that bind are broken... in the boiler room... must be referring to a breakdown in ranks. Is that why we are here? For some punishment? We disobeyed superiors and prevented advancement?"

Harriet responded so that Dr. Oberst wouldn't have to, purely because his hoarse voice grew grating, "How would that make sense? Only two of us were in the military. And I have never disobeyed anyone I have worked for. I don't think I have ever done anything worthy of punishment, not this sort of punishment anyway."

She ripped the skirt of her dress. Deftly, she wove a

shoddy and feeble cast to wrap Semyonov's arm. Parisa donated a string of golden thread that adorned her neck, and the cast was fastened.

Dr. Gage craned his neck over to watch the process, saying nothing. If he was impressed with the craftsmanship, he did not make it obvious. Just a limp, "Hm, innovative."

Renard said, her attention only at half-mast, "Scarecrow is right, I have done no wrong either."

Harriet recoiled, "Huh? Scarecrow?"

"Hm? Oh, apologies, I misspoke."

Dr. Gage hoisted himself out of his chair, placing his full weight onto his feeble little cane, "Kitagawa, your father is in the Imperial Navy. Shahidi, your father serves the Shah. Dr. Oberst, you were a foot soldier for the villains of recent years. I carried out my duties too. That is four of us, four out of eleven. All those too young, you Foster, and the Chinese boy and the Soviet, Morrelli, you must be related somehow. Perhaps you do not know it. While strangers, we must have something in common, something we have not considered."

Parisa and Harriet looked at each other. The well-practiced silent discussion commenced. Harriet prompted Parisa with a nod, who took in a confident breath and squared her shoulders.

"I saw Wassermann in Zürich. He was a stranger to me then, as he was to me here. But I saw him. He introduced himself to me and my uncle as Jonas. That was his first name, I remember. He spoke the truth; I saw it here on his passport. Perhaps, yes. We may have some connection."

"Why were you in Zürich?" Harriet asked, nudging her shoulder.

"Holiday. Nothing grave. With my uncle, who went to Zürich on business. Wassermann… he was the clerk in the travel office. He wanted to see our papers. He was friendly.

His colleague was not friendly. Not friendly and not Swiss. Colleague looked Turkic. I tried to practice my Turkish on him, but he didn't speak Turkish…he was very rude. It is the last memory I have before the bunker," Parisa said, then waited in hope for someone to spark with a sudden revelation.

Her hope was immediately dashed. Kitagawa replied, "I would not think too much on it. It may be just proximity bias. Perhaps you were already a target, and Wassermann was a mere obstacle. I last remember Paris. Kovacevic and Oberst said the same thing. Last in Paris." He faced Harriet, "You were traveling to Stockholm, correct? Where do you remember last?"

"We had just docked in London."

Kitagawa replied, "Indeed, London. Perhaps we each bumped across each other unknowingly. That only leaves the Russian boy—"

"Russian!" Parisa jolted, "Colleague! Turkic Russian. My uncle asked him if he was Soviet, and he got very angry. My uncle then guessed Tatar. The man said nothing, then left. Wassermann apologized to us."

Kitagawa sucked his teeth, "Maybe the Soviet knew him. If only he had also learned the alphabet, perhaps communication with him would have been feasible. Too late now, I suppose."

Harriet called from the floor, "No. It's not too late. Look. His color is returning. Dr. Gage, see, is there hope?"

Indeed, the blue had faded into a grayish hue. Still ghastly, but not ghoulish anymore. The gold thread did gleam extra brilliantly against such a pallor.

Dr. Gage grunted, not belaying any undue optimism, "Not out of the woods yet. Change out the bandage every so often. Infection is worse."

"Location matters?" Alessandra asked, "I was in Apulia, I met no strangers and not one of you. Will this help answer the questions?"

"Better than doing nothing at all, I say," Dr. Gage huffed and turned his attention back to Semyonov, "The Soviet has evaded cyanosis, for now at least. Death is no longer imminent but perhaps delayed. Organ failure may still loom. Keep him warm unless you wish to be free of the burden."

Harriet complied, but muttered without breath, "Wonder how you fared in private practice..."

Dr. Gage scoffed, "Do you have scruples with my diagnosis, Miss Foster?"

"I thought doctors were supposed to have bedside manners."

"What would be the point, child? He likely does not hear, understand, or care. Shock often claims life, even if the body leads all to believe it is recovering. It would be a disservice to speak softly, and let disappointment have the surprise advantage. I have seen it thousands of times over. Certainly, I do not wish death for him out of selfish reasons. As the bodies of Kovacevic, Wassermann, and the Polish man had to be cleared out while we were unconscious, I am sure we will once again be gassed to oblivion if he fades too. I am readying my faculties for it again."

"But us, Dr. Gage. It is cruel to us," Harriet protested.

"Oh, come off it now, don't give me any of that. You cannot grow fond of any stranger after such a short period of time. Especially one who barely has the capacity to talk." Dr. Gage's voice cracked. Abruptly, he fell silent and stern.

Harriet readied another complaint, but Parisa grabbed her arm and shook her head.

Dr. Oberst swallowed a dry cough, fiddling with his own injury. The hasty bandage he had fastened around the gash in his right hand had been soaked and crusted over. His fingertips were yellowing. He sucked on them to stir the nerves but only stirred a disgusted grimace from Kitagawa.

Inappropriately timed, but said nonetheless, Renard announced, "If there is but one good thing to think of, it is the boy here. YiMing is a quick learner. Go on. Say it YiMing, say elephant."

"Elephant," Gao said hesitantly. He repeated himself with more confidence. Then, he said it a third time with full force. Then he kept on saying it. A good dozen times, to the point where elephant no longer became a word, until Kitagawa shot him an ego-shattering scowl.

Kitagawa said, "Neither impressive nor useful. Again, how will sounding out animals help us?"

"As the doctor here prepares himself to succumb to death, I prepare myself and the boy for the surface. I have hope we will think it out thoroughly," Renard replied with a weary smile, "Have you not heard Alessandra and Parisa? Their speaking improves by the hour. It is a sign. There is hope still in this bunker, *hein*?"

"By the hour or by the day, do you wonder?" Kitagawa's tone sharply turned from stoic to pensive, as if he was now lost in a daydream. "I just now noticed. My own facial hair, I can feel it coming in. Admittedly, I am incapable of growing much at all and especially not quick. I feel it now, the same when I tried to grow out a beard replicating older Shinto monks. We may have been down here for the better half of a month, our unconscious hours longer than we assumed."

Surprisingly, it was a fairly accurate guess. If there were indeed observers watching them from behind the walls, they maybe were impressed.

Dr. Oberst exclaimed, "My mustache! No! It's my most valuable quality! So tidy, so neatly manicured. Now I must look like a barbarian."

Dr. Gage snorted, "You look like a drunkard."

Parisa cut off Dr. Oberst's reply, "If so, then our families have noticed our absence. There may be an effort to find us."

Dr. Gage scratched at the scraggly start of his own beard, no optimism going unpunished under his guard, "If that is the case, then we can be certain we are in such a remote location that we are absolutely undiscoverable. Why, someone of your status certainly would have a full spectrum of search and recovery deployed."

Alessandra nibbled her bottom lip and drummed her fingers on the table, "But that is just it, no? Why would I, a farmer's daughter, and Harriet, a seamstress, be stolen with Shahidi and Kitagawa? It feels, what is the word in English?"

"Random?" Harriet offered, "It must not be random. Certainly not. Now, I am not too sure if our occupation or status matters much. But our origins do seem to matter. Think on it, why one person from each place? Why Persia, or Yugoslavia, or France, and Italy? What do they all have to do with each other? If there is some military explanation here, it could not possibly be the war, could it? Persia had no part, I think."

Kitagawa whipped his attention away from his facial hair, "Neither did Japan for that matter. But there may be a point there. A string to pull. Let me think, Germany and England are at odds, and the rest of Europe has been divided with almost none left to any neutral position. Similarly in East Asia, there are those friendly to the emperor and those unfriendly. Hm, all of us from such contenders."

"Switzerland…." Dr. Oberst said lightly.

Kitagawa grunted, then seemed to drop his rationale altogether, "Each room has a formula, which one was the most obvious? We can start there."

Harriet said, timidly looking down on Semyonov, "The

lever in the boiler room. Practically dying to be pulled, but I don't know, seems like it will also certainly cause injury."

His disposition had shifted, but to the untrained eye, it was hard to tell if it improved or worsened. Semyonov squeezed his eyes shut, and they trembled under great strain. His curdled rasping simmered into something fainter as Dr. Oberst checked his pulse and temperature.

His eyebrows faintly wilted, and he stooped down over Semyonov's mouth, "I do believe his chest is returning. The shock may be ebbing now."

Dr. Gage spoke from his perch, "That could always be a bad sign, though. In the final stages, you think recovery but then death comes not much later."

Harriet continued to tear off bits of her skirt, stockpiling more bandages than necessary. She used up practically half of the remaining water on cleaning his wound, much to the annoyance of the more pragmatic thinkers around the table, but nobody stopped her, yet.

Uneasily, and with much time, Semyonov regained his faculties. He sat up and could slowly blink. Out of habit, he asked something to Parisa and Harriet, who could only clap with delight. Reflexively, he tried to clap too. The effort went punished by his own injury.

Of course, the rest of the group were either apathetic, or pleased solely that a trap was survivable. But that notion didn't matter, not to Semyonov's arm at least.

❋ ❋ ❋

Dr. Oberst waited a socially appropriate amount of time, after hours of stillness, to re-address the group with their objective. Semyonov made as good a recovery as any could hope. His arm was mutilated, but at least he was alive and in relatively decent health given his conditions, which was more than Dr. Oberst could say about his lung capacity. Even better, morale seemed to increase with Semyonov's recovery.

"So, the boiler room?" Dr. Oberst prodded Harriet, "I do recall you saying something earlier."

She nodded, "I'll go back then. To the boiler room. I will continue to do what is necessary; it is my turn, after all."

"How valiant," Kitagawa said, succeeding in eroding her newfound bravado.

Parisa got up to follow Harriet, but the seamstress halted her, "It's fine, we should try to keep as many safe as possible. Besides, as Dr. Oberst is good at Latin, you are a sharp mind. It would be a major blow to us all if you were incapacitated."

"No, Harriet. I go too. Every room you go to, I go to as well. That is fair. The two of us will find out the boiler room like we found out the navigation room." She squeezed Harriet's bony little wrist.

Harriet's face was sunken, her eye sockets reddened, but she allowed the echoes of a smile to lift the corners of her mouth.

Parisa looked around the room. No ready volunteers among the older members. However, Semyonov still got to his feet. The two women immediately protested, pointing to his still-fresh injury. But he dismissed their cries with a shake of the head and a back-patting ritual. He took a skull-rattling step straight into the wall. A shudder, a gentle redirection by Harriet, and he took another, less obstructed, step. A limp shrug, an even limper pat on the back to Harriet, and he nodded his readiness.

Renard did not budge from her seat next to Gao, nor even raise her eyes to meet anyone else. Harriet and Parisa ducked out the back door, and Semyonov followed, accidentally slamming his shoulder against the frame.

"I suppose brute force is one way through," Kitagawa lilted, picking up a piece of literature to bide the time. "If the

Chinese boy didn't find himself such an ardent guardian, I may suggest that it is his turn to contribute."

Renard wrinkled her nose. "No, he is far too precious."

Kitagawa wrinkled his own nose, in a way not precious at all.

Dr. Oberst posed the stinging question to the group amid an awkward silence, "Are we cowards?"

In a fashion indicating shame and humility were eternal strangers to him, Kitagawa replied, "Never. It only makes sense that there are those who are fit to serve with their bodies and those fit to serve with their minds. You, me, and several others here, we must preserve our thinking abilities. It is for the communal benefit, of course. But Semyonov, well, I suppose he is fit for one thing and one thing alone."

Renard said under her breath, "Yes, I am. I could not do it, forgive me. I could not do what Semyonov had done, I would never even allow the blade to pierce my skin." She softly pat Gao on the head, who gave her a blissfully ignorant smile, "But maybe it is for the best. No one else could have survived it."

Alessandra slumped next to Renard and clasped her hands, "For me, I will give what is asked when I must. But first, I will want to know I do not bleed for no gain." She craned her head to address Kitagawa, "Would you do too? If needed?"

He didn't respond but looked back through *The Wealth of Nations*.

There were a few minutes of silence, only disturbed by Gao still sounding aloud English words, and Dr. Gage sputtering out corrections.

Chapter Thirteen

Back towards the stifling heat, the three went together. Semyonov was breathing heavily, and he picked at some of the scabs surfacing at the edges of the bandage. Every couple of steps, he'd saunter his way against the walls with a mighty slam. Harriet linked an elbow and thus became a nursemaid attending a geriatric patient.

At the fork in the corridor, Parisa seized, gripped Harriet by the hand, and tugged her to the left at a quickened pace. Before Harriet could even ask her for an explanation, Parisa stopped short of the bend. Eagerly, she pointed towards the corner. The radio was gone. Removed in its entirety. A wavering groan erupted from Parisa's throat, and she looked upwards into the cramped ceiling corners.

"They sure are diligent," Harriet said wryly, and patted Semyonov on the back, "Maybe they're upset they don't have a corpse to come snatch." He proudly completed the patting ritual with his mutilated arm.

Parisa muttered, "Very bold, is it? We are all awake. How could they know we would not see them take the radio?"

"Probably because they knew we were all idling in the dining room. Maybe that should be our next task, to look around and find out how they can watch us."

"Maybe, yes. But now, let us go to the other boiler room. The lever should be pulled, does it seem that way?"

A shuddering reluctance halted Harriet, forcing her to steady herself before responding, "Yes, I think that is what is being prompted of us. Don't worry, I will be the one to pull it." She let out a weak chuckle, "Maybe it will give me the same shock as Wassermann and maybe produce a blade from the handle and cut me open. Who knows. In that case, I will expect you to resuscitate me, Parisa."

"I can only promise to try," she said, and gave Semyonov a once-over. Maybe it was because the name Semyonov was too long, too convoluted, or because he didn't look old enough to have such an aggrandized title, she asked, "Pyotr, yes? Pyotr is your first name?"

He nodded. A little glimmer, a far cry from a smile, but something close enough.

"Pyotr," he said in a small rasp.

Harriet said, "Pyotr."

"Pyotr," he repeated.

Parisa added, "Yes, Pyotr!"

Harriet gave it another go, "Pyotr!"

He pointed at them with a shaky finger, "Parishya. Kharryet."

Harriet shrugged, "Good enough." He shrugged back. Another back-patting ritual commenced.

Parisa beckoned them back down the hallway, and within minutes, they were in front of the hellhole boiler room. The heat stifled the corridor well before they even broke entry.

Parisa said, "When the lever pulls, and you see something happen, let me know."

She pantomimed the same message to Pyotr. Maybe about half was understood through her artistic hand motions, which was good enough to be considered a victory. They congratulated themselves for their succinct communication with yet another circular round of nods and shoulder shakes.

Taking a deep breath in, Parisa pushed the boiler room door. It swung wide open and banged shut as soon as Pyotr's heels passed the threshold. A reverberating click punctured the air. Pyotr warily gave the door a shake. Bolted. Somehow.

He gestured to the two women in a panic, but they were surprisingly unmoved. Harriet commenced the shrug, nod, pat language.

Pyotr's worry did not dissipate, so Harriet squeezed his shoulder.

She mumbled, "I suspect it will be unbolted once we pull on the lever. The wardens here are playing a trick on us. Sometimes, I can hear them giggling. Giggling to themselves between the walls."

As he screwed his face tighter, she mimed it all out, punctuating with a shrug, nod, pat, and a stuck-out tongue. He returned with his own pantomime, putting a finger gun to his temple. A bit of a grim addition to the language, but they continued.

Back into the maze of churning machines and the hiss of steam, the three went straight for the lever, in all its special presentation. Parisa craned her head towards the swinging chains. Like the wires around the ship wheel, the tails of the chain disappeared into the walls, their anchoring and webbing hidden. She stuck out her hand to steady Harriet, who happily yielded.

Parisa murmured, "The chains and the machines, it looks like a measuring thing. See the design?"

Harriet murmured, "Huh? Oh yes, yes, I see it. The chains that bind are shattered. So... something heavy?"

She began to thump on her chest so hard it threatened to crack her ribcage. A shiver rattled down her body. Her eye sockets began to flush bright pink. But she weakly chuckled, "Well then, I will have a go at the lever. Parisa, maybe you should go stand in the middle, you may be able to see more that way."

Parisa gave a firm nod, gripped Pyotr by the hand, and darted away. Harriet took more uneasy breaths, bouncing to jostle her nerves loose. With a yelp, she wedged herself in between the narrow opening, the sole place free from the steaming heat of the boilers. Feeding into the nervous drive, she stuck her hand out and yanked the lever down. It required much force, almost the entirety of her paltry back and shoulder muscles. The lever scraped against itself, refusing to budge. The slightest ease of force, and the stupid thing was quick to return upright like a soldier to attention.

Disturbing the lever demanded punishment. Immediate and boiling. The lights cut. The boiler room pitched into darkness. Fire erupted within the chasms of the machines on either side of Harriet, and scorching steam burst out with great ferocity, singeing and blistering her sides.

Instinctually, Harriet released her grip and took several blind steps backward. The steam subsided, and the lights flickered on as the lever quickly reset. In numb dread, Harriet felt her arms and hands. The steam had quickly penetrated the thin linen of her dress, and her whole arms were sufficiently roasted. The skin on her hand had bubbled into sea foam. Despite the pain, the damage was not too bad—at least that was the permitted delusion she gurgled to herself.

Parisa called from the center, "What has happened. It went dark. I saw nothing; it went by too fast."

"Stay there. The dark must be necessary," Harriet said, trying to keep her voice steady, and failing into a warble. She tried to wrap the skirt of her dress around her arm for extra protection—the second permitted delusion, "I'm going to try again, it burns a little."

Banishing thought, or self-preservation, she leaned forward, burying her face towards her chest, and yanked the lever down again. The steam was even heavier and piercing this time. The second delusion held fast for not even five seconds, and she relented her grip in six.

"It is not the ceiling. It is the wall. Something lights in the dark. What I saw earlier. It is the Latin. I cannot write in the dark, please pull again and I will try remember and write it down," Parisa called out, her voice bouncing around the metal cauldrons.

Harriet couldn't muster a call back but groaned a response. Quietly, she began to sniffle and curled into her lap.

Pyotr, likely feeling abjectly useless with Parisa, made his way back to Harriet. He found her on the floor, shaking into herself. All of the exposed skin on her limbs had reddened, peeling off in thin, white layers. The side of her neck had a massive yellow and white boil. Harriet shot him a meek universal *it's fine, all is well, no worries here* sign with her raw hand. He tried to collect her, but she didn't budge, so Pyotr stepped back.

Refilling her chest with the heavy, wet air, she hid her face then pulled down on the lever again and held it fast. Five seconds passed, and the steam that plagued her sides became unbearable. She tried to stop herself from crying out, but it escaped her mouth regardless. Her grip around the lever waned under the fiery assault of the steam, and the lever began to slide upright again. Her ears filled with the deafening roar of the fire, as if the boilers supernaturally scooted closer. The lever escaped from her grasp and flung upwards. The lights flickered back on again.

"I need more time," Parisa called, strained and apologetic, "Just one more. Please."

The small *Please* was enough. Probably the first utterance in the bunker.

Harriet slowly nodded to herself, gasping and choking. Feebly, she placed her hand around the knob of the lever, trying to put her failing strength into it. Pytor came behind her, firmly placing his good hand over hers on the knob. He yanked down easily. The steam came, but none reached Harriet. Pytor strained and grunted under the blast from the fire and steam but held on. Five seconds passed, then ten, then twenty. Harriet could feel his body shaking, but as the darkness endured, so did he.

A heavy clang vibrated the metallic cauldrons. A jingle and chime. The swinging chains began to enthusiastically dance in the blackness. A red halo flared among the pitch. Then came the fire's roar, which sounded like a bloodhound's siren.

"I have it," Parisa shrieked beyond the dark.

Too eagerly, Pyotr relented his grip. He collapsed backwards and softly groaned. Too eagerly, Harriet joined his groaning. His clothes were even thinner than Harriet's linens, and it looked like his entire torso and arms were blistered over. Several layers of skin were peeling off his hand and forearm. His shoddy cast was all but evaporated. Yet, he had no tears. He tried to get up; too painful to lie on his back, but now his strength finally failed. Exhausted and frail, Harriet tried to help the best that she could and used the damp cloth around her skirt to wipe his face down. Thin layers of skin rubbed off, so she stopped. Instead, she used the back of her hand, which was similarly ineffective.

Parisa then joined the two and tried to politely halt a retch in her throat. She was unsuccessful. They were so red and pulpy, and the stench was unbearably heavy and sulfuric. She clutched her little notebook so hard her knuckles turned white. A meager contribution, and now she was ashamed of it even more. Paralyzed in place, she could only watch the two clumsily get to their feet.

"Did you get it? Any box of sorts?" Harriet asked faintly,

holding up Pytor, who was more carcass than man.

Parisa shook her head and stuttered, "The chains lowered. The clear ink caught fire. I heard a howl. There was a question mark, must be the prompt. Kitagawa or Gage or Oberst can help."

Parisa uneasily made her way back towards the front of the boiler room and tugged on the door handle. Unbolted. Snarkily unbolted.

Harriet sneered and whipped her head around to address nobody in particular, "I hate you."

Another chuckle leaked out from the vents.

✳ ✳ ✳

"The injuries are severe, and prone to infection if you are not careful, but are not mortal as they stand now," Dr. Gage said, following an inspection of the expansive burns on Harriet and Pyotr. "Try to keep them dry, and un-irritated. I suppose our jailors would not be so kind as to give you both a change of clothes but stay away from any moisture the best you can. Boy, I think you've had enough with this self-mutilation. Three strikes and you're out, I do say."

Kitagawa and Dr. Oberst had taken up the task of looking at Parisa's notes, ripping it from her hands without a second consideration.

"*Quid pondus fregerit...* What has broken the balance," Oberst said, leaning onto Kitagawa's shoulder, who certainly wasn't appreciative but didn't overtly protest.

Kitagawa responded, "A better translation would be *What has broken the scale. Pondus* here can mean both, but is used to refer in philosophical discourses to law and legality. Those statues that hold the scales in front of courtrooms, that is the *pondus*. And this Greek sign here, if your drawing is accurate, it was illuminated above the Greek sign?"

Parisa nodded, about to add her own thoughts, but was

cut off at her nod.

He continued, "That is the Greek sign Beta, a 'B' in the alphabet." He reclined back with utter self-satisfaction and looked at Alessandra. Not knowing what he expected from her, she clapped.

Dr. Oberst said, "So, all together in the boiler room – *The chains that bind are shattered. What has broken the scale?* Is that it?"

Parisa exclaimed, "The scale. Yes, the way the chains were arranged in the ceiling. I thought it looked familiar. It looks like those scales. When dark, chains lowered and connected to central machine. Flame lit above."

Kitagawa lilted, "Yes, yes, you are very clever. Now, if the chains that have been shattered are indeed referring to a breakdown in ranks, what scale could it be referring to? Balance of power, maybe? What turned the tide in the war?"

Dr. Oberst meekly proposed, "Battle of the Marne, maybe? German forces were halted indefinitely."

Dr. Gage grumbled, "No, too literal. The scale is a clue here, surely. The trials of Leipzig. Finally, German officers were held accountable."

Dr. Oberst cocked his mouth in an irate grimace and shook his head intensely. He stood up and paced the room, railing against the squeezing in his chest. Every so often, he would stop dead behind Dr. Gage, then abruptly start his pacing again.

Renard groaned, "That is just as literal, I fear. If the navigation office's answer is territory, then this answer must be just as vague, no? It could be 'power', as the answer. You said yourself, the balance of power was thrown off, especially in a time of chaos and violence?"

"Yes, but no," Dr. Gage responded.

"What does that mean?" Renard asked.

Kitagawa cut in, "He doesn't know."

"Yes, I do."

"Then tell us."

"Pah, you wouldn't understand it."

The elders started a circular grousing to refresh their sudden collective mental fatigue.

Alessandra yawned and optioned the best entertainment was to scrutinize Kitagawa's face. Amid deep reflection, he intensely frowned and wrinkled his nose and sucked on his teeth. She began to parody him to a surprisingly accurate imitation. He didn't notice at first, so she flopped onto the table and wrinkled her nose straight at him.

He drew his mouth down and let out a sheepish, "What?"

Alessandra laughed, scurried back to her seat, and whispered something in Renard's ear. It was likely intended to be a secret, but Renard shared it with the group regardless, "Alessandra thinks maybe this must not be due in Europe. The navigation office, maps are of Europe, but not the boiler room. Maybe more with the globe. She is interested in exploring the East, *hein* Kitagawa?"

"Could not possibly be," he responded with a strangely high-pitched timbre.

"Why not?"

"Why Latin and Greek symbols? Why not Chinese characters, or Arabic script? No, it's Western surely. I think that maybe I am a victim of circumstance here. But I do appreciate Alessandra thinking of such an inclusion."

His temperament was hard to gauge. Somewhere between indignant but earnestly grateful, both yet none. But he certainly was bashful; the red flush on his neck being his most disloyal attribute.

Harriet slowly paced circles around the table, following Dr. Oberst's lead, rubbing the gummy skin from her arms.

Harriet gave her pacing a chorus of free word association,

"Lever, pull, dark. Dark and fire. Darkness, chains, scales... what else..."

Parisa joined her pacing, "The scale. It weighs the law. Perhaps balance has been broken." Habit made her grip Harriet's hand, but sensibility retracted it after a glimpse of the massive bubble on the knuckles.

The three paced, weaving around each other like old crows around a garden; the flowers being the sullen intellectuals. Pyotr joined after a while. No explicit intent, outside of it still hurt to sit.

Not the academics heavyweights, rather the simple cow maid made the first declaration. Alessandra stood, orating to the human garden, "It is not darkness, but blindness. The law is blind."

Renard giggled and patted Alessandra's hand, "So close, dear. The saying is not law is blind, it is justice is blind."

Dr. Gage remarked, "Is that it? The law binds society together and was broken in wartime. What breaks the scale? Justice, is that it? Or rather, injustice."

An immediate, and certainly premature, burst of congratulations erupted amid the congress. Harriet and Parisa cried out, jostling each other by the elbows, crooning 'injustice' to each other, and tried to share their joy by shaking Pyotr's pulpy shoulders; no idea what happened but pleased to be included.

Gao looked to Kitagawa for some explanation and was only met with a clipped, "What?"

Gao repeated, "What!"

Kitagawa apparently didn't like Gao's *What* very much, as announced by an eye roll and a self-indulgent snort.

Dr. Oberst feebly exclaimed, "Injustice. Yes. That makes sense,"

He leaned forward and gripped Dr. Gage around the

Hal Enzinga

shoulders, jostling the old man around, in a moment forgetting all past transgressions. Dr. Gage, for once, didn't even seem to mind. He just poked at his own temple with a knowing smirk.

Kitagawa grinned and was only three seconds away from patting himself on the back, "Yes, it does. A Western notion from our Western imprisoners."

Renard asked giddily, "You mean to say that law and justice is unknown to the Far East?" To her, a joke.

Yet, Kitagawa responded with a returning seriousness, true to the most steadfast component of his nature, "No, but the concept of *blind* justice would be very wrong. It's almost a hateful construction." The fleeting joviality vacated the room as he continued, "Justice applies to everyone per their condition. It would be wrong to hold everyone to the same standard, a standard that may be easily upheld by some, more so than by others."

Dr. Gage jabbed, also returning to his nature, "An excuse to allow the emperor to do whatever he pleases."

"Not at all. But as I illustrate, if you indulged in the national habit of neglecting dental hygiene, and if it was considered a crime in France not to brush one's teeth, would you bellow if imprisoned at the border during holiday?"

Dr. Gage spluttered, "What does that even mean? Was that an insult? I do brush my teeth!"

"So, you disagree with our answer?" Dr. Oberst asked, entirely in good faith, but Kitagawa enjoyed being offended anyway.

"No, no, of course I agree. It would make sense, and I am beginning to puzzle together the implications of the Greek letters. But I do find the prompts a bit unfair. If this room were comprised entirely of my countrymen, they would be left empty-handed. Not for lack of intelligence, mind you, but because the conceptions are so vastly different."

Dr. Oberst hesitantly asked, "Impartiality is not valued?"

Kitagawa almost jumped out of his seat, ready to dive into some diatribe, "No, not saying that. Find the nuance. It's obvious we are meant to be working off assumptions taken from the Western lexicon, that is all. It's a construction for justice to be blind, most preferring justice to be fully lucid to an alleged perpetrator's customs. I'd say, if he was capable of such a cerebral puzzle, Mrs. Renard's pet would agree."

"Why don't you ask him?" Dr. Oberst asked, fully earnest, but Kitagawa indignantly drew his face thin anyway.

Kitagawa said, "To be completely honest, my comprehension is eroded by his inability to speak properly. Believe me, in academic pursuit it may be worthwhile, but I am certain such an elevated principle would not translate down to the necessary level. It's as you said, Mrs. Renard, some ideas are simply lost on those not equipped to understand."

Alessandra rolled her eyes, but still smiled, even snorted, "You speak of me? I am equipped to understand more than you think."

Kitagawa stammered and buried his eyes into his lap, "I didn't mean it as an insult. Just an observation is all. Indeed, you have surprised me."

Dr. Oberst flew into the seat next to Kitagawa, so close, so fast that Kitagawa practically jumped, "No, Kitagawa, please tell me, I'm greatly interested. So, justice understands our circumstances. What drives us, what pushes us? It's more merciful than something as harsh as a blind leveling?"

Kitagawa collected himself again, banishing the flush from his neck, "Well, if that is how you choose to interpret it, then fine. I find it better that way. We are all slaves to our own circumstances, and justice should know this."

"Yes. Yes, I see what you mean." Dr. Oberst grabbed Kitagawa by the shoulders, who looked none too pleased with the contact.

The energy that Dr. Oberst subjected Kitagawa to was not explicitly unnerving, but rather bizarre; staring at Kitagawa as though they had been childhood inseparables, knowing each other through and through, holding each other in the highest esteem. Dr. Oberst's posture and blaze of a grin suggested he was about to pull Kitagawa into an embrace, but much to Kitagawa's relief, he did not.

Harriet listened, gnawing her lip, picking at a boil. She mumbled to herself, "Slave of circumstance. Yes. I've been a slave of circumstance." Her private musing went unheard.

Renard called, "This is tiring. Gao! To me!"

He trotted over and stood beside her. She took up one of the books from the navigation office, *Discourse on Inequality,* and flipped to a random line on a random page. She pointed it out, and he spoke, "Beings perfectly abstract are perceivable in the same manner or are only conceivable by the assistance of speech."

Gasps of pleasant delight flooded the room, and even faint applause from Parisa and Alessandra.

Kitagawa scoffed, shrugging Dr. Oberst's grip off of him, "Oh please, he may as well be babbling. He can sound words out but cannot articulate the meaning."

"No, that comes next," Renard beamed, "We have good fortune as of late. Two of the rooms have been answered. We shall be saved. Our capabilities grow stronger by each minute."

"Pessimism is more practical," Dr. Gage cautioned and punctuated with a pat on his belly.

Renard scoffed, "Can we not have a moment of amity? Finally, some peace to cut down the bleak and dreariness?"

"That will only make reality more sobering," Dr. Gage closed his eyes again and leaned back. His breathing was palpable, old, and croaking. It stopped sporadically and grunted back to rhythm again. He fumbled with the little pocket watch, flourishing it between his fingers.

Harriet had resumed her pacing around the room, stopping short of Dr. Gage's seat. A wretched snicker clawed its way down from her brain into her throat. Under her breath, something spiteful scratched its way into existence... "sobering".

Dr. Gage didn't reopen his eyes and didn't provide any acknowledgement. Embracing invisibility, spite shook her ribcage in another silent giggle. Then, whatever nasty creature that possessed her momentarily retreated. It emerged and dissipated with a flash, and Harriet clamped her hand over her mouth, but the tremble lingered. It grew ferocious yet died in the next blink.

"Sobering," she murmured into her hand. The nasty creature dwelled within her, muzzled but crouching.

Gao started intently into the novel of English gibberish. With a sudden clap of energy, he flung it aside and began to dig through the other texts. He rifled through each page erratically, and despite Renard's gentle attempts to calm his sudden bout of frenzy, he kept on plowing through. His young brow broke out in sweat, he began to grind his teeth, and foreign mutterings came out from him in a sharp staccato.

At first, Kitagawa didn't seem to notice or care, but after a minute, he shouted a command at Gao—the words unknown, but the intent obvious—cut out the racket.

Gao began to scratch his head and pace in a circle, then suddenly dropped to his hands and knees and began to bark. He paused, waiting for a response from anybody. Receiving nothing except Renard's concerned stare and Alessandra's giggle, he barked again and again, then shouted Chinese back to Kitagawa.

Parisa whispered, "What is he saying?"

Kitagawa spluttered out, "Nothing. He's insane. Saying stupid things about a stupid fairytale."

Parisa continued, "What fairytale? Please, he must know something."

"He knows nothing," Kitagawa said with much venom. He snapped something to Gao. Gao stood back up and began to cry. Renard immediately wrapped him in an embrace, which he sullenly returned.

Chapter Fourteen

It was the second time Kitagawa left the dining hall without much notice. Long after Gao stunned all with his newfound skills and then stunned them with his fit of insanity, everyone fell back into melancholy half-consciousness. Kitagawa paced back down towards the observation chamber with precise intent, grumbling all the way. His face was screwed up in a petulance indicating he was something akin to jealous. Of course, someone like him could never be jealous. Jealousy was for ugly people.

He gave the supposed exit door a cursory tug. Still bolted. So, he entered the observation room with double petulance. Walking in like it was his own foyer, he circled around the periscope with great interest, running his fingers along the metallic tube. Peeking back inside, the sharp threads lay in wait, greeting him with a smug flash. The looking glass's glint still reflected a darker amber color against the black. He spoke to himself, softly, as if giving himself a private confession, "What do the chains see that the masters cannot? What can I see?"

A hard voice startled him, "Yes, what can you see?"

Whipping around, he was met with the displeased frown of Alessandra, standing in the doorframe with her arms crossed. His skin broke into a cold sweat.

She barked, "Why have you come here alone?"

"Why did you? Where is Renard? Has she not elected you her surrogate daughter? Or is it that she abandoned you for her surrogate son?" He brusquely returned his attention to the periscope, continuing to circle it with his hands gripped behind his back like an old man inspecting an art piece, and furrowed his chin into his collar to hide the faint gooseflesh.

"Yes, she attends to Gao. She likes to hear him say words. She likes the accent. I saw you leave. You said nothing. You do not fear the danger?"

"I have already found out what is dangerous here, so no. I merely need to think of a way to circumvent it; that is all. Apologies. I mean, *avoid* it if that is more understandable," he said, refusing to fully address her for dignity's sake. "You cast suspicion on me; I can feel it. If I cared, I'd call it hurtful."

"You walk off, saying nothing, like a cat. Yes, I have suspicion, suspicion that your pride will lead to injury."

"Do not worry, I would not allow myself to be mutilated. I confess that I am led by pride, but so are the rest. I am not so unaware I cannot see that I am locked in some battle of intellect with the others and must readily take up an offensive. Make no mistake, however, I am a willing participant."

Alessandra walked up next to him and lightly grabbed his elbow, halting his pacing, "But why? We all have the same goal. Any competition for most smart does not matter."

He clutched his chest as though to stifle a heart palpitation. He responded, finally facing her, "Maybe to you it does not matter, but it must for me. I envy you, to some extent. You are exempt from the race. I have been a contender since birth. And there is no grace in losing but cowardly forfeit is even worse."

"Mr. Junichi, what are you saying?"

He stuttered and blinked erratically, "I don't know. That once you have achieved some standard, you have to try your whole life to maintain it, and to prove it to others. It gets worse once you must represent not only yourself, but the whole of your people."

She pouted, cocked her head to the side, and widened her eyes to a bulge, "You think I must not do the same?"

It was an odd expression. He struggled to find a way to respond to it.

"It's different. Despite what you may have understood, I would never imply peasantry is stupid or irrational. But it's a different league among scholars. If you were to sit back and contribute nothing, nobody would think any less of you. The same cannot be said for me."

A boisterous laugh boomed from Alessandra. She gripped his shoulders and aggressively shook him.

Despite the overly familiar gesture, he did not protest, but begged, "What is it? What is so funny? Why must you always laugh at me?"

"I don't laugh at you. Not just you. Scholars, academics, all the smart men, you are all the same around the world. Please tell me, Junichi, when was the last time you visited a farm? Visited the common people? Visited those that must live in the world that you make?"

Standing still under her grip, he responded, "Often, I will have you know. I have been to the Italian countryside."

As if he had somehow continued the joke, she laughed and shook her head, "What an answer. Come on, Junichi, let me help you look through the room."

"Not necessary, I believe I have found all I needed to find, I simply am thinking it through." He broke free from her at last and peered back up the periscope, "I only wish we had paid more attention to the time. The light here, that reflects from the looking glass. It changes colors as does the sky. We may have been able to keep some record of time had we noticed it earlier."

"Oh? Well, we can start now," she said, about to poke her head into the dome of the periscope. Kitagawa yanked her back, accidentally sending her careening to the ground.

He forwent an apology and substituted an unintentionally haughty explanation, "It's a trap, surely. There are thin wires that trigger a blade. It will undoubtedly slice your neck if you were to actually try to look through the scope. I have been thinking about a way to disarm it."

"What have others said?" Alessandra said and rubbed her smarting backside.

"It has not been discussed. I would rather think of it myself. I only trust the highest intellectual authority at my disposal, so thereby I seek counsel inward."

"Well then, I suppose I must leave you to your thinking. I must not disrupt your counsel," she replied, turning to start for the door.

Kitagawa muttered, "No, it's fine. You may stay if you like. Your company is bearable. More so than the others at least. As long as you don't ask me anything stupid. Only if you want to, of course. I am sure Renard misses you."

With just the smallest waver in his voice, the thinnest peel of his bravado, at once Alessandra had to rancorously laugh.

The bravado peeled even more, his goose-flesh tripled, and Kitagawa asked a wobbly, "What?"

She sat on the ground, "Fine, I stand here and will watch you think. Perhaps I tell you about my hometown, Matera. You may ask any questions you like. I am not easily angry."

And so, they started. Kitagawa ambled around the room, striding out his thoughts. Alessandra chatted on, mostly to herself, but sometimes requesting some commentary from Kitagawa. He responded in overlong sentences and would conclude each thought with a long stare, as though silently prompting her to request another monologue.

He ran out of things inside the observation room to feign interest in but probably didn't want the migraine of returning to the dining room. So, he did something unthinkable—asking her questions about herself. Things he surely didn't even care to know.

"You don't get the opportunity to leave the circumstances of your birth, do you?" Kitagawa started. He took a seat on the step stool, something a bit below his dignity but would suffice in the austere environment.

"Eh?" She remained sitting by his feet, unbothered by the place relegated to her.

"Don't travel much?"

"What? No. I travel much," she said, and feigned indignity with crossed arms. No doubt Renard's influence.

"No. Travel, like for fun, go to another place for no reason other than you want to go?"

"Huh? Oh. Yes, yes, yes, I understand now. But I do not get holidays much, this is true. Without me, who else will do the work?" She began to untie and retie his shoelaces, then licked her thumb and rubbed a dull scuff clean again on his right shoe. He was instinctively annoyed for a half-second, then intrigued, then pushed his left foot closer to her. She obliged, polishing the left without hesitation.

He said, "A pity. One can only expand their mind and challenge their predisposed preconceptions and perspectives if they are not relegated to their lone corner of the Earth."

She said, "Please, sir. I am already impressed, do not do that."

"Apologies. Force of habit. Please, let me know what it's

like. I cannot fathom it, only knowing one way. Does it feel, oh, what's a good word, limiting? Your neural pathways? Restrictive? Fastened? I am jealous. Every moment you spend here must be in pure awe of unadulterated discovery."

"You think I enjoy the underground?"

"Not what I meant. No, I dare say nobody would enjoy this. I mean that I envy those who still can hold wonder in their eyes for the unknown. When you become like me, and everything is so knowable, the world loses its luster. It must be fun to be someone like you. Almost childlike. Playing with your hair the way you do. You must tell me, where did you learn such a habit? A common quirk among your community?"

Alessandra laughed and slapped him on the knee, "I have almost thirty years. Not a child. And I know a lot. And I never learned any habit; I just started one day. What person needs a community to play with hair?"

Surprising, and a bit close for him, but he continued, "Never said you didn't, never said you did. I am sure if I were to spend a day in your shoes, I would run the farm into the ground. But alas, I do know what a farm is, and what a cow is, and what hard labor is. That is not what I am getting at. But if you were to spend a day in my shoes, well, you'd become cognizant of more than you could ever dream."

A shallow frown creased her brow. "Hmmm. You think I'm stupid?"

A strange pang of panic ripped through his face, and it contorted into a comically wide expression of fright, "No. Not at all. Please understand, I am jealous. Truly."

"I think I know more than you in things that matter."

"Things that matter? What, a geopolitical expert? Transcontinental economist? Interplanetary gravitational physics?"

"No, things that actually happen to people. Things that you must do every day. Let me think. When is the last time you spoke to a woman?" Alessandra snorted and scratched her nose with a teasing wickedness.

Kitagawa muttered, "Roughly four or five seconds ago."

"No, you know what I mean."

"Oh. I think perhaps last December at an embassy function. I was invited for a Christmas—"

"And how did it go?"

"I know what you are going to suggest, and I do not appreciate it."

Alessandra gasped and clapped like they were neighbors sitting in the fields of a shared land plot, gossiping in a manner most catty. "I expect correctly?"

"I'd never say," Kitagawa said and pulled his mouth thin.

"Please tell me then, in as few words as you can try, why you think you did not do well?"

Kitagawa began to yank on his sweat-stained collar. "What an assumption. The fault hardly rested with me. She was a dull conversationalist."

"There are two in a conversation, no? Maybe she thought you were a difficult conversationalist. I can understand her feelings. And, if she was dull, why think of her at all?"

Kitagawa suddenly cried out, "Because you asked me."

"Which tells me many things, all at once. If that encounter comes to mind first, then it is a sad way your life is in, I fear. You see? I know this matter well, better than you," Alessandra said and could hardly contain her laughter.

"Well, hardly noteworthy. It's a common affliction."

Alessandra couldn't help but continue to giggle at Kitagawa's expression: he furrowed his brow, crossed his arms, and upturned his nose. An overgrown toddler. She was compelled to mirror it.

Kitagawa said, "Oh, I'm sorry, is this amusing to you?"

"Yes. You are a funny man."

"I certainly do not try to be. I've been laughed at plenty in my lifetime. I try to avoid it whenever possible."

"Then do not make that face. So, how's the word, like when pressing down on cake?"

"Squishy?"

"Yes. Your face is funny when it is squishy."

"Your voice is funny when you can't pronounce squishy properly." He recoiled at his own jab.

Luckily, she did not care, "Aww, do not be angry. Why not laugh at yourself?"

"Because as soon as you do, that gives permission for others. I refuse to give that sort of permission. It's uncouth. I am a person of dignity, so I shall behave and thus be treated as such."

"Well, I am a lady of dignity, and you shall no longer use words that make me confused."

"You cannot pronounce yourself a lady of dignity."

Alessandra shrugged, "But you did."

"That is different. I have fought my way to such a position."

"Oh? Being the son of an important man did not help?"

"Well, yes, but I've done the bulwark of my accomplishments on my own merit, I will have you know."

Alessandra squeezed him on the knee, "Yes, yes, I know. Anyways, to answer your question. I do not travel much, but when I can, I like to go to Lisbon. Only have been once."

Kitagawa responded, suddenly entranced by the pressure on his joint, "What? Oh, right. Yes, Lisbon is lovely. Myself, if I could spend the rest of my days confined to one town, it would be Beirut. Real crossroads of culture, so much to see. Whenever I have the chance to escape the doldrums of the mid-term, I must go. It is the one place where wanton giddiness finds its way back into the crevices of my mind."

"Is it too difficult to say 'I like Beirut'?"

"I thought Italians liked poetry? Not one for descriptive language?"

"No, I like poetry. When done good. Because you use more words in confusing ways, does not make poetry," Alessandra concluded with another knee slap. "Ah well, if we are to argue, then we may include the others, yes?"

Kitagawa hesitated and stared at the door. He took one step towards it and froze again. He took another step and groaned. He tugged at his hair, maybe wondering if it would offer him comfort. From the looks of it, it didn't. Alessandra laughed and yanked on his elbow to force him back into the company of others. He groaned the entire way down the hall.

※ ※ ※

A dismal scene greeted them. At first, the two believed the room had soured in their longing for Alessandra and Kitagawa's company. But it was another matter, much more stupid. Dr. Gage and Dr. Oberst had erupted into a lopsided verbal joust again. Something about reparations, or maybe it was something about chemistry. It was hard to tell. Dr. Gage was shouting and coughing interchangeably, and Dr. Oberst only sullenly crooned into his lap.

Renard had thrown her entire attention onto Gao, not allowing herself to perceive the argument. The others lay about in varying stages of idling. Harriet was absentmindedly gnawing on her raw knuckle. She met Kitagawa's quick once-over. She grinned at him, grotesquely roguish, teeth crusted with red.

Alessandra muttered into Kitagawa's ear, "Keep away from her. Bad sense."

"Yes, she does look...deteriorated..."

As if on cue, gas leaked back into the room. They all wearily succumbed to its effects after finding a comfortable place to sit.

Only Pyotr retained consciousness long enough to hear a dull shout vibrate beyond the metal. He pressed his ear with a fading perception against the wall. The unseen voice struck a chord, and he began to bang a weakening fist against the metal. Not his mother tongue, not quite, but something painfully recent.

He grunted before the drugs claimed him, "*Tatr...znam.*"

It was a good thing all those within the dining room were unconscious. The slap that came from behind the walls was clear as day.

Chapter Fifteen

Now a routine. Awakening in their place. More of that hellish hardtack. More jugs of water with a film of dust on the surface. An alarming stretch of time required for Dr. Gage and Dr. Oberst to recover. Renard and Kitagawa were similarly stifled. Everything muddy: senses fogged, sanity wisping away, jaws slack, eyes half-lidded. Harriet and Pyotr's cuts, burns, and blisters still oozed pus. No grave infection. Not yet, at least. If it did come, neither would ask for confirmation. It didn't matter anyway.

The atmosphere was still. Silent. None moved. Not for a while. Fatigue had won temporarily, and nothingness filled the vacancy that the deprivation of energy left in its wake. Everyone resumed their postures that offered them the most comfort.

It was the rough nothingness that was perhaps a bigger trial than being burned, scarred, or confused by archaic tongues. In the absence of stimulation, there was nothing else to do but sit and stare at each other, sometimes passively, sometimes impishly, sometimes hatefully, for no reason other than to puncture boredom.

As all the nerves and excitement from the boiler room settled into flatness, Kitagawa took up his usual habit of his tight-mouthed stare at Renard, who was locking her arms and humming, murmuring, and otherwise verbally dribbling to the only half-willing Gao. After a couple minutes of his attention being ignored, he cleared his throat.

Renard didn't give Kitagawa the dignity of directly regarding him, and opted to speak out of the perched corner of her mouth, "Why be so disturbed?"

"It's a matter of the proper economy of language. Don't waste the few words afforded throughout the course of life on those who cannot understand, it only serves to pollute the air and my senses, and as you should know, any good society refuses to exercise histrionic logorrhea unless absolutely necessary."

"Then your society is dreary."

"Fine then, this side of the table is civilization, and on your side is prattle."

Dr. Gage decided to object, as expected, "No, civilization is wherever I sit."

"Then get up and move," Kitagawa responded.

"No. You move over here, and Renard, you take your lot over there."

"Why must I be the one to move? This is my perch, and it will stay my perch."

Kitagawa said, "Then your perch will be the crown jewel of the prattle side of the room."

Dr. Oberst, in a foggy stupor, asked, "What are we meant to do on the civilized side of the room?"

Kitagawa responded, "We will have discussions. Intellectually stimulating discussions!"

"About what?"

"About life, politics, history, things that matter," Kitagawa said, yanking his chair further from the table and sitting back down with an esteemed huff. Dr. Oberst dragged his chair beside him, perhaps a bit too close, and smiled with cautious pleasure that he was now a patron of the established civilized sector of the bunker.

Dr. Gage scowled, enveloping his watery eyes under his saggy lids, "You can demark any filth-soaked hovel as civilization, but it will be nothing but mere imitation if I am not there."

Kitagawa returned, "You are welcome to drag yourself over here."

Somehow, Dr. Gage's scowl soured even further.

Renard scoffed, "I have a better idea, over there are the boring parts of society, and over here are the better parts. You discuss all things dreary, we shall discuss art. Go on Alessandra, say something about Roman poetry."

"Eh?"

"Recite a portion of the Iliad for us over here in the better part of society."

"What is Iliad?"

Kitagawa spoke up, almost shouting across the room, "The Iliad is Greek."

Renard flicked his interjection away with a flap of her wrist, "Then allow me, 'Tell me Muse, of the man of many ways'—"

"That's the Odyssey," Kitagawa continued.

"It's the same thing."

"No, it isn't. Don't try to argue with me on such a subject, I've spent more time reading those texts than you've spent doing just about anything."

Renard snorted, "Can the boring part of society not keep to themselves?"

"Not if the worst part of society refuses to do things accurately."

Harriet, slumped against the wall, nibbling her knuckle skin off, a dozing Parisa and Pyotr on either shoulder, said, "They are two parts of the same story, aren't they? I'm not certain, but I think I recall it from one lesson I had."

"That's right enough," Kitagawa said, "Fine, Miss Foster, you may join our side of civilization once you stop biting your hand."

"Really?"

Dr. Gage said, "Don't bother. None of this nonsense is real."

Kitagawa snipped, "Matters become real once they are put into practice. Don't be upset that you're stuck on the worse side. As Weber once said—"

Dr. Gage spouted out again, "Oh don't go bringing Weber into all this like that name means anything. Every first-years of any school read Weber, invoking him is not the achievement you believe it is."

"Weber?" Alessandra whispered to Renard, "Is he Greek too?"

The round of indignant sighs was immediate and self-sustaining, as though there was some competition over who could be most offended.

After a groggy gurgle, Parisa rubbed her eyes into half-lucidity, "What is happening?"

Harriet whispered, "Not sure, I think the right side of the room is art and the left is school things."

"Oh, silly," Parisa said, and let sleepiness take her again.

"You know," Dr. Gage started, "True civilization is wherever Miss Shahidi is. True life and order started in the Levant."

"Oh, excellent, so I'm in the civilized corner then?" Harriet asked, "Great, now I don't have to move."

"Proximity means nothing," Kitagawa said. "Is the court jester royalty because he sits next to the throne of a king?"

Dr. Oberst blinked, "I'm confused, so why are we drawing a boundary between the right and left room?"

Kitagawa responded, "There's a nuance to be had here, doctor. It was a necessity in our case, because I can't stand to listen to Mrs. Renard chant her dumb songs to a dumb boy any longer."

"Who is Weber?" Alessandra asked again.

Dr. Oberst finally responded to her pleas, "A proprietor of social theory."

"Social theory? Social like friends? Fun! I want to sit over there," she responded, but Renard clamped her back down in her seat.

"I will not permit you to make a choice I know you will regret. You will stay beside me and little YiMing here. Won't she, YiMing, won't she regret it?"

Gao blinked at her, blinked around the room, came to some private conclusion, and said, "*Hao.*"

Just the unintelligible word was enough to re-invigorate Renard's better spirits, and she jostled him and clapped with glee, which served to only further irritate Kitagawa, and further confuse Gao.

The matter at hand was forgotten in an instant, and once again, the room fell into awkward uneasiness, but at least the uneasiness was separated between art and pedagogy.

Strangely, Gao began to mutter across the room to Kitagawa. A frenzied mutter. He barked again. Kitagawa flicked his hand, and Gao was rendered silent.

Kitagawa's temperament reached some sort of peak, and he stood up without a word, and departed the dining room yet again. His departure was noticed but he left pointedly undisturbed.

❋ ❋ ❋

In the hallway, Kitagawa rubbed his chest, blew out a huff of air, and reset his composure back into a feigned plainness.

Kitagawa stalked towards the observation room but was suddenly halted in the hallway as two presences, one more welcome than the other, whipped him around.

Dr. Oberst, only tepidly confrontational, asked, "Would you share what you know about the observation room? You've spent quite a long time there. That's where you are heading, is it not?"

The decidedly non-confrontational Alessandra chirped, "His sanctuary!"

Kitagawa sighed. "Nothing to share. I'm just getting away from all the prattle."

Startled, Dr. Oberst said, "Prattle? But I'm not part of the prattle! I thought we had some agreement! The civilized sector of the dining room?"

"Oh please, that's not real, I only wanted Renard to shut her jaw, and I have no obligation to escort you around the bunker like a valet. I want to be alone."

"You let Alessandra join you last time," Dr. Oberst said, jutting a thumb at Alessandra. For whatever reason, she found this wholly amusing, and the iron halls echoed her laughs.

Kitagawa replied, "I didn't ask her to join, she smashed her way in, and I couldn't get her to leave."

"Could not make me leave? That is not how I remember," she said. "You like my talking."

"I never said that."

"You do not need to."

"This isn't fair," Dr. Oberst moaned. "Everyone has a collective, even the mute slob."

"If you want to be part of a collective so badly, then go beg Shahidi to join her little circle of self-mutilators."

"That would make me look pathetic!"

Kitagawa kept a snarky scoff at bay, but only barely,

"There's no collective to be had here. Leave me be, I want a moment of solitude to collect my thoughts. When we are free, and I get my day in court, I'll need to recount this whole dismal affair with succinct precision to ensure I am duly reimbursed for my tribulations."

Alessandra grabbed him by the arm and gave it a good shake, "Go to court? I want to come. Help me practice what I will say when I also go to court!"

Kitagawa stuttered, "Fine. That's a worthwhile expenditure of my effort."

Dr. Oberst moaned again, "Are you serious? Moment of solitude? That's not solitude if she's with you!"

"Go complain about the parameters of solitude to someone else. When we must testify, it is the role of us with a strong command of language to instruct others on how to best outline their case to ensure maximum reparations."

"What are reparations?" Alessandra asked.

"Money."

"Yes, I want money."

"Don't we all," Kitagawa responded, "Fine, doctor, I'll meet you halfway. Feel free to sit in as I prepare and align our testimonies, as long as you don't complain so much."

"I'm not complaining!" Dr. Oberst said, then flew past Kitagawa to take point.

Kitagawa trudged behind, followed by a prancing Alessandra.

Inside their destination, Dr. Oberst started up a feeble pace around the circular walls of the observatory. He whistled as he traced his fingers along the etching of the mirrors.

Kitagawa took up his favored perch on the short stool, and Alessandra dropped to the floor before him as a dutiful student. At once, Kitagawa began to outline his testimony, sparing no details, particularly none that pertained to how offended his sensibilities were, and Alessandra started off by listening, but then took up the habit of untying and retying his shoelaces again. He ignored it at first but then had to ask for her intentions once he realized that Dr. Oberst was watching the habit intently, and likely judgmentally.

"You did a bad job of the bow," she responded.

"Hardly, you just like to fidget."

From the periphery, Dr. Oberst asked, "What is the best deduction you can make from all of this?"

"Don't worry too much about it. I'll get it sorted for us," Kitagawa responded, "I'll restart the whole riddle affair again, but I must pay attention to my other priority too. That's the true mark of civility, actually, dual-tasking. Now, Alessandra, you must remember this word, *criminal mischief*. If no other charges can be levied, criminal mischief must be."

"Mischief? This is a crime?"

"It certainly should be."

Dr. Oberst wafted his way over to their congress and crashed down to the floor on his knees, rubbing and huffing out breath from his chest. "Not to pester, but could we by chance get it sorted in the near term?"

Alessandra gave him a limp pat on the back.

Kitagawa responded from his perch, "Fine, fine. I have early plans formulating for other rooms. Not this room however, this room demands something meticulous. Would you mind coughing away from me?"

Dr. Oberst obliged.

Alessandra said, tugging on Kitagawa's elbow, "Will the police let me keep the plates?"

"Why? They look worthless. Fool's gold, not worth the weight to carry them. If you like the design so much, I have many of a much better quality and aesthetic. You can have them."

She clapped her hands and then tugged his elbow some more for no explicit reason other than it was within her reach.

Dr. Oberst weakly smiled. "Is that an open offer? I'm not too well-off with personal finances either."

"What man flatters another man with fine dining ware? That would be rather vulgar. Upon our release, I can offer you a firm handshake and maybe a referral to my benefactor to consider a foreign application for educational financing, but that's about as much generosity as I can be expected to bestow. That's a much better gift than paltry service plates. Besides, I doubt she'll ever come into finery on her own account, and Alessandra deserves at least a couple nice things."

Dr. Oberst blinked at Kitagawa, then to Alessandra, then back to Kitagawa. His face screwed up, "Here? In the midst of all this?"

Kitagawa grew frosty. "Silence."

"You cannot be serious. She's taller than you."

"I don't know what you're talking about."

"I'm certain you don't," Dr. Oberst then started to laugh, as much as his frail lungs would allow.

"Don't laugh at me, doctor."

"Please, you must find it absurd."

"Yes, as absurd as it is embarrassing. If you breathe a word to anybody on the surface, I'll vehemently deny it and then have you committed to a ward for the insane."

"Fair enough, I'll likely be assigned to the same ward I did my preliminary research in. Don't worry, such confined spaces make the brain perceive things in ways that trespass standards. I'm sure you will come to your senses upon release and find someone that you won't have to flatter with dinnerware."

Alessandra frowned, "I do deserve nice things. It is not an insane idea. If you do not keep your promise, Mr. Junichi, I will burn down your house. In England or in Japan. I will swim there if I must."

He said, suddenly overcome with a bout of meekness, "I believe you. But I always make good on my promises, do not fear. You will have your reward."

The room suddenly began to creak and groan, and the three snapped their eyes towards the ceiling.

Dr. Oberst muttered, almost voicelessly, "Somebody must be walking atop us."

Kitagawa craned his head, peeking up the periscope, "The trap is still set."

"Think it must be help?" Alessandra asked, jolting to her feet, and pressing her ear against the curved wall, "I hear things. Like steps."

She rapped her knuckles against the wall. No response.

Kitagawa sucked his teeth, "It could be any number of things, but I would never assume it's help."

Alessandra flapped her hand, shushing both men, and kept her ear pressed to the iron.

She said, "I hear talking. There are people behind the walls. They are silent now."

Kitagawa raced to her side and listened in for a moment before shaking his head.

"Damn it, well, what did they say, what language?"

She murmured, "It sounded like how the boy talks."

"The boy? Chinese?"

"No, the Soviet, in that way, but not that language. Maybe English. But I do not know."

Dr. Oberst coughed, and then sputtered, "What does that mean? Just the accent then? I knew it, I knew it must be him, in some way. How else could he survive all that mutilation? He's being helped. It's him!"

Kitagawa furrowed into an angry contemplation, tapping a finger to his chin, and said, "He isn't smart enough for this sort of intricacy. But it may be worth keeping in mind."

Dr. Oberst drew near, precariously pressing his mouth to Kitagawa's ear, "Should we tell the others that we heard our captors?"

Kitagawa made a quick retraction of his head, wiping spit crusts off his cartilage, "No. No, let's keep that among ourselves. They'll stupidly muddle about and draw idiotic conclusions and get us nowhere. Just between us, you both understand, just us. Let's go before we get locked in."

"Just us?" Dr. Oberst said, briefly brightening, "Sounds fine, us."

Kitagawa scoffed, "Don't whisper it like we're betrothed. It's becoming desperate."

"Us! We have an us!" Alessandra said, precariously chattering the words on top of Kitagawa's other ear. He made no retraction of the head. Instead, he escorted her by the arm towards the door in a manner indicating they were exiting some regal gala.

Dr. Oberst scratched his overgrown mustache and limply followed the two out.

In the hallway, Kitagawa suddenly seized.

"You know, doctor," he said in a low mumble, "I remember something. Three months before my Paris soirée, I did meet a Russian. A Turkic Russian…"

Dr. Oberst flailed to get to his side, but Alessandra nudged him out of the way, drooping her arms around Kitagawa's shoulders and pulling him close, "With Wassermann? Same man with Wassermann?"

"Maybe, but not with Wassermann," Kitagawa said, voicelessly, darting his eyes up towards the vents, "No, he was with some old Italian philanthropist. A real peacock sort. With the consular coordinator…a very ill-tempered Turkic Russian. But it was so long ago. The Russian talked to me about my publications. He had read all my publications. All of them. Even those published in Japanese. The Italian…the Italian was funding a grant I won. A grant I didn't remember applying for…"

Dr. Oberst flushed, "I knew it, it's that serf! The Russian is his father or something!"

Kitagawa vacantly shook his head, "No, it was as Shahidi said…he looked too Eurasian. A Tatar-Slav type. There's no resemblance."

Alessandra gripped Kitagawa around the neck, re-shoving her mouth into his ear, "The Italian, tan, pointy beard? Wears expensive? Talks like poetry?"

"Pointy beard…yes… poetic phrasing…definitely."

"Rodolfo Pisano, he is famous. He came to my farm last year. He was stranger to my family but wanted to buy our farm. Asked much questions, but none about farm. My father said no. Pisano wore expensive, even walking in mud with nice trousers. Saw once. Never again. I had bad sense! But no Russian man. Came with a Senegalese! Senegalese did not speak, but my sister said he drew our farm on paper while Pisano looked around. Pisano has a reputation. Erh, what's the word…man of bad religion."

Dr. Oberst coughed, "Rodolfo Pisano? I never… I met a Rudolf Pine… my onboarding contact… he told me he was a German-American…but that accent…I just knew he was Mediterranean. I was supposed to meet with him before I went to the SPP. His assistant was some Swedish fellow."

Kitagawa's breathing became unsteady and shallow. He darted his eyes in every single direction before asking, "What do you mean by man of bad religion?"

Alessandra sucked in a wet breath, "*Occulta.*"

Dr. Oberst said without a voice, "Occulta? You mean a cult? That's nonsense… there are no cults in Europe!"

"Make no mention of it," Kitagawa said after a cold quietness. "Privileged information, just for us."

Alessandra whispered, "What good in secrets?"

"Because then everyone will want to share every single person they've ever met in their life and it will get us nowhere."

Dr. Oberst asked, "It'll be annoying, yes, but maybe—"

Kitagawa blurted out, "Pride is at stake, doctor. Can you imagine if the serf last saw a German, what sort of accusations the others would make on his behalf?"

He left in a quick hurry. Alessandra and Dr. Oberst shared a confused concern, and without warning, Alessandra kicked the metal wall adjacent to the door and exclaimed a curse. Both the kick and the curse were very loud and very annoying. If there were indeed hidden observers beyond the wall, they were likely extremely offended and feeling slightly vindictive.

The three recongregated back into the dining room, keeping good to their promise of *us*. Alessandra accepted a small castigation from Renard, who bemoaned her abandonment and false-friendship, forcing her back into her relegated side of the bunker. Dr. Oberst sat in his seat with a dull wheeze, and began to stare at Pyotr, who was still in the midst of a restless rest against Harriet's shoulder. He muttered anger under his breath.

Chapter Sixteen

After hatefulness waned, mortal pain waxed, and Dr. Oberst suppressed another coughing fit.

"We must be quicker now. My chest feels so tight. I am beginning to feel a bit... delirious," Dr. Oberst pleaded. His murmurs bubbled over to something more comforting—something angry.

Harriet asked weakly, rousing Pyotr from his slumber, "I can try the next room, can I wait for some of my burns to scab over first though?"

Dr. Oberst groggily stood up, "No, no, I must contribute. As a proper man ought to. I must be responsible for my own condition."

Parisa reluctantly extended out her notes, but forgot to let them go entirely, making Dr. Oberst tug them from her hands.

Dr. Gage coughed, "Mr. Kitagawa, you have been off, traipsing about by yourself?"

"Yes, what of it? I am working on my own scheme regarding the observation room. No need for any consternation. You'll know when I settle upon an idea."

Dr. Oberst nodded in the midst of his own coughing fit, "Oh, then perhaps we should try someplace else. The kitchen maybe? It is close by, and I do not want to overexert myself right now. Shall we go? I think between us both, we may find some answer. You know, us?"

Alessandra bolted upright, almost swooning, "Yes! Us!"

Kitagawa mulled over the proposal, and the wick of his mouth flicked into a smirk.

He stared at Gao. Gao stared back and barked yet again, then started a foreign-tongued monologue that started off calm but soon became frantic. Renard patted his head in a manner indicating she had come to accept, and even love, this odd behavioral tick. Kitagawa sucked on his bottom lip and came to a private decision.

Kitagawa announced, "Fine, but only if we bring the Chinese boy along."

Dr. Oberst drew his mouth into a fine point, and wheezed, "Well, only you are capable of asking. But may I inquire as to why?"

"If the kitchen follows the same trend as other rooms, then a young man, without ailments, may withstand physical tests better, correct? Do not worry, I will ask him beforehand. I am sure, as many peasants have a workman's pride, that he will consent."

Kitagawa paused. A slight tremor shook his eyelids. With a possessed jerk of the neck, he snapped his attention to Gao, who gasped then waved at him. Strangely, Kitagawa waved back, and Gao brightened.

A hushed, fluid stream of words left Kitagawa, and Gao suddenly burst into a cheer and coupled clap. Kitagawa nodded, beckoning Gao forward with a supernaturally rigid spine.

Gao trotted up to the door leading to the kitchen and waited for his elders to pass through first. He waved to Renard, "Bye bye. Bye, Agnes."

She clapped her hands with a small delight, "YiMing learns so fast. Shout if you need any of us, we are so near."

Alessandra gleefully followed suit, even linking her arm into Kitagawa's, but he immediately stuttered, "No, not you. You need to sit here and read something."

"Read what?"

"I don't know... the book on discourse. Yes, read about discourse."

"Why read about discourse?"

"Because we need it. Us," Kitagawa said, and spun on his heels.

The three shortly thereafter disappeared, much to Alessandra's chagrin. She slumped in a seat, picked up a random book, gave it a thirty second skim, then tossed it over her shoulder.

Renard chuckled and decided to poke, "I told you, he doesn't think you're smart."

Alessandra plucked up another book and threw it at her. Renard scoffed, slipped off her shoe, and sent a volley right back. Alessandra returned it with an airborne chair.

Renard cried, narrowly ducking under the catapulted furniture, "It was a joke!"

"I know!" Alessandra said with a boisterous laugh, "So is this."

Renard cried out, "Parisa! Make the Soviet come to my aid! I need reinforcements!"

"I fear this is your own battle, Mrs. Renard."

Alessandra leapt onto the table in a pantherine crouch, "I used to play lion with my mother. Go on, Lucie, you are the deer, I am the lion."

"No, I think I'm best as a woman. If not, perhaps a pretty little dove."

Alessandra pounced onto the dove anyway. As expected,

the middle-aged dove was no match for a cow maid lion. Renard cried for mercy after twenty seconds, then groaned as she tried to stand, and collapsed with a bang of her forehead against the table.

Alessandra gave a shout of triumph, parsed over the spectators, then pointed a finger at Pyotr, "Him! A worthy challenger!"

Pyotr needed no charade, no pantomime, no translation. He just shook his head. Alessandra pounced regardless. He let her. Without struggle, she put him in a headlock, jostled him about, and asked him, "Do you submit to my strength?"

He grunted, then used his fingers to shoot himself in the head. Alessandra was unaware how easy he went on her.

Alessandra giddily took back up her seat at the head of the table, "I am Chief of Bunker now!"

Parisa imbued her with a small applause. A mistake. Alessandra promptly assigned her the role of maid in waiting.

Harriet asked Dr. Gage, "Our wits are leaving us. Is it an effect of the drug?"

"Certainly," he said, tilting his head upwards, confronting some ethereal being, "Prolonged exposure of almost any substance will certainly cause some psychosis. We may be coming to some critical apex shortly."

"How shortly?" Harriet prodded.

"Cannot say, we still do not know what it is," he huffed, "But in times like these we must be reminded of our progress. It is not much, assuredly, but two answers. Two more than how we arrived."

Renard gave him a quiet blink before saying, "I did not take you for such an optimist." At last, the histrionics seemed to tire her out, and she settled into something resembling sincerity.

"Certainly, I am not. But it is senseless in certain cases to allow pessimism to weaken action. This is such a case," Dr. Gage responded, "If it's to be my role to straighten out the manners of you all, then so be it. As unnatural as it is for me to provide, oh what's that term, esprit de corps, then so be it."

A pause, sincerity short lived, Renard and Alessandra burst into a fit of giggles.

"How absurd, but ah, we welcome your support for our morale," Renard said to the even more indignant Dr. Gage. "Indeed, you are best fit for nurturing our *bonnes espirits*. For all know the amiable and merciful airs of the English."

Pyotr was unaware of everything, except that the Italian woman was now Chief, and did not care to remedy his ignorance. He relegated himself back to another corner of the room, picking at the boils, scabs, and blisters on his arm. Parisa had tried to get him to cease, but it wasn't of any use. It was a small comfort to him, so she eventually let him be.

When he ran out of scabs to rip off, he began to scratch his head. His shaved head had grown quite rapidly, and an inch of flaxen blond hair hung from his brow. Stubble outlined where there would soon be some semblance of facial hair, giving him the appearance of a burgeoning pensioner.

Her knuckles thoroughly gnawed raw, Harriet began to root through the old box that housed all of their identification cards and passports, giggling like a heretic, muttering to herself, "Sobering. Be sober. Yes, sober."

She fished out a bright red little identification book, with lettering that looked reminiscent of English words but not quite. She giggled even louder.

"Look at this dyslexic little language," she proclaimed to the room.

Dr. Gage squinted, then said, "Cyrillic. Must be the Soviet's."

"Ah," she responded, "Quite a limbo of an alphabet.

Makes my brain fuzzy looking at it."

She flipped to Pyotr Semyonov Volga's personal page. His birthday: 17 March 1913.

"So, he just turned twenty-three. The last date I recalled was, what was it, 20 March?" Harriet said, hunching over to look down at Pyotr. "So strange, when I first saw him, I would have figured him nineteen or so. Now, he appears about forty. I wonder how poorly I also aged these past weeks."

"Well, the Latin mirror is right there, have a look for yourself. Fair warning, it'll be a grim discovery," Dr. Gage said plainly. Parisa swatted him on the shoulder, which didn't disturb him in the slightest.

Pyotr stuck out his hand, and Harriet plopped his little book into his palm. A quick glance at it, he lifted into a soft gap-toothed smile and stowed it in his trousers. Harriet tossed her own passport over to Pyotr.

"I was born January 17. Similar birthdays," she said, "I'm only two years older. You could be my little brother. Baby brother Pete. I'd substitute you for my older brother Andrew in a blink."

Parisa said, eagerly rejoining their little chorus, "I am jealous. I love the winter. I wish I was born then. I am a summer child. August the 25th. I will be twenty."

"Only twenty?" Harriet started, "Jesus. A child... God, I feel old."

"Then am I ancient," Renard moaned, "But if I am ancient, then you are dust, Dr. Gage."

Dr. Gage lifted his brow, "Not dust. Too unstable. I would liken myself to some archaic ruin."

Renard said giddily, "I think when I am your age, I will not be a ruin. No, preserved, like a fine artwork."

"Me like wine," Alessandra added, taking up a cross-legged seat on the table, the Chief overseeing her domain. "Or maybe cheese. If you cut the mold."

Renard reached up and tousled her scalp, "My dear cow maid, you are more similar to leather, or perhaps a cured meat."

"Not funny. Not clever," Alessandra responded, but then hitched her breath. An explosion of laughter followed, accompanied by a rain of spittle, straight over Renard's brow.

Renard wiped it off with the back of her hand, pouted, then said, "A camel."

An unseen observer would have agreed to Renard's assessment.

Chapter Seventeen

The kitchen remained barren of anything interesting, save for the hatch in the floor. The three crowded around it like pensioners to a public garden. They limply looked among themselves for which three had the strength to raise the iron hatch. None, apparently. Kitagawa prompted Gao forward.

Gao asked Kitagawa something in a clipped mutter, trying to squirrel out from under Kitagawa's hand clenched around his arm.

Kitagawa sputtered something fiery right back, tightening his vice grip.

Dr. Oberst stayed silent, awkwardly plucked at his shirt sleeve, and peevishly asked, "Should I know what's going on?"

Kitagawa said, "It makes the boy nervous, but don't worry, I will convince him. You are too frail, and I do not have the same strength as a peasant, they're born for such tasks."

Dr. Oberst clapped him on the back gratefully, and Kitagawa for once let the offending touch go unprotested. Kitagawa turned back to Gao, and said some more things, this time hazardously forcefully, even approaching a shout. Gao eventually submitted and knelt down to heave the heavy door upwards. It took a great amount of effort, the two elders not even pretending to assist, but Gao managed to wrestle the lid up and over, letting it fall with a heavy clang on the ground.

Kitagawa chided him for producing such an accosting noise but then peered over into the cellar—flooded almost halfway. All of the paltry furnishings had drowned; there was still a nerve-shaking drop from the opening until breaching the surface of the waters. The black waters wafted a putrid scent so egregious that Kitagawa's nose began to twitch.

Dr. Oberst decided to state the obvious as a means of exercising utility. "Are we meant to climb inside? Surely not, there is no way to exit. We would drown."

Kitagawa provided no response at first, just gawked at the still waters. A dazzling rainbow glimmered in the reflection. He murmured, "Look at the waters, against the black water do you see the red and white. Do you think what I think? Something is written on the ceiling and is reflected back into the water."

Dr. Oberst narrowed his eyes, "You are right. I see it now, but it's too fuzzy for my eyes."

"Mine too," Kitagawa said breathlessly. "If only the waters could remain still."

Dr. Oberst asked, "But that is what we are meant to do, to go down and read back up?"

Kitagawa smiled. "Certainly."

Glee rattled their frail bodies. The two men shook each other's hands in congratulations at their good attention. But then the next step dawned on them, and the congratulations died immediately.

"Well… who will do it then? One of us must wade inside," Dr. Oberst said slowly, backing away, pinching his nose, halting vomit in his throat.

"Not a question at all, the boy must," Kitagawa nodded, "I figured something such as this might happen. It has to be him. Renard and Gage would surely refuse. Shahidi, Foster, and the Soviet have formed some sort of coalition. We two are too important to risk any injury. It must be the peasant. He looks healthy enough to wade in. Besides, it will put those English lessons to good use, as well as give him something to do, something worthwhile at least. Here, we may even practice his speaking now just to be sure."

"What about Alessandra? She can speak good English now, and likely even better Latin. Undoubtedly, that is what is written on the ceiling, probably not English."

Kitagawa's throat tightened, and he fervently shook his head. "No, she may have another purpose yet." He shook his head so hard he became dizzy, "No, no, it must be it—him—that one."

"Should we first find a means of pulling him outward? Perhaps we should go get a curtain or something."

"No use, it would not reach down far enough."

"What do you propose? We toss him in? Seems a little…"

"Not until after this," Kitagawa spoke lightly, in a daze. A shadow of a sickly smirk drew up on his face. He produced his notes on the Latin and presented it to the confused Gao. He gave some sort of directive, and Gao read off the notes. Gao's pronunciation of the Latin was poor, but intelligible to Kitagawa—the only thing that mattered.

"Yes, yes, I think he will do fine."

Kitagawa then prompted Gao to look further into the flooded cellar, dismissing the boy's anxieties. Gao peered over, his knuckles turning white as he gripped the edges, his chin quivering. Kitagawa placed his hand centrally on the boy's back. Gao recoiled and almost started up to make a dash, but it was futile.

In a flash, Kitagawa tipped Gao over, sending the poor boy flailing into the waters. A heavy splash rang around the kitchen, followed by the desperate cries of Gao. Kitagawa quickly yelled down an order. Gao, trying his best to tread water, yelled back up. Dr. Oberst elected to stare at the ceiling.

The smirk flared into a grin on Kitagawa's face, who turned to Dr. Oberst with utmost delight, "The boy says something is written, but not with paint, with pearls. A fascinating discovery. He says the little beads are even falling down, loosened. And yes… a dog in the pearls…a dog."

"But what does it say?" Dr. Oberst's breath rattled, and good sense finally abandoned him.

Kitagawa yelled down another command, but Gao was too panicked and was quickly fatiguing from treading water. Kitagawa grew impatient and exasperated and continued to shout at Gao. Dr. Oberst placed a hand on Kitagawa's shoulder, steadying his anger. Kitagawa, in turn, was silent for a couple seconds, and then muttered down to Gao in a gentler tone. Another pause, silence interrupted by some splashes.

The boy finally cried out after wiping mildew out of his eyes, "Quay pooeenaa deket dominoos kw eye ambulant… in cawato superb, eye ah?"

Another pause. Kitagawa called out, "What?"

Exasperated, the boy tried to sound it out again, struggling with the pronunciation and the water. His pronunciation was still poor, but Kitagawa began to write down the phonetics. Again and again, he yelled for the boy to repeat the pronunciations, only promising salvation if he did so.

Kitagawa then got another idea, a better idea. An idea deserving a ghoulish little giggle. He yelled for the boy to simply spell out the words with each English letter. And so, the boy obeyed, eager for his help to arrive.

Finally, Kitagawa and Oberst had their prize.

Quae poena decet dominos qui ambulant incauto superbia?

Dr. Oberst exclaimed, "This with the Theta painted on the trapdoor, this is the next puzzle. And the pearls, they must mean something, it must be significant."

"Yes, and I feel like this translation is even easier. Easier or we got better at it. *What punishment befits masters who walk with blinded pride*, do you agree, doctor?"

"I certainly do, sir." Dr. Oberst grew a repulsive grin, "This may be even easier yet. It is so plain, the theological allusions here. The pearls, the sin *superbia*, the blindness like the boiler room alluded too. Am I insane or is this now too easy?"

"Yes. Yes. It is easy," Kitagawa shook Dr. Oberst in a childish, manic delight. "The others will be so pleased. They will know we did it. We did it ourselves, not needing to conspire with them."

The two men grasped hands and shook on it like some business shareholders.

Then, just as rapidly as his grin came, it subsided, and Dr. Oberst's face grew pale, "How are we going to get him out? Gao?"

The two barely peeked over the edge at the overexerted Gao; the slightest glance, a courtesy more than anything else. His face was sickly pale, streaked with mildew, his heavy breathing echoed up and out of the cellar, yet Gao still reached out a mossy hand. Kitagawa drummed his fingers on the edge of the cellar.

"Nothing is long enough. The curtains surely aren't…" Kitagawa murmured.

"But what if we tie them together," Dr. Oberst suggested, color re-appearing at this brilliant if crude idea. He started to get up to head towards the door, but Kitagawa stopped him in his tracks with a tug to his jacket skirt.

Kitagawa spoke rapidly, yet his words flowed with an elite grace,

"Doctor, what do you think the peasant will tell the others? No, he does not speak English, but he will find some way. Renard will know what he says, somehow, and she will despise us both. She does not trust you, especially. You know how she feels about your people, you heard her earlier, all those days ago, did you not? Dr. Gage, who undoubtedly would do the same thing in our position, how do you think he will now treat you? And how do you think Alessandra will regard me? A murderer rather than our savior? We may go back into the dining room to tie together some sheets, which may not boast enough strength to hoist the peasant out, but they will all ask why. If we tell them why, they will spurn us and judge us, as if they had any right to. The peasant will then be a victim, not a contributor. That is what he would want, that is the way of his type. Forever the victim. Do you not see it? How us men, who do what is necessary to find the proper advancements, how we are made to be the villains? Do you not remember Kovacevic? Was he not right to be defensive, because all soon became suspicious of him? Do you want them to view you as some villain, doctor? Where is the justice in that? We bring solutions, they spurn it?"

"Surely this would be murder. And what could we even say if we go back without him? They will find us to be villains regardless?"

Kitagawa gripped Dr. Oberst's arm tightly and yanked him down to meet his ear, "It is not murder, we did not flood the cellar, and we did not imprison ourselves in this iron cage. And no, as Wassermann and Kovacevic had perished, we did not find the others to be villains. For all we know, they may have been subjects of intentional harm, but we never pried. If we were to return, and if we were to be vague, and even referential of the sacrifice the boy made, we will not be held in the same suspicion. If we admit we had used him knowingly to find our clue, then we will then become murderers to them. Although, I find it is impossible to be considered a murderer if the deceased is a Kunming peasant."

Inappropriately, Dr. Oberst chuckled, and his head began to sway while he groped the ground as if it was slipping away from him, "This feels personal, Mr. Kitagawa. You have personal distaste for the boy? I thought I smelled jealousy."

"I will not lie to you, doctor. Tell me you do not feel it. If you could throw in Gage, and with it all the misery and grief of his ilk, would you not do the same?"

Dr. Oberst stuttered, "Why... yes. I suppose I would. Not malevolently, but it does feel like justice. Why...you're right. I can see it now. Die a martyr, not a victim..."

"Besides, there's nothing we can do now..."

"Yes...nothing we can do now..."

"What's done is done, doctor."

"Yes, what's done is indeed done, sir."

The two heard Gao's weakening cries and looked at each other. Each perspiring profusely, and Kitagawa's hands shook as he remained clenched around Dr. Oberst's arm. Then, silently and obediently, Dr. Oberst bolstered himself and then went over to the metallic door. With the last of failing muscles, they tried to hoist it back up and over. It took an embarrassing amount of tries, further disturbed by Gao's increasingly anxious shouts. When they finally managed to heave the weighty door up straight, they both sucked in a foul breath, and gave it a final push. The door clanged shut. The echo lingered. Gao's cries muffled into a deafening silence as he was then sealed inside the watery tomb. Kitagawa knelt on top of the trap door, hands crossed, with a pearl-toothed grin and a twitching eyelid.

First came relief. Then came the urgency. The urgency to provide an answer to his slow suffocation, the urgency to kill remorse in its fetal stage. The remedy was forging the lie.

The two colluded briefly and came to a succinct point. The boy died willingly, accepting despair and losing hope of ever being set free from the bunker. The boy loved Mrs. Renard and did it for her. The boy didn't want to go back home to the dirty streets of Kunming. It was short, vague, and irrefutable.

They waited over a half-hour, barricading the door with their sweaty hands, waiting to be sure the boy had fully drowned. They could not risk Parisa or Alessandra coming up with some rescue method, who would then point the finger to his assassins. It would be embarrassing.

It was silent at first as the two blocked the entry shoulder to shoulder, sweating and shaking.

Kitagawa finally spoke, breaking out of his feverish delirium, "It's funny almost. We have similar personal names. Almost the same. I wonder if he too was the firstborn son…"

"Pardon?"

"Yi Ming. Junichi. They are similar. Junichi, first to obey. Yi Ming, first cry. Interesting thing. Names. Isn't it?"

"Your names don't sound alike. What are you talking about?"

"Nothing. You wouldn't understand."

A lengthy, mind-numbing pause, then Kitagawa continued, "First day. Gao asked me if I knew who captured him. He remembered his kidnapping. Fully. In the fields, he drank from his canteen. He tasted the drug. He vomited it out. He tried to run home. Men snatched him on the road. He was beaten, then stowed in a car."

"Beaten? By who?"

"Three people. One spoke Chinese to him with a Mongolian accent, one looked European, and the driver was Japanese. The driver injected a needle in his arm to make him sleep when they arrived at the docks a day later. Everyone at the docks was Japanese. He said his clan knew of this group. Apparently, they're bogeymen that haunted his dirt patch for centuries. It was as Alessandra said—men of bad faith. His clan used to warn him the bogeymen do black magic. He was so certain a cult of Nippon wizards abducted us. I just…I ignored him, how could I not?"

"Well…did you know about any of it? Did you know any of the Japanese?"

Kitagawa said without breath, "No."

"Then why didn't you tell us this earlier?"

Still no breath, "You wouldn't understand."

"You can't keep saying that!"

Kitagawa spoke like it was a prayer, "Pride, doctor."

"Pride? Come now, there's a Tatar-Slav, an Italian, a Mongolian, and a Senegalese in the mix! The blame doesn't fully—"

Kitagawa mumbled, "When Gao said it, it was so stupid. But when Alessandra said it…I just…just…you wouldn't understand."

Kitagawa and Dr. Oberst jolted as a bang vibrated from behind the walls on the far end of the kitchen, as if one of their unseen captors pounded a fist against it in utmost aggravation, as if that Mongolian captor wasn't even Mongolian, but was Chinese as well and merely had a speech impediment. Kitagawa and Dr. Oberst didn't jolt a second time as they heard another slap coming from beyond the walls, as if one highly scornful Tatar-Slav struck that same Not-Mongolian for his lack of noise-discipline.

Dr. Oberst muttered, "We are being watched by a cult?"

Kitagawa responded, "We are being watched by a cult."

❋ ❋ ❋

"Those three have been gone for much longer than I would have thought," Renard announced, scanning the room for any similar sentiment, and grousing when Alessandra yawned with her chin on her knuckles—still in her chiefly perch.

Dr. Gage snorted, "I thought the Germans were known for diligence. I guess not. Another disappointment." He stifled a yawn with his thick hand.

Harriet and Parisa had not noticed the length of the absence. They followed Gao's example and began looking through the books to learn something new. Parisa tried to teach Harriet the Persian script at her request, but it was far too difficult to grasp. Instead, Parisa taught Harriet a mathematics game. Confusing rules about doubling even digits, and subtracting odd digits, then multiplying the differences, then incorporating the nearest prime integer—all in the mind before putting it to paper. A game from her prior tutor that was supposed to turn Parisa into a young genius. Harriet spectacularly failed. Parisa attempted to mime the rules out to Pyotr. Somehow, a spectacular success. Somehow, even beyond success. With only an hour of practice, he could beat her at her own game.

Not the most invigorating entertainment, but it did consume their attention for a good stretch of time. Once the math game grew dull, which happened after Parisa's fourth consecutive loss, Pyotr and Harriet took back up a shrug, pat, nod ritual. Parisa tried to join in, but didn't know the rules. Harriet didn't either but did it anyway. Just something to do other than sit around and spurn on an argument.

Alessandra decided to spurn on one anyway, "What do you think of Kitagawa and Gao? I do not know anything about China, or Japan, or Korea, or any of Far East."

Assuredly, Dr. Gage had an opinion. Presumably a

negative one. Yet, he grunted, "The lands are beautiful, I will say as much. China is wide open, and large. It makes one feel so small, and insignificant." A surprisingly reverent statement from the old man. He continued earnestly and serenely, "If I have a chance again, to see the surface world. I'd go back. I will take Bernadette and even ask Thomas to go back. I would love to see Xi'an again, just once more." His voice trailed off, succumbing to daydream, "Bernadette would love it. She has a keen mind, always curious, always adventurous. She would love it, just as I do."

"A surprise. He has love for at least one place," Alessandra chuckled. "And can express it in better terms than Junichi about Beirut."

It was then that Kitagawa and Dr. Oberst re-emerged, as if summoned from mere mention. Renard perked up, encouraged by the queasily satisfied look on the two men's faces. But it was only the two.

Renard's temperament sharpened. She harshly asked, "Where is YiMing? Where is my boy?"

Dr. Oberst scratched at his overgrown mustache apologetically, and spoke in a brisk stutter, "He threw himself into the cellar. It was flooded. But through his sacrifice we found our next piece of the puzzle. He told Kitagawa to tell you all he wishes you well, and to not worry about him anymore. Says that he loves you, Mrs. Renard."

A collective choke. Renard was about to shout something with an outstretched finger as an accessory, but Kitagawa cut her off with a preemptive counter, "We have already found the appropriate translation for what was written on the ceiling of the cellar. It was written with pasted-down pearls. *What punishment befits masters who walk with blinded pride.* Now, let us think on what an appropriate response to this is." He hastily took his seat, and produced his notes, joining them with the collection of other scraps from the other rooms.

Nobody said anything but sat with it. Sat with it and ground their fists into their guts. Renard's face soured into a sneer.

Kitagawa re-prompted the group, "Any ideas then? What punishment befits masters who walk with blinded pride?"

"You appear to be much in shock," Alessandra said. "You look faint. Like sick sheep."

Dr. Oberst remained standing, dumbly, but Kitagawa yanked him into an adjacent seat with a sweaty grip.

Pyotr looked towards the kitchen door patiently, still waiting for Gao to make his entrance. Harriet gripped his nape and shook her head. He tried to nod, and shrug, and pat, but he couldn't get past the first step—Harriet just kept shaking her head.

Kitagawa said, slurring his words together in a haste, "We really must thank you, Mrs. Renard. Your lessons, I admit I thought it was a stupid venture at first, gave the boy enough ability to spell out the phrase. Truly helpful, so I must thank you! *Quae poena decet dominos qui ambulant incauto superbia.* What say you to our translation, Alessandra? Very accurate, isn't it?"

He similarly yanked Alessandra into the seat next to him, with an even sweatier grip. She sat stunned, and shrunk away from the accosting leer of Renard.

After a moment, Alessandra leaned and whispered, "Junichi, you shake. What has happened?"

Renard's sneer darkened her face into a vibrant purple.

Kitagawa markedly ignored said stare, and chirped, "Dr. Oberst has said it all, no need to delay on it. Now, what could possibly be the answer? Let us all think. The key words I find to be punishment, master, and blinded pride. We mustn't forget the importance of the Theta, nor that the manner of inscription was different. Pearls, if it is to be believed."

The silence that followed was suffocating and sickly. Some

were in contemplation, others in scrutiny, one in particular frozen with scorn.

"Theta, Mu, and Beta..." Parisa finally said aloud, giving reprieve to the sweating Kitagawa and Oberst against her better judgment, "What order do they appear in the alphabet?"

"Beta, Theta, Mu. Why?" Dr. Gage responded but kept most of his attention on continuing his scrutiny. With each heavy breath, his brow seemed to sink further into speculation.

"Pairs of each. May be an order. I have a thought, a simple thought. If we put the answer to each room in order it forms the answer to the 'truth'. What do you think?" Parisa continued, nervously running her fingers through her hair.

"Maybe a worthy venture once it is decided what the answer to each room is." Dr. Gage replied, finally turning towards Parisa. He even gave her a small smile. It was not condescending for once, rather grandfatherly. Perhaps the gas was getting to his head as well and stripping down his irony and caustic sarcasm.

"Blind, that's strange, maybe it is also to do with justice?" Harriet added, "Or something else in the same figurative manner."

Alessandra turned to Renard and asked a quick question in French. Renard spat, "literal". Alessandra then addressed the group, "I think maybe it is literal. The pearls and pride are very Catholic to me. They say the first sin was pride. The evil that is prideful, Lucifero, fell out of Heavens. The gates made of gold and pearls, do you remember in your studies, Junichi?"

He nodded, gasping out a sigh. "Yes, it is familiar to me."

"His punishment was..." Alessandra then asked Renard for more help formulating her thoughts into English, which she did rather curtly, "His punishment was to be cast out of heaven. I think there is an answer. Cast out. Or thrown out, whichever suits the translation best I think."

"Alessandra, you are certainly more shrewd than I have given credit for," Kitagawa said, very uncharacteristically respectfully.

Alessandra was about to render her own compliment when a shrill scoff shot out of Renard's mouth. Thus, Alessandra presented Kitagawa with a shaky half-smile and proceeded to braid and unbraid her hair.

Harriet asked, "What is the application to the military, though? Was that not our basis for assumptions?"

Dr. Gage croaked from his seat, "Yes, we all think too hastily. Settle your nerves, Kitagawa and Oberst. Then, let us rethink. Both of you are jumpy and too excited. Irrationality will be the death of us. As I am sure irrationality was the death of Gao."

Everyone fell silent. Renard let out another shrill scoff. Harriet turned her head to Pyotr and blew off her temple with a finger gun.

Chapter Eighteen

The angry silence continued for hours. Then the deliberation took the reins, and harrowingly, that commanded many hours more. Prudent approximation dictated a good forty-eight hours. A waste of forty-eight hours. Circular dribble, forever returning to a fifteen-minute lapse of sullen contempt, then reigniting with the same analysis, and the same thinly veiled accusations.

No delineation between the civilized side and the uncivilized side. Both stunk like a chamber pot, and the only remedy, for those able, was drifting about to prevent any odor from lingering too long. Those unable sat with it, trying to turn displeasure to tepid enjoyment of the briny funk. It made temperaments stormy which made deliberation stormier which was the sole surviving amusement.

Harriet said, pacing in circles with Parisa at her side, "Pairs of symbols. Two Thetas, two of the Mu, but only one Beta. Shouldn't there be two?"

Like a call and response, Parisa thought in tune, "The first room we went to. It was locked, remember? Perhaps unlocked now, or we have missed a Beta somewhere. We must find the second, I can feel there must be two as well."

Alessandra hummed aloud, mechanically still fiddling with

her hair, "We may think all wrong. This is not about military, no, I think religious instead. That is why Greek and Latin. The riddles talk about punishment, and many sins. Very Catholic."

She turned to Kitagawa with an impish smile, "Very, how you say, Western, you think?"

Kitagawa allowed himself to lightly laugh, with as much dignity that he was still capable of, "Indeed, very Western. I would love to see a similar trap of an Eastern make. It would be a very interesting design."

Alessandra joined his laughter, violently louder, "I would like to see this too. No hope I would have, too tricky for someone like me. Perhaps only you and maybe Dr. Oberst could think on it."

She scooted in closer to Kitagawa. Too close for Renard's liking, as punctuated by the most theatrically inclined sneer. But Alessandra was Chief of the Bunker, as punctuated by a quick flex of the bicep. Thus, as Chief, she felt fully at ease resting a head against his shoulder, sending his neck into a crimson flush.

She whispered, "Next we go, just us? I will not read about discourse."

"Fine," Kitagawa responded in a quick staccato.

Dr. Oberst, sitting morosely to himself, likely no longer a part of the illustrious 'us' stewing in some private, peevish emotion, finally spoke, "Please, Dr. This and Dr. That. It seems unfair that I keep my title while everyone else has abandoned theirs. Josef is fine for me. I hardly feel like a doctor here. My practice has been of no use, unlike Dr. Gage. Only he should be called doctor."

"Quite right, I daresay I would rather perish than hear those my junior call me William," Dr. Gage said. He looked at the room expectantly, swallowing bated breath. Perhaps it was a joke from him, but it came across intensely sincere. He shot a watery blink to Parisa, who obliged a chuckle. He rewarded her by directing her to sit by his side.

Renard said, "Well, let us put your practice to use then, so we may continue to call you doctor, hein?" She sat on the floor, haunting where Gao used to practice English letters, tracing her fingers on the ground, "It has been so long since I last saw daylight, I am forgetting the sight of it. How do we keep away from insanity? Tell me then, student psychiatrist, member of the *Société Psychanalytique de Paris*."

"I am afraid I cannot say. Well then, I am no longer a doctor. Just Josef."

"Alors, as you have been stripped of your title as you are unable to provide treatment, so will Junichi, as he was unable to philosophize to save YiMing from throwing himself to the cellar. Let us not forget him. Not while his body is likely still warm."

Alessandra whispered in Kitagawa's ear, "Do not mind her. She will heal in time. Please, have patience with her."

He whispered back, "She does not concern me."

Renard suddenly shrieked, "And you. Alessandra. You laugh and joke and whisper and do all this when Gao has been taken from me. You lost all your care. You shame me. Disgusting."

Alessandra gave her a sympathetic smile, not ashamed, but ironically remorseful, likely even hinting towards sarcasm.

Harriet interrupted another burst from Renard, "The other two riddles, from the armory and the observation room. Let me think on those for a bit. What makes sins new? Well, what does make sins new? Repentance? How could that fit in?"

Dr. Gage responded, "Not on the armory, but on the observation room. I think that I have the answer." He took one of the old, crusted maps from the navigation room in hand. "I think if we were to look through the periscope, we would see that the glass is pointed eastward. The enemy lies to the east, for you lot at least. The maps are indeed of Europe, and the enemy of Europe was the Austrians and Hungarians, and yes, the Germans. The master can see the enemy. The chains, the foot soldiers, cannot. They are too close to the battlefield. I think we can answer that without having to risk our necks. This answer is as literal as being cast out of heaven."

Harriet responded, pulling a thick scab off her bottom lip, "That is a very broad assumption to make, but I'll take it as long as I won't be asked to verify."

"If it comes to it, and to be certain, who will look through it?" Alessandra asked, but then promptly answered her own question. "I think it must be me. I am what is left. My role! Chief of the Bunker!"

Kitagawa said in a fluster, "Chief of what? But unnecessary. It can be us. You know, it's not necessary to accept undue risk. No, I will think of a way where we can verify without having to succumb to the trap."

"Like how you did with the cellar?" Renard spat on the floor—abrupt and uncouth.

Kitagawa ignored her and continued, "I ask you to wait until I make some decision on how to proceed. Next, we shall engage again with the armory. The trap is laid bare, that I feel. Those guns may be made to shoot towards that wooden chair. I do not know the trigger, but if we are careful enough, we may avoid it."

"Well, then, I will await your command. I will take your warning. Hopefully, if I am to die, you will ensure it is a noble one," Alessandra replied, then squeezed Kitagawa's hand. He no longer reddened, but a full-on boyish blush. The sort that went scalp to collar. A blush didn't suit him.

Harriet, Parisa, and even Dr. Gage watched the exchange

like a grand opera. Harriet smirked and leaned to whisper privately to Parisa, "Children become schoolboys. Schoolboys become men. Change very little, don't they?"

Parisa raised an eyebrow, whispering back, "How quickly schoolboys become smitten," and then shook with a silent giggle.

Addressing the smelly congregation, she said, "Then to spare time, should I go to armory now? Or should I wait? Harriet's wounds are not yet healed. I want her to join me but want no more injury to come."

"Yes, yes, we know. May as well wait for it to scab over, as I said," Dr. Gage replied, "Get her to stop plucking at it! She's disfiguring herself!"

Harriet limply responded, "Disfigured? Probably an improvement. Scars are in fashion, I hear."

Alessandra abruptly called out, "Actually, I go now. I think I am indeed clever and can find some answer. No argument, I win the fight. I am Chief."

Kitagawa exclaimed, "But what about waiting for my command?"

"That was for observation room. For armory, I think we have been there safely once, so we will be safely twice. I have yet to find answer myself, I wish to do so. I must—I am Chief!"

Kitagawa cried, "What on earth is this Chief nonsense?"

Alessandra bounded onto the table, "Yes, we have tribes, art tribe and boring tribe, and I am Chief of all tribe. So, as Chief, I find answer for tribe. Now, yes, now. I want to go! I always want to be a Chief, now I am Chief, until one wins in a fight. Now, yes now, I go!"

"The mercurial moods that besiege Italians," Dr. Gage chuckled to himself, delighting in Kitagawa's subsequent stuttering, "Surely, you would like to join Ms. Morrelli, Mr.

Kitagawa? You as well Mrs. Renard? That will not be too large a hunting party."

"I shall remain here," Renard said sourly, "As should you, Alessandra. Let Oberst and Kitagawa go again, since they find answers so easily. Let them bleed from their own flock." Her contempt had not mellowed with time, only fermented, and Alessandra snorted at it.

"I am fine to go on my own. I am a grown woman," Alessandra declared and hopped back onto the floor.

Kitagawa similarly got to his feet, "Certainly you should not go alone."

"Why not? You have gone alone to the observation room, then leave me when go to kitchen. I thought you called me shrewd? Not shrewd enough to be alone?"

Dr. Gage let out a sudden burst of laughter, "Morrelli let the poor sap go with you."

For the next minute, Alessandra enjoyed poking at Kitagawa. A couple Nos and couple Maybes, one Perhaps, but relented and took him by the forearm.

"Who knows what those two will get into. It makes sense, a man does get lonesome all these days with little affection," Dr. Gage laughed to himself, wiping a tear from his eye. "By God, if I am to die in here, at least it will be accompanied by some comedy."

"Dr. Gage, don't be crude, there's a princess present," Harriet cried.

Parisa shrugged, "I've read stories before."

"He best not push the barrel of some gun into her stomach," muttered Renard. "I do not trust him. He is pretentious, and conniving. I saw the way he looked at Gao. Hateful ass. I do not doubt he feels the same for all of us. You should have heard how he talks."

Dr. Gage snorted, "I hear him talk quite enough, I think."

Parisa quietly knelt Renard, who didn't accept nor encourage any other comfort, "I can understand him though. It is not understandable to you all, but I can know it. We are made to feel lesser, you see."

Dr. Gage wagged a finger towards Renard, "I doubt he has any violent or hateful intention towards Morrelli. Those scholarly bookish types are always so desperate for the attention of a woman, even one as rough as she. He is probably overcome with satisfaction. Mrs. Renard, I do believe you are jealous that you do not command Morrelli's full attention now."

Dr. Oberst grew even sicklier. His pallor was almost yellow.

Harriet asked. "Dr. Oberst, or sorry, Josef, are you alright? Do you feel your allergy flare?"

He nodded and said nothing.

She continued, "Well, hopefully those two find more answers, for all our sakes. The drugs are even weakening me, and I am still in good health."

He still only nodded.

Parisa continued her own thought, "I understand Mr. Kitagawa. I myself am similar. I fear the shame of losing and must race to prove worth. You understand?"

Renard grumbled and dismissed her with a flick of the hand. So, Parisa gave up trying to reason with her, and found more comfort in joining Harriet's pacing. Pyotr joined the pacing, nothing else to do. After a good five minutes, Harriet halted, tapped his shoulder, nodded, grunted, blinked, and that was enough. Pyotr lifted her onto his back and became a valiant steed to Harriet, the cowboy. No explanation offered, none really needed. Truly—nothing else to do, nothing else that promised no injury.

Dr. Gage listlessly watched it, rolled his eyes, and said,

"Took me years to break such sport from Alfred and Thomas."

Parisa watched the two as if she was considering asking for her own turn but never did. She optioned to entertain Dr. Oberst. The kindred third wheel.

She asked him, "How do you feel, doctor?"

"Neglected."

✳ ✳ ✳

Alessandra sauntered around the armory once again, chatting away in a confusing mixture of English and Italian. Without Renard, nothing stopped her from poking and prodding at all the cages and anything of interest.

Kitagawa took back up interest in the chair with the Theta. As seen by the crinkle on his nose, the sulfuric smell was almost unbearable, but pride forbade leaving, and thus, he diverted attention back onto the furnishing. Upon further inspection, the chair was bolted to the floor.

"Well, context would beckon one of us to sit down on the chair. Undoubtedly, that would start some sort of trap. In that case, we should refuse to sit in it," Kitagawa called. "What are you doing over there? I thought we decided nothing of interest was in the weapon cages?"

"Yes. But maybe something changed. We must be certain," she called back. "Also, Junichi, may I ask you something? I promise it is not about being a funny man."

"Well then, certainly."

She re-emerged in front of him with a pleasant, if a bit serious, expression, "Do you have trust with me?"

"In what regard, my dutiful Chief?"

"In a natural regard. You know that I will do nothing to injure you and only want all of us to return home. Do you trust this?"

"Yes, we all want that."

"Well, then please answer two questions from me. Please answer honestly. If you do, then I will not speak about it any further. When you went to observation room alone, if passage out of bunker was found, would you have told the rest of us? I feared you would have left us, saved only yourself."

Kitagawa recoiled, and furrowed his brow, but he responded truthfully to her, "Maybe, I would have only known if that circumstance came to pass. But that was then. Now, no, I would have told you before I left. Do not fear that."

"I am happy. Second. Forgive me for asking, but did Dr. Oberst say the truth? What happened to Gao? Your faces... like a lie. It was so open. Please tell me it was the truth."

Without any hesitation, he responded, "It was the truth. We were shaken is all. We discussed it before coming back, how you all would respond. We know that we are the two most disliked among the group, and that misgivings would arise shortly upon our return. It was nerves, we did not want to upset you, any of you."

Alessandra sighed, hand to heart, "I am so happy to hear this. Then I will be angry with Lucie if she says rude words again. I will punish her, as Chief."

Unflinchingly, Kitagawa nodded, even smiled. An ally. A fervent ally. A young, fervent ally. The self-proclaimed Chief as his ally.

He sucked in his breath and asked, "Alessandra, about this Pisano? He is a cultist?"

She shrugged, "Yes, is rumors, but my father say rumors have seed of truth. Pisano was famous theater owner but goes away to other countries often, and has home in Italy, but lives in a place called Eden. The cult maestro is a half-God, I hear. So strong, wealthy men like Pisano kneel. Don't know which is truth and which is stories. But yes, I think we are tortured by that religion. I think they want to torture me for my father not selling our farm. I think maybe they want to torture everyone else because they also don't sell a farm."

"I haven't sold, nor marketed, anything!"

She shrugged again, "Eh, I think we are all punished by them, but reasons, maybe different. We are cast out because injustice, so we solve bunker to earn forgiveness."

Kitagawa began to gnaw on his lip and slapped a bead of sweat off his neck. He looked uneasily around the armory, as if the captors' invisible eyes bore straight into his skull and directly voiced displeasure on such an insulting assumption of their noble business being a cult.

He snapped his neck to point at the chair, like a child in a bout of show-and-tell.

"About this chair, let us try an experiment, shall we? The guns pointed to the chair must be loaded, I do not have the capability to tell as I have never touched such an infernal thing, but I think it works that if one were to be seated on the chair, the guns would trigger. Maybe then some other clue would be revealed. How about this, you pull the trigger manually, and I will stand out of the door, just enough to see the perspective of the seated person. That way, perhaps if we trigger the trap ourselves but with nobody in the seat, we can receive the clue without injury. I will assume some risk by being somewhat close to the seat. But surely, you will be safe behind the guns. Wait, as a farmgirl, do you have any experience with a rifle?"

"No, my father owns some to ward off wolves, but I never touch them. I like to hold axes more," she responded.

Quickly, the two inspected the lined rifles. Cocked and loaded, but no wires or springs were attached. Not readily apparent to the naked eye.

"But how can we be sure you will be safe? The door is so close to the fire line of the guns. A stray bullet may hit you?" she asked, tightening her mouth into a flat line. "Much like red hair boy, we may injure ourselves if not enough thinking."

He rested a hand on her shoulder to guide her away, "Do not worry about that. Have we not all agreed, each of us may assume some risk of injury?"

Alessandra let out a slow exhale, and gave a shaky smile, "Yes, yes, I agree. My duty, as Chief!"

"How much longer will you keep up this Chief business?"

"I am Chief, and you will be my courtesan!" Alessandra stuck out her hand for a shake on the matter.

Kitagawa pouted but shook her hand regardless, "Courtesan of a farmer? A chapter to be excluded from my biography."

They each took their places—the Chief and the courtesan. Kitagawa stood with one foot out in the hallway and one foot toeing the threshold of the door. His eyes were trained on the chair and its surroundings. Alessandra stood behind the row of guns. She shouted to her courtesan—readying her command. Unlike his character, he hesitated again.

Physics was never his strong suit. Too objective. Yet, he obviously deluded himself into thinking rough calculations in his head were just as serviceable as a doctoral degree on the subject. Thus, the two would be safe in their respective stances. Full of self-deceiving courage, he nodded for her to pull the trigger.

And so, she did.

A small explosion erupted out of the tip of the barrel of the gun, as expected. But the armory flickered alive. The whole room exploded. An instant furnace. The concussive thrust shoved Kitagawa back into the hall, slamming his head against the opposite wall. The front of him was singed, and the inside of the room continued to burn. He scrambled to his feet, his face drawn and paralyzed in front of a wall of smoke and flame. Nothing heard but the roaring of fire.

The barrier of flame was too thick, and the embers licked beyond the doorway, threatening to tickle his nose. All thoughts left him, and he slumped against the wall, stuck in place with nothing but a hot terror for a companion. The fires did not die out quickly, rather yawned to a prolonged death.

He muttered through chattering teeth, "They won't believe me… they won't believe me…"

The smoky haze inside the armory finally dissipated. He gingerly stepped inside, a sweltering blast immediately curling his eyelashes and compressing his lungs into complete flatness. Charred remains slumped over the buttstock of the rifle. The sulfuric stink congealed in its halo. He vomited but was unaware that he did.

A drip of glycerin plopped on his head. Amid the charred ceiling, out radiated a taunt fashioned through the gel.

Redemptio tua ex Purgatorio

Chapter Nineteen

Renard cried, "Did you all hear that? That thunder coming from the hallway? Something must have happened. I knew it." She began to claw her face, yet as her fingernails drew up faint pinpricks of blood, she turned her talons onto Pyotr and began to rake his already raked arm.

Parisa tried to take Renard's hands in her own but was subsequently slapped away. Still, Parisa tried, "Relax, do not be hasty. It could have been a plan. It must have been a plan."

Renard continued to wail, "I knew something would happen. I knew it. That thunder."

Harriet joined Renard's other side, trying to put a gentle arm around her, and was met with an elbow to the gut. Nevertheless, Harriet joined Parisa's effort, "Can we even hear thunder while underground? It does sound like it's coming from the hallway, whatever it is. Well, should we go check?"

Parisa shook her head, "That would anger Kitagawa and Alessandra. No use bothering them, they will feel we do not trust them. It will only annoy." She leaned over the top of Renard's hanging head to whisper in private to Harriet, "No, something certainly happened. Something bad, let us wait a bit. See what is made from it."

So, they waited. Renard hovered near the bookcases,

gnawing on her knuckles, flipping through the whole range of emotions available to her: anger, frustration, sorrow, optimism, despondency.

Dr. Oberst grew even more sickly, his skin almost the color of old parchment with his eyes shadowed in red. He had vomited in the corner soon after Kitagawa and Alessandra had left and now cowered over it to conceal the sight from the others, likely to save himself the headache of their protests. They could hear, see, and smell it anyway. To turn his senses away from the squeezing in his chest, he also began to gnaw on his bottom lip—the favored pastime of many of the bunker's dwellers. Through time, it too became a scabby, shredded mess of a lip. But the metallic taste of blood was preferable over the putrid sourness of vomit.

It was another agonizingly long stretch of time later when Kitagawa returned from the hot shadows, alone. Sooty and blackened, wide and frantic, he emerged like a mountain cryptid into the dining room. He sat down. Saying nothing, doing nothing, emoting nothing, sitting woodenly.

Renard bolted upwards, raced around the table's perimeter, and gripped him by the collar, "Well? The noise? Alessandra? Our Chief?"

Kitagawa shrugged. A maneuver that sat well with nobody, not even himself.

Renard began to violently shake him, repeating the same questions. He locked his focus downward and kept on shrugging.

Dr. Gage nodded to Parisa, "Now is the time to go find the thunder."

Kitagawa halted his meek muteness, darting a wide, twitching eye to Dr. Oberst. He grunted, pointing his eye towards the hallway door and back to Dr. Oberst, "Us. Doctor."

"I can do it. I will go and check," Dr. Oberst said quickly, trying to fasten Parisa and Harriet in their place, "Seems like something deadly happened. I will go and see what I can make of it."

Renard spat on the ground, "No. Certainly not. I must see, you may only follow if you wish. I will see what you have done."

Dr. Oberst uneasily chuckled, "No, no, in this state, it would not be good for your psychosis."

"Damn your psychosis, you aren't a real doctor," Renard shouted back, "You won't cover for him, I see this. I see this and I rebuke it."

"I intend no such thing," Dr. Oberst stuttered. "I have objective eyes. You will see what you want to see."

Harriet tried to place a calming hand on Renard's back, "We can all go. Don't worry, me, Parisa, and Pyotr can assure —"

The calming hand had the opposite effect, and Renard ripped it away, "You can assure nothing you ugly creature."

They all scrambled for the door, eager to be first to the scene. All except Dr. Gage and Kitagawa, each choosing to lock focus on the floor.

❋ ❋ ❋

As they all ran nearer to the armory the putrid smell of smoke and burning clogged all throats, and a choir of hacks and coughs rang around the iron.

The hallway was scorched. Ash and dust settled in great mountains, clinging to the baseboards. A hellish tundra.

Renard ran in first, elbowing and shoving Dr. Oberst to the floor several times, yet at once fell to her hands as Alessandra's charcoal flesh greeted her. Grisly, yet Renard could not look away. With her forceful and prolonged stare, Renard hoped to intimidate the corpse into reanimation. She should have her way. Death should submit to fame. Yet, it was final, and Renard was left displeased with death's refusal to answer her demand.

Harriet came up behind her and gently tried to lift her back to her feet by the shoulders.

"Look away Lucie, we shouldn't perturb the dead. It was an accident. It must have been. Just like the box that shocked Wassermann. An accident. Don't touch anything."

"Yes. Accident. Nothing more to it, I think," Dr. Oberst chewed on his lip even more, pinching his nostrils together. Mouth breathing only worsened the chest ache, but the smell was soul-bleaching, so he picked the lesser battle.

Renard immediately began to shout, "What if it was not? What if it was how Semyonov bled himself, or how YiMing threw himself down the cellar. What if he forced her to do this? He tricked her, he must have. How could such a thing be an accident? He wants death for each of us, it is what he wants. Don't you dare defend him, you cretin."

Swiveling around the half-raw half-roasted stump of a body, Parisa cried out, "Look, above."

Dr. Oberst eagerly followed up, making wide, histrionic gestures, "Your redemption out of purgatory. Or also, your payment out of purgatory. That is what the ceiling says."

He flung a haphazard arm around Pyotr and Parisa, meandering towards the back of the armory as though the three strolled throughout a promenade. Parisa didn't notice. The ceiling demanded her full attention. Pyotr let it happen, better than staring at a quasi-cremated carcass.

Harriet struggled to keep the wailing Renard from touching Alessandra, desperately pleading to not meddle with the deceased. Renard strained against Harriet's grasp, and something wolfish entered her spirit. She swiveled around and punched Harriet hard in the face.

"Do not keep me from mourning Alessandra. Both my babies are murdered. See how she leans against some *fusils*? It must have been a trap. He led her to a trap."

"You don't know that Lucie—" Harriet muttered, patting her face like it wasn't her own.

Within the gratifying boundary of rage, Renard fervently pushed Harriet to the ground, knelt onto her frail ribcage, and began to rail a closed fist down on her, freeing all of her anger onto the woman's head. Against the dull thuds and squelches followed a sickening crunch.

Renard screamed at Harriet, the receptacle for all hate and sadness' burden, "You ugly, disgusting cretin. You defend a murderer? You love a monster? You want to be one. I saw how you look, how you goad. You want to be like him, *hein*? Ugly little beast. You cannot tell me what to do. You ugly little nothing."

Harriet shrieked. The black particles suspended in the air started to rain down. Pyotr ripped away from the doctor's grip.

Grabbing the back of Renard's dress, he yanked her up and then slammed her back down on the floor like she was a bear to be wrestled.

Harriet's lip split, and blood trickled from her nose. Her left eye was bright red and began to swell. She sat up and gingerly groped her face. A long strand of red-tinged saliva looped out of her mouth, intertwining with her fingertips. Like a ghost lifting from a corpse, she got to her feet, and stood vacantly above Renard, who still flailed, cursed, and screamed against Pyotr. Underneath him, she had nowhere to direct her rage, and began to rip out her own hair, kicking her feet hard against the floor. Harriet watched and a snarl crawled out of her throat. She lightly tapped Pyotr and beckoned him to shift backwards. He did, grimly ducking his head to her.

Harriet drew her foot back and then propelled her heel firmly into Renard's side. She kicked again. And again. And again. Something crunched. Harriet then mindlessly lurched forward onto the woman and held her down with an iron grip to the jaw.

It was permanently her turn. She pummeled her fist down on Renard, with a torrent of screeches. At first, nothing intelligible, but then the chaos forged a meaning.

"I am not nothing. You cannot do this to me. Not nothing," Harriet beat and beat and beat, blood, puss, and sweat pouring down her face. "Hate you, hate you." Red droplets splashed up like a geyser.

Renard became sufficiently demolished. Only then, Pyotr grabbed Harriet's swinging fist. Her rage melted into nothingness. She stood, wordlessly, patted Pyotr on the shoulder, who relinquished her hand, then drifted away. Before vacating the armory, she halted, then proclaimed, "I hear them giggling."

She left.

Pyotr knelt down to jostle Renard back to her senses, but the woman gave no response. She coiled inward and pressed her face into the ground, heaving in great plumes of ash.

Parisa stood paralyzed. Dr. Oberst was not paralyzed, decidedly not paralyzed. If anything, he was never more energetic. He pranced around, touching all things immolated, whistling with strained breath as he continued his gleeful little inspection.

Nothing remained of the armory. All charred. All brittle. All ravaged. Not a hindrance. An advantage. The 'us' took the lead. The civilized tribe.

Dr. Oberst crept up behind Parisa, and whispered without warning, "I think me and Kitagawa can answer this room. We should be off. Do not dwell here."

Turning to meet his face startled the life out of her. Pulpy. Crusted by sickness. Smiling. A ghoulish smile. Etiquette failed to stifle her recoil.

With a hand covering her nose, she nodded, then darted off to collect Pyotr. A gentle tap to his shoulder, and he hesitantly released Renard from his clutch. The brutish scowl endured, as did Renard's coil on the ground. She moaned, gripping her gut, and spat out a large puddle of mucus. She only ceased her moaning when all abandoned her at the feet of Alessandra.

✳ ✳ ✳

The attitude back in the dining room was just as sullen. Dr. Gage had ripped off a piece of his dress shirt and dabbed away at Harriet's nose, all the while trying to instruct her on boxing defensives. Among his vast expanse of cataloged knowledge, he informed her that he too knew all things combative and martial, and that she should never get into scuffles that she couldn't win. As he continued the lecture, Harriet's eye twitched with pain, then with a small irritation, then a prick of hatred.

Kitagawa was in an indescribable mood. He sat back at his seat at the table. His pride had taken his body over and he tried his best to look wholly undisturbed. His straining neck tendons betrayed otherwise. The thin protective veneer of arrogance was cracking, and he put a great mental strain into trying to keep his faults at bay. He sucked his teeth and preened his nails, sitting up rigid in his chair, pretending not to notice or care when the three others re-entered.

Dr. Oberst engaged the room with his findings, spluttering out spittle, blood, and flecks of vomit with each word.

"The ceiling, *Redemptio tue ex Purgatario*. Your redemption out of Purgatory. That with the Theta that Kitagawa said was on the chair, and the first phrase *What makes sins anew*, I think we may have more religious imagery on our hands—"

Dr. Gage interrupted, "Yes, yes, this was easy. The Lake of Fire, from Dante's *Purgatorio*. It is the barrier between purgatory and heaven. Fire in hell cleanses sins. We know the answer is fire."

Dr. Gage turned his attention towards Parisa, and said in geriatric amity, "Come here, child. You are sweating too much. Here, my waistcoat is still relatively clean, use it to wipe your face. Come on then, you will become ill otherwise. Hurry up."

He struggled to unbutton the waistcoat and then instructed Parisa to do it for him. He blotted her face, asking her again and again if any part of her was injured. She shook her head but let him inspect her head, face and hands all the same.

He said, after thumbing her wrist, "Rapid heartbeat, but you've had quite a shock. Hopefully it settles soon. Otherwise, your condition is fine. Much better than your peer at the very least. I would suggest waiting a while until your next venture. Let your nerves calm."

Harriet took her seat again, cradling her sore face. Pyotr sat next to her, still violently irate. The best comfort he could offer was staring at her broken nose while shaking his head, patting her on the back, and putting a finger gun to his head. Harriet shrugged, then directed his gun at her own temple.

She said, grimacing as blood continued to trickle, "This has me thinking we were all wrong about the military angle. I mean, justice, cast out, fire cleansing sins. The first place we went to, the navigation office. The book choices are starting to make more sense to me. The books matter. What was the age of reason called in Europe? I have since forgotten the name, but I learned about it in school. What was the time period all those books were written? I checked the publishing dates and they were only a few decades apart at the most."

"Those books?" Dr. Oberst leaned forward over the

table—too jerky to be a natural movement. "The Enlightenment. But that does not answer the question 'Through bloodshed comes beauty, what hope does the master have', now does it?"

Harriet closed her eyes and slightly bobbed her head to rock the aches away, "No, no, it is starting to make sense to me. The Enlightenment, age of reason, it also had another name. It makes sense. There was bloodshed, right? During that time, monarchies were killed off, and brought about democracy and liberal values, right? What was the name of it... it had another name..."

"The age of progress," Dr. Gage answered, still wiping Parisa's brow.

Harriet opened her eyes and then furiously reached for some paper and a pen. She began to scribble down a collection of thoughts: Beta, Theta, Theta, Mu, Mu, Unjust, Cast out, Fire, and Progress.

Blood continued to trickle down her nose, but she no longer wiped it away, allowing it to drip down her mouth and onto the paper. "If we get the answer to the observation room, we may finish out the sentence. Look here, 'cast out to fire' maybe will make a coherent sentence. Then we may tweak it a little bit to answer the 'truth'."

Parisa leaned over her, "The pattern... there may be two Beta, do you remember?"

"Yes, we should try, but slowly. We may be so close. No need to risk it all now, we are figuring it out, piece by piece," Harriet beamed, her teeth reddened, "Or should we rip off the bandage? What's the harm now?"

Pyotr placed a hand on her scalp. No ritual followed. Just a flat mouth. She tried to nod and shrug, but he shook his head and darted his eyes towards the door. Harriet spat on the ground, some of it splashing onto Pyotr's feet.

Renard had finally crawled her way back to the dining room, downtrodden and dejected. She furled into the corner, offering no explanation nor apology. A strange look passed around the others. The awkward sort, like a faux pas interrupted a wedding.

Harriet snorted, "Well, I'm certainly not going to make some hasty forgiveness. But if you want Parisa, you can clue her in. Don't expect me to say anything to her."

Dr. Gage chided from the safety of his chair, "Don't say that; it's disgraceful. Not very becoming of a young lady, and you'll regret ever holding such a sentiment once we return to the surface. Apologies will be made in due time. Such resentment will only hamper our escape here."

No wave of the hand, no grunt, no grimace, not even a dismissal, Renard had lost all interest in the matters at hand, and she sought solace on the floor. She groveled in her corner, her fraying curls hiding her face from the judgmental eyes of the room.

Parisa whispered to the jeering chorus, "She'll be well soon! Let's give her patience!"

"The people's champion," Kitagawa muttered.

Several grumbling minutes passed, and Dr. Oberst leaned towards Kitagawa's side in an unvoiced whisper, "What say you to their theorizing?"

Kitagawa mumbled back, "No reason, progress, or anything rational to be had here."

"What does that mean?"

"You wouldn't understand."

Kitagawa suddenly sucked in a mighty breath, ground his teeth together, and darted a stony leer at each of the bunker's living inhabitants.

He finally made every single person an *Us*, when he announced, "Our captors are a cult that has been stalking us.

Some of us for years."

A frost swept the room. Mouths slackened, eyes bulged, stomachs gurgled.

Dr. Gage asked, in a strangely calm manner, "How long have you suspected this?"

"Only recently," Kitagawa said faintly. "Recently. Hence, all the religious nonsense. Hence, the patched-up theology smashed together with insipid philosophy. Whether each of you realized it or not, at some point, a cultist had poked their nose into your life."

Harriet spat out, "Is that the truth then?"

Parisa shook her head, "No. It must be something personal. The truth is why we are here." She suddenly seized up. Without a word, not even a silent request to her typical escorts to follow, she darted out of the back door.

She raced to the armory. The door was shut. She gave it a tug. Locked. She raced to the boiler room. Another tug. Locked. To the frigid navigation room. Locked. She ran back to the dining room, darting through it without looking at the others, bursting towards the door to the observatory. Open. But she did not enter. She lingered in the hallway and pressed her forehead against the wall.

"Locked if correct?" she asked the invisible wardens. No response. Nothing audible, at least. She was ignorant of it, but on the other side of the wall, an observer pressed their hand against the metal.

She continued to talk despite never receiving a reply, "Why am I punished?"

If only she knew that she didn't have to speak English. If she spoke her native tongue, at least one of the observers would've understood.

Harriet stumbled her way into the hallway with Pyotr in tow. Gently, but forcefully, they escorted Parisa back to the dining room.

Chapter Twenty

Kitagawa sat still, heavily breathing, eyes fixed to Renard. Inappropriately, he was calm and somewhat smug. He swung his eyes over to the other corner of the room, indulging with a flagrant stare at the petulance emanating from Harriet. There was something so quaint and comedic about it. A mousy girl, raw and hateful towards a woman over a decade older and over twice her esteem. Maybe because it was reminiscent of uprisings, riots, and revolutions he had been forced to toil over in school—dull and predictable moments of history with dismal outcomes, perhaps it was because she drew some of the ire directed towards him. Whatever it may be, he answered the urge to exploit such an odd fervor. Even as she lay hunched over in a seat, resting her bruised face in her hand, she peeked a satanic eye out between her fingers.

Kitagawa broke the silence that had shackled the room for well over three hours, "Miss Foster, come sit next to me."

A sullen scrutiny quickly shuddered the room. Dr. Gage, the torchbearer of the scrutiny, leering with his watery pupils and thumbing his pocket watch.

"Why?" Harriet stuttered and dropped her claw from her face. There was hardly a clean patch of skin left on her head. Dried blood and grime fashioned the ugliest warpaint imaginable, and sweat matted her hair close to her forehead. But her voice returned to a gentle timbre, and her question was earnest and not interrogative. A prime subject.

"Yes, why?" Dr. Oberst leaned forward, as though he expected Kitagawa to share some secret.

"It is bad for the psyche to be so close to your tormentor. Next to me, she can keep both eyes on Mrs. Renard, as well as enjoy a bit more physical distance. A matter of brain health, nothing more. Would you not agree, Dr. Oberst?"

Kitagawa's friendliness was cold, his posture stiff as though sitting for a portrait, and he raked his fingers through his hair as though the long-gone wax still held any strands.

Dr. Oberst recoiled and furrowed his brow and mustache. He tried to pass a silent message to Kitagawa: a question, a request for clarification, an inquiry that it was he who was Kitagawa's appointed bunker friend—implausible that someone like Kitagawa made such a baseless, senseless statement. It must have been a deception, but a deception lacking any reward. And there was no way Harriet was better company than a doctor, psychiatric or otherwise.

Yet he responded, not in a convincing tone nor with a convincing posture, "Yes, I agree."

But it didn't matter. Harriet had already shuffled her way from the periphery to the head of the table, taking the seat that the dead Pole Nowak once occupied. Between Dr. Gage and Kitagawa, either side of her burned fiery or icy.

"What do you really want from me," she asked Kitagawa, in the same docile candor. She kept her tremoring eyes on Renard, but her mouth had dropped into a frightened part. "You've never once talked to me about anything before."

Kitagawa stretched out his hand, slow and stiff, and patted her on the shoulder. It was mechanical, ill-practiced, and imparted no apparent comfort to either party. But he committed to the action, so he let it linger.

"I truly wish you to know I agree. I think you have the right notion about the burden to forget placed on society."

Dr. Gage interjected, "When did she ever display such a notion?" He leaned towards Harriet, trying to drag her entirely into his orbit. She remained steadfast in the center, most of her attention still retained by Renard.

Kitagawa spoke only to Harriet, "Forgiveness should never be an expectation, only a gift by one wholly giving. There's too much arrogance in half-forgiveness, or undue forgiveness." His voice dropped to a whisper, "It is an ill of society. The eradication of shame. The fetishization of sympathy. Truly, it does little more than spread harm. As you see it now, forgiveness allows poor behavior. Stay like a rock. When we return to the surface, do not forget what Mrs. Renard did to you, as she tries to return to her former life, as she is able to, as is permitted solely that she is who she is. She will forget it, as it would suit her, but don't you forget it. Because maybe then you really will be a... scarecrow."

Kitagawa turned his sharp jaw toward Dr. Gage, "Don't you see it the same, sir? Doctor?"

Dr. Gage sputtered and fumbled about his breast pocket. His knuckles, wrapped around his cane, began to shake. His head rattled, knocking fragments of thoughts and anecdotes together, trying to fashion some response that exonerated him from any hypocrisy. None existed. Humiliating silence resumed. A glance from the side lit up Dr. Oberst's face, and snarkiness nestled into his greasy skin.

Dr. Oberst coughed, "Yes, I do believe he does agree."

"When the context is right, surely," Dr. Gage sputtered, "And this is hardly the right context. We are hot on the trail. Freedom from this prison is nigh. No time for such talk."

Harriet spoke again, gentility fading, "But who decides

what the right context is?" Finally, she broke her gaze from Renard, scanned over Parisa and Pyotr, then faced Kitagawa, "Do you think it is possible for someone like me to decide? Or must it be you? The bastions of the people? The way I see it, this may be as good a place as any. On the surface, I'd hardly get a word in. I've been silent. A slave. A slave of my circumstance."

Kitagawa gave her a crooked smile, "Slave or pawn?"

Dr. Gage protested, "What are you even thinking? None of us decide. It's the natural way, the proper way. Why hold a grudge now, it only sours what little air we have left in this bunker. See the Soviet? God knows what filth Kovacevic put in his brain about us, but see, he's forgiven it!"

"A strange thing to say," Dr. Oberst said with a chuckle, sucking his teeth and scratching his mustache, "You seem awfully keen on forgiveness now, doctor, when you favor the subject, for whatever infernal reason. No matter how mute the subject is. Perhaps consider, I was once such a mute subject."

Dr. Gage darkened his scowl, "You are a buffoon, and nothing more, if you don't understand where the discernment lies. Both of you."

Only Parisa saw it. The brewing. The stinging. The first sands ripped up before a storm. Harriet as the eye. Parisa pulled herself back to the wall, far from where the dust would settle, lightly tugging on Pyotr's elbow.

Dr. Oberst coughed and hacked, infecting the air with the stench of phlegm. All his preparation to ready his voice, to give weight in his chest, went unused, as Kitagawa leaned in closer to Harriet, and ignored the other two parties to his sermon.

"I think you can decide, in time. Same as I will decide, in time. Perhaps therein lies the truth of it all..." Kitagawa looked through her, like his eyes rested on a ghost, "Maybe it should sooner come to the self, than anyone else. Dignity lives and dies with the holder."

Dr. Gage interjected yet again, "You are rambling. You have lost all senses."

Harriet's words tumbled out of her, "You want to know something, Mr. Kitagawa? I think I'm jealous of you."

Kitagawa's crooked smile straightened out, "As is your right to be, but it is unnecessary. Once I find our means of salvation, I do think we shall know the same reality. You want to be a king too."

Dr. Gage slammed his cane on the ground with a shout, "Hold on there, I see what you are doing, just as you did to Morrelli, trying to find yourself a new crony. Stole them both from Renard, now stealing one from Parisa, I won't have it."

A soft whimper shook out of Renard.

Dr. Oberst murmured from the corner of his mouth, "No need for such accusations, what happened to releasing grudges?"

"May it be one of us who wins," Kitagawa said to Harriet. "If we could start thinking like a king, less of a pawn. That's what this whole game is. An opportunity to be a king. The Tatar-Slav read all my papers, even the Japanese ones; he knows I have what it takes to be a king. I just need to prove it. Prove it here."

She broke into a fevered smile, matching his own. The rhythm of breathing accelerated and jolted to an off-kilter rhythm. A fog clouded both their eyes.

Dr. Gage made a grim, sly face over to Parisa, and slightly bobbed his head towards the table. A clear directive: intervene in whatever misshapen, unspoken, alliance that was forming.

Fumbling with her own nails and fingers, she gently trod back over and softly leaned over Harriet's shoulder.

"Will you now join me over by my seat? I think we

should share ideas with each other, I'm still thinking about those Greek letters. Perhaps you may have some good idea?"

Harriet spun her head around, eyes wide, her neck veins spasming, like Parisa had given her the fright of her life, or that she had been ripped from a dream.

She said, airy and vacant, "Sorry, Parisa, you didn't scare me, I just… lost in thought. Yes. Yes, I'll join you wherever. Whatever you need me to do."

Standing was labor-intensive, so Harriet hoisted herself up from the table by bending over in the most geriatric of fashion. Ambling back to her original chair, her back towards Renard's sniveling corner, she plopped back down. The pupils and irises of her eyes had contracted into pinpoints, and she focused on nothing in particular.

Parisa sprawled out the entirety of her notes in front of them both and tried to make another effort to brainstorm, but it was a vain attempt. But she persisted, talking each and every thought aloud, often repeating herself, often allowing herself to be interrupted by Dr. Gage, which was tepidly helpful.

But then Dr. Oberst began to mutter under his breath, very unhelpfully, leering at the ever-watchful Pyotr, "I was like him too once. A silent follower, dumb to whatever intention I was led to. He has your mercy, but not me. Not me. I wonder why that is. A real mystery…"

Dr. Gage didn't render him the dignity of looking him in the eye, "Semyonov may one day be a man. You will never be."

They all did not notice that once again, Kitagawa had slipped from the room.

Chapter Twenty-One

Kitagawa lurched, lunged, and limped his way back up the hallway to the observation room. His legs had grown loose, and his whole body weakened from refusal to eat the hardtack. Fatigue wore down his eyes, his teeth chattered with unspent anxiety, and an ache vibrated his chest. But this could all be ignored; the anxiety to find the last answer could not.

He didn't even bother checking the supposed exit door this time and flung himself back into the observation room. The room felt different. No longer cold, dingy, and dark. Bright, each curved mirror smiling at him, begging him to enter.

"What does the master see that the chains cannot?" he uttered to himself and answered the mirror's call, looking back into the dome of the periscope. Eyes are deceptive, so he squinted, glaring so hard his head veins pulsed. It must have been a trick of the eyes, but he delicately reached in his hand, and a cry leapt from his throat. No threads.

He groped along the perimeter. The blades were fully retracted. Reflecting off the looking glass was bright, orange warmth. The promise of safety, of daylight. His nerves stayed him. Surely, another trap.

Gingerly, he stuck his left arm through and braced for it to be ripped apart like Kovacevic's. Nothing happened. Another pause. He tried again. Nothing happened. A manic grin stretched open his mouth. Finally, he did it.

He stuck his head up into the periscope and peeked out the looking glass.

There it was, plainly. The surface. Illuminated with a gorgeous pink and yellow light. The sun, a stranger for so long, beginning to peek above the horizon. Kitagawa's eyes began to well. His mouth agape with a pant as he stood there, dumbstruck by the enchanting first light of a new day. His purpose forgotten, he stood there staring, unable to rip his eyes away.

At first, he voiced a suspicion that this was just an evil joke, and that he saw something fictional. However, the longer he stared, the more the sun vibrated above the horizon, the more it became reality. Moments like that, pure bliss, when poetry sprang to the mind, when all the great thinkers, philosophers, and literaries crafted masterpieces. Too beautiful for rational words, only adjectives, similes, or other rhetorical devices.

"The sun is my friend, he welcomes me world weary, let me live again," he recited to himself, lightheaded and giddy. Bouts of delirium washed over him, and the armory melted from consciousness.

He voiced another poor excuse for a poetic musing, "I will see the sun shine on Ueno again, as I see it now." Then, finally, one haiku from an actual poet, "*Hitori bocchi, yakümo kuu, koto wo yuruse.*"

The landscape begged all who had seen it to wander into a daydream. Stretching towards the sunlit horizon rolled long, green hills, covered in frostbitten dew. Enraptured in the ethereal beauty of the landscape, Kitagawa stayed entranced.

✻ ✻ ✻

Renard babbled to herself in the corner. Only Parisa understood her words but kept their meaning private, despite several requests from Dr. Oberst.

Instead, she whispered to Harriet, "Do not be too angry with her, she is going mad with misery."

Harriet responded, "I only promise I will try, but why must her misery break my nose. If I had a worser mind, I'd ask Pyotr to knock her head loose."

After the fervor of configuring some of the 'truth' died down, the pain of her injuries re-ignited. Her burns and blisters flaked and popped, and her face throbbed red. She had run out of places on her sleeves to wipe off specks of nose blood, and just let it dribble.

"Miss Shahidi is quite right, do not waste your thoughts or energy on such matters," Dr. Gage added from afar. "I, too, understand your sentiments, Miss Foster, but as my wife would remind me, pay your mind to only those worth spending the thoughts on. Ignore all those who rally against it, little devils on the shoulder."

Dr. Oberst furrowed his brow with much to say, completely lacking the proper lung capacity to say much. His long-practiced defense was scowling, so that's all he did. Sat and scowled. But Dr. Gage was no longer the sole target. It was the other one. The little serf becoming a little tyrant.

Pyotr kept his eye on Renard. He sat back in his chair, placed squarely in front of her little hovel: a schoolmaster supervising an unruly child. Arms crossed, knee bouncing, an astern glare cautioning against sudden movement. Whatever spades of anger and contempt he harbored were stowed away, but there was no outreach of any sympathy. All became subservient to plain prudency. It was just a known fact: Renard was a lunatic and needed a warden. A role that didn't go unappreciated by Harriet or Parisa, probably for opposite reasons. If Renard were to lash out, Pyotr would put a stop to it. Parisa expected Pyotr to do so gently, as Harriet expected mortal force.

Parisa quietly murmured to Dr. Gage, hoping Renard was not within earshot, for her own sake, "Why has no more gas come? Two more are dead, but no more gas. Do they not wish to collect the bodies?"

Dr. Gage, whose face had grown as pale as Dr. Oberst's and even more leathered, shrugged, "Perhaps there was no need to. They're already sequestered away."

The reality of the situation was that some of the releases were unintentional, and much to a scarily irate Tatar-Slav's aggravation, the unseen wardens only had a precious few doses left. A few, but still enough. The bodies would have to stink up the bunker.

Dr. Gage coughed so hard the sound of trapped mucus rattled the room. "If anything, I am grateful." He produced his pocket watch, rubbing his thumb over the lid, "I must be frank with you all, so that you are not consumed in fright upon it happening. If another dose of that drug plagues us, I doubt I will awaken. If I do, it will certainly not be with a sound mind. Anything you wish to know, on medicine, on Latin, on theology, on war, ask it now."

Parisa lightly rubbed the mound of his back, "Don't say that. Please find it within yourself to endure it some more. We are so close, as soon as my mind resettles and my nerves calm, I will go to the observation room, I will do what is necessary to find the last answer."

"Do not waste your thoughts on me. Instead, I will ask, if I die, and you see my lifeless body before it is taken away, please take my pocket watch. Please take it and return it to my wife, Bernadette Gage. In Brighton, will you remember this? Bernadette Gage. Need me to write it down?" he said with fleeting gruffness, flicking away Parisa's saccharine pleas.

"Yes, I promise if that comes to pass, I will do it. One of

us will. But it will not come to pass. We are so close," Parisa gripped his arm. Her spindly fingers could barely wrap around his thick forearm, but she tried all the same. She was rewarded by his coarse hand patting the top of hers.

"Yes. I think she would like you. Very much, I think she would," Dr. Gage uttered. A hidden observer found himself agreeing.

Dr. Oberst whispered, "Despite everything, if I do manage to survive, even I will do it. Maybe in death will you forgive but a poor German soldier boy." He managed a weak smile, but it was hollow. Nothing warm was behind it. His complexion had turned from a ghostly pallor to almost green. His crusted lips had blackened, and he reeked so badly that a circumference of solitude forged around him.

Parisa left Dr. Gage's side and began rummaging around the dining room. She began to flip through every book that lay on the shelf, even looking under every single chair and furnishing. "No. No Beta in here. Must be in that room that was locked first, the one with the dog on the front."

Another anxiety pricked Parisa. Increasingly, she buzzed about, becoming an expert on every inch of the dining room. Outwardly, she was a crazed, sweaty bumble bee, locked in a metal jar, bumping from wall to wall, pressing her ear against the carpets, the faux windows, the walls, and even the floor. It was tempting, way too tempting, diabolically tempting, to whisper a brief greeting to her—but that would make a permanently angry Tatar-Slav violently furious and a never-angry, as Kitagawa had put it, Peacock Italian lightly peeved.

The furnace from the armory seemed to have expanded and covertly surrounded them. The dining room grew sweltering. They all sat sweating, the carpet dampening with collective leaking body fluids, but Pyotr, one from a land without true heat, grew harrowingly distressed. He wheezed, tugging his shirt, scraping salty crusts from his reddening brow.

Against better judgment and standard decency, he ripped his shirt off and began to fan himself with the maps from the navigation room. Parisa and Harriet looked away, as was befitting the last remnants of their etiquette. Dr. Oberst briefly moved to do the same undressing but relented to being a slave to his more superficial courtesies. The heat worsened his condition, but if he were to perish, he would do so properly dressed.

Dr. Gage suddenly cried, and jut his rotund finger towards the crimson Pyotr, "What's that there? On his back? My word, I believe he must have spent time in prison."

Dr. Oberst grunted out, "I wonder what it means. I heard tattoos in an eastern prison have a meaning. Perhaps he was a murderer or a thief. Maybe he was the spy all along. Can't trust those serfs. Certainly, he has that barbarian jaw. I knew it. I knew we had a criminal among us."

Harriet shed her shame and looked at Pyotr's back. Inflamed flesh, warding off infection, but there it was. Engraved within the ropes of muscle and fascia on his back was a thick, dark outline of St. Peter's cross, intertwined with an abstract image of a howling hound, adorned by many intricate roses. A beautiful, blessed marking. Divine in nature. Important beyond what any of them may assume. None knew the splendor of such a marking. Not yet.

Abandoning any etiquette, Harriet halted his intense self-fanning and pulled the skin taught, running her fingers over the deep etching. Pyotr gestured for some level of explanation. Harriet gestured back, punctuated with a shrug, nod, and pat right on top of the hound's head. Confused, he began to scratch at his back. First brush of fingertip against the ink, and red worry screwed up his face. Something hideous sank into Harriet, and she began to scratch at her own back.

"Parisa, can you look at my back too," Harriet cried, frantically trying to undo the buttons.

Parisa, still with a fragment of decorum, took over the task and tried to covertly unbutton the back of the linen dress after pulling Harriet into a corner. As she undid each button as rapidly as her sweating fingers would allow, a lump stuck gagged her throat as a black line flushed against the frail spine. Quickly thereafter, Harriet peeked down the back of Parisa's dress. The same horrifically beautiful symbol.

Harriet began to shake. "Oh God, it must not be permanent. It can't be. How could it." She began to claw at it, hoping to rip up the ink with her overgrown nails, shredding the thin fibers of linen.

"Do not. You hurt yourself," Parisa said and grabbed her hands, accidentally rupturing a blister on Harriet's palm.

"I am already hurt. Oh God, what is this? Are these permanent? Please, tell me. Just pen, right? It's only pen and ink," she choked out. Nobody else bothered checking.

Dr. Oberst moaned, "Why do this to us? Was it not enough to kidnap, to bring us under the Earth, to confuse and pester us with torments and riddles? When will it be enough for them? Why can they not suffocate me at last? How can I be taken seriously now? SPP will never allow me in. Carrying the same mark as a Soviet felon." A very short-sided statement coming from an over-educated man.

"It will fade with time," Dr. Gage said to the others, completely unfazed. "I once, very long ago, took the graphite, ink, and water from a comrade. We took an iron hanger and stripped it to a point. We burned it and poked it through our skins. Our unit mark, right onto our arm. We shared a tattoo of fraternity, to carry with us for the rest of our lives into death. The tattoo faded from my skin not five years afterwards. If it is also of such a rudimentary design, it will fade. Do not worry yourselves." A rather insulting statement, which was not unexpected coming from Dr. Gage. The mark was anything but a tattoo of rudimentary design.

Harriet flopped forward, scratching at her head, moaning into herself, "Why? Why would you mark yourself like that?"

"Life has been horrible to me, and I wanted to remember some things that are good," he replied, some semblance of sincerity peeking through. "I see the nasty irony in its fading, of course. But I did what I could, so I would always remember what it was like. Among friends, surrounded by hostility. At least the memory of it is permanent, even as my mind weakens, I recall it. The sensation, pricking my skin. The smell of the searing rod. The scabs it produced. Roger's face. I can still see it. He cried. Thirty years old and he cried. Two days later, he was blinded by trench gas. Four days later, he died." He picked back up the pocket watch and began to rub it, "Now, I carry more tangible tokens. I have learned my lesson." His watery eyes glazed over, and his jaw remained slack. His breathing mellowed as he drifted deep in the bowels of memory.

Harriet sniffled, gripping onto Parisa's hand and resting her head on the table, "I don't think I would even want to remember this, even if we do all make it out."

"It would be crueler to remember," Renard softly spoke from her furled position, almost entranced, "I could spend years at the hypnotist. I could have the skin ripped off my back. I could forget seeing the sight of the armory, or of Kovacevic's arm, or Semyonov's gash, but I could feel them. I could smell them. Tell me, Dr. Gage, do senses fade with memory? I beg that age ruins my senses."

"Maybe as you meet the grave yourself," he responded.

Dr. Oberst moaned, "Is that why the tattoos are there, to make us always remember? What would be the purpose if we are expected to die anyway, if this all is some punishment, or if we all fail this grand test?"

His groggy head slowly swung left and right. He tried clutching his scalp with his hands to settle it back in place but no longer could tell where that place was. Now, it looked like that to him everything was a bother, everything that touched his skin felt perverse. Even his mustache, teeming with disease, mocked his face. He brimmed with a stupid sort of resentment, scratching his graying stubble, probably hating how it sprouted without consent, how it itched the chin, how it was a poor design of the body.

"Maybe that is a wrong question," Renard chirped, as if all cares suddenly dropped from her shoulders. "On the subject of memory, we have not seen Kitagawa. Has it not been several hours? Has it been a day? Longer? What did Alessandra tell me before? Where she caught him? Yes, she said in observatory… she kept him company there…" Her voice trailed off as her eyes clouded over, catatonia inbound.

Harriet gulped down her misery and got to her aching feet. Parisa joined her, and they ambled towards the door, murmuring only a cursory confirmation of their destination. Pyotr in turn, had quickly reclothed himself and scurried after them. He shook his head furiously to wrestle his wits alive again, sending a spray of perspiration off his hair. Dr. Oberst wrinkled his nose as the sprinkle fell atop his brow. With a rigid wrist, he smeared it off and wiped his hand on the table.

Dr. Gage spoke aloud to nobody in particular, "I wonder which of them will be next. Not Miss Shahidi, God won't allow it."

Dr. Oberst responded, despite himself, "I hope it's the felon."

Dr. Gage muttered, "Save it, he's not a felon. If he once was, he's not anymore."

"Would you extend that sympathy to me?"

Dr. Gage promptly dozed off.

Dr. Oberst grunted and decided to pass the time by indulging in a German text. At first, it was a mindless endeavor, just sullenly flipping through the pages. Yet, as he landed on a particular page, he clutched his chest like a heart attack had pounced.

There was the mark. The same on their backs. Next to thaumaturgical translations.

Dr. Oberst muttered to himself in the privacy of his mother tongue, "Men of bad faith…" He read the handwritten dedication on the inner cover, "The masters are grateful to you…"

He looked around the room and then settled on the mirror hanging on the wall. He stood, ambled over to it, and pressed his face right against the glass.

"Masters?" he asked the ghosts behind the walls. "You are grateful to us?"

If those ghosts were permitted to respond, they would have raised their voices in a resounding cheer, *Yes*. But none did, because none could. Not yet.

Chapter Twenty-Two

As they passed the left-hand door, Parisa and Harriet shook it gently. Forever locked. Gleefully rattling. The rattle was no longer a bother. Something meaner. Something begging for hatred. And it earned that desired hatred. Harriet hated it. Hated that rattle. Hated the insentient little gremlin of a lock. Known because she spat on the handle. Something clawed its way back up from her chest into her brain. She cackled to herself. Madness blossomed. Violent and meaningless madness. The madness demanded an answer, immediately. A violent, painful answer. She obliged an answer.

Harriet slammed her body against the door, begging it to crack under her hatred. Parisa tried to pull her away, but it was futile. Harriet beat and beat herself against the door, happily, the pain remaining fresh, numbness dying. Blood splattered from her nose and forehead against the paneling. Boils and blister bubbles on her skin popped and sent pus spewing. Parisa put a gentle hand on her back, but Harriet pushed her away and continuously slammed herself against the exit. The one promise of escape that was kept jeeringly within arm's reach. The hurt prompted a wider grin. The grin welcomed a rumbling cackle. The cackle coddled the newborn madness. The madness must have felt good; Harriet was licking her grin like the taste was sweet.

Parisa clawed at Pyotr, pleading for action, to muscle her away, to lord over her with the same brutish intimidation he did to Renard. He did nothing. Only waited, only picking at his own scabs.

Harriet continued to beat her head into the door, more and more violently and intensely as though she intended to knock it down through sheer brutality. Primal rage refused to subside once the skin on her forehead split; it only worsened. Saliva streamed down her tensely ajar mouth. More hound than human, snarling, snapping, and howling at her restraints. Squelches and slapping punctuated the air as her forehead's raw skin and bone continued to slam against the door.

Madness never died. Only wilted as her neck fatigued, the rigidity in her muscles slackened. Left, bruised, bloodied, and panting, resting her head against the crimson-smeared door, her throat kept on clenching, mustering the strength to howl and scream.

Only then did Pyotr approach her, gently guiding her to rest onto him, as though she was some scorned infant. A natural, familiar response. One without any judgment.

"Why be timid, or gentle, or docile anymore? A luxury we can't afford," Harriet finally spat. "I'm so tired of it. Tired of being afraid, or of being sad. There's more pleasure in anger."

Unspent wrath sent a shiver down her nerves. Her braids fell from their fastening and lay in matted tendrils down her shoulders and back. Her eyes were blackened, the pupils fully expanded.

Parisa was certainly always afraid, but now alone. Now, she was another Pyotr, muted and cut off, abandoned to dwell inside herself, nobody left to understand her words, nobody that she could see before her. She turned away and continued towards the observatory door, fully intending to go alone now. Surprisingly, Pyotr and Harriet followed her, walking together, bonded by a new common tongue. He kept her upright. Her spine had lost its firmness, and she flopped and whipped around, letting the whims of hysteria wrench her about like a dead animal in the jaws of a hyena. And Pyotr became the shepherd.

Cautiously, Parisa opened the observation door, ensuring her expression was blank before daring to peek inside.

Gruesome sights no longer instigated panic, only silent and grim acceptance. Kitagawa's body dangled above the step stool; his head fastened into the periscope. Blood rained down his suit, and his arms hung still and limp beside him. A deep, hateful cackle erupted as soon as Harriet came in behind Parisa and immediately released her unadulterated thoughts.

"Suicide? Does not seem a death he would choose for himself," Harriet said, hinting at a satanic pleasure. She crept up beside his body and inspected it like one does to a well-tended garden and poked his body. It swung gently, and a bit more blood trickled downward from the tube that concealed the damage done to his neck and head. "Seems that his body is propped up by the wires wrapping around his neck." She craned her head underneath and gawked upwards, "Knives are stabbing into his throat as well. Do you think we should wrestle his body down? Or would that be too much of a mess?"

Parisa shuddered and shook her head. "No, I do not think so. He was so cautious before. He must not have known that placing his head into the looking tube would do this. I think he must have found it open, or thought he took down the trap."

Harriet indulged in the imagination and then doubled over laughing. Pyotr stood beside her, gently patting her back, still without judgment.

Parisa traced the Mu on the step stool, smudged under Kitagawa's feet, and traced a finger over the etchings in the curved mirrors.

"Harriet, do you remember what he said this meant? Something about seeing chains?"

"Hmm? Oh yes, actually I am beginning to recognize a bit of the Latin words myself. Me. A seamstress. Surely, he would have found this wholly amusing. Well, I believe it was 'What does the master see that the chains cannot', or something of that nature," Harriet said, finally dimming her merriment. In a blink, a semblance of sanity returned. Her voice mellowed, "So do you think he saw it? The answer? Or even, the surface?"

"We can only know what he saw if we look up ourselves," Parisa said, "I think that maybe we can find how Kitagawa stopped or delayed the trap."

"That is where he failed." Harriet's simmering madness flared again, "But who can we get to test it out first? My vote is for Renard. I think she has been the most useless, so she should try it first. Actually, let's ask her to stick her head in regardless, just for fun. She probably won't even have a fuss, with her babies being dead and all, nothing else for her to live for. Doubt she even has a career to return to."

Shaking, Parisa allowed a release, "Harriet please, I am at the end of my mind. Don't speak like this, not you too. I first came to you and left the dining room with you because you are safe. The most safe and the most gentle. Please, do not be like this. I still need you safe and gentle. Please return to how you are, how you truly are, naturally, before all of this."

With the same haughty candor and cadence of Kitagawa and Oberst when they prattled on their scholastic diatribes, Harriet said, "Parisa, I was safe and gentle because I was confused and afraid. Now, I am confused and enraged. I have grown closer to my natural state, as I am in my home, afflicted with the troubles of daily life. Please don't ask me to be anything but what I am, or what I can be." She sucked her teeth and swiveled her head to take a gander around the room, her body followed in a peculiarly detached fashion, like the two entities were entirely separate. Staring at herself through a dirty, cracked mirror, she began to giggle, scratching the rest of her hair loose, the bunker swallowing the rest of her mind.

Chapter Twenty-Three

Inventiveness struck Parisa. To those with a modicum of superstition, it would have been prescribed as divine inspiration.

"We may have to wait for a long while. I do not know how long, but I think maybe it will open again, at some point. Kitagawa came back here often, I think one of the times he came back here, it was open."

Still sucking on her teeth and picking her nails, Harriet responded, "Sounds fine to me. Better than waiting back in the dining room with all the invalids. If he could talk, I'm sure Pyotr would agree with me. By the way, doesn't it seem perverse? Talking about him right in front of him and he doesn't know about what. Maybe he recognizes his own name, but that's really about it, don't you think?"

Her gaze snapped to the mirror etching, and she pranced up and pressed her face directly against it. Blood, saliva, and snot smeared against the glass, and she giggled, "I have been thinking about it. Wouldn't it have been very funny if we were all taken down here, below Earth, trapped between home and Hell. And then, not one of us could read Latin. We would have salvation right in front of us, but because some of us were not raised Catholic or couldn't afford university, we would be left to rot. It got me thinking is all. Same as Kitagawa said, imagine a group of pagans in here, unfamiliar with the fall from Heaven. How on Earth would they know the significance of a pearl? Funny, right?"

She finally ripped her face away from the mirror, back to Kitagawa's body, wantonly fiddling with his sinewy leg, "Well, if I am to wait here for that damned trap to release him, or for it to open, or for more gas to pour in, may as well enjoy the comedy. The one time I dare to leave my township, the one time I am stolen. There's a lesson here, do not strive to be greater than anything that you are. Some should be relegated to obscurity, lest face damnation deep within the bowels of dirt, poisoned by our breath, surrounded by those who would avoid you under any other circumstance. Tell me, on the surface, would a Persian princess have anything to do with me?"

Parisa whispered, "I'm no princess."

Harriet continued, words intensified, bordering on a shriek, "I'm not delusional. Would I want to know you on the surface? Surely. But you cannot say the same. You'd never let me in your palace. Would I want to know Pyotr on the surface? Who could say? Would I find him a raw brute like the rest do? I'll never know for sure, but I could suspect it." She began to violently laugh, hacking up bile.

With a sigh, Parisa silently took a seat on the floor next to the step stool, not looking at Harriet nor Pyotr. Pyotr was still intently watching Harriet course through her bouts of hysteria. If he had recognized his name, he did not make it known, and the lack of response did not perturb her fever.

"Actually, I have changed my mind. About Kitagawa that is. I can respect that he did what was necessary. We have been so slow, so prodding, too patient. We felt the need to rest after every injury, after every affliction. Why? This has only given more time to our tormentors! They laugh at us! I hear it! We have been here for over a month. My menstrual clock still ticks! And we have nobody to blame but ourselves. That's right. I blame myself. Why did I cower from the steam? Why could I not withstand it like Pyotr did? Why could I not figure out the navigation room, like you? And Kovacevic, the one man that could connect us to Pyotr, why did I not extend an olive branch? Gone too soon, in such a stupid way. In such a stupid, stupid way. Why did I do nothing but watch him throw his tantrums? Did I hate him? I hated that he argued and screamed about things that I have no idea about. What does a seamstress from New Hampshire have to do with Yugoslavian affairs?"

Tears streaked red down her face and her mouth pulled tightly into a grimace. Frozen as gargoyle, until another shift occurred, and she flung her arms around the dangling legs, "Kitagawa is right. I will be like him. I will walk among kings and queens and princesses. Or let this bunker be my grave. Mark me now, either way, the seamstress dies here."

Parisa said nothing. No movements. Not a shrug, nod, nose scratch. Like the rant never happened.

Pyotr kept his unfazed, non-judgmental gaze still. Slowly he reached out and wrapped his large hand around Harriet's thin wrist and clamped down tight. A forceful squeeze, right over raw blisters, yet not painful or uncomfortable. A soothing sting. A strange catharsis. Harriet's voice trailed off. Then she stuck out her other wrist. Pyotr wrapped his other hand around that one too and firmly clamped down. He gave them a small rattle. She fell silent and lost all agitation. A dainty smile lifted the corner of her mouth. A small, tight giggle. Another shake of the wrists. The smile faded into flat serenity. The newfound ritual worked.

✳ ✳ ✳

The three waited in the observation room until the room began to swell with the metallic and rotten stench of

Kitagawa's corpse. Then they waited some more, until they had adapted to the smell. Whenever a fit of hysteria rose up within Harriet, Pyotr clamped down again as if vaulting over the condition. Parisa muttered to herself in her mother tongue, churning her mind for some explanation to the effectiveness of the remedy but came to nothing. It was the product of some experience that she had never come to know, and she hoped, would never have to know. She debated aloud with herself on whether to inform the dining hall about discovering Kitagawa's corpse but concluded against it. No reason other than she didn't know what English words would have been appropriate.

Every hour or so, Harriet would demand to Parisa to tell her what the mutterings were about, and Parisa would say, "My daily prayers."

After telling the lie, Parisa would then boost her head up near the opening of the periscope and look again at Kitagawa's bloated neck. His hands and fingers were vibrantly purple and nose-bleedingly pungent, but Parisa forced herself to stare at them.

The body was a sundial. The stages of decomposition, even to those uninitiated, ticked away the hours. Parisa stared and stared. The bloating thickened before her eyes. Lost in her deep thoughts, Harriet disturbed the tense peace once again.

"Funny how the most manicured man has the most revolting carcass. When it is my turn to go, drain all of the blood out of me so that I don't become so swollen and disgusting. Do you think they return the bodies to our homes? Do you think my father will have to see me like this? Eviscerated? I hope not, but also, I want them to know. Something happened to me. Something grand, and horrible. Is that a better fate than having a small life, never leaving my own borders. Maybe they will pretend I died valiantly, fighting off my attackers. I can picture the funeral now. It will be beautiful. Everyone will be sobbing. Maybe that is Renard's use after all. Make her go to my funeral and cause a stirring scene. Is that not a mark of a person's worth? How hard people mourn at the funeral? I'd say so, it makes me blush thinking about it."

She rambled on, "Parisa, if you were to attend, my social standing would go beyond reproach. In death I finally reached above myself. How could someone like me know someone like you? Now, I am a woman of mystery. Or Pyotr. Make sure he attends as well. The distant unknown, an elusive Soviet. And no. Don't get a translator, it's better that way." Her jaw then suddenly locked up. Through gnashing teeth she snickered.

Parisa finally responded, serenely as she could, "What will it take, Harriet? To find calm again?"

Harriet put a finger to her mouth, a mocking thoughtful stance, and pranced about the curved room, ridiculing the pacing she did so many times before.

"Death or daylight. Whenever it pleases you, I will stick my head into the death tube. If I am decapitated, then I am cured. If I see the sun again, then I am cured. That is my final purpose. Rather than to slowly feel my body turn against me like those two old cretins. Better that than become some husk like Renard, some sniveling husk. Better instance than that. I'd rather jam my thumbs into my eye sockets and pry out my eyes than live to see myself stooped in a corner. Then this would all be for nothing."

"Then I grant your wish," Parisa said, draining all emotion. "I will not stop you. I do not want your death, or any other death. If this is how you choose, then it will be. But I will be here for it, as I wait here with you through each hour. So please understand that if you choose death, you will not die alone and without care." A firmer breath, "We know each other through this one place. Yes, I held to you because of this place. But for me, it is just as truthful if we were to meet on the surface."

Harriet shrugged her shoulders, her mangle of hair flopping about, and continued to prance about, keeping herself occupied. Pyotr remained unchanged, leaning against the wall. He adopted the habit of gnawing on his bottom lip. Soon, it became shredded, barely attached to his face, which proved to be no hindrance.

Even more time passed. Parisa must have grown sore from sitting, but still didn't budge. Drowsiness loomed, and she was quickly losing the ability to fight it. Pyotr did not appear to be afflicted by fatigue, or by anything, not even the dribble of blood plopping down from his chin. Like a stone guardian, he watched over the room, keeping manic spirits at bay and the room under a temporary spell of silence.

But not until it was finally heard. A slick metallic scrape, as though a sword had been re-sheathed. A squelch. Kitagawa's body collapsed to the floor. His face was paralyzed in an agape shock. He was rigid and red. Blood gummed around open wounds, and each thick vein bulged from his head and neck.

The wretched odor refreshed itself. Parisa peeked up towards the periscope shaft, "The blades pulled back. No wire. No thread."

Pyotr did not hesitate to pull Kitagawa's body away from the step stool. With the indecent tossing of the bloated corpse, Harriet's expression stretched back into a mawkish smirk.

She planted her foot decisively on the step stool, hugged her arms around the metal tube, and threatened to pop her head into the opening, "Well then, let me have a look."

Pyotr stopped her with a yank of her neck. She returned with a mighty shove, sending him reeling back. In one second, Harriet was mightily self-satisfied. In the next, histrionic remorse. She collapsed to her knees and attempted their sacred ritual over and over again. Nodding, blinking, extending out an arm to give him a pat. He stood, crossed his arms, and shook his head. Harriet began to convulse in hysterics, gurgling out ample apology. After ten seconds, he craned over, patted her on the head, and she ceased.

She murmured, "I'm sorry. Let me repent. I'll look now."

Parisa gently knelt next to her, softly whispering, "Wait, one moment, before you do, because we both know what may happen. Please, in case I have not said it, I will remember you as we first met. And you will do no wrong in my memory."

Harriet optioned to blink up at the ceiling. An eye-scrunching smile broke onto her face, and a fit of giggles leapt from her mouth. Yet, in a minute, it melted away. Pyotr lifted her up by the shoulders, nodded, blinked, and patted her on the back.

Harriet huffed out a sigh and took back up another grip around the metal tube.

"Well, here's to hoping this is the end of my brain fever." Harriet's smile loosened into something resembling sincerity. As if suddenly struck by nerves, she hesitated before poking her head up towards the looking glass. But she did so, with an animalistic grunt.

Nothing happened. Not until a gasp escaped from Harriet's lip, echoing back down the periscope shaft. Her hands began to tremble.

"I can see it. The surface. The sun is rising up from some hills… grassy areas stretching outwards. It's daybreak. I can see it. Slow, but the sun is rising," she shouted. Her hands strengthened their grip on the outer perimeter of the tube, so forcefully the knuckles blanched white. Harriet began to shake, and drips of wetness plopped out from the tube onto the ground. Not blood. She was crying.

Parisa asked, "What else can you see? What could you see that chains could not? Are there any chains there?"

Harriet said, her voice echoing from inside the tube, "No chains. Nothing else. Only daybreak. Dawn."

Pyotr tapped on the tube, likely instructing Harriet to pull out, but she did no such thing.

Parisa began counting. At first, no expressed intention as to why.

"I cannot see anything pertaining to *enemies*, like Dr. Gage said. No soldiers, no weapons, nothing like that. It's pastoral," Harriet continued.

"What time does it look?"

"Very early, I would guess five in the morning, perhaps."

"I see, Harriet, please pull your head down. Do not get too attached to it. I think this is what may happen to Kitagawa," Parisa said without breath. It took too long for Harriet to obey. But another tug from Pyotr, and Harriet retreated from the periscope. Tears streamed down her face, creating a dull glow, illuminated with happiness for once. The ghoulish veneer had been stripped from her face—almost sane again. Without hesitation, Parisa yanked her into a tight embrace, all the while muttering a count.

She was up to three hundred seconds. Then, she began to count louder. Three hundred one, three hundred two, three hundred three. Harriet quickly continued the unsaid assignment when Parisa reached one thousand. They switched back again at two thousand, then for the third time at three thousand. It was at three thousand six hundred and twenty-eight that the metal tube shrieked. Pyotr peered into the periscope mouth and nodded. The wires returned.

Parisa asked, "Sixty times sixty is three thousand and six hundred, correct? Is my mathematics correct? We were close to that number. It was open for an hour. An hour in the morning."

"But how does that help us with the riddle?" Harriet continued, rational intelligence briefly making a reappearance. She paced about again, this time in her usual habit.

"Much like the armory, it is more literal than we believe. We can see dawn. The masters see dawn. Think about the symbol on the stool, the Mu. Like the answer from the navigation office. Progress. Together it is figurative. The Dawn of Progress. Let us go back now. Tell the others." Parisa excitedly leapt towards the door, but Harriet lingered.

"So, you think it will be open at dawn again tomorrow, or some other time? I want to see it again. I want to see the sun again." She started to cry harder. "We can all see it if it's open for an hour. We can take turns."

Parisa was about to respond, but Pyotr ushered Harriet away. His boils and blisters had hardened into yellow calluses which toughened his appearance into something truly harsh and inhuman, but yet he still seemed so soft, and aged. He simply gestured back down the hall, and Harriet obeyed. He shut the door behind him, loudly and firmly. Another metallic shriek. Bolted. Again, the three would swear it—a chuckle from behind the walls.

It was from the Italian Peacock, so the Tatar-Slav was not allowed to admonish him.

Chapter Twenty-Four

The three had been gone for such a stretch of time that Dr. Gage surmised aloud all three must have perished. Of the two others, neither felt up to the task of checking. The cause was too hopeless, and they only waited for more gas to come for bodies to be taken away, wherever they may lie. Upon their return, he was not disappointed that they were alive, merely that he had been proven wrong.

Invigoration only struck the room when Parisa presented their findings. None asked Harriet why she looked beaten beyond measure. It hardly mattered. Parisa made no pause and rapidly explained the findings of their previous venture. News of Kitagawa's death went largely ignored but certainly did not go unheard. Renard didn't sneer, smile, or spit. Just huffed. Interest was snatched up by the more pressing matter —the answer.

Dr. Gage was the most active audience, the most active he could be. A wheat stalk was more stable than he, and likely more articulate at that point. Tremors shook his hands violently, and he had great difficulty keeping a grasp around his cane. His eyes had dulled over. Dr. Gage had Parisa repeat herself over and over, sparing no details, prompting "and what else" in the middle of sentences. The two talked in swirls, eclipsing and conjoining sentences and thoughts together. They came to some convoluted and incomplete conclusion that neither understood, but both agreed to it regardless.

"Do you suspect none of this matters?" Dr. Oberst's voice strained under his squeezing esophagus, "Even if we are right about every single room, every single one of these vague riddles is answered, what is to say that we can even leave?" His eyes had yellowed but were pierced with something angry.

Harriet clapped, sharpened her posture, then clung onto Pyotr's backside, "Yes. Yes. I have thought about that. At length. Parisa can tell you. In all honesty, I hope it is all for nothing. It would be funnier that way. This cannot be punishment. I have done nothing wrong and am upstanding. I knew none of you before this, but some of you bumped up against each other by chance or fate, or maybe even by design. So, I thought, it's random. It's random and it's pointless. None of it matters, wouldn't that be wonderful? Then, finally, we are free from the burden of being wrong; we didn't kill ourselves, it was all too stacked against us. You cannot blame the gambler against a cheating house. Comic, isn't it? Simply comic?"

Pyotr reached around. She stuck out her wrist. He gave it a delicate squeeze.

Observing Parisa's lack of surprise, denoted by a small shake of the head and a sigh, Dr. Gage decided to ignore the ravings, and likely ignore the girl all together. Now they were effectively down to two good minds. The others: one mute, two crazy, one German.

Dr. Oberst spat out dryly, "What if the gambler had cheated, why hasn't the dealer intervened? I am beginning to suspect there may be no dealer, no house. The bodies still lay where they were, the house has vacated this bunker. We are left to our own. Left to rot underground. Comic or not, that is going to be our fate."

"Yes, it is, you know everything," Renard yelped from her corner, jolting all with her sudden noise. "Know all, see all. Without fault, done nothing wrong." She spat phlegm onto the floor, leaving a dark, red mark on the carpeting, then began to play with the muck of it, "I can believe this from a young woman, a woman with no interesting life. But one like you, in war, in university, older. This, I do not believe. You have done wrong. This is deserved for you."

Parisa pleaded, "Please, we are abandoning our task. Please let us return to the answer." Her pleas went unheard. Venom was boiling up again, ruining the sparse good hopes that followed their meager discovery.

Harriet added to the mounting tempest, still clinging onto her rock, "At twenty-five, I am hardly without my own sins, but yes, I would love to hear of yours. I have always held educated men in such regard, I'd love to be proven either right or wrong."

In a jolt, she ripped herself away from Pyotr and attached herself behind Renard. With a feigned pout, she began to ruffle and coil her hair, a smug grin contorting her scorched face. Renard didn't stir, letting her frayed hair be turned into a rat's nest. Pyotr only shook his head. Harriet stuck out her wrist again without losing her smugness, but he didn't budge, nor cease his head shaking. Her smugness evaporated, but she still ground her fingers deeper into Renard's knot of hair.

Dr. Oberst was too sickly and indifferent to properly protest, but not too insensible to forgo responding, "If there is one thing to do that will please you, then let it be done." He spoke only to Renard, "But only if you come back to the table. I will not say anything if you stay huddled in the corner. It isn't gentlemanly to speak down to someone in such a state, and I will die how I lived, properly."

Renard stirred. Paying no mind to her nonconsensual

hairdresser, she hoisted herself up with much struggle, teetered to the table, then collapsed in the chair squarely across from Dr. Oberst. Despite her limpness, her neck and head stored the rest of her strength and vitriol. Her jaw and fists clenched, the muscles twitching at the hinges, and she embarked on her masterful performance of her final hateful leer.

"What is there that you could possibly say to me that I will find pleasant?" she said at last. Dr. Oberst sucked in a breath, and indignance bled into remorse. The hollowness in sallow cheeks drew in and out as his breathing quickened, as if mustering the force to push something from his white-crusted mouth. The remorse was fleeting; he became indignant again.

He studied Renard. Then, he must have acknowledged it. And it certainly brought freedom. He hated her. Nothing else to do but snap the thin wire keeping confession at bay.

"Perhaps some of your suspicions were right. But you also faltered in a proper adjudication. You have all been against me from the start, and never even gave me the benefit of the doubt."

Dr. Gage interrupted, trying to crack through the heavy phlegm and saliva coating his throat, "What are you talking about? No more of this word-buffering, say what you mean or don't waste the oxygen."

Dr. Oberst's face lowered into a harsh violet, "I mean to say you both owe me an apology. I have done nothing wrong. You think that boy drowned because of us. I demand an apology."

"We did defend you though! And I took the beating for it," Harriet called from the side. "We've forgotten about him already, let the issue die."

Dr. Oberst ignored her, but locked onto Renard across from him, silent and seething, "No, I have done nothing wrong, I had no part in Gao's death, so I want an apology from you, Renard. The truth of the matter is I did nothing, it was all Kitagawa. When my attention was turned, trying to figure out something to free us all from this cage, he threw the boy in and clamped the door down. My only fault is I was not quick enough to stop it. I have suffered even more than the boy, I had to sit in all of your hateful presence for, oh I cannot even say how long. A worse fate, don't you think? Rather than a quick death? A death that brought about even more progress. So then, William and Agnes, an apology is in order, I do think. Or else you all will not live to be remorseful."

"A threat, is it?" Dr. Gage coughed, "I never once levied any accusation, yet I find myself now thinking I must do so. Have you just told on yourself?"

Dr. Oberst began to furiously scratch the crust off his eyes, then raked his fingernails through his mustache, "No. You blamed me for things I did when I was seventeen, just as Agnes blamed me for things I was not party to. Thus, if we are all to suffocate beneath ground, I want you both to suffocate absolved of your misplaced hatred or suffocate knowing you were idiotically wrong. We aren't going to escape, I'm not at least, but my conscience is clear, and none of you can say the same."

Dr. Gage flapped his jaw, trying to choose an emotion to settle on, "Just like the girl, you are raving and insane. Oh, why don't you rot in the hallway and leave us all alone?"

"I just might," Dr. Oberst yelled but remained seated. Instead, Renard got to her feet, her jaw locked firmly, her hands gripping her own shoulders, still in an incensed daze. She returned to her corner, without a word. She hunched inward and began to claw her hair out, throwing large clumps over her shoulder.

Parisa scanned the dining room for some semblance of proper distraction. Quite perversely, the room carried a sickly, homely sentiment, expounded by its complete disarray. The carpet was stained and eaten by filth and mold. The bookshelves were bare and picked apart, the previous content stacked around in a chaotic mess. The odor was putrid and hung heavy in the air, which was so dense it was nearly visible. Everything was soiled. A biome of festering bacteria. The hallway was a preferable venue to sit and rot. But it wasn't home. The dining room was home. Complete with angry relatives. And there was no giggling from unseen voyeurs. Not then at least, none that she could hear.

As her cause had been lost, and any hope of returning to their task at hand was moot, she picked up a nearby book. The title in that dyslexic Cyrillic. It was constructed of a thicker paper, and each page only had a spare few words and sentences in some foreign language, complete with brightly colored pictures.

She cautiously turned her head to see Pyotr, who had taken back up a seat at the table, silent and stony as ever. Slowly, she made her way over to him and presented the book. With little interest, he nodded with a small smile. He tapped it, then pointed to Renard. Parisa narrowed her eyes at the book that Renard was clutching to her chest. It was the Chinese picture book that first intrigued Gao. Parisa doubled her eyes back to the Cyrillic book. The same cover, same paper material, likely the same texts, but in two translations.

Clenching the book underarm, she began to root through the stacks and piles of papers and books. Nobody asked, nor likely cared, what she was doing. She found one dictionary, English to French, then French to Japanese, then found two copies of some novels but in Japanese and Chinese. Her face brightened. An idea formed. Perhaps a plan of no help or progress, but it would be merely something to do, and merely a means of drawing Pyotr into a small level of contact. Diligently, she wrote out a couple of random phrases in French with a good variety of nouns and verbs that may be useful. She traced the French words to Japanese, largely ignoring grammar, as most people tend to do.

With the help of punctuation and small amounts of recognition, she then traced some words from Japanese to Chinese in the two copies of the novel. Now set with a crude translation of French to Chinese, she shirked a glance at Renard—a crazed, semi-sentient stumbling block. Surely, Renard was not apt to assist. She wasn't in any mood. She was a shell.

Harriet, who sat with a lazy wildness in her, studied Parisa's every move. Old sentimentality flaring, Harriet got to her feet and violently snatched the book out from under Renard's grasp. The woman shrieked and tried to claw at Harriet for its return.

Harriet's fury won, and she viciously kicked the woman away, subduing her with much unneeded force. Renard tried to get up and win it back out of principle, but her attempts were in vain as an unleashed primal rage railed back down on her. Like a rabid cat dropping a dead mouse before a master, Harriet then presented the prize delicately to Parisa. Accepting the gift given the manner of its accrual was perhaps a cruel thing, but Parisa took it anyway with a sheepish nod of gratitude.

Dr. Gage looked at Harriet, shook his head with a hint of untimely judgment. He made no attempts to reason or chide her, only said, "About time it has finally got to one of us. Brutality will always have a say. Since the dawn of the Hittites, violence always had a vote."

Parisa ignored the rest and refocused on her task for the next couple of hours. Against the off-and-on again ravings of Harriet, the moaning despondency of Renard and Dr. Oberst, and the odd rebuke from Dr. Gage, she kept on. Paying great attention and focus, she meticulously followed her Chinese translation to match the Russian words in the picture book.

She followed the translation back, and after another hour, the entirety of the Russian picture book had a rudimentary French translation. Feeling a dim, if useless, accomplishment, she tried to engage with Pyotr. He remained seated the entire time, no longer quelling Harriet's violent outbursts, only giving it a passing eye. If insanity had gripped him too, it was entirely internal.

She approached him, hoping he would meet her gaze halfway. He did not. Plunging into her initiative, she pointed to some words in the Russian picture book, stoking only mild interest. She pointed to more, hoping that stringing scraps of nouns together, the intent would be made clear. At first, he remained impartial to whatever effort she was making, but as she continued to point things out, her labor finally paid off. Something clicked, and he sat upright, lit up in understanding. It was simple, and the vocabulary was bound to only the couple hundred words found in the picture book. He pointed words back to her, finally shaking off muteness.

After an exhale of spent effort, Parisa finally remarked, "He is doing well."

"Oh? How did you figure that?" Dr. Gage asked. "Fashion yourself a Rosetta stone?"

"I do not know. I think he is staying hopeful. We only have the words in the book, so not much else can be explained, unless we should ask something about family life on a farm."

"Farm...farm..." Renard muttered to herself in the corner, squeezing her stomach. Parisa quickly attempted to give back the Chinese picture book. Renard didn't take it, but kept her arms folded close to her gut, and rocked.

Parisa said, "But with these words, if my translation is accurate, we can ask if he agrees or disagrees with things. It will not be perfect."

Only Harriet responded. "Excellent. Is there a way for us

to translate the words from each room back to him? Maybe there's a way to fasten it all together?"

Gasping and beating her forehead, Parisa cursed her memory, which only cursed her back as she apparently only drew blanks. Flipping through the picture book translations, suddenly it was spitefully obvious. There, among hundreds of other words, lay *Dawn, Fire, Progress, Unjustly, Cast*.

She exclaimed, "We should have done this first! Looked through each book first!"

Somebody beyond the walls scoffed with much indignity, but she didn't hear it.

"Or coincidence, or confirmation bias." Dr. Oberst's voice was thick with mucus and lacking any reverberation. "Don't be too pleased with yourself."

"Farm...farm..." came from Renard again.

"The Greek Symbols, the order. Unjustly Fire Cast Dawn Progress. Is that the truth? How can those words for the 'truth'," Parisa said urgently as she saw the light of rationality leave Harriet again. She gripped onto her shoulders, as though to hold the lucidity in place.

"Dawn of Progress makes sense, surely." Harriet's voice had only a vapor of rationality left, the wildness emerging. "Unjustly Fire. That's strange. Or Fire being Cast down, hmmm. Don't know. Did you tell Pyotr these words are in the book? Tell him to point them out."

Parisa did so. With a mixture of gestures to each door and pantomiming each trap, she pointed to the translated words. His eyes widened in understanding, finally speaking aloud, "*Bezzakonno. Ogne. Brosayutsya. Rassvet. Progressa.*"

Dr. Gage proclaimed, "We must be missing that other Beta, the pattern. The room you two went to on the first day. Go back again. Why didn't we think to do this sooner? The books were here for such a purpose, although a roundabout one. That one man, what's his name, was right. We could have reasoned with everyone so much sooner. What a waste."

Another scoff behind the walls, more audible than permissible. Pyotr's ears twitched. But his attention was shortly diverted.

Renard had climbed her way back to her feet. It took an even greater effort than previously, and she had to rip herself from the ground, heaving up with furniture. Looking at nobody, she padded across the room to the door leading to the kitchen. All watched her, none halted her.

Only once she disappeared into the door, Dr. Gage asked the room, "Well then, should someone see what she intends to do?"

As soon as he spoke, she returned. But only briefly. She picked up a chair, straining under its weight, and carried it back out through the door to the kitchen. Harriet followed her, her head swaying side to side in a rather serpentine manner.

After a couple steps, Pyotr trailed after, but Harriet pushed him away. A silent, rolling anger in the push seized Pyotr in place. He gnawed on his lip and returned to his seat. He was still for a second, then slammed his head down on the table.

"No use. Murder is permitted..." Dr. Gage said.

Parisa pounded on her chest, like trying to break through a sudden shield of ice, "It shouldn't be."

"But somehow it is."

Chapter Twenty-Five

Standing in the kitchen entryway, Harriet watched Renard. The weak woman lifted up the heavy hatch just a little and slid the leg of the chair underneath it. Through the command of physics and mechanics, she was able to pry the cellar open, albeit with all the remaining force left in her. The hatch door fell open with a jarring clang.

Harriet watched and did not interfere at first, but she couldn't help but jeer, "Do us all a favor. Throw yourself in. I say it is your turn."

Paying no attention to the interruption, Renard looked down the cellar, a pained grimace soured her otherwise once-beautiful face. After a deep breath, she looked backward to the young woman, beckoning her over. The grimace melted into a faint, sincere smile, and her eyes drooped to a half-lid.

Surprised, Harriet obeyed, lacking any reason, but stiffened her spine. As she crept closer, she squinted at Renard's neck. It was long and delicate, like a swan, but fine lines illustrated the marks of aging, and the skin was powdery and tactile. Easy to grip and snap. Harriet's hands shook. But she clenched them to her side and stood behind Renard, peering over the crown of her head into the cellar.

Gao's body was green, swollen, and floating listlessly. The

stench was acidic and nauseating. A propulsion of vomit flooded Harriet's mouth, and she looked away to release her sickness.

"To dust I will never return, but maybe sewage. Please close it over me if you can..." Renard said, "I know you want to. I know you wish this. You want to know what it feels like, yes? To be a king? Do it. Consider this a reparation, a gift. A gift given once you promise you will close the hatch over me." Renard kept her smile frozen on her face and gently stretched her hand up to bring the hair out of Harriet's eyes.

A hard gulp gripped Harriet's throat, "I don't know what you are talking about. Are you planning to throw yourself in? Fine, I'll close the hatch over you."

A faint, airy chuckle escaped from Renard, "No, you want to kill me. To be a king. To own another's life, dictate how it ends, to be in that rank of man. You had a taste of it when you beat me, which I do not disagree that it was deserved, but you want to know more. I can smell it. It's in your blood. I've met many like you before, long ago and very recent. Do it. Just please, close the hatch over me, so we can decompose together. Then may we both be satisfied."

Harriet stared down at Renard, wide-eyed and panting hard. Her hands shook. Jolted into action without hesitation or consciousness, they struck out and wrapped themselves around the woman's thin neck. All watching could feel it as Harriet did. The pop and squeeze of the tendons. Renard's nails instinctively dig into her forearm. Fiery sweat dripping down her back. The throat crushing inside itself. The pulse waning into oblivion. Perhaps it took an hour, perhaps it took an instant. As Renard's eyes shuddered closed, Harriet tipped the woman into the abyss. Harriet craned her ear down and sighed with relief when she heard the soft splash.

With a triumphant giggle, Harriet slammed the hatch down again, resealing the awful smell of rancid death, a feat she would never be able to do under other circumstances. No waves or struggles were heard beneath the metal hatch.

Harriet stayed kneeling on top of the Theta, and her throat and hands continued to shake. Another bout of hysteria intruded. A perverse humor possessed her. The shrill giggle bolted from her mouth with no restraint and pierced through the door, down the short passageway, into the dining room. It was so loud and so inhuman that all could hear it.

Heavy drops rained down Harriet's eyes, splattering onto the metal with a sturdy plop. Her laughter continued. Saliva began to stream down her lip to her chin, before reaching the same fate as her tears. She couldn't stop laughing. Then she began to scratch herself like a furious itch tortured her skin. Laughing, she ripped open her blisters and calluses that dotted all around her skin, tearing herself open, pus and blood streaming down onto the floor. Hysteria persisted and she kept on howling.

✳ ✳ ✳

None in the dining room hazarded themselves to check the kitchen. All except Pyotr. Standing in the kitchen doorway, he said nothing and stared at the ground. He waited until the thrush of catharsis subsided and her fit weakened before he went to her. She resembled little more than a hyena, hunched and howling. He did nothing other than sit next to her. Not touching, not talking, not judging. Perhaps it was this steady nature that finally ripped away the fog.

Her voice cracked deep against her shrieking laughs, and her wretched smile dimmed in intensity, "There is nothing left of me."

The Theta held her eyes downward; it would have been too great a task to lift her head to meet her companion. But she didn't need to, he didn't force her.

Waiting through the course of hysteria, he gently raised her up by the shoulders once her temper was docile, and ushered her back, away from the stench.

❋ ❋ ❋

Dr. Gage directed Pyotr to plop Harriet down in the far corner of the room, away from the ordered minds. Harriet did not need to make any excuse or explanation for what happened. They just knew.

Strangely, Dr. Oberst had a look of abject jealousy, as though displeased that Renard didn't provoke him to accompany her to her death. But perhaps it was for the better; his body was at war with itself.

Against the grinding, constricting flesh of his neck, he tried to give a voice to his thoughts, "So, is that it then? Are we done? Finished? I'm free?"

Dr. Gage said, "No, no, not yet. That one room Miss Shahidi mentioned before was locked. We need to try again, try everything again. If that is fruitless, then we may submit to death."

Parisa looked around, skirting her eyes around Harriet; only she and Pyotr were fit to do anything. She nodded, "I will go. Alone, if I have to. I feel it will be revealed to me. Indeed, if there is a Beta to be found, then we are not done." Uneasily, she stood up and took firm strides towards the head door. Someone tugged at her skirt.

Harriet looked up with bloodshot eyes, a crusty mouth, and all orifices deep sunken in reddened skin. "Let me go with you. We left together first, and please forgive my mental capacity. I know I am failing, but I can't be left to dissolve by myself."

Parisa looked at her, and her stomach groaned with an ache. The rotation of Harriet's sanity and neurosis was accelerating. And the obvious risk was unspoken but understood. But in the face of destruction, there was little reason to inhibit any help. Parisa nodded uneasily.

With relief, Harriet nodded her gratitude, got to her feet, and softly squeezed her hand. A small apology, a plead for mercy. Parisa was all too ready to provide it. Pyotr stood up in turn, snatching up the picture book, hugging it tight to his chest.

Dr. Oberst coughed out, "You know something, I think I should go too, if I stay seated, I may forget to breathe entirely." He shakily stood up, his knees buckling under the burden of his weight, grinning to himself. "Unless you protest solitude, Gage?"

"No choice, now do I? Go on then. If I am struck dead in this seat, then so be it. Like it would make any difference. Go on then, go find your own escape. Let me sit here, let me remember Bernadette…"

Pyotr's body seized, and he gripped tightly onto Harriet's elbow. Dr. Oberst lumbered behind them like some monster but was docile enough. The doctor looked down onto Pyotr, and gave a smirk, a paltry attempt to appease, but it was pointless regardless. He was to tag along against any protest. Parisa and Harriet forged ahead, and Pyotr lingered next to the trailing Dr. Oberst, with a gaze fixed like a hawk.

✳ ✳ ✳

Opening back up the door, the hallway felt colder and damp, as though some imaginary window had let morning dew mold in the corners. There was no draft, but a dull groan spun the hallway like a ghost. Parisa took the first couple of steps into the hallway. Against good discretion, she stuck her hand behind her, patiently waiting for Harriet to grasp it like she had done many times before. At first her request went unanswered, but then Harriet's cold and clammy hand gripped hers. Parisa tugged her in closer. Unexpectedly, Harriet wrapped a sweaty, curdled arm around her shoulders.

Harriet whispered, "I will even go first in if you want. Please, forgive me, let me be of use again. I can only keep my mind and the rest of me when it's at work."

Parisa responded, "No, we can go together. We may be heading into death, but we can go together."

Harriet sighed, and rubbed sanity back into her temples, "Together. Like day one. Safer together. You're right. You've always been right."

And so, the two walked forward towards the last room; Pyotr and Dr. Oberst slowly following.

Chapter Twenty-Six

Shortly, they met with the iron door with the engraved hound. It was such a simple door, yet it felt so heavy and grand, and malicious. Parisa gave Harriet's hand a squeeze, a warning, then reached for the knob. Unlocked. With the gentlest effort, Parisa opened it.

A stupor followed. The only appropriate reaction. A large domed church. Larger than the observation room, larger than the boiler room, probably larger than the rest of the bunker. Large and ornate. Ornate beyond immediate belief. And, for once, it smelled nice. A deep incense. Sandalwood.

Rows and rows of wooden pews lined up to a pulpit, befit with a large crystalline podium with delicate golden embellishments. The stand was gargantuan, fit only for a Goliath pastor, at least three meters tall. Centrally carved into the crystal lay the gold Beta. The symbol captured all of their attention at once, but it was quickly ripped away by the extravagant glassworks that paneled the concrete walls of the chapel. On the back wall, behind the pulpit, hung an intricate depiction of men sleeping in a huddle in a cave. A large beast, a dog of sorts, guarded their slumber. The fangs were drawn, dripping with gore, but the eyes remained pleasant, its posture was friendly and outstretched. A strange animal.

"The Companions of the Cave…" Parisa said, "It is a story in the Quran. Why? Why in such a chapel, the other arts are Christian in nature, I think."

The right wall was another man who was casting pearls downward, a dog was sitting at his feet in a snarl. The man gripped in his left hand, and with his right hand threw the pearls, which spiraled into dust. The man had a sinister grimace, as though conjuring some evil deed. On the left wall was a stag being ripped to shreds by hounds, similar to the painting in the dining room. Its face bleating and desperate, the hounds tearing flesh from its ribcage. Each dog had a red mark—the same engraved on their backs. The glasswork that constructed the deep, bloody gashes of the stag glinted with rubied crystals, gorgeously polished and lustered, but the subject was so realistically agonized it stung to gaze at it for any length of time.

Making quick work of the room, the wooden pews were upended and reset. Just nakedness, no holy texts in sight.

Parisa scoured the pulpit. The podium housed nothing in a rather blasphemous fashion. It was just the four of them, the pews, the podium, and the artwork. Nothing else. They all attached their hands to their hips, spun around, and the beauty of the chapel quickly faded to a facade of sarcasm.

"Latin? There must be something here. There's the symbol… where's the phrase?" Harriet snapped and then stifled a giggle.

"We are missing something, or it's hidden," Dr. Oberst coughed out. Flopping in a pew, he wiped down his glasses and let out an exasperated sigh. "Why can this room not be any easier? It is the last after all."

Harriet gargled phlegm into her throat, spat it on the ground, and said, "Maybe that is the thing, it was locked before, it has some other importance, something new. We are trying to speak *truth*, right? This is the bunker chapel, that is what it looks like, there's something there. Some connections. Why was this locked before? Because it was meant to be seen last. Why last…" She took a seat next to him, resting her chin on her fist, her eyes wild. He used failing energy to scoot away.

Harriet muttered, "The motif here, scenes from the Quran, but in a chapel. It was locked, hidden. Let me think. The rooms have been more literal than we have been giving credit for. What could be literal here? Why is there no phrase? Perhaps this is where we are meant to speak the *truth*? But no, there's a Beta. There must be something here."

Pyotr walked extremely close to the cave's stained-glass, almost pressing his nose against it. The glasswork looked almost fuzzy up close, as opposed to the crystal-clear lines of the other two walls. He tapped on it. It echoed. He began to knock furiously with his bruised knuckles. A deep echo.

Parisa made her way over in a hurry, doing the same, "It is hollow, or no, that is not correct word. It is a fake wall, something lay beneath. Pyotr. You have done it! We may be free finally. We are close. So close!"

Parisa pulled him into a hug. He returned a limp pat on the back before he freed himself and pointed to words in the picture book.

"Animals. Animal and…sheep…I think…" Parisa spoke the image aloud. She tried to render the shrug and blink ritual, but without practice, it failed. Pyotr frowned, whipped around, and pointed to Harriet.

"He probably thinks the animals are important here," Harriet called out. "Well, is the exit on the other side of the glass wall then? Is that our means of escape? Are we done?" She hobbled to her feet but soon collapsed again.

Parisa huffed, knocking on the glass eight more times, "Only way to see."

With the violence and energy of the turbulent first winds

of a storm, Parisa grasped the podium and smashed a small hole into the center of the glass wall. The strength was surprising, unprecedented, but above all, unrelenting. Through repeated bashes, each growing in intensity, the small hole grew a modicum bigger but sent splinters up the glass.

Something lay on the other side, at first promising, then abjectly disappointing. Just another concrete wall, but the beginnings of another painting winked at them from beyond the jagged glass.

"We are going to have to rip shards out by hand," Parisa said, and wrapped a bit of cloth from her sleeve around her hand and yanked a shard down. The glass was tempered into layers. The serrated edge ripped through her cloth instantly, easier than a hot knife through butter.

A deep, red gash dug through her hand. Dark blood began to ooze. Yet it did not sting. A surgical slice. It fed the fervor. The end was close. So close. Tantalizingly close. Skin continued to shred, yet glass continued to splinter and crack away.

Harriet swaggered to her feet and tried to hobble over, "Wait. Let me help. Wait a moment."

Parisa acquiesced to the budding mania, "No. None in my way. I will be quicker. Let me do it all. Quickly. We may be free at last. Finally. So close."

Impulsively, thoughtlessly, ecstatically, Parisa ripped the shards down, creating a twinkling shimmer of hard rain. The showers of glass dug into her palms and hands. But it didn't hurt. Out loud, she told herself it didn't hurt.

Pyotr copied her bashing, but couldn't match her haste or her vigor, nor her wanton disregard for the sharp debris.

Dr. Oberst remained seated, a useless supervisor. A resentful, useless supervisor. Resentful because Pyotr dared to cast an eye back, as though to silently mock him into raising to his feet, knowing damn well Dr. Oberst was incapable of such an activity.

Parisa released a gruff cry. A shard fastened at the base. Five tugs at it. Spitefully, it endured, already slickened with blood. So, she began to kick at it, piercing through her silken slippers. Only then did it snap off, yet the shard won a slight concession, grinding a deep puncture into the sole of her foot.

But that was no matter, the lower half of the concrete wall lay exposed. It was hard to decipher what it was, but a first guess implied something gruesome and gory happening on a battlefield. There were grassy plains, hooves of some kind, and red splattered about—maybe painted blood, maybe drawn from Parisa and Pyotr.

"I have to knock down glass from the top," Parisa said through pants and gasps, wiping sweat off her forehead. Blood smeared her face, and her hands were in tatters. A trifling bother. She beckoned for Pyotr to set the podium upright again. Then, she had him hoist her to stand on it. With an outstretched hand and a precarious hop, she grazed the ceiling. A triumphant laugh, and she began to bang her fists against the top sheet of glass.

Harriet weakly called, "Oh God, please be careful."

Parisa flapped her hand behind her and let out a desperate groan. She continued to knock the shards down. Hopping higher and higher, her feet teetering close to the edge of the podium.

Glass rained down. Pyotr stepped back to avoid the little daggers. Finally, she knocked all the glass away from the central portion of the top. The first blush of the prize. One word uncovered in totality: *vinculum*.

The central strip of imagery peeked beyond the double bluff—a cow being slaughtered by a still hidden figure. Parisa, pleased with her good work, gleefully hopped down from the podium, straight onto a bed of needle-like debris.

She prompted Pyotr to shift the stand to the left. Hoisting her way back up, she continued to ravage and rip at the glasswork. While the pain had grown dull, the blood loss didn't. Parisa grew pale, and her speed began to rapidly wane. Yet, she kept on. Clashing and bashing, she broke and ripped even more of the left side down until it too became glass hail. With two-thirds of the concrete wall exposed, the first portion of the phrase made itself known.

Amicus qui numquam vinculum rumpet

Parisa, tired yet fevered, jumped down carelessly and eagerly made Pyotr move the podium to the right.

Only then, Dr. Oberst decided to put himself to some use, "*Vinculum*. Chains. The same as other rooms, the theme continues. *Amicus*... friends. *Numquam*, never. *Rumpet*... I'm not too sure... I don't know. It is so hard to think, impossible to remember."

Harriet tried to spurn him on, flapping her hands in a daze, "Friend who never chain.... Never chain what? What could make sense? Wait, *rumpet*... seems familiar. Other rooms talked a lot about chains. *Confracti*, *fregereti*, I don't know I can't remember how to pronounce them. *Rumpet*, is it another work for breaking?"

"*Rumpet*.... Yes... must be breaking... The friend who will never break the chains. This is my guess." Dr. Oberst wheezed and moaned. He tilted forward, leaning his head against the pew. "Who is the friend then, that must be the answer. Should you tell her... Tell Parisa she can stop."

"No. There is more. I can see it," Parisa called out. She balanced on her tiptoes on the podium, fervently ripping away glass. All were slick with sweat and blood: hands, feet, the shards, the podium. Pyotr shot a nervous glance at Harriet as he weathered the downpour of shards and stood beneath her with arms outstretched.

"Parisa, be careful. You're teetering. You're going to fall,"

Harriet cried, then shrieked and clutched her head.

Parisa flapped her hand behind her again, and her energy was reborn. Her little hops turned into full jumps. Her little pounds against the glass turned into grips, forcing the glass to snap and fall down with her. The podium began to rock. Pyotr waffled from left and right, trying to position himself beneath her. But there was no true 'beneath her'. Teetering left, right, forward, backward, the podium became a dreidel. Parisa paid no mind, too close to knocking the last bit of glass from the wall. One last chunk remained that obscured the last word on the second half of the Latin.

The scenery unveiled another violent display. Cows being pitilessly slaughtered by jeering men in dark robes, each cow branded with the red Greek letters. Sticks and stones were painted at the feet of each cow, constructing a bizarre symbol. A cross. Then, the illusion of an intertwined hound.

Pyotr saw it first—struck dumb. Without thinking, he stretched his arm around his shoulder to feel at the raised edges of the divine marking on his back. And then the inevitable happened.

A yelp. A crash. A squelch. Parisa tumbled. Skull against cement. Eyes shuttering, teeth chattering, then stillness, then an immediate back-arching spasm. The glitter of glass rain followed.

She let out a loud, inhuman retch, then began to convulse violently. Neck muscles bulging and tensing. Her irises disappeared, and the whites became red. Blood pooled out the base of her skull.

Harriet shrieked, jolted upright, and tried to run to the pulpit, but her legs lost coordination, and she crashed and sprawled along the ground. With a fading grunt, she began to crawl like she was deep in a mud trench. Dr. Oberst roused in turn, and each step produced a wheeze.

"Don't touch her," Dr. Oberst cautioned Harriet, who

hazarded to grab Parisa's face with her hands.

"What can we do?"

Despite Harriet's frenzy, her face began to twist into a sick grin, and chuckling started to rattle her ribcage. Another manic fit inbound. "Dr. Gage. We must go get Dr. Gage. He will know. Head injury, he should know, right?"

Dr. Oberst said quietly, a smile began twitching up his face, "Maybe yes, go get him. Yes, brain injuries are severe."

Pyotr clawed at the hem of his shirt, and his legs shook, watching the life fade from Parisa. Strange groans tumbled from Pyotr's tremoring mouth. Articulate groans. Self-castigations, known by the slow and coarse gurglings of it.

Harriet chattered, "Alright, fine, alright, alright, fine, I'll go get him then. I can go. I get him. I get Gage. I get him now, fine, no worries, not a problem. I go. I go now."

Swaying back and forth, she used momentum to get back upright but seized in place. Strength, in its entirety, deserted Harriet. She fell back down to her knees hard. The sick grin was fastened. Her body ran dry.

She crawled to cower over Parisa, running her hand into Parisa's scalp, "No, can't, sorry, can't. Can't be me. Can't do it. Get up. Now. Get up. Do math. You can!"

Dr. Oberst slapped Harriet across the face, "What are you doing, girl? Go get him, run. Now." He yanked her up by the scruff and shoved her towards the door. In a daze, she ambled away, bumping into each pew. At the doorway, she keeled over briefly, let out a siren howl, and in a limp, she left.

Dr. Oberst was now alone with Pyotr, and the resentment bubbled to the surface.

Chapter Twenty-Seven

Pyotr could only stand there, ashamed and stupefied, watching Parisa's body go cold. He hardly noticed Dr. Oberst reaching up towards him.

A grip around his shirt. A firm yank. Pyotr's skull met the ground. Dr. Oberst's hands met with his throat, his thumbs right on top of the bony bump.

Pyotr did not cry out. No shock. No pain. Not even confusion. Just acceptance. Just staring up at Dr. Oberst.

Dr. Oberst was seething. His plaque-encrusted teeth bared. His saliva splattered onto Pyotr's forehead. Pyotr let him seethe.

Dr. Oberst was wholly incapable of doing any real damage, which only aggravated his hatred. He squeezed and squeezed on the bony throat and even spat hot bile into Pyotr's eyes. Pyotr did nothing. Not even blink. Laying on a bed of bloody shards. Almost peaceful. The murderous furor whimpered and ceded to a striking embarrassment.

Dr. Oberst's yellow, greasy skin began to sweat feverishly.

With a grunt, he tried to pitch his embarrassment back into anger, "Why can't you die, you stupid, mute, dumb child. Stupid dimwit. You think you can intimidate me? You don't, you can't. You'll kill me, I know it. Then, I'll do it to the doctor. He deserves it, like you. Deserves it the most even. I was a boy, too, once. A boy. Stupid boy, and also mute. Nothing to say. A boy once too, how could he not see it?"

His anger momentarily swelled again, yet apexed without conclusion. Pyotr even seemed to relax into his strangulation, letting the bile roll off his face without interruption.

So, the rage broke. No immediate satisfaction, no quelled bloodlust. Vacant. The snarl left his face. He released his grip but stayed kneeling on top of the boy. Then, a sob shook his chest.

"Yes, I was there. The kitchen. I did it. I helped," he uttered down onto Pyotr. "I did it. They were all right. But… could you blame me? It seemed so necessary, so necessary at the time. How could I be judged?"

He began to shake. His cracked lips trembled, and he finally fell back onto his haunches. He grabbed Pyotr up, limply dusted him off as a grim apology, and began to force his confession onto him.

"There were a hundred solutions, a hundred ways to bring him back up. But it was easier that way. And better. It felt better. It happened to me. It should happen to others…"

Despite everything, Pyotr patted Dr. Oberst on the shoulder, and the man began to cry.

"How did you do it? You can't even talk? Yet, yet, why would they choose you over me? You don't talk, but you matter more than me. You dumb, mute thing. I was a boy too, once," Dr. Oberst continued. In his final throes, he switched from English to German, both of which were lost to Pyotr. But at least it felt good on the tongue, "My last words, deaf ears. What can I possibly say that would be worth saying? There's no way to articulate it…"

Harriet's voice rang down the hallway, "Dr. Gage fell back into his chair! Oh God, I don't know if he is going to last much longer. Can we bring her over there to him? What can we do?"

"Nothing. We can do nothing," Dr. Oberst mumbled to himself, and he gripped onto Pyotr.

Compelled by some spiritual whim, he clung onto the Soviet, resting all of his weight onto his bony shoulders. Silently, he wept. Pyotr patted him on the back, shrugged, then gave him a nod. Dr. Oberst's sob broke into a chuckle, and he nodded back. Slowly, he brought his hands back up to Pyotr's neck and gave it a playful squeeze, as though his prior murderous furor was little more than a shared joke.

It was interrupted by a hard bash against the doctor's head. Neither had noticed Harriet stalk up behind them.

Her hysteria flared into something beyond rage. She gripped Dr. Oberst's skull with her clammy hands and began to bash his fragile cranium against the ground.

She sputtered, "I saw. I saw you strangle him. I'll kill you."

Pyotr defended his would-be murderer, prying her fingers away, furrowing the doctor into his chest against Harriet's righteous indignation. She still struggled to bring her brutality to completion, but Pyotr kept the doctor locked in close.

Protected by his almost-victim, Dr. Oberst began his comprehensible confession.

"Yes. Don't know why, I wanted Semyonov dead. I'm sorry. Sorry. I think it will be you three. It won't be me. I won't live past this. I know it. And I didn't want him to live as well, but he will." He shook so hard, even Pyotr struggled to keep a grip around him.

Harriet still spat, "No, you won't. You don't deserve it. If the gas doesn't take you. I will bash your head in."

Slowly, Dr. Oberst turned his head upwards, "I'll hold you to that."

Amicus qui numquam vinculum rumpet.

Through the thick sludge clouding Dr. Oberst's mind, looming death awakened his focus.

He muttered, "Is the master to be held responsible? The friend who will never break the chains, is the master to be held responsible?"

Parisa's lungs let out the death rattle. The Italian Peacock made the call. The Senegalese obeyed.

Vapors began to pour into the chapel, thick and hot. With urgency, Dr. Oberst ripped himself away from Pyotr and gripped Harriet's face, shaking her head with failing force,

"Harriet. Remember this. *The friend who will never break the chains is the master to be held responsible.* Restructure your thinking. The masters are the cult, and they are grateful to us. The German novel. By my seat. Look through it. Remember all of that if you still want everyone else to carry on. They are a grateful cult. The truth of why we are here goes in hand with why they are grateful. That must be it. I promise you that I won't wake up, so you must remember."

Harriet didn't have the time, nor the energy, to respond. She just spat on the ground, shoved the doctor away, then crawled over to Parisa, furling against her.

Holding onto consciousness a little longer against the torment of the drug, Dr. Oberst yanked Pyotr's ear in close with a grip to the nape and muttered more last confessions to Pyotr. As the gas carried off the other two into darkness and himself to death, Dr. Oberst kept his mouth to Pyotr's ear.

❋ ❋ ❋

They woke back up at the dining room table. The three of them. Surprisingly, Dr. Gage awakened first and immediately attempted to return to slumber once he noticed the absence of Parisa.

Pyotr became conscious next. He kept his head on the

table. He picked at his scabs. He sighed. He gnawed on his lips. He did nothing else. Then, Harriet grunted, alert. She was silent for all of seven seconds, and then she let out a cackle. The cackle morphed into a giggle, which melted into a mutter, which melted into muteness.

Dr. Gage gently inquired, "What became of Parisa? Brain hemorrhage? From the fall in the chapel?"

Harriet nodded, whispering something unintelligible that even the native English speakers observing behind the wall had no clue what it was.

Dr. Gage murmured to himself, "I should not have awoken from the gas. When I was needed, my body failed. I should have not awoken."

Pyotr shook Harriet's shoulder. A blink, a nod, a shaky twitch of the mouth. Then, he mooed.

Begrudgingly, Harriet obliged, "The friend who will never break the chains is the master to be held responsible. That was on the wall behind a false wall. Parisa ripped down the glass at a great cost. She said it was at first some parable from the Quran. Some companions in a cave with a guard dog. The other walls, a stag being eaten alive by hounds, and then some wizard doing magic. On the wall behind the glass, there were cows being murdered by some more wizards. What do you make of that?"

Pyotr gestured to his back in a frenzy.

"Oh yes, I suppose that may be important. The glasswork had our tattoos. The Beta was on the cows," Harriet said plainly, as if the subject no longer interested her. She, vacant and bereft of any life, drifted her hand down the table, snapped up the German occultist novel, and flung it at Dr. Gage, "Oberst said this is important. Something about the masters being the cult and they're happy for some godforsaken reason."

"What's the reason for that suspicion?"

"How should I know? He died a loon," she said with an angry yawn.

Dr. Gage flipped through it, marked his pleasure with a weary sigh, then did something remarkable. He stood up.

The cane groaned under the strain of his weight. He swayed and swooned on his feet, always a moment's notice from toppling over. He spoke, his voice coming deep within his gut, "My German is rudimentary, but I saw a confirming chapter. The Companions of the Cave. Seven people protected in a cave, protected by a dog. Then a depiction of a hunt—a deer being ravaged by dogs. Then, casting omens, the dog being a creature of darkness as depicted in the more occult faiths. But it is the cows, that is what intrigues me. Why the cows are being slaughtered, that is the question."

Slowly, he ambled about the room. His brain churning against fatigue and against the drugs, "The cows... must they be separate? Separate from the dogs, hidden behind a veil of glass. And the Latin, it is a yes or no answer. This is different."

"But why? Is there any good in thinking on it? From what I have seen, no," Harriet said. "The bunker has won."

Chapter Twenty-Eight

A mute hour ticked by.

Harriet continued to shred the scabs off her skin. Dr. Gage's chin wobbled, and he picked through the cultist texts. Pyotr ground his forehead onto the floor.

Harriet murmured at long last, "Parisa and Dr. Oberst, they died in the same room, only perhaps an hour from each other. Those two were incomparable except for the place of death. One good, one villainous. If they deserved such a fate, then so do I. I should die, here, beneath the ground. If I don't, I will lose the rest of my mind at last."

Dr. Gage said, "You are letting your mind be lost. Wrangle it back in, blast it. Wrangle it back in, or it is an insult to the deceased."

"Wrangle?" Harriet said, her nose scrunching, "Wrangle... I was wrangled...I was drugged...then I was wrangled... wrangled by the Swede who leant me a pocket dictionary on the boat... at the shore...he bought me water...not just a Swede...he had one directing him...an old man...a mafioso man. Italian grandpa, I guessed."

"A Swede?" Dr. Gage grumbled, "A Swede... I recall the fuzziest recollection. Given a cigar at the bus stop. I left my tobacco sleeve at home. My last memory. A Swede gave me a cigar…My God, Kitagawa was right. A cultist had a nose in my business. Good news. We are close! So close!"

As though prompted, Pyotr got to his feet and weakly sauntered over to the door that led to the observation room. The gas had ripped away any lingering mind-body calibration, and he moved like a drunkard. He tried to pry open the door. Fastened tight. Another door yanked. Fastened even tighter. Bolted inside the cramped and musty dining room, which stunk of flesh rot. This worried Pyotr, excited Dr. Gage, and didn't move Harriet.

"We are truly close. Our captors know it, the truth is close," Dr. Gage wheezed, "Speak the truth. What is the truth? What is the missing piece? Think with me girl. With my aged brain and your crazed one, together we may forge the answer."

Harriet sighed with every ounce of reluctance in her body but acquiesced, "Well, chains and masters are appropriate in the chapel, it being a subject of religion and all. But a yes or no wouldn't do for an answer, not that I can think. Yes, unjustly… No unjustly… I don't know, the two Beta symbols wouldn't make sense."

"Read out them all, Harriet, every answer we have discerned," Dr. Gage asked and attempted to lean forward to brute force some sense into her through sheer will alone but began to gag so violently he slunk back into his seat.

Harriet choked out, "Let's see again. Unjust, Cast, Fire, Dawn, Progress. Together, these must make some sort of truth to be spoken. I think we agreed that *dawn of progress* would be a natural connection, as well as *cast into fire*, but the first bit makes no sense, as well as the whole. I don't know, my memory fails." She returned to silence.

"The whole… the whole…" Dr. Gage's watery, rumbling voice became fluid, "That's it. We are missing the whole. We are trying to find some truth, and we have been too granular.

We must look at the whole, at ourselves. The reason why we are here. Us in particular. Why us? You asked it yourself, Harriet. Why us? Why one person from a smattering of countries around the globe. Altogether, disregarding nothing. Why the terrain maps…You! Boy! Pyotr. Take your seat."

Pyotr plopped down and promptly began to claw at his rug of hair. Dr. Gage shoved the maps from the navigation room in front of him. Dr. Gage pointed to the USSR, "Mark it. Russia. Yes? Understand? X on Russia."

Handing over a pen. Pyotr obliged the request, placing an X over the USSR. Dr. Gage continued, "France, Italy, Germany, mark it." Pyotr did so, and then took the liberty of marking the UK, the US, Yugoslavia, and Persia. He drew in two crude circles on the side for Japan and China.

"There it is! The progress," Dr. Gage exclaimed in a voice so loud it shook Harriet from her sullenness.

"What do you mean?"

"I mean to say, girl, that the progress is directed pointedly. These nations. These are us. The truth is what is happening now, to us, and is the truth of the nations. This bunker, this fire, this is the inferno."

"We are in hell?"

"No, no child, not literally, figuratively. Hence the religious imagery, hence the Latin, hence the philosophy. Blast it all. It is us referred to in the riddles. Not some abstract militia, not some grand idea about the state of mankind. Us. The chains. We see something the masters cannot about our homes. These terrain maps have our homelands on them. One of us from each homeland. We see the progress of our homes, the destinies manifest!"

"The masters…the cult…the captors," Harriet mumbled, "Our payment out of purgatory, friend that has broken the chain. I cannot possibly see how that relates to us, and the solutions have been more literal, have they not been?"

Dr. Gage grunted in his seat as the winds left his sails, and age knotted his joints. Harriet sat at the table drumming her fingers, gazing intently into nothing. Pyotr leapt to his feet, hopped in place with a strange, zealous expression, then dug back into the picture book, settling on an image of a cow.

"Yes, the cows were being slaughtered," Harriet nodded her head with undue apathy. Thus, Pyotr committed to an awkward charade. He gathered up pencils, then dropped them. He did it again. Then again. Then again. Each time, he looked to her for some revelation to strike her. No such thing occurred. She clapped him on regardless.

After five minutes of the game, she asked, "Dr. Gage, what do you think he is doing?"

"Hmmmm, gathering firewood perhaps? Dropping the firewood? No, maybe not so literal. I do not know, some ritual of sorts?"

Harriet sighed. "A ritual that may relate to cows, or more so the slaughter of cows?"

Pyotr gathered up and dropped the pencils again, making a marked display of counting each one and sectioning off pencils into groups. He pointed to the picture of the cow, and then to himself. Harriet clapped again, which spurred on a more frantic gathering and dropping of the pencils.

Harriet said, fighting back the onslaught of brewing mania, "He is a cow? No, not right. A cow and a bunch of pencils…"

Pyotr gave up and tried a different pantomime. He resumed a stance reminiscent of the old man on the wall, the one with the dog at his feet, conducting magic. Again, he pointed to the picture of the cow.

"So, a wizard, pencils, cows, and himself." Dr. Gage's eyes traced the movements of the pencils, then fumbled through the text, "Casting lots. That is what he is doing, casting lots, as is common among the superstitious peasantry. Ritualistic cattle slaughter. Fortune telling."

In frustration, Pyotr cried out, then ripped his shirt off, exposing the back marking. He then dropped the pencils while holding the stance of the man in the painting. And just then, it happened. An arrow in the dark. An arrow shot by neurosis. A crazed affliction bearing a crazed speculation.

"Restructure our thinking," Harriet jolted. "We are wrong. About the whole. About the truth. Never a ransom kidnapping. Never an insult. Never a punishment. An opportunity. An opportunity to become a king!"

Harriet began to cackle, ripping hair out, a perverse ecstasy, "We came in with a stupid assumption. A self-pitying one. Like a pawn. But no. Now. Now I think like the master. The master is grateful to us."

It went silent, only wheezing breath disturbed the stifling air. Another arrow in the dark.

Harriet warbled, "The answer to the chapel. It's been everywhere. Dogs. Dogs are the friend who will never break the chain, the dogs so marked to be important. Dogs are there, always protective. The dogs look over the ritual of cattle slaughter. The wizard, the master, cannot be held responsible. No. It is the dogs. Those entrusted with the ritual. Cattle are the ones being slaughtered. They are the victims of fire. Protecting, observing, foreseeing. Evil or good, they are the first barrier, the first victim of the fires. The dogs see the dawn. They see the progress. The cows, though, the cows maybe something else."

Dr. Gage frantically thumbed through more pages, "Haruspicy. The slaughter of cattle, the examination of their organs for divination. These rooms, the cows, picked apart."

With frenzy, Harriet cried, "This is the divination! This is our opportunity, between masters and fire! And they are grateful to us."

Dr. Gage groaned out, face buried in the book, "The divination... meant to speak the truth. This is no haruspicy. No. The divination from the dogs. Here it is! The stages of the divination! The first stage: Casting. Then Observing. Then Divining. Or, as the founders of such rituals would call it: *Ballo, Theoreo, Manteuomai*. Beta, Theta, Mu. Together, they make a cynomancy."

Harriet began flapping around, "Dr. Gage, I know it. The rooms are ordered by their stage, and so are the answers. Unjustly, Dogs are Cast into Fire for the Dawn of Progress."

She waited. Nothing happened.

She began to ghoulishly smirk, "That's not the truth. That's the final prompt. The prompt that begs towards the truth. The truth of why we are here. And I know the truth. I have the masters' lucidity. We are the dogs of the cynomancy in flesh. We are fortune-telling. Right now. In these rooms. That's why they are grateful to us. We are going through hell for a prophecy."

She screeched again, staring right into the mirror, so unnecessarily loudly, "That's it then? This is a fortunetelling ritual? All you there behind the walls, we are your dogs?"

The Italian Peacock blew a sigh of relief, then made that long-awaited call to release the final dosage.

A deep groaning shook the dining chamber. The metallic walls reverberated, as if some slumbering beast awoke deep within the Earth. Then, a faint hiss. The gas began to trickle in from the vents.

Dr. Gage covered his mouth with his sleeve with a dire panic. Harriet's jaw slackened, and she jolted upright. With a yelp, she darted towards the lead door and began to pound on it, yank on it, thrust herself against it.

A steely sound emerged from the vents, permeating the

air. It was at first not discernible as anything human, rather some scrapes and groans from industrial machinery. But then, it materialized.

Harriet felt along her back, feeling the edges of the mark, and she fell serene. The darkness shuddered her eyes. Vision failing, but hearing still holding on for life, she heard a wailing, like there had been some invisible eruption of celebration and congratulations. Their cheers and congratulations. The unseen ghosts celebrating. Then, another deep groan and scrape. A release and a gush of air.

Pyotr held on the longest, his constitution withstanding only mere seconds more. He tried to crawl his way to Harriet to jostle life back into her chest, yet the room grew hazier and distant. Unreal. Swirling around. His head lolled back and forth and he blinked erratically. A stern voice demanded that he submit, rest, and give up. It spoke Russian. In such an altered state, he had no choice but to obey. Not a second after his eyes shuttered closed, the lead door finally opened.

The Proctor permitted the scribe observers to cease their transcriptions and informed them that no mention of the leadership's monikers was permitted in the finalized report. One weary scribe made the note to himself – *Replace 'Italian Peacock' with Proctor, replace 'Tatar-Slav' with Executor, replace 'cult' with 'industry'*

It officially concluded.

Chapter Twenty-Nine

The pounding in her skull wrenched Harriet out of subconsciousness. Shuddering her eyes open, blinding light burned her sockets. Natural light, bright and striking, unfiltered, not from some dusty bulb.

Harriet shot up, finding herself sitting atop a massive over-cushioned bed in the middle of a large, over-ornate room. The throbbing in her head prevented her from sudden movements, as did a refreshed acute sense of fear. With a slight instinctive twitch of her spinal column, she felt her hair hang loose down her back. No longer greasy and matted, rather soft and thoroughly combed. She smelled her skin. No odor. Just faint detergent. Her tattered red linen dress was gone, swapped for a dense cotton sleeping gown. Fresh bandages, properly dressed, were plastered up and down her arm and other parts of her skin. After the crushing pain ceased in her skull, she slipped her bare feet onto the floor, her ankles creaking and cracking. There was a window on the side wall; wide open, a breeze wafting in. A distant rumble vibrated the air.

Harriet scrambled as fast as her rickety joints would allow to confirm reality or confirm self-deception. She stuck her head out through the window, and at once was met with the lofty view of a street. There were people outside, real, anonymous people, dressed for the day's occasions. A deep breath in. The odor was fresh yet carried that same smoky undertone of city air. She pinched herself: a dream, or purgatory. Either way, a welcome relief, but she would have preferred purgatory.

Then, a heavy creak ruptured her moment of semi-lucid serenity. Whipping around, she was met with an old woman standing in the oak doorway. Carrying the air of refined proto-aristocracy, a relic from years past, she was around seventy, clad in dark velvet finery, and ordained with pearls and silver. She held a large silver platter, home to a cup and a parcel.

Waiting for the first blush of astonishment to die, she spoke in a surprisingly robust, Germanic voice, "Yes, I presume you believe this all to be some vision, some dream? I can say this is very real. Please go sit back down on the bed. I would not want you to collapse, Miss Foster. Please sit."

Doing as she was told, Harriet took a seat at the foot of the bed, facing the woman. Questions or protests, or any other means of verbal defense, felt silly and futile at best, and embarrassing at worst. The woman appeared appreciative of this, but her odd expression, fixed with trained neutrality, would leave almost anyone guessing, and she quickly walked forward, placing the platter on Harriet's lap.

"Here you will find some tea. Earl Grey, I was told it's your favorite. A decent choice. And here is your dress, washed and mended. If you prefer, I can send for something else to be purchased for you. Go on now, drink up. I will not rush you, but know the others have been awake for ninety minutes already and patiently wait for you. So, be cooperative, do not dawdle. But, ah, listen to me, hurrying you against my own words. Our physicians say you may still be fragile, both in mental and physical capacity, so you must not exceed the limits of your faculties."

Drowning in a waking daze, Harriet grasped her cup but did not drink it. She only blankly stared at the elderly woman, her jaw slack, her shoulders drooped as low as ligaments would allow. The woman sighed and shook her head, "I cannot answer any of the more pointed questions you may have, but only the general. Please ask if it will help you get moving."

Cognition found its place with Harriet again, and she asked through a rusted voice, "Who are you? Where am I? What is going on?"

"Brigitte. Zürich. For all else, you must come before the presiding Proctor. The Proctor will not repeat himself, so he waits for all to join. Go on then, drink your tea, put on your dress, make yourself presentable. Hurry up now, don't be rude."

Harriet did nothing but grip her tea and stare. Brigitte, with gentle exasperation, wrapped her hand around Harriet's grip and forcefully lifted it to her mouth. Most spilled down Harriet's front, but some managed to make its way down her throat. The warm liquid revived some of her senses, just the polite part, and Harriet stumbled out a thanks.

Brigitte asked, "Would you like me to help you braid your hair? Or put on your dress?"

"I think I'll keep my hair down."

"Hair down? Very uncouth, very unladylike. Please, not in front of the Proctor." Forgoing permission, Brigitte combed Harriet's hair away from her face, fastening it back neatly with a band without concern for any potential tension headaches.

"Why are you doing this?"

"To make you presentable for the Proctor, it's my job."

"No. I mean, all this…why? Was I right?"

"I won't be the one to answer that."

Dialogue died in its infancy, so Harriet's fingers wandered to her back. The raised edges endured.

As if on cue, Brigitte said, "Yes, Miss Foster, it's permanent. View it as a prize. Almost none walk through life carrying the mark."

Gingerly, Harriet unfolded and inspected her dress. It had been so refurbished that it scarcely resembled its original make. Nonetheless, she slipped it on.

Brigitte ushered her over to a vanity mirror, craning her head to look at the corner clock every five seconds, each time punctuated with an impatient tut. But it didn't matter. The mirror was being cruel to Harriet.

The reflection was a stranger: a scrawny, patched up, hideous thing. Harriet felt heavy, burning, drops form in her eyes. Even the dress mocked its position. It had become too large, floating away, like the fabric detested touching her body.

"Don't cry, you will return to yourself in time. In time," Brigitte muttered behind her. "It is a shock, I know. Trust me, I am very grateful for what you have done for us. We all are, you will feel this in time. Come then, let us not linger. The Proctor awaits, Harriet Foster."

Hairs tensed and bristled at that sound. Her own name. An ugly name. A waste of words. But there was no time to ease her nerves, Brigitte pushed her towards the oak door, firmly but gently, in a manner most well-practiced.

✹ ✹ ✹

The floor was extravagant. More expensive than any fishing baron in New Hampshire could ever fathom. A château of a Victorian monarch, constructed of dark wood, fixed with heavy velvet draperies, adorned with delicate candelabras. Each room, of which there was a stomach-churning number, all had the same copper and oak door, all locked, all without any hint of life beyond the wood. Palatial yet bereft of any people. A vacant beauty. All noise came filtered in from the outside muffled and distant.

Fear and apprehension left Harriet. If this was another trap, and death lay in wait in some corner, it hardly mattered. If Brigitte was some wolf in sheep's wool, it was just as well. Better to die in a castle than a bunker. At least her fresh corpse wouldn't be so musty.

Harriet allowed herself to be pushed along the hallway, down the swirling staircase. After a couple steps, her knees and ankles failed.

Brigitte said, "Not too long now, in the lounge we go, lock those joints up."

A harder task than one would suspect—descending down the staircase. Four stories. Still lifeless. Yet somehow more heavily decorated with paintings and portraits and chandeliers and furnishings of unknown origins. A scent swirled up from the ground floor, a deep woodland scent.

Harriet stumbled down four more steps before her grip found salvation around the banister. While her feet caught up, she gazed at the curved wall.

Hung before her was a seven-foot-wide portrait of grim faced, muddy, bleeding men. True brutes. The caption: *1888 The Prison, Sortelha*. More paintings shouldered the staircase. *1902 The Tower, Riga*, *1910 The Dreadnought, Bermuda*, then came an empty frame *1936 The Bunker, Rhineland*.

Brigitte expedited Harriet's pace with more force than necessary.

She clucked, "Some of your recent predecessors. Laudable memories. To be completely honest, The Bunker was forgiving. The Prison was merciless."

Chapter Thirty

And then, there they were. Another large room, one wall entirely made of colored windowpane, letting in copious amounts of pastel daylight. People meandered the streets beyond the glass, separated only by a well-manicured garden that lay right beyond the window. But the draw of escaping to the outside commanded no attention; the man sitting at a cherry-wood desk did.

Unfortunately, he was familiar. The mafioso from the docks. He looked how he smelled—expensive. His face was tanned and ancient, and his suit was dark and stiff. Both meticulously clean. His neatly trimmed goatee formed a sharp point, extending his chin in a Byzantine fashion. Heavy red and purple jewels hung from a thick chain around his neck.

He sat diligently at his desk, leather gloved hands clasped on top. No expression readily discernible on his face, the same clinical nothingness as Brigitte. Unnerving, but anxiety had lost its potency.

Two others sat across from him, their backs to Harriet, but recognizable at once. Dr. Gage, wearing his refreshed suit, and Pyotr, wearing a new set of trousers and a well-pressed shirt, their eyes affixed to the man. Without a word, Harriet took a seat between the two.

She turned to the left to face Pyotr. Her heart stopped. His face was similarly weary but tentatively calm, yet still prematurely aged. To her right, Dr. Gage offered her a small smile.

"We have been waiting for ages," he said with a gentle nudge to her elbow.

Rolling breeze from the window fluttered through his sparse hair. Faint laughter coming from children playing in the streets drafted through the room.

Dr. Gage continued, "You sure did take all the time in the world, didn't you?"

It was probably a gentle jest, but it stung regardless.

"Sorry," Harriet mumbled.

The mafioso behind the desk, the supposed Proctor, cleared his throat and beckoned Brigitte forward. He whispered in her ear, and she promptly left the room. Not a minute passed when she returned accompanying yet another man: middle-aged, dark haired, olive-skinned, sharp featured, probably handsome at some point but a debonair haughtiness ruined his face.

The Proctor silently gestured to Pyotr. The new man immediately took a position standing behind him, a healthy distance away. Pyotr still furled inward, as though he was already acquainted with the man, and decidedly didn't like him.

The Proctor spoke in a deep voice, eloquent and methodical. Each sound, each syllable, placed and punctuated. He had an accent, one not readily identifiable, one different from the feigned Italian inflection he gave Harriet at the London docks. But coupled with his appearance, he bestowed the impression of a Hellenistic noble plucked from a bygone era.

He said, "We may begin. Mr. Mikhailov will translate for our friend Mr. Semyonov Volga. So then, please ask any and all questions you may have. This is your one chance to do so. I will respond to all, within reason. You all still have reason, don't you?"

The man, Mikhailov, leaned forward and began whispering in Pyotr's ear, whose face twisted into a curt frown.

Immediately, Dr. Gage took point. "So what was all this? What's the ruse? Murderers? Kidnappers? Ransomers?" With each word, his composure and gentility dissolved, and his face began to flush.

Harriet blurted out, "Was I right? This was a fortune-telling nightmare?"

The Proctor said, "Let me start from our genesis. Centuries ago, a small group of men, fearfully intelligent men, gloriously faithful men, could not stand their lives and fortunes to be ransacked and ravaged by the chaos and turmoil of the common world. They formed a clandestine defense against such travesties, a procedure of divination, heavenly inspired, forever concealed, eternally protected from the commons. The industry of cynomancy was born. This is us. We elevate ourselves above the mortal impositions of those commons. We do not seek to control the commons, but to be separated from the commons. We seek to carve out pockets of Eden on Earth to dwell in, and to do so, we must know what catastrophes will plague the globe. And we thank you for this. Your participation, although nonconsensual, was necessary. If this makes us kidnappers to you, then so be it. But know it is more than that. Unfathomably more."

Dr. Gage said, "Kidnappers from a street gang or kidnappers from a cult... kidnappers all the same." He leaned forward as though he intended to strike out at the Proctor and was only corralled by his fragile constitution and lack of wingspan.

The Proctor's nose twitched. "It is a shame you feel so,

but this is an industry, not a cult."

Harriet said, "The purpose... the truth... is that real? I was right?" She hated how she sounded: feeble, pathetic, thoughtless.

The Proctor said, "The purpose was grand. Yes, you are our Dogs. Our bearers of prophecy. We thank you for revealing fate to us." His face morphed from some unfeeling stranger to something amiable.

He smiled at Harriet and leaned his weight forward, the desk deeply croaking with the shift. "Let me speak simply through example from decades prior. Our master felt such a great distress festering between the divine and the common. A war would rattle our Eden. He alerted us, his disciples, thousands around the world, and we executed the noble mission. The master instructed that the 1910 divination must take place among a drifting ship in the hellish Bermuda seas. Eight Dogs to predict eight lands. It was a logistical nightmare to conduct, observe, and analyze. Worse so, the American Navy ran across our dreadnought, and it took much financial persuasion for them to not perturb our effort. Strangely, we had not included an American nor any from the Western frontier in our divination. Alas, it was a part of the divination, as our master foresaw. Duly, when the war he prophesied finally struck, those states of the Western frontier emerged forth after some time. The blessed divination, the actions of the Dog and the actions of the common world. Even our mistakes are, as errors are woven into the fabric of people. For you: an unintentional releasing of our toxin, allowing a transmission through to the radio, overdosing our Polish Dog, we are only human ourselves. Uncommon, but still human. Do you see now? The intertwining with our common agents, our Dogs, with us, the uncommon disciples. Our divinations, to you these may be tortures, yet these tortures produce our prophecy. All those to be victors, all those to be vanquished, all those to be undisturbed. Valuable prophecies, and our master leads the interpretation."

Harriet's mouth hung low. "So you're saying you can predict war?"

"We target the larger game. Not mere victors or vanquished. Each step you took, each word you uttered, from the time you first woke up to the time you knew yourselves to be Dogs and understood the role you play in the divine ritual, it is a piece of fate. Yes, war, but religious schisms, droughts, famines, all things that trouble the commons. Our master finds the divinely ordained future, and we, the disciples, share the good word among our selective herd, who pay mighty fortunes to know of impending catastrophes. We have helped our clientèle survive the unsurvivable and steady themselves against economic ruin. A noble goal indeed."

Dr. Gage scoffed, "So then…what is it? What is the prophecy? What fate for Poland? The man you killed upon arrival?"

The Proctor responded, "I can only speculate, but our master will know after the divine tells him."

Brigitte chirped to herself, "I think I may have an idea…"

Mikhailov interjected, "Semyonov Volga wishes to ask if he had a choice in leaving the cynomancy?"

The Proctor's mouth curled into a cheery smile. "It is a great honor. An honor beyond refusal. No, once selected by merit of all things, be it age, occupation, birthdate, attitude, proclivities, you are forever a Dog as divinely orchestrated. Our master beseeches the heavens to illustrate the characteristics befitting the champion of each land we wish to prophesize. Once the characters of our Dogs are selected, our network scours the lands for those suitable. Once our Dogs are in place, we have the shepherd commence the divination among the dogs before taking his leave. The shepherd must bear the mark of the Dog themselves and thus understand they must leave when appropriate to not interrupt the divination. Regrettably, we must forfeit the prophecies of the shepherd's land."

Mikhailov recited this back to Pyotr, who in turn stomped on the ground.

Dr. Gage sputtered, "You kidnapped me because of my age and birth date?!"

The Proctor said, "Our master decreed our Dog of the United Kingdom must be elderly, disgruntled, war-scarred, and grief-stricken, and for reasons only known to him, born in January. A dutiful scout found you out among the commons, and our master accepted you! However, for others, it is less random, as you asked within the bunker, Harriet. Two disciples in our industry heard of the qualifications for the Dog of Persia and the Dog of Japan, and both had relatives they thought to be suitable for the position. Parisa Shahidi's uncle volunteered her, as the Dog needed to be a young, affluent, secularized woman, and our master accepted the offering. Junichi Kitagawa's father did the same, as the Dog of Japan needed to be a man with the emotional combustibility of a child and hold political views some in the commons would find unsavory. He also needed to be thirty-four, again for reasons only the master can discern. However, you three here, you were found through faith-guided chance."

Dr. Gage's face fell. He murmured, "Her uncle? Her uncle…"

Harriet would have felt a similar pang of depression, but another thought struck her mind. "The shepherd… you mean there was a mole? I always had my suspicions. Who? Who was it?"

"Oh yes, Brigitte, please fetch him. He will have the gift of seeing those who stayed the course."

Again, Brigitte left the lounge and returned shortly with another set of footsteps in tow. Dr. Gage turned around immediately, almost snapping his neck in the process.

Dr. Gage voiced, emotionless, "Christ… I knew it all along."

Pyotr and Harriet didn't bother turning. They opted to stare at each other, and to match their reactions. The footsteps drew near, as did a sudden onslaught of tobacco's scent.

The Proctor spoke, "Stand beside me, Jonas."

Wassermann, dressed in a fashionable Sunday suit, promptly stood next to the Proctor, his hands politely resting behind his back. His mousy hair was slicked back much like Mikhailov, his eyes sympathetic but unremorseful. A small smile graced his lips. Same bureaucratic appearance, but no longer a charisma vampire, a primordial vampire. A hateful, grotesque creature wrapped in expensive wool.

Dr. Gage shed his coldness to foster his growing contempt. "You Judas. How could you do such a thing?"

"If I may speak," Wassermann waited for the Proctor's nod. "My purpose was simple: to start you all on the path to find salvation. No more, no less. When the role was fulfilled, I made an exit. Despite it all, I am pleased to see so many have survived, especially fully intact. It has been said, but I will reiterate, with time and with the bounty you will gain, you will come to respect the cynomancy. It took me almost two decades after I was made a Dog, but I too came to see the cynomancy's use, to know the true power of being privy to the future, to know it's an honor to be in such a divination. Further, it was an honor to be your shepherd."

Harriet's voice trembled, "In 1910? A divination to predict the Great War? How could you go through that, and still agree to put us through similar torture?"

She began to scratch at the bandages plastered on her skin, and Brigitte leaned over to swat her hands away. Mikhailov diligently kept his translation flowing.

Wassermann responded with too much ironic mirth, "Yes, 1910, I was there. I was twenty, the youngest in my cohort. On that iron ship for a month. A floating hell. In fact, most deaths during my divination were not accidental nor self-imposed, but murder. We became rabid on that ship, ripping and tearing and breaking one another until only two remained. Our shepherd was some Swede, Hedlund, a very morose fellow. When I came to know it, I hated him too. So, in turn, I accept your hatred of me."

Harriet sharply cleared her throat. "You said three is a lot to survive. But you survived with two... how can three be a lot and two be a little?"

The Proctor responded, "Nobody had to perish. All deaths were self- or peer-selected; this is true for each cynomancy. It is entirely possible that one day we will have such a cynomancy without death. But as it stands now, not one has passed since the inception of the practice without casualty. For our bunker, three were plenty. So many of us were certain maybe one would survive, some even thought it would be a red cynomancy—no survivors and the bunker left unsolved. Yet for The Dreadnought cynomancy, we were all astounded that only two survived."

Wassermann started a thought, "Through no fault of ours —"

"Jonas," Mikhailov said, and a strange darting look passed between them. Wassermann shut his jaw and exhaled a slow, lumbering breath.

Pyotr frantically blurted out another question.

Mikhailov relayed, "He wishes to know the date."

The Proctor looked down at his watch. "Today is May the 5th, precisely 11:42 in the morning. The cynomancy commenced on March the 23rd of this same year, 1936. Six weeks and one day, you three were underground in our bunker, as were we."

The Proctor looked back at the group with a new expression, quizzical, and borderline disappointed. "If I may gently submit, of course I will not judge the actions of any who find themselves in your position, but I was surprised not one, even among the more philosophical and well-read, bothered to read all the texts we provided in the bookshelves early on, not save it for the fading hours. We disciples are not so harsh to leave our Dogs without any bearings."

"If I recall, I did point it out at the onset, almost immediately," Wassermann cautiously interjected. "But it was forgotten in favor of the picture books, which they used for other purposes." His tone illustrated he was somewhat miffed.

The Proctor responded, "I am very intrigued by what our master will come to know through that. Alas, what happened was always meant to happen. It will be an interesting prophecy, I am sure."

Wassermann yet again interjected, "I told you all there was something worthwhile in those shelves… You all would have been in and out in a week. But fine, I did suspect you all would continuously ignore the prompting."

Harriet spluttered, "You thought we'd read books after waking up in a strange place full of strange people?"

Wassermann shrugged. "You all thought I'd willingly electrocute myself? Now that is surprising."

Dr. Gage blurted, "You behaved like a buffoonish dullard! Of course, you'd be the type to get electrocuted!"

Harriet sighed, "To be honest, I didn't think much of it. I've met buffoons before…Now, I think I join your ranks, Mr. Wassermann."

Wassermann kept a rigid, smug smile. "If it eases your temper, Miss Shahidi was so close to labeling me as an insider. I was so certain when she gave me that death glare in the navigation room. But I suppose it's just as well. Even if she did, it likely wouldn't have mattered."

Mikhailov said, strangely bitterly, "It would have mattered, as part of the divination."

Wassermann immediately responded, "My apologies, it would have mattered."

Pyotr was growing livid and spitting out words directly at Mikhailov, accosts likely not meant to be translated. Mikhailov pinched the bridge of his nose, let out a sharp sigh, and spat a sentence down to Pyotr. Whatever it was, it did not quell Pyotr's fury. Pyotr shot up, but Mikhailov clamped him back down with a surprisingly strong arm.

"Semyonov Volga is upset. He's concerned that his mother worries," Mikhailov explained, shooting a pointedly irate expression down to Pyotr. Pyotr sneered right back.

The Proctor maintained his serenity. "You may tell him it has all been arranged, we have prepared suitable alibis. All the stories to tell your family, friends, employers. If you wish to embellish, we will make it so. We will supply any documentation, hospital receipts, academic records, travel vouchers, anything at all. Not one of you will walk away empty-handed."

"But what about those that didn't return… what about Parisa?" Harriet asked, "What about her? What about Renard? Kitagawa? People will know they have disappeared. People will care. Important people will care. Even unimportant people. I will care."

"We will make it just. We have had much practice. A Persian socialite and an actress of the stage are trivial. We have seen greater beings. Leaders of nations, even," the Proctor replied. "And you are not unimportant. Not anymore. You have transcended your own station."

Harriet's anxieties faded. Something gleeful and burning took root.

Dr. Gage yelled, "Damn all of that nonsense, what about us in the bodily sense? I am old! I cannot recover from such a thing. How am I supposed to return to my wife, playing pretend I was on some grand holiday? My lungs have never felt weaker."

"We will make it just," the Proctor repeated, "You have played your part, of which we are thankful. Of course, we must insist on secrecy. The consequences of breaking this are severe. Ask any in the room. We have all been witnesses to it. Otherwise, you may return to your life and have as much or as little contact with us as you deem fit. If you find our cause righteous, we welcome you as a disciple into our industry. If you wish to never hear from us again, then we will make it so. Regardless of how you choose to continue life, know that suffering will become a stranger to you."

He suddenly grew animated, "Whatever you desire, it is yours. We have disciples in every common industry, in every common land, among every common class, and they are grateful to you, our Dogs who bear the mark of our master. Dogs above all. Even I am beneath you."

Wassermann eagerly followed the Proctor's words with his own, "This is truly a magnificent gift. A privilege! Trust me, I understand better than anyone what you feel. Do not rob yourself to appease your anger."

Dr. Gage resettled himself in his chair, his hands resting upon his newly polished cane. The room fell silent. In the burdening quiet, Harriet began to shake, wrestling with something blasphemously ecstatic. Pyotr reached over and indelicately squeezed Harriet's forearm.

The Proctor gave the three two minutes of silence, which should have been contemplative but instead was just awkward. It wasn't even Wassermann's fault. It was Pyotr's. He kept swiveling his head up to Mikhailov and sneering. Mikhailov returned with a cold expression of dispossession.

The Proctor finally concluded, "I cannot say when our master will formalize his prophecy, but once he does, we will send notice to you. Accept our invitation or don't, as is your privilege. Brigitte and Mikhailov can see you off to the Hauptbahnhof to recommence common life."

"Recommence common life? I can't...not like this," Harriet said. "I can't go back. I'm a king now. Aren't you a king?"

The Proctor sighed. "Were you not listening?"

Dr. Gage re-engaged, "The barracks, the exit door. They never opened like the chapel did, why?"

The Proctor responded, "The barracks were simply where the observers rested when not between the walls, in the vents, or under the floor. Surely, we couldn't have you intrude on them. And that one door was not the exit, merely an empty broom closet. Upon reflection, perhaps leaving it unlocked would have blunted its unnecessary intrigue."

Dr. Gage stuttered, "But...that's not fair, that's not fair at all!"

Wassermann's nose twitched, and he stifled a small laugh with the back of his hand. "Perhaps not, but to be completely honest, I'd say my cynomancy was the most unfair."

"Jonas, enough," Mikhailov said. Another stormy look bounced between them. Mikhailov continued, "It doesn't have to be fair. It has to be correct. And this cynomancy, and all others, were correct."

Pyotr spoke some more, his tone shifting to something harrowingly defeated. Mikhailov scrunched his nose and responded directly to his ward. Pyotr rolled his eyes, grabbed and tousled Mikhailov's arm, forcing his translator to address the Proctor.

"Semyonov Volga stated the same ill-thinking argument. He says it's unfair. Why must the instigations be in Latin and

Greek, or why must there be religious illusions beyond his understanding?"

The Proctor's eyes sparkled. "Because it is global. We must represent the globe."

Mikhailov snorted, "That's what I told him. He's not convinced."

Dr. Gage spouted, "And there's no way to convince anyone with sensibility. Where was the room written in Sanskrit? Or in Navajo? You put Islamic iconography in a chapel? You jumble Greek and Latin together with the inane presumption they are inherently linked? Self-important cretins. It was, as Kitagawa said, a farce. You think this is global. Your group is so cosmopolitan. Your types are all like this, global cultists. Thinking you can know everything, can see everything, can predict everything, but are still so curtailed by what you are so sunken in. Lunatics. Freakish lunatics. Idiotic freakish lunatics."

The Proctor dismissed the jab with a wave of the hand, like a parent pushing aside childish impunity, and locked up his jaw. No more questions would be tolerated, which was acceptable; nobody had anything left to say.

Harriet stared at her lap, unaware of her gaping smile.

The Proctor gestured vaguely, and Wassermann took his leave. The Proctor stood up, restructured his jacket, then said, "Dogs above all—whatever you decide to do, know that."

He left at a rigid, slow pace.

Chapter Thirty-One

Silence befell the lounge except for the faint rumblings of daily life echoing from the outdoor afternoon. Brigitte and Mikhailov had a private deliberation in each other's ears.

Brigitte groaned, likely on the losing side of the private deliberation, and addressed the three, "Thus, your decision?"

Dr. Gage started to blink rapidly, and a tear began to leak from the corner of his eye as he muttered, "Damn this. Damn all of this. Take me back home. Take me back to Bernadette."

"Very well," Brigitte said, and without any prompt, people burst in through the ivory doors.

Well-groomed people. Ornately decorated people. Nationally vague people of all varieties. Flooding in two by two. All as anonymous yet superbly made. A parade of cultists.

Harriet wanted to stare, yet common courtesy found staring to be rude. But she gawked at her hands and then began to grope her smile. She could stare; common courtesy had no place among the uncommon, so she stared.

One cultist began to murmur in Dr. Gage's ear.

Dr. Gage mumbled, "Surgical conference in Lisbon?"

He sighed, then blearily turned to Harriet, "If the story I

am given is to be carried through, we all met on some important surgical conference in Lisbon." To this, he gave a despondent chuckle. "What a strange thing to suggest to Bernadette, but I will do my best."

Swelling with some unseen ego, Harriet reached out to him to wipe the tear from his cheek, "We are better now, Dr. Gage. Better." Her hands began to twitch.

Dr. Gage sighed and allowed cultists to usher him towards the doors. "We are alive, and for me, that's not so much better."

He hobbled away, escorted by no less than four of the newly arrived strangers.

Mikhailov whispered back into Brigitte's ear, then sharply swiveled on his heels to tail Dr. Gage's procession out of the door. Yet, Pyotr dashed up and grabbed Mikhailov before he had a chance to leave. He released a frantic spew of questions.

"Semyonov Volga wants me to ask you for your decision. He is incapable of making any choice on his own, apparently," Mikhailov said, his voice still flat, yet betrayed a simmering irritation.

Harriet began to gnaw on her lip as she scanned the sunlit faces swarming around her. Without explicit entrance, even more anonymous faces began to populate the lounge, and noise from the inner château began to leak in. They all looked at her in a strange way. Respectable, inquisitive, somewhat worried, yet wholly in admiration.

"I don't know yet," Harriet said. "I need…I need to speak with Wass…I need…don't know."

Mikhailov said what sounded like two rude words to Pyotr, who in turn began to jostle Mikhailov on the forearm and launched even more questions. Mikhailov grimaced but produced a notebook out of his slicker jacket. On a scrap of paper, Pyotr scribbled down something and proudly presented it to Harriet.

Mikhailov yawned again, which was likely a feigned yawn. "It's the location of his filthy commune and some insipid pleasantries. Alright then. He's going back to St. Petersburg, or Leningrad, whatever the Soviets call it nowadays."

Strangely, all the anonymous people in the room turned to each other and began to worriedly murmur. An unwanted giggle leapt from Harriet's throat.

Mikhailov directed a pointed glare at a young, swarthy cultist, "Take Semyonov Volga to the Hauptbanhof, then make an itinerary for future travel to New Hampshire." Mikhailov turned his scrutiny down to Harriet, "He wants to visit it, for some reason."

The young cultist said in a nervous chitter, "Sir, I don't speak Russian."

"That doesn't matter, he says nothing worthwhile."

Pyotr didn't allow himself to be escorted away as promptly as Dr. Gage did. He kept by Harriet's side, and for one last time, squeezed her around the forearm. It stung.

He mumbled more, and Harriet turned her head expectantly to Mikhailov.

Mikhailov, already making good distance towards his exit, called back, "He warns you against your desires."

"What does that mean?"

"Not even I know," he said, then left by diving through a swarm of people like a ship in a storm.

Harriet stood and scanned Pyotr's face. It was there. A bizarre mortal panic. She patted him on the back as her means of goodbye, but he blew off her head with a finger gun.

Brigitte, in the middle of a congress with two strangers, grumbled, "Shall one go fetch Mr. Mikhailov again? Just in case Mr. Semyonov Volga has questions about his story?"

"Ma'am, he told us he would only speak Russian for no

more than fifteen minutes."

Brigitte scratched her temple, appearing abjectly lost, but Pyotr took quiet steps over to her and tugged on her elbow. He pointed to the door, then quietly left without an escort. Harriet felt her heart begin to pulse rapidly. It no longer felt like a heartbeat, but rather a seizure.

Brigitte mused, "He's a lot more agreeable than Mr. Mikhailov led us to believe." She turned to face Harriet. "Would you like us to arrange transport back to New Hampshire? Or would you like direct transit to Stockholm? We have already sent representatives from the line company to inform your brother that you embarked on the wrong ship and are now in Morocco."

"Do I have to go back?" Harriet whispered.

A good dozen faces in the lounge suddenly grew wide, like she had run around the room and slapped them all across the jaws. Yet as soon as they made the expression, they curbed it. Flat stoniness.

Brigitte responded, "You'd prefer to stay?"

Harriet mulled it over. Her pulse began to hurt. She shot to her feet, then broke into a sprint for the door.

Chapter Thirty-Two

She ran down the foyer, frantically darting into each hallway on the ground floor. People appeared to emerge out of nowhere. They all shot her bewildered glances, but then they all brightened. Some smiled. A few even clapped.

Finally, she caught a small glimpse of Wassermann heading up the staircase. As she followed, she halted right before the dreadnought painting.

There Jonas Wassermann was. A mopey little man tortured amidst a throng of fellow Dogs, illustrated through delicate paint strokes. Strapped to a chair, blood dripping from his jaw, tears dripping from his eyes, scattered teeth and entrails around his feet, a frightfully hellish figure's hands around his throat. Harriet snorted, then continued her chase.

Wassermann took notice of his pursuer and quickened his stride, but Harriet's frenzy served her well.

Gripping onto the back of his suit before he could evade her clutch, a volley of interrogations poured out from her. "How does it feel? Honestly? Knowing you looked each of us in the face, knowing what was going to happen? And when you survived, what was inside you?"

Wassermann turned around, dropping the stiffness in his posture. As he looked her up and down, he pulled his mouth back into a tight smile. A flippant wave to the pursuing Brigitte, he nodded towards another room nearby. He guided Harriet by the shoulder into a drawing parlor of sorts.

With the modicum of privacy, he relaxed even further, sinking his shoulders down and scratching his head.

He spoke, abandoning all pretense, finally back to the mundane European, "Inside me? You mean to ask if I went as rabid as you did? Well, I couldn't help it. No matter what Andrey, I mean Mr. Mikhailov, says, it was unfair. I lived it. He only watched it. I was rabid. And did I care? I care about the cynomancy, the purpose of it all. The Dogs drive the purpose, so it is possible to get loosely invested in your survival, but never enough to pollute the cynomancy's benevolence. Before my own time as a Dog, I had little purpose, just as you."

He leaned in further. "But I suppose that does not answer what you wish to know."

Harriet picked at the toughened scabs on her hands and closed the dwindling distance between herself and Wassermann, so close their foreheads nigh touched.

"What happened to you? Why did you go… rabid," she whispered.

A twitch twinged up the side of Wassermann's face, "You should thank me, I was a decent shepherd. My shepherd? Cruel. Cruel to the highest order. I never pretended to care for any of you. But he pretended. He made me rabid through heartache. Painful heartache. Blistering heartache. Parallel maybe to your hatred, but not the same."

"Hatred? That's not the right word for it."

He gave a slanted smile. "Don't forget, I watched for the whole of those six weeks, side by side with the legions. I know your nature. It may take a decade for you to know it as well."

"That's not my nature. Desperate, but not murderous."

"I found my nature in the dreadnought. The engine room, precisely. I identified your nature in the bunker's kitchen. Tell me, was Renard right? Did you like how it felt?"

Harriet stared at her veiny hands. They seemed to glow. "Yes, yes, I suppose I did."

He concluded, "Then indulge."

The door suddenly ripped open. In stalked Mikhailov, who had an indescribable expression. Same trained neutrality, yet a boiling aggravation.

He was about to embark on some manner of interrogation, but a frantic crackle jumped out of Harriet's teeth as she pointed to him.

"You nabbed Parisa? You're the Tatar?"

He recoiled, earnestly startled, but quickly reset his neutrality. "I am nationless. And I didn't nab, only identified, as due my role as counsel to our master. We have younger, more limber disciples to do said *nabbing*."

"Ah, I was wondering…I don't think Pyotr liked you very much."

Mikhailov took a deep breath. "The sentiment is shared. He didn't succumb without a fight. Put our only decent Caucus disciple in the infirmary. Unfortunately, that was one *nabbing* I did have to do myself. On the subject of sentimentality—"

Wassermann took several steps backward and began to fidget with his hands as though he were a chastised schoolboy. Mikhailov was about to say something to him, probably something searing, but Harriet interrupted.

She asked, "Who was the Swede who nabbed me? The same as the shepherd from The Dreadnought?"

Wassermann choked behind her.

"No," Mikhailov said, and anger flickered up in his face. "That was some lowly scout. The shepherd, the morose

Swede as he was indelicately referred to, is no longer in our service. A redundant but necessary word of caution—don't yap about this practice to anyone. Not even those you become particularly affectionate towards."

Wassermann choked again.

Harriet shuffled on her feet and weakly chuckled. "Who's this master that man downstairs talked about?"

Mikhailov responded, "The only one above a Dog. No more questions on him."

Harriet paused, another shuffle, then impishly continued, "So, do you have to do everything I say?"

"No, we are equals. I also bear the mark. But I am obliged to some courtesy."

"Brigitte told me Dogs in the industry are rare."

"We are. Less than a dozen are still alive. Only two in the industry. And they're in this room," Mikhailov said, and turned his gaze back to the peevish Wassermann. Wassermann directed his own gaze at the floor.

Harriet continued, "You were a Dog in The Dreadnought with him?"

"No. At fifteen, I was in The Tower."

"What did you represent, if you are nationless?"

Mikhailov allowed himself a slight grimace. "I was born shackled to the Czar. Liberated through my Doghood before I became shackled to the Bolshie mob."

"That's a convoluted way of saying Russian Empire?"

Mikhailov allowed himself a stronger grimace.

Sensing the presence of an aggressively sore subject, Harriet pivoted to likely another sore subject. "Were you also tortured?"

"The practice isn't torture. Wassermann wasn't tortured; don't believe him if he says anything different. He earned what happened to him, as he earned the dentures we paid for after the fact," Mikhailov spat and then addressed Wassermann directly, "She's not even indoctrinated, and here you are, sowing your self-pity."

Wassermann sighed, then shrugged.

It was too tantalizing; dipping into grudges between such people, so Harriet asked, "What did happen to him?"

"Justice. As is what happened to his shepherd," Mikhailov said.

Wassermann cried out, "Justice? That Welsh she-devil ripped out my teeth, goddammit! For no goddamn reason!"

Mikhailov leaned down and whispered to Harriet, "The shepherd helped him cheat. The Welsh Dog took issue with that. Rightfully so."

"Ah," Harriet said, and swiveled around to tut at Wassermann. "And there you were, judging us for our lack of book-reading."

"I didn't cheat," Wassermann protested, "Oh please. You cannot judge me! The Tower cynomancy was so easy. I heard the stories! Not even two weeks. All fun and games. Only one accidental death! All warm and cozy with one another."

Mikhailov snipped, "But not one of us cheated."

"I didn't cheat!" Wassermann proclaimed, "What more can I say?"

"You've said quite enough," Mikhailov responded, "Pity's sake, I could probably write your biography given how much you've said. Not once during The Bunker did you shut up. Giggling at every little thing like a simpleton."

Wassermann suddenly grew indignant. "Was I supposed to be silent for six weeks? Hell, I recall you encouraging me to break up the monotony."

Mikhailov paused, pursed his lips, and replied, "That's fair. Truth be told, shared history considered, I do find you quite amiable. Certain sins of decades prior now…make more sense. And at least your cologne isn't so appallingly outrageous as Pine's."

"Oh," Wassermann said in a slight shock, "Well…thank you." He let out a simpleton's chuckle, the very one Harriet heard emanating from behind the bunker's walls, "I believe one of them called Pine an Italian peacock. Quite accurate, if I may say."

Mikhailov snorted, "I'm obliged to agree."

Harriet started chuckling too, for a reason that she didn't yet realize, "Now, who here is Pine?"

Mikhailov sucked his teeth, "That's the Proctor's name, one of them at least."

Wassermann said, in such a casual way that one would assume this was a bout of small talk in a local market, rather than a headquarters of such an industry, "Whatever happened to Proctor Kebede? I was told he'd shadow the cynomancy."

Mikhailov responded, "He was, but a week before initiation, his hemorrhoids flared up again."

"Ahhh, is that why nobody in the bunker told me when I asked them?"

"Likely. That man…hemorrhoids should be the least of his worries. Eighty-seven, if you can believe it. Eh, the odd case of hemorrhoids is dismissible."

And just like that, Wassermann and Mikhailov were simply chatting with one another. She then took notice of each article of their clothing, how perfectly maintained their hair and skin was, how they spoke without any sort of heavy burden, how they were purely better than anybody she'd ever seen before. Better than her parents, than her pretentious brother Andrew, better than any of her dull classmates. Purely better.

Harriet's organs began to stir as she listened to their chatter. The idea was delicious: let in on some gossip. Gossip different from the stupid affairs of the common world.

Different from the snipes and barbs thrown around the bunker. Gossip of kings. An elevated clique. A civilization with history and tragedy, separate from all others, known only to those within their clique. Surely, it sounded the same, but it carried a different odor.

When Mikhailov noticed the obvious delight of the in-plain-sight eavesdropper, Mikhailov reset his shoulders, then spoke to Harriet, "All are awaiting your decision for the immediacy. To commit yourself to us is a heavy decision; do not feel pressured to make such a choice now."

"No," Harriet said with a shaking giggle. "I stay. I want to stay. Make it three. Three in the industry. Tell them. Tell my father, tell my mother, tell Andrew. Harriet Foster died. Died at sea. Tossed to the waves. I've died."

Mikhailov and Wassermann shared a passing glance.

Mikhailov said after a lengthy pause, "I will tell the master. Jonas, acquaint her with the industry." He left at that same slow, rigid pace, pulling a flask out of his jacket, and sucking hard on it.

When Wassermann escorted her back down the stairs, she stopped to gawk at the empty frame of The Bunker. She let out an exhilarated cackle. She would be there, immortalized in paint, at some point. Next to those laudable predecessors. Next to those that bridged the common from the uncommon.

The exhilaration doubled as Wassermann mused, "Maybe you'll be heralded as something truly remarkable. The first woman to survive."

He raised his voice as people began to trickle onto the floor below, staring quizzically up at them, "Send word out to all quarters around the globe. Miss Foster, Dog of the Americas, shall be among our congregation."

The exhilaration tripled as the people on the floor began

to clap as though it were a scripted round of applause. The applause rang into cheers. Suddenly, the château was alight with resounding joy. No longer an empty beauty.

As she made her way down to the ground floor, circles and circles of people fastened themselves around her. Mainly men, a few women, all anonymous, but all in adoration. They let out collective praise, a chorus of earnest gratitude, many on the verge of tears. Some turned their faces away, as though the sight of Harriet was so grand they could never hope to be worthy enough to gaze upon her.

Harriet said to Wassermann, her words almost lost among the gleeful celebration, "A Dog is above all of them?"

"Second only to the master."

Harriet studied his appearance for the last time. He was no longer what he was. The disciples loved him too, as they loved her. She swiveled her head around at all the finery in the château. Truly, a palace of Eden. Crystalline baubles dangled from the curtains, from the wide pastel glass windows, and lined the carpet. She realized that each bust embedded into the soaring walls that stretched up beyond the heavens was pure gold. With three or four blinks, she realized that each terraced level had countless corridors, each promising a new nook of paradise. And the people, the disciples, the patrons of the industry, kept pouring from every corner, every hallway, out from thin air. All beautiful, all grateful, all so completely awestruck at her presence.

The mark on her back began to burn. A deep scent flooded her nose. The lights began to dim, and a waft of thick incense emerged from unreality. The celebration grew frenzied.

Wassermann said in a light chime, "The master approved."

Another cackle reared, but this one was not so unwanted.

About the Author

Hal Enzinga, a former soldier and Pentagon analyst, draws from a global patchwork of experience living in Beijing, Tokyo, and Washington D.C. Their academic background in global studies and religious fundamentalism threads uneasily through *Deusetta*'s cryptic rituals and moral rot.

Find Hal Enzinga at www.haldanae.com or on X/twitter @halenzinga

Please consider leaving a review!